WATCHING ALICE

ALSO BY SUE WATSON

Psychological Thrillers

Our Little Lies

The Woman Next Door

The Empty Nest

The Sister-in-Law

First Date

The Forever Home

The New Wife

The Resort

The Nursery

The Wedding Day

The Lodge

You Me Her

Wife Mother Liar

His First Wife

Wanting Daisy Dead

Fiction

Love, Lies and Lemon Cake

Snow Angels, Secrets & Christmas Cake

Summer Flings and Dancing Dreams

We'll Always Have Paris

Bella's Christmas Bake Off

The Christmas Cake Café

Ella's Ice Cream Summer

Curves, Kisses and Chocolate Ice Cream

Snowflakes, Iced Cakes and Second Chances

Love, Lies and Wedding Cake

WATCHING ALICE

SUE WATSON

This is a work of fiction. Names, characters, organizations, places, events, and incidents are either products of the author's imagination or are used fictitiously. Any resemblance to actual persons, living or dead, or actual events is purely coincidental.

Published by Thomas & Mercer, Seattle

www.apub.com

Amazon, the Amazon logo, and Thomas & Mercer are trademarks of Amazon.com, Inc., or its affiliates.

EU Product Safety Contact:
Amazon Media EU S.à r.l.
38, avenue John F. Kennedy, L-1855 Luxembourg
amazonpublishing-gpsr@amazon.com

ISBN-13: 9781662523885
eISBN: 9781662523878

Cover design by The Brewster Project
Cover image: © New Africa © Henry Djiauw / Shutterstock; © Lori Mann / ArcAngel Images

Printed in the United States of America

For Nick, who's always there for me – even when he'd rather be at the football.

Prologue

It's the smell that hits me first, a thick metallic stench of blood and urine.

I walk through the front door and down the hallway, my heart beating hard. At first I can't make sense of the tableau. Josh is on his knees at the bottom of the stairs with his back to me; the sound is coming from somewhere inside him. Is he laughing, is he crying?

'Darling, what is it? What . . . ?' I can barely get the words out; a lump of panic sits in my throat. Then I see the trickle of blood meandering along the black-and-white floor tiles. I bend down. 'Josh, are you hurt?' *Has he tried to take his own life?*

'There's no pulse, Mum . . .' He moves away slightly, and that's when I see what he's been hiding. There's so much blood I don't recognise the body at first, but when I do I hear myself whimper in horror . . .

1

It isn't what he said, it was the way he said it.

'Hey you.' There was a warmth in my husband's voice that I hadn't heard for a long time. I held my phone in both hands, listening intently to his voice note.

'I called you earlier, where are you?' A heavy sigh. 'I miss you, babe,' he said, his words honeyed with lust. 'I've been sitting at my desk all day, just thinking about you. I *want* you, Ellie.'

His tone was soft – yet burning, intimate.

'Ellie, I *need* you,' he moaned.

My heart began to beat so fast the blood pumping through my ears deafened me. But what I remember most is the sheer panic ricocheting through me. Because my name isn't Ellie . . . my name is Alice.

And in that moment, life as I knew it was over.

It's been a month since I listened to the voice note on Jason's phone. A whole month since I discovered that my husband was in love with someone called Ellie.

Apparently, Ellie is someone he works with, but refuses to talk about. Which is okay, because I don't want to listen.

I realise now that our marriage was over before he even met her. She was the final straw. I'd been fooling myself; I should have ended things years ago. Our life was designed to work around him, his career and his needs – but it took that voice note for me to actually see that. Crazy, I know. How does a grown woman live in a life that doesn't fit her? It's like wearing a dress that's too tight and in an unflattering shade, and just not knowing. Or perhaps I didn't look close enough, because I didn't want to see? It wasn't the first time Jason had been unfaithful. I knew there had been women in the past, but he was clever – he'd tell me I was jealous and had a wild imagination. I began to question myself, because until that voice note, I'd never had any proof. He'd say I was being ridiculous, and even when I protested, he'd somehow convince me I was wrong, hinting at my 'instability' and suggesting I needed 'help'.

When I first confronted him with the voice note, he accused me of 'overreacting' – a word he often produces from his portfolio of 'mad, hysterical women' tropes.

But after hearing the note, his face paled and he realised he'd been caught. 'It was a one-night stand, she means nothing to me . . .' he tried, playing it down, denying the woman's relevance, as I'm sure he's done to me throughout our marriage. But I realise now his rampant gaslighting made me doubt myself more than him, and the feisty, sparky woman I had been was slowly being swallowed whole.

I can't believe I never saw this, never saw him – but now I have, and I'm done. I want him cut out, before he destroys me. But fifteen years, two children, a cat and a beautiful house – there's a lot to cut at.

I think we both know there's no future for us, but neither of us wants to hurt the kids or leave the house. Currently we're locked in a stalemate, living together but *not* together. I sleep in the spare room, leaving him alone in our king-size bed, where I sometimes hear him on the phone – talking to Ellie, I presume?

'Have you thought about partitioning the place into two?' my friend Martha suggests when we meet for coffee. 'A sort of his and hers?'

'Oh God, you mean *My Husband Next Door*? Sounds like a naff seventies sitcom,' I groan. 'No. I don't want to be in the same house as him at all. I can't bear the sound of his voice, the way he chews his food, the same old stock phrases . . . and don't get me started on the fake laugh. Nope,' I conclude, 'there's no partition strong enough, or thick enough, to block him out.'

'True. So you want to split. What does he want to do?'

'Oh, you know Jason, he's inscrutable, that's why he's such a good lawyer. I used to find his lack of openness a turn-on, a challenge, but not anymore.'

She rolls her eyes. 'Yeah, I remember, you called him your "man of mystery". Man of *misery* more like. You were so lovesick it used to make me want to puke.'

'So you've said, like a million times. I was young and stupid – and now I'm older and stupid for putting up with him all these years. But I'm not so stupid to leave our home so he can move his new girlfriend in to eat dinner in my designer kitchen and stand under my rainfall showerhead. *I'm* going nowhere. I'm not leaving my house, or my kids . . .'

'No *way*, your kids need you, and your home is a bloody work of art. *Your* work of art – you virtually rebuilt that house, it's your signature as a designer, your showcase for Sundrenched Interiors. It's breathtaking, and all down to you.' She reaches over and grabs my hand. 'I'm glad things are finally working out with the business. After all your training, and dreaming, you deserve this break.' She sips her coffee. 'And with my marketing hat on, I do think you need to be advertising a little bit more?'

'Yeah, but I can't really afford to take out big ads.'

'No, but I was thinking – why don't you use what's there, that's what most businesses do. Sundrenched Interiors has a Facebook page, so why don't you post on other groups and pages on there? Our old school has an alumni page for folks who want to brag about how well they're doing.' She smiles.

'Er, I'm about to get divorced, possibly lose my house, and though I'm cautiously optimistic about Sundrenched Interiors, I ain't Kelly Hoppen yet. What do I have to brag about?'

'Nothing, you're a huge failure,' she jokes (at least I think she's joking). 'But it's all advertising dressed up as socialising. It lets people know what you do and how to contact you. You don't have to mention anything personal, just say "here's my business, this is my number if you want me to *Sundrench* your home".'

'Using "Sundrench" as a verb, eh? I like it. You've done this before.'

'Every day of my bloody life to be precise. Shall I put something on the message boards for you?'

'That would be great. I just don't have time or the talent to write enticing stuff like you.'

'Leave it with me, I can have it on there in ten minutes.'

Delighted with her offer, I give her my passwords. 'I have enough clients at the moment to make some decent money, but I need regular work to live independently. That's the real dream, to have enough income to keep the house and kids . . .'

'And lose the husband,' she murmurs, then in a flash of vulnerability she reaches across the table and covers my hand in hers. 'Divorce is horrible, and expensive. Take it from me.'

'I know. He says if we split, we'd have to sell the house. Apparently he can't afford to pay the mortgage on that and buy another one for himself.'

'He's such a liar, of course he could. He's never been honest with you about anything – least of all money. You said so yourself. So just tell him to move out and you stay in the house with the kids.'

Martha's right. Why don't I just kick him out?

Because of the secrets between us – things Martha doesn't know. Stuff I can't share, even with my best friend.

'If the business continued to build, in twelve months I could afford to take on the mortgage, and he'd have no excuse to stay, he could take his money and buy himself a bachelor pad.'

'He could afford to do that now, and still pay your mortgage, but he doesn't want to give up the house. For Jason it's a status symbol.'

'Yeah, perhaps. He's the one who had the affair, and I hoped he'd run away with her and that would be my ticket out, all expenses paid. But he's dragging his feet, says we should wait.'

'You'd think he'd want to run away and be with *Ellie* – or whoever he's sleeping with this week?' she says flippantly. 'Is he still with her?'

'I don't know. He doesn't really tell me anything. I'm sure he's seeing someone though. He's away a lot, supposedly working.'

'Meanwhile, he holds all the cards. God!' she groans, exasperated.

'I have to be patient, Martha. If I push too hard, he'll do the opposite of what I want.'

'You want a divorce, so demand one.'

'It's not just what I want though, is it? What about the kids? I can't uproot them right now – Josh is about to take his A levels, and Ruby's happy, her friends live nearby. But later on, in a year or . . .'

'A year? Can you stick it out that long?'

'Probably not,' I say, defeated, with no answers.

'Thing is, Alice, if you're both determined to stay, it could go on forever – save for putting arsenic in his tea or dishing up a toadstool fricassee, you're fucked.'

'No, there are alternatives. If I work really hard the business will give me financial independence, I just have to focus. And anyway, there's a chance he'll get serious with Ellie or meet someone else and move out.'

'I disagree. He'll hate that you're regaining your independence, that you don't need him anymore, and he'll stay just to make it tougher. There'll never be an easy way to get rid of Jason.'

'I know, but . . . I just have to hang on until the time is right.' I know I sound weak, like I'm allowing this to happen to me, but I'm determined to get myself out of this, I just need time.

'He's taken the piss for years with his womanising, his lack of appreciation for you or anything you've done. When you were first together, you worked and paid all the bills while he carried on training to be a hotshot lawyer, then the minute he qualified, you had the kids. You've never had a break, always been doing stuff for others, never been able to do things for you.'

'But now the business is on its feet I can work for me – and the kids of course.'

'I hope so, because you have to start believing in yourself. Jason has never acknowledged or supported your talent, never given you the credit – but your potential screams through that house. The understated shades, warm open fire, cool sofas and tongue-in-cheek art. It's just *pure* Alice! Whatever lawyer tricks he thinks he can play, he can't take it from you – you are the beating heart of that house.'

'And I feel it, you know? I really want to stay. But he said if I stayed there with the kids, it wouldn't be fair.'

'Fair? Wow. He's never played fair. Anyway, as Ruby's only twelve, a court would probably allow you, the primary caregiver, the right to live in the house with the kids until she's eighteen.'

This is awkward – I don't know how to respond, given that there are other reasons I don't want this to go to court.

'You know what he's like, he'd only find some legal loophole, I can't fight him on stuff like that.'

She shrugs. 'I wish someone would, he's never played fair – my brother used to say he even cheated when he was playing cricket.'

Everything he's ever done has been tainted by something. The more I know my husband, the more I grow to hate him.

'Yeah, he doesn't play fair, and despite the fact I have a legal right to half the house, I'm sure he'd find a loophole, and I could end up with nothing.'

She shakes her head in disbelief and we sit facing each other at the little wooden table in the café where we often meet. The café's been here – under different names and management – for so long, we used to come here after school. I'm reminded of our schooldays now, leaning on our desks talking boys, and lipstick, all those teenage plans and dreams we had yet to realise. Martha was always the wild one; she had this inherent belief that if she wanted something badly enough, she could have it. She once made us both fake passports so we could run away to Italy for a holiday. We were twelve, and we didn't get as far as the driveway.

'Hang on,' she says dramatically, picking up her phone, red lips pursed, long fingernails now tapping the screen. 'Give me a moment.' Her eyes are bright. God only knows what twisted plan she's come up with. I wait patiently until the shiny nails slow down, and she looks up at me like she's just found the cure for cancer.

'What?'

'What about *nesting*?'

'Sounds weird, what is it?'

'It's a thing. It popped up the other day on my newsfeed!' She pings the article she's referring to straight to my phone.

'When a couple split, but don't want the children to live in two places . . .' I read out loud, scrolling slowly. 'The parents fly in and out of the nest, each spending half the week at the family home, while the children continue to live there, uninterrupted.'

I look questioningly at Martha.

'It's genius,' she says, already swept up in the idea. 'The kids can stay put, and you can keep the house until you work out what to do, or make enough money to buy him out.'

It's mad, almost as crazy as making fake passports to run away to Italy. But despite all the reasons to reject this idea as utter madness, I suddenly feel a little spark of hope. '. . . nesting?' I look into the distance to think it through. 'I've never even considered something like this – but could it work, just for a few weeks or months?'

She nods. 'Given there's no alternative, has to be worth considering.'

I nod with certainty, while feeling uncertain.

'Where will you live on the nights you aren't at the house?' she asks. 'You're welcome to stay with me.'

'Thanks, but I'm going to stay with Mum – she's close by and it's convenient. Besides, I'd like to spend some time with her – but I may well take you up on the odd sleepover now and then.'

'Well, there's always room at mine if you need it.' She sips on her coffee.

Over the years, I'm aware that Martha has judged me for putting up with Jason and abandoning my own career to support his. But she doesn't know the full story and has no idea how hard it's been, how I've struggled with the ties that bind Jason and me. We've kept the past hidden for so long we've managed to convince ourselves that we had no choice. But we did, and the truth is always there to remind us. It lives under the floorboards of our lives, walks past windows, and knocks on the door in the middle of the night. Jason and I buried this long ago, but now we're splitting up, and for everything to stay hidden we'll just have to trust each other. But we don't.

2

It's three weeks and two days since I suggested the idea of nesting to Jason. At first he was horrified. 'You and Martha never grew up,' he said. 'You're still those two schoolgirls coming up with stupid, hare-brained ideas.'

It took me a while to convince him, and only when he couldn't come up with a better idea did he grudgingly agree to give it a go.

So, tonight is our last night living at the family home together. The schedule starts in the morning, when Jason leaves and I stay with the kids until he returns to take over in four days' time.

It's been a mammoth task, cross-referencing his work, my work, the kids' timetables, their after-school and social stuff too. But tonight, with the kids upstairs in their rooms, we sit in the living room together, him lying on the sofa, and me trapped in the easy chair. I know I should feel something after all these years, but there's no sadness, no regrets for me, just relief that we're finally moving towards the endgame.

'Will you be okay on your own with the kids?' he asks.

'Yeah, of course. It's only like you're working away.'

He looks up from the TV screen. 'It's not too late to try again.'

'Oh, it is.' I almost laugh at this.

He shrugs. 'Okay, you've obviously made up your mind.'

'I have,' I say, before adding softly: 'And we should start the divorce proceedings as soon as possible. No point prolonging the agony.'

He nods, sadly, playing the victim when this is all his own making, but I've moved on. I'm not playing his stupid games anymore.

◆ ◆ ◆

'You're doing what?' Mum looks bewildered. She's seventy-eight, and in her day people stayed married regardless, they didn't divorce. But this half-in, half-out thing is freaking her out. 'Nesting? What the bloody hell's *nesting*?' Her face contorts like the word tastes sour on her tongue.

We sit across from each other at a table, eating lunch in her favourite café.

'We want to do this with kindness to each other and consideration for the kids,' I hear myself say, aware my rehearsed words sound ridiculous, and not unlike a press release issued by Gwyneth Paltrow and Chris Martin. And as Mum is already looking at me like I'm mad, I move quickly into a clear and gentle explanation, resisting the urge to declare this 'a conscious uncoupling'. When I've finished Mum looks even more confused.

'So, what do you think?' I ask, shuffling a stash of sugar sachets in my fingers like a mini pack of cards.

'I don't know. What do Josh and Ruby think?'

'They're very accepting.' I smile, remembering how Jason and I braced ourselves to tell the kids.

We sat them both down together and told them what was happening, clearly and without emotion as the parenting books advised. When we'd both finished speaking, we asked if they had any questions, and Josh said, 'I have a question,' while Jason and I glanced at each other anxiously, ready for the emotional fallout.

'What is it, Josh?' I was ready with a box of tissues.

'Can I still go to that gig with James next week?'

'Of course. Is that all you're concerned about?' I almost laughed out loud with relief.

Then Ruby said, 'I don't like this. I don't want to do the nesting.'

'Why, darling?' I asked, scared of our only solution slipping away.

'Because it's so lame. Why can't you and Dad have a whole house each? Then I could have *two* bedrooms in different places, like Maisie does!'

Afterwards, when the kids were in bed, Jason and I opened a bottle of wine while I silently congratulated us on behaving like grown-ups. 'They're so resilient, aren't they?' I remarked, relieved they'd taken it so well.

'Resilient? More like self-preserving little bastards,' he laughed, with grudging admiration.

I lifted my glass to his. 'Well, if we needed any confirmation that we're doing the right thing, those self-preserving little bastards have just provided it,' I giggled. It felt good to laugh with Jason again; the relief of us not being an 'us' anymore must've gone to my head.

'The kids are just fine about it,' I say to Mum now. 'Are you? Is there anything bothering you, Mum?'

Her expression is vacant, as if the shock of what I've just told her has erased everything from her mind. It's a lot for her to take in. She knew we were splitting up, but this nesting thing must sound insane to her.

How can she possibly understand? Mum and Dad were happily married for thirty years, until he died. They adored each other, and she still talks to the photo she keeps on her bedside table, even though he's been dead for twenty years.

'So, you're okay with everything? You understand what we're doing?' I ask, unsure if she's heard me.

But then she looks at me intently, her head to one side. 'I don't see why you don't just carry on living together, as a family.' Then she adds loudly: 'No one needs to know you and Jason aren't having sex.'

I look around to check if anyone's heard. 'Okay, Mum, I don't think we need the café to know either,' I joke. I expect her to chuckle at this, but she doesn't. She's going a bit deaf – maybe that's why she seems confused. She hasn't heard a bloody word I've said.

The waitress asks if we'd like dessert, and brings menus, as Mum leans towards me across the table. 'Jason's always had an eye for the ladies, hasn't he, Alice?'

I don't really want to get into it right now; this isn't the place to discuss my husband's infidelity. Looe is a small Cornish town, and everyone knows everyone else here, so I attempt to change the subject.

'Was your quiche nice, Mum?' I ask, in an attempt to distract her.

But she's not interested, still focused on pursuing Jason's womanising ways.

'He's what the youngsters call a "man slag".' She enunciates the two words slowly, and at cringingly high volume.

'Mum, shh,' I chide gently, while smiling at the ladies at the next table, hoping they didn't hear.

But judging by their amused expressions, they heard every word.

'Mum, do you have your hearing aids in?'

'What?'

'Can you hear me?' I say, loudly.

'I can hear you perfectly well, I don't need you to bloody shout!'

I pause for a moment, take a sip of water; she's being unusually sharp today, and as I'm feeling rather fragile, I don't say any more. If I do, I might end up in tears.

Her lips are tightened as she sits in angry silence. I'm not used to her being like this and I'm not sure how to continue the conversation, so I suggest dessert.

I order us two lemon meringue pies, and venture back into the thorny territory of our nesting plan. 'It won't be forever,' I say. 'Josh will be off to uni next year, and perhaps by then Jason will have moved on and Ruby and I could stay.'

'Won't you have to sell the house if Jason moves on?'

Mum might be deaf, but she's as shrewd as ever. A dark shadow slips into my mind – the prospect of anyone else living there fills me with overwhelming sadness. 'I don't know. We'll just have to see how it goes.'

I try not to let her see the well of sadness filling my eyes.

'Do you remember what it was like when we first moved in?' I ask, longing to revisit the past, when everything was perfect. Or *seemed* to be.

'It was a big pile of bricks,' Mum chuckles, probably seeing my pain and rallying.

'You turned up at the house and yelled at me for climbing a ladder.' I smile.

'Of course I yelled, you were pregnant. You shouldn't have been climbing a ladder!' she admonishes, gently.

'That summer was so hot, and Josh was only little, rushing everywhere, hurling himself around the garden.'

'And you were waddling around after him. I worried about you, Alice. You were exhausted, working on the house and dealing with a boisterous four-year-old. Where was your husband?'

'He was away working.'

'Well, you had a tough pregnancy, and very little support from him. I'm glad I was there. We thought Ruby would never come, didn't we. But when she did, we knew about it, a noisy little hurricane she was – still is,' she chuckles.

'Yeah, a long hot summer, and a long hot labour, but worth every moment to get Ruby,' I murmur.

'Oh, I did feel for you, love, but some of your problems were self-inflicted. I mean, who goes to a property auction at four months pregnant and buys an old relic?' She's shaking her head, but I hear something like pride in her voice.

I'd spotted the neglected Edwardian house in the property pages of our local paper, and something about it just stopped me in my tracks. I kept turning the page back to gaze at the cracked facade, the damp creeping up the outside walls, the overgrown tangle of garden. It was my inspiration, and proved to be my liberation too, when later I left my boring job at the council and began a course in interior design. I loved it, but had to give up the course when Jason was promoted and had to start travelling with his job, so there was no one around in the evenings to be with Josh. Mum did a few nights for me, but she was still working full-time herself back then and it was a lot for her, and by then we had Ruby. I was disappointed, but the children came first, and I always said I'd go back and complete the course when the kids were older. Two years ago I started an online course, and now have the qualifications I need without neglecting the childcare or compromising my husband's career (God forbid!). And once I had the letters after my name, I went to the bank with my business proposal, and was given a business loan to start Sundrenched Interiors.

I've already made one dream come true by starting up my business, and now I'm going to realise another dream by becoming single. I also need financial independence, but that might take a little longer. I just need to play nice with Jason until I'm ready to take what's mine.

3

I adored Jason from the moment I saw him, and sometimes, if I close my eyes and really concentrate, I remember loving him. And later, when the children came along, they were enough for me to ignore the red flags, the jarring smell of unfamiliar perfume, an auburn wavy hair caught in the seat belt of his car, the late-night phone calls whispered in the dark.

It took me a while to realise that the ghosts of other women were always between us. He always had a plausible excuse, and my concerns were greeted with incredulity, accusations of jealousy and paranoia. Eventually, I started to believe what he told me – that I was the problem, because it was easier to doubt myself than face the pain of what was really happening.

So I focused on my children, who healed the open wounds left by my husband. But eventually the truth emerged, pushing itself to the surface, and after many years of doubt, whispered rumours, and other women's pitying looks, I faced up to what I'd always known. And that careless voice note was the evidence I needed; it gave me the proof to realise I was right, and the courage to finally say 'enough'.

Reaching across the café table, I touch Mum's hand. She still wears her wedding ring; her vows were important to her, and I know she's disappointed and sad about my decision to end the marriage.

Dad was only fifty-eight when he died. They'd had so many plans: to retire early, cruise the Mediterranean, buy a house by the sea, and get a little dog to walk along the dunes. I remember their laughter, the way he'd dance with her in the kitchen, drive her to work on cold, icy mornings, and cherish her. They were a team, both equals, and I wanted the same for myself when I married. I didn't get it.

After lunch, I drop Mum at her place, and head home. Pulling up outside our house, I feel that familiar rush of happiness. *Home.* I step from the car and walk up to the house, where my two perfect bay trees wait patiently for me under a rustle of roses around the door.

Thirteen years ago this summer, I saw this beautiful, broken building up for sale and it changed everything. I had scrawled the date of the auction on the calendar, and as my baby girl grew inside me, so did my dream. We were renting a small but lovely cottage by the sea in Looe, but with a second baby on the way it just wasn't big enough. This house was derelict, and needed so much work it was going for a song, and Jason was keen to make things up to me after what had happened *before* we were married. He wanted me to be happy, so I didn't try to leave, or tell anyone his secrets, but I had no intention of doing either – I adored him.

In my hormone-induced madness, I longed to fix up this house, despite being pregnant and with one child already. And Jason was so desperate to 'live the dream', I only had to show him the thumbed newspaper photo, tell him my insane idea, and he readily agreed.

The property auction was tense – with just Jason's small inheritance from his father, our budget was tight. We couldn't go a penny over one hundred thousand, and unfortunately there were people in the room that day who could. As the auctioneer raised the stakes, my nerves were shredded, and sweat gathered on my upper lip. I'd never wanted anything so much in my life – except Josh and Ruby of course – and I clung tightly to Jason as another stranger nodded at the auctioneer from the crowd.

Jason then lifted his hand, and for several long seconds we waited for the inevitable counter-bid. I held my breath, scared we wouldn't win it, but at the same time knowing we *had to, or I would die*. And in those terrifying moments of limbo, I really thought I might throw up, or cry or faint. As the gavel landed with a thump, Ruby kicked for the first time, and I was so overwhelmed I didn't know if it was ours or not, until I looked at Jason, smiling, victorious. I'd never been so exhilarated and terrified in my life . . . it felt a bit like falling in love.

Within weeks, Jason had taken out a loan and the transformation began. As my baby grew inside me, I built my palace, while Jason spent long hours at the office making the money to pay for my crazy dream. Jason revelled in the fact he'd made my dream come true, and I was grateful, but he saw the potential and wanted it as much as I did, though sometimes I worried about the financial commitment. I didn't need to worry, because my husband let nothing stand in the way of what he wanted – even money.

So, with an army of builders, and Josh toddling beside me, I began the slow and often stressful process of tending, nurturing, and healing the wounds of neglect experienced by this once-beautiful house. What kept me going through it all was that it was going to be our family home, and one day I'd plant frothy lavender wisteria where the dark, creeping damp had been.

And thirteen years later here I am, walking into my home, knowing every little crevice as well as I know my children's faces. I open the kitchen door with the handles made by a local artist from Cornish sea glass collected on the beach. Each chunky piece of pottery displayed on the shelves in the kitchen holds a memory – a family holiday somewhere warm, a birthday gift, a special day.

I take off my shoes and sink my feet into rugs inspired by the ones I'd loved in a souk in Morocco on a girls' weekend with Martha. Once home, I sourced a local rug-maker, who imbued the earthy tones of the sun-baked walls of Marrakesh with the soft limestone ivory of the Cornish cliffs and the sea fused with Atlantic light. My home is a travelogue for our lives, each perfect moment caught, like an insect in amber. This is where I'm happiest, where my kids grew up and where my new baby, Sundrenched Interiors, was born.

I missed you, I think, as I walk through the house, my fingertips caressing the mink-and-blush walls like a forgotten lover. I take it all in, wondering how long I'll be able to live this in-and-out half-life and never truly possessing it all. I get along with my mum, but it's a long time since I lived with her, and for me to stay at her apartment every week won't be easy for either of us.

My phone rings. I don't recognise the number; it's probably someone trying to sell something or scam me. I reject the call; I don't have time for that right now, I have to collect Ruby from school. Josh texted earlier to say he'd be staying late to revise as he has his exams soon. I'm grateful he's so focused, not hanging around nearby parks vaping like most of his peers.

I'm just locking the front door when this weird feeling of unease washes over me. I instinctively turn and look behind me but can't see anything – am I imagining things now? I tell myself to stop being silly, but just as I'm about to get into the car, I glance at the trees that line the front garden and swear I see something move. The planting is high to give an illusion of privacy on a busy road, but it doesn't stop people from peering in. And right now, *someone* is doing just that from behind the lacy canopy of leaves.

What the hell? I'm trying to make out the shape, but need to get closer. So I walk cautiously towards the trees, ready to run if they jump out. I'm nervous, but remind myself it's broad daylight, and it might be a kid or someone who's just passing. But as I get closer, my eyes slowly make out a face in the leaves. I gasp audibly, and whoever it is seems to realise I've seen them and they move quickly away.

Are they completely innocent – someone merely wanting to look at the house? I can understand that; it's been featured in magazines, it could easily attract interest from someone walking past, but why stand there so still and then move away? I can't help it – I immediately think of Ellie. Jason said it's over, but that could be a lie. She could be checking up on him, or seeking some kind of revenge on me if he *has* dumped her. I'm not interested in knowing everything, but I *am* interested to see if she's decided to hang around outside the house. It wouldn't be the first time.

I've been watched by one of Jason's 'lady friends' before; there was a woman a few years ago who used to stalk my social media. She'd sometimes write vile stuff about me in the comments, and I'd block her, but she'd then pop up again under a different name. The remarks she made were so disgusting, so hateful, that I knew it was the same woman. It was only when I threatened to get the police involved that she stopped. I knew she had a connection to Jason because she would direct-message me to say he was with her, but of course he denied it. I wasn't sure I believed him, even when she eventually stopped. But the feeling of being watched has never really gone away.

For a few seconds, I hold back, then move slowly out past the trees, my keys now in my fist, and look left and right down the road. It seems clear, but the trees and scattering of parked cars could easily hide someone, though all I see is an old man walking his dog. I breathe again. What's wrong with me? Whoever it was, perhaps they were just passing our house and peeped in through the trees to look at the scramble of white roses around my pale pink door? Or the beautiful handmade shutters painted in vintage eau de Nil?

Suddenly the air is filled with the sound of a car's engine revving really fast. I turn quickly, just as a mint-green Fiat flies past me and disappears into the distance. Was the driver of the car the same person standing behind the trees? Or is it just a coincidence and I'm overthinking things again?

I climb into my car, shivering a little despite the warm spring sunshine, and start the engine. I head off down the road for school, slightly comforted by the fact that most of the houses lining this road have door cameras. People are out walking their dogs, as the trickle of mums and pushchairs head slowly along the pavement for the primary school pick-up. Surely no one with any bad intent would be hanging around outside our home on a sunny afternoon in early summer. Would they?

4

Pulling in at the school ten minutes later, I manage to convince myself there was no one hanging around near the house. It's just my overactive mind – something Jason always said when I remarked on how he smelled of another woman's perfume. It may be over, but the scars from my marriage are always with me; they run so deep.

The burgeoning crowd of teens soon begins to spill from the school gates. Boys launch book bags at each other's heads, girls gossip and embrace like they'll never see each other again. And in the middle of this teenage maelstrom, I spot Ruby, school tie wrapped around her head bandana-style; she's laughing with her gaggle of girlfriends and I feel a rush of love. On spotting me, my daughter abandons her friends and runs towards the car, waving at me as she simultaneously waves at the girls behind her. *Hello goodbye.*

Throwing her bag in first, she explodes into the car, long legs in laddered tights, scuffed shoes, clutching a file stuffed with papers. Her beauty takes my breath away.

'Muuum, let's go to the coffee shop? *Pleeease?* I *need* hot chocolate with lashings of cream!'

That angelic face is gazing at me in hope. How can I say no? This might be the last time Ruby will want to drink hot chocolate with her uncool mother in public. It's hard to comprehend when your children are young, but there's a last time for everything, like the last time she squeezed into our bed, the last time she asked me to brush her hair and fasten her buttons. The last time her little hand held mine.

'Mum?' She's still waiting for my response, her eyebrow raised hopefully as I haven't yet said no. I smile indulgently, which she sees as victory and claps the ends of her fingers together in celebration. I start the car, about to pull away, when my phone buzzes, and Ruby grabs it while I move off.

'Ugh!' She pulls a face.

'What?'

'Josh says his revision is cancelled and can he get a lift. Can I text him back on your phone and say "no, you knob". *Pleeeeease?*

I shouldn't, but I laugh. 'No Ruby, you *can't*,' I say in mock outrage. 'And don't say "knob".'

'Can I say "no, you dick" then?' Her finger is poised to type the text, so I pull up on the pavement a little further down the road. And to avoid any confusion or obscene texting, I gently take the phone from her, and text him to say where I'm parked. He immediately responds with a thumbs up, and a few minutes later, he's sitting in the back of the car waiting to be chauffeured home.

'Why was revision cancelled?' I ask.

'Mr Roberts had a family emergency.'

'His wife's having a baby,' Ruby pipes up. My daughter's always on it with the gossip.

Josh reacts with unnecessary horror at this. 'He's about a hundred years old, his wife can't be pregnant, you *dick*.'

'*You* dick!' she replies.

'No more dicks please,' I say breezily. 'And as for Mr Roberts, you may be surprised to learn that even if he is a hundred years old, which I doubt, he's technically capable of reproducing.'

'Yuck,' Ruby says, while Josh grunts his disapproval.

I'm aware that the lifespan of human sperm probably isn't a discussion for school pick-up, but I enjoy making my kids cringe.

'Sadly the same can't be said for women,' I continue, 'who often have to abandon or compromise their careers in order to make use of the small window they have to give birth. But Ruby could be right, even as a centenarian, Mr Roberts *may* have impregnated his wife.'

'Eww,' they chorus.

'Anyway, I'm glad revision is cancelled, because now you get to join me and Ruby for hot chocolate at the coffee shop.'

I glance in my mirror to gauge his reaction. It's full-blown horror.

'That's *so* lame. What if my mates are there?'

'Oh, I hadn't thought of that, damn. Perhaps Ruby and I could have our drinks in the toilets so your friends don't see us?'

'Or we could wear fake moustaches and sit on the other side of the café. That wouldn't be weird at all,' Ruby adds.

'You don't need a fake moustache, Ruby,' he teases. 'You've got a real one.'

She leans into the back seat to whack him, but he quickly ducks out of the way and they're now play-fighting as I try to steer the car through traffic.

'I'll order the drinks, Mum,' Josh says once we're in the coffee shop. He's already done a quick scan to check none of his friends are in the vicinity to witness the fact he's out with his mother and sister. The shame of it.

I give him my credit card and walk towards a window table, while Ruby skips off after him, heading for the queue.

They seem to have hardly registered the fact Dad won't be staying tonight, and I will be staying at Nan's later in the week. And their usual irreverence and swapped insults tell me nothing's changed and everything's okay.

My phone rings. It's the same number that called just before I left the house. I decide I'd better answer it or they'll just keep calling, so I pick up.

'Er, hello, is this Alice? Alice Pemberton?'

'Oh . . . yes, that's me.' It's my name from before I married so it takes a moment to register, but I'll soon be Pemberton again, so I might as well start getting used to it again now.

'Alice – er, yes, this is a bit awkward. I'm not sure if you'll remember me, but we were at school together.'

'Oh?' I'm intrigued.

'Daniel Prescott, we were in the same year for a while.'

I see him in my mind's eye, year 12, we'd have been sixteen, going on seventeen. He was posh, his family had moved from London. I feel a sudden flush rise up my neck as I remember how much I fancied him. God yes, it's all coming back. He had a party when his parents were away, the house was huge, they were very rich, and I'd always liked him. He began to show an interest in me, flirting and teasing me the way teenagers do when they like someone. On the night of his party, he asked me to go out with him, and we kissed awkwardly in a bedroom on a bed piled with coats. After that, I waited for him to invite me to the cinema or something, but he didn't and soon after that Jason started to show an interest in me. But I always held a torch for Daniel and the blood has now rushed to my face at the memory, and I'm glad my children aren't here to witness their mother blushing over a high-school crush.

There's an awkward pause, then he says, 'I've just moved back here. I saw on Facebook that you're an interior designer now, and have your own business, Sundrenched?'

So Martha's not wasted any time posting on Facebook.

'I hope you don't mind me calling out of the blue like this.'

'No, not at all, it's nice to hear from you.'

'I've been in London,' he's saying, 'but I've come home to the south-west. I've bought Silvercliff, near Salcombe.'

'Lovely.' I'm vaguely aware of the house. It used to belong to some old-money family. That was many years ago. They went broke, or disappeared, I don't know. And there was something else . . . I think one of the family died in the house, but I don't remember much about it, and I can't really ask Daniel, so I'll google it later.

'Yes, it's beautiful, high up on the cliffs, amazing views. I'm excited to be back,' he adds. His voice is gentle, with a spark of enthusiasm. As he talks, the years roll back, and I recall how Daniel's quiet voice always drew me in, like he might know a secret. I haven't forgotten him, and wonder if he's still as good-looking as he was almost twenty years ago.

'So, Alice . . . you probably know what I'm going to say next?'

I haven't a clue, unless he's having a party at this new house and wants to kiss me awkwardly again on a pile of coats. I flush slightly at the memory.

'No, I can't imagine what you're going to say,' I giggle. My voice sounds girlish, but more finessed than usual. Again, a silent prayer that the kids aren't here to witness my 'posh voice'.

'Well, I'm calling because you're an interior designer?'

'Yes, I—'

'And I'd love for you to come and visit the place, cast your eye over things and see what you think?' he adds with the foppish awkwardness of Hugh Grant. People sometimes used to say he looked a bit like the actor when he was younger. I wonder if he still does?

'Yeah, I'd love to see your place,' I say. 'My business is relatively new, a couple of years old, but I have all the qualifications.'

He chuckles at this. 'Alice, I don't need your CV. I'm sure you're brilliant, you had such a unique style back in the day.'

Did I? My face flushes even warmer. I don't recall being particularly stylish. I hope he isn't mixing me up with someone else.

'So, I suppose the best thing is for you to come over here as soon as possible to take a look?' Daniel's saying. 'Would tomorrow work for you, or is that too short notice? I'll send my address.'

'No, that's fine . . . great.' He seems very keen, and it is short notice – but I can move a few things around. I'm thrilled at the prospect of working on a no doubt big and beautiful house in Devon.

I put down my phone after we say goodbye. Wow! What just happened? I can only just quell the urge to bang my fist on the table and shout *YESS!*

I do a quick google and find out that Daniel Prescott's family still own half the county. This could be very good for business – I have to really impress him tomorrow.

I'm slightly panicked at the prospect of such a huge undertaking, but if I get it right, this could be the breakthrough I need. I feel quite giddy, and can't take the smile off my face as I wait for Josh and Ruby to return with the drinks.

I'm making notes on my phone by the time they arrive back at the table. They're fighting over what was apparently the last millionaire's slice, but it's good-natured, and as they sit down, Josh quite sweetly gives in to his sister.

'That's really nice of you, Josh,' I say, giving him a wink. There are five years between them, and Ruby really looks up to him. It matters that he's a kind big brother.

'Mum, did you see that woman talking to us in the queue?' Ruby asks.

'No, I was on my phone . . . what woman?'

'She's gone now. She was a bit weird,' Josh says, taking a brownie from the tray.

'Weird how? I ask absently, still thinking about the phone call from Daniel.

'She was wearing these dark glasses.'

'It's a sunny day, you knob,' Ruby butts in.

'It's not sunny *inside*, dickwad.'

'Okay, okay, enough of the insults, guys.' I gaze around, vaguely intrigued to see this 'weird' woman wearing sunglasses indoors. 'Where is she?'

'She left,' Josh says.

I take my coffee from the tray, my head now full of fabrics and colours.

'But when she was in the queue, she asked if we live nearby.'

And suddenly I'm on red alert. 'Josh, you didn't tell her, did you?'

'No, I asked her why she wanted to know,' Josh replies. 'But she didn't answer, just started talking to Ruby, asking her weird stuff.'

'She wasn't that weird. You were,' Ruby interjects. 'She was only being polite, Mum, and Josh was really rude. She was asking about school, she was, like, "Oh, so what's your favourite subject?" And I told her I like drama. I mean, she wasn't, like, weird-weird.'

I can feel that familiar tenderness across my flesh, my breathing now shallow.

'When she left, did you see which way she went?' I try to sound calm.

'No, she scuttled off, like she didn't want anyone to see her.' Being older and more aware, Josh's reaction to this is completely different to Ruby's.

'Neither of you told her where we live, did you?'

A glint of guilt flits across Ruby's face.

'Ruby?' I ask.

'Nooo. I'm not, like, a toddler.' She hesitates. 'But she asked if we live at the house with the pink door, and I said yes.'

Fuck! 'Where's this woman now?' I ask, still trying to contain my panic and not let the kids see how much this has shaken me.

Josh shrugs. 'She's gone, didn't even wait for the coffee she paid for.'

I start to drink my coffee, my mind filled with possibilities – and none of them good. Am I being ridiculous, and the woman was a genuine stranger making genuine small talk with my kids? *But she knows we live in a house with a pink door.* Okay, stay calm. Is this woman Jason's lover Ellie? Is she circling my house and kids? Jason wants to keep the 'perfect' house and family, he hates the idea of divorce, to him it's failure – and Jason doesn't fail. So is Ellie my replacement, and she's checking out her new life and kids? Nothing would surprise me about my husband. *Jason likes to have his cake and eat it*, I think, watching the kids devour their pastries. And then, out of the corner of my eye, I see something through the window. My mouth goes dry and my heart starts to thud in my head as I watch a mint-green Fiat peel out of the car park.

5

Driving home from the coffee shop, I'm feeling so uneasy. Was the woman talking to my kids, the woman in the Fiat, the woman Jason sent the voice note to? Was it Ellie? And if so, why was she asking my children where they live? Doesn't she know where her lover lives with his family? And was *she* the person peering through the trees at our house before I picked the kids up? Did she follow me to the school and then the coffee shop? If so, why?

Jason may not want to lose everything by rocking the boat. But what if Ellie wants more? What if she wants to *capsize* it?

As soon as we get home, the kids go off to their rooms saying they have homework (no doubt a cover for texting, gaming and FaceTiming) and I text Jason.

Hey do you know anyone that
has a mint green Fiat?

He doesn't answer straight away, which is nothing new, so I try to distract myself by starting the lasagne for dinner. As it's our first time in the house during this new regime, I wanted tonight to be special, but the staring eyes through the trees and the strange encounter in the coffee shop have shaken me. So I lock the front door, and though it's still light outside, I close the downstairs curtains, looking out first to check there's no one loitering.

Back in the kitchen, my phone pings. It's a text from Jason.

No, I don't know anyone with a Fiat. Why do you ask?

I saw a woman looking at the house today. And a woman at the coffee shop asked the kids if they live in a house with a pink door.

Oh, do you know who it was?

I didn't see her, but if it's your new girlfriend can you tell her to back off? The last thing we need right now is a bunny boiler.

It isn't, and as I said I don't know anyone who drives a Fiat

I put down the phone, still trying to come up with an innocent explanation, but as I empty two tins of tomatoes on to the sizzling beef mince I'm damned if I can think of it.

Later, the three of us eat dinner, and I try to put aside my concerns. I want us to enjoy our first night of nesting together, so I have a glass of red and pour Vimto into wine glasses for Josh and Ruby.

'Cheers!' I say, and Josh rolls his eyes while Ruby sips her drink like wine and demands a toast.

'To the Taylors!' I add, attempting to toast family unity in a way that doesn't exclude their father. The books about how to have a healthy divorce say you should avoid any negative chatter about either partner. Despite Jason's behaviour towards me, or lack of respect for our marital vows, he is still their father.

After dinner, I'm loading the dishwasher and chatting to the kids with my back to them. 'This is your job from now on. You can take it in turns, and make your beds, and try and keep things tidy. And don't leave your shoes all over the hall where your dad trips over them. Things are different now. Dad will be on his own and will need your help – so you have to step up.' I turn around. 'Guys . . . guys?'

They've obviously both sneaked off upstairs, thinking it was hilarious to go while I was talking to them. Okay, I was probably nagging, and in all honesty how is me at home on my own with the kids any different than our usual weeknights, or weekends come to that. But I want them to feel part of a team, not a broken family, and it's not like Jason's the most reliable at housework. So once I've cleared everything away, I take a large whiteboard from my office and create a family rota that covers the whole week. It takes me a while, but it's a labour of love, and when I'm finished I prop it against the wall on the kitchen counter. I love the way the week is now blocked into neat lines and squares, the colour coding an extra safety net – there's everything on there from school pick-ups to after-school activities, Josh's revision, and repeat prescriptions for Ruby's asthma inhaler. If we all check the board, this new life will pose few problems, and we will all be on the same page – literally. I stand back to admire my handiwork. Doing this has given me some peace of mind, but not enough, so I go back into the hallway to check I locked the door.

It's raining really hard outside, and sounds windy too, like a storm, but as always this big old house feels sturdy and safe. *You can huff and puff but you can't blow my house down.*

It's late, but the porch light illuminates the stained-glass panel of blossoms layered in shades of pink, lavender, lilac and deep violet. I painted the door frame myself, in soft, pale pink, the colour of a rose petal faded by the sun.

There's a faint crack in the glass: it's been there since forever, a beautiful, familiar flaw, like Ruby's crooked smile and Josh's gait. I glance down, loving the way the coloured glass projects shards of jewelled shades on to the pale wooden floor. The illuminated refractions stripe the ground. I gaze at them, enjoying the small, silent spectacle, until suddenly they stop. I look up at the stained glass in the door: it's dark, a shadow is blocking the light. *Someone is standing on the doorstep.*

I stand very still in the hallway for a few seconds; whoever is on the other side of the glass also stays very still. I hear a noise behind me, or is it above? It must be the cat – but when I turn back and look towards the front door, there's no one there. *Or perhaps there never was?*

I think of the kids. 'Josh, Ruby, are you still upstairs?' I call, standing by the half-open front door, a hovering dusk waiting to be let in. Frozen, I listen for my children's voices.

'Yeah,' I hear from Ruby, then 'What?' from Josh. I breathe a sigh of relief. Everyone and everything is fine, I'm just over-tired and over-anxious. I need to get out of my own head. So I make sure the door is double-locked, take my laptop, head for the living room, and peep through the curtains to check there's no one outside. Now reassured, I sit on the sofa to search for Daniel Prescott's house on Google Earth.

I'm still a little nervous, but soon distracted by Daniel's gorgeous, white clifftop home overlooking the sea, and I have no doubt it must be worth several million. My mind flies over the house, imagining the interior, the kind of lives that have been lived there, and I wonder idly if Daniel's single.

Then, like the other Alice who went to Wonderland, I go down the rabbit hole, and through a few articles and newspaper cuttings I discover there was a death in the house. But going deeper, it becomes curiouser and curiouser – it looks like the death was suspect, the woman of the house died from a fall, but no one was ever charged or convicted. Now I remember as a teenager seeing the lurid newspaper headlines, and Mum and Dad talking in whispers about Silvercliff and the 'goings on' there. I google further, but can't seem to find any more. I'm sure Daniel's aware of the dark history of the house and might be able to fill me in?

I google him again, and this time put 'Daniel Prescott wife' as the search term. I don't see any evidence of a wife.

I wonder idly what it would be like to be married to someone like Daniel – what would my life be like now if I'd made different choices all those years ago?

The exterior of the house is pure inspiration, and as he hasn't been there long, I'm imagining the inside is likely in need of some TLC. I decide to use the cliffs and the glittering white stone as my starting point for the design. This will be luxury coastal living, life by the sea, nothing nautical or clichéd but sun-drenched shades, golden beaches and changing sunsets. As yet, I don't have any idea of what he wants, or needs, or his taste in decor, but one thing I do know is that I need this job.

Outside, the summer storm continues, puncturing the building heat of the past few days. Ombre shades of blue and slashes of pink are smeared across a smoky sky – and my creative mind goes into overdrive. Colours, shapes and textures are inspired by the swirling storm, the rugged cliffs and rough sand, while the sea provides soft furnishings in whirly waves of silks and frothy cream fur.

I immerse myself in paint samples, creating mood boards and rough sketches, a palette of light and shadow, land and sea. Blues and greys and shades of white reflect the misty morning fog rolling off the cliffs, softened by the warm gold of sand. This is morphing into something far more important than an interior – the fee for this transformation will be my escape!

I feel the same at the start of any project, and it always takes me back to my own project: this house on Seafern Road.

Jason hadn't been convinced I could do our home justice, offering to bring in 'real' interior designers. He would complain bitterly about me wasting money 'on ridiculously priced paints, with ridiculous names to match!' But when what he'd referred to as 'Alice's folly' was transformed into a stunning home with a beautiful interior, his attitude changed. When we invited our friends round for a 'house-warming' he took most of the credit for my hard work, and when someone asked about the colour palette, Jason waxed lyrically about 'the hint of purple' in Elephant's Breath. He also banged on enthusiastically about 'the yellow undertones', and 'echoes of sunlight' in Cooking Apple Green, the colour on our kitchen walls. One of the neighbours was so impressed by his knowledge of high-end paint, she started sleeping with him.

It wasn't the first time, and it wouldn't be the last, but when I asked him about the neighbour, he denied everything as always.

I blame myself for staying, for allowing him to treat me like that, but I realise now that I wanted him to lie. If he'd admitted it, I'd have to have done something about it. And what could I do? If we split up he might try to keep the children, the house, take everything I loved and leave me with nothing. Being a lawyer, the threat was real, and during our marriage he'd sometimes hinted at what he could do if he had to, and I never wanted to find out.

But now I feel stronger. The children are older, my business is growing enough for me to dream of financial independence – and I can finally break free. The opportunity to work on Daniel Prescott's house feels like fate, like the universe is giving me something back for all those years of pain and suffering. Working for him could be just the beginning – his family own hotels and holiday homes, and if he likes what I do to his house . . . then who knows? Anything is possible.

Suddenly I become aware of a scratching noise coming from the hall. It must be Willow, our cat. Is she scratching at the front door to come in? There it is again – the scratching. It must be Willow. I get off the sofa to go and let her in, but when I move, I see Willow is here, watching me from the chair. My flesh prickles. If Willow's in here with me, then who's at the front door?

6

Standing up, I go to the doorway of the sitting room where I can look into the hall. It's dark, but the outside light is on and I can see the outline of someone. My heart jumps, and when they press against the front door and start peering through the stained glass, the blood pounding in my ears is louder than the sound of the storm. Then the shadow steps back, and my heart begins to slow. Are they leaving? I walk into the hall to check they're gone, and move slowly towards the door, one step at a time. And just as I reach the door, I see the definite shape of a human still standing in the doorway. It's 10 p.m., and it's dark. No way am I unlocking that door. But what if it's someone here to tell me Mum's been taken ill? I *have* to answer. In my mind's eye I see the same figure I saw earlier peering through the trees.

Can they see me? It's dark, I don't think so, but now I see movement. Whoever was peering inside is going away. I continue to stand rigid, a few feet away from the door, in case they return. Maybe I should call the police, but my phone's still in the sitting room. I'm worried about the kids upstairs, so need to make sure that whoever it is hasn't gone round the back of the house. *Shit!* I just remembered there's a ladder out there. I used it yesterday to paint the bedroom window frame. What if someone knows I'm here on my own with the children tonight? What if they see the ladder and use it to climb in?

I could kick myself. How could I forget to move it? Turning away from the door, I head cautiously back down the hall, and through the kitchen to see if anyone is out there. As I turn on the kitchen light, I see movement in the back garden and freeze. Only to realise it's my own terrified reflection, stiff and scared. The bespoke floor-to-ceiling windows are also betraying me to whoever may have walked around to the back of the house. I watch myself walk towards the black mirror, and reach for the switch for the outdoor lights: one click and the patio and garden are illuminated. Now I turn off the inside lights, giving myself the advantage if anyone is out there.

Scanning the area, I see nothing, no one, just rain lashing diagonally across the garden, and trees shaking in the wind.

Satisfied I'm alone, I leave the kitchen, walk down the hall, and unlock and open the front door wide. The safety lights are on, and I see that one of my two beautiful bay trees has fallen, and realise with huge relief that it probably landed against the door. As I pick it up, it makes a scratching sound against the glass of the door, and I want to laugh. That was the scratching sound – the bay tree against the glass. I'm so ridiculously relieved and delighted by this that I step outside, and throwing back my head I let the summer rain land on my hair and face. I take in the trees that line the road outside our front garden wall, loving their blackness against the deep grey of the sky. Thunder fills the air, rumbling through the garden and into the house. Flashes of lightning follow, illuminating the trees, now black against the bright sky, before darkness lands again. The residue of fear still sits in my stomach but I'm okay, and my children are sleeping peacefully upstairs. I need to go and check on them, to settle my mind that all is safe, so I leave the storm for the calm of the house. Inside, I slip off my shoes and climb the stairs on autopilot, avoiding the steps with the noisy creaks. I love this house, and all of its quirks.

I slip through the open door of Ruby's room, where she's sleeping soundly, but the carpet is damp under my bare feet. She's left her window open, and I pull it shut firmly. It lands with a loud bump, and she stirs briefly. I look at my sleeping child, who doesn't even wake to a storm raging through her window.

Then I tiptoe across the landing to her brother's room, and listen for a moment. I can't hear him, so slowly open the door, something I wouldn't normally do but I allow myself this intrusion on his privacy. Tonight, I just need to check on them both, and now I can go to bed and sleep as peacefully as them.

I walk back downstairs. This is my first night without Jason, alone with the kids, in the house. I've been alone before plenty of times, but there's a strange, heightened feeling, a mix of fear and excitement. I don't quite understand it, but I'm feeling exposed. I don't miss Jason though – he wouldn't do anything anyway. He'd just say I was being paranoid.

After checking the locks again downstairs, I head back upstairs to bed. The first night of nesting hasn't quite been the success I'd hoped for.

All the 'activity' has put me on edge, and on top of that I'm feeling an undercurrent of anxiety regarding tomorrow's meeting with Daniel Prescott. He's my biggest prospective client to date, and I have to impress him. What if he hates all my ideas?

Consequently, when my alarm goes off at seven-thirty, I have barely slept at all.

'Time to get up!' I yell in my loudest voice thirty minutes later as I trudge down the stairs in my best trouser suit and full make-up. I'm exhausted, but my nerves are providing me with a dose of adrenalin I sorely need today. I have to be at the house in

Salcombe by ten, so go straight into the kitchen to throw several slices of bread into the toaster and make myself a strong coffee.

Damn, I can hear water running upstairs. Ruby's obviously having a shower. God knows how long she'll be, but knowing her there will be no rush to get to school. I stir my coffee. hoping her last-minute ablutions don't make me late. They could both, in theory, set off early and walk to school, but after yesterday I feel uneasy about that.

I keep checking the time, and eventually Josh wanders in. I ask about his revision, he rolls his eyes, and then Ruby appears.

'You okay, sweetie?' I ask, relieved to see she's dressed, even if her hair is wringing wet.

She flops on a stool at the kitchen island. 'Yeah, I didn't sleep too good.'

'Oh, I'm sorry, you look a bit tired.'

'Do I? Shit, I need more concealer.' With that, she rushes out of the room to deal with this 'emergency'.

Josh gives me a look.

'You aren't worried about your exams, are you, love?' I ask.

'No . . . it isn't *that*.' He butters his toast, eating the first slice while buttering the second.

'What then?'

He walks from the toaster to the island, toast in his hand, and sits down.

'What?'

'Ruby asked me not to say anything. But . . . she's worried.'

I sigh deeply and join him at the island.

'Why?' I ask quietly. He glances at the door to make sure she isn't within hearing distance.

'She's been having nightmares. She's worried she's going to end up in care.'

'Oh no.'

'Yeah – one of her friends had to be fostered or went to a children's home or something when her parents split up.'

'That's her friend Rosie, she was placed in temporary care. But their situation was quite different. Her parents were struggling.'

He shrugs, already bored or uncomfortable with the conversation.

'I should have realised,' I murmur, angry with myself for not picking up on Ruby's concerns.

He's now standing up, about to abandon our exchange, so I have to be quick with my interrogation.

'You say she's having nightmares? Did she tell you what they were?'

'Dunno, she said something about dreaming that someone was trying to get into her bedroom window.'

I feel like I've just been punched. 'Who, when?'

'Last night I think, but chill, Mum, it was only a dream . . . and don't tell her I told you.'

'No, of course, but thanks for letting me know.'

He pushes his plate away. 'Then . . .' I can see he's debating whether to say this. 'She might be wrong, but she said when she woke up this morning, her bedroom window was open. She reckons she'd closed it before she went to bed last night.'

7

'But I closed her window last night, when I went in to check on her,' I say, knowing I'm right. But even if I didn't, Ruby said she did. We can't both be wrong . . . can we?

'Well, it was open this morning, I saw it – she probably did it herself in her sleep.' He grabs his bag. 'I need to get off,' he says, shutting down the conversation. But I can't leave it there. I need to work it out, this doesn't feel right. I'm hemmed in by self-doubt, and fear – but what am I scared of?

'Hang on, I'll drop you both at school,' I say, maternal instincts flooding through me as thoughts of the woman in the coffee bar, the face in the trees, and last night rush at me.

'No, I don't need a lift. I'm calling for Elliot.'

'Okay . . . if you're sure.' I wouldn't normally think twice about Josh going to school with a mate – he's seventeen, not seven. But today the idea of my kids leaving the house unnerves me, though I can't let either of them see that.

'Josh . . .' I say as he turns to go. 'All this change isn't easy for you, I know. But you're okay, aren't you?'

'I'm sweet as,' he replies dismissively.

I suppose it's natural, he's been pulling a fraction more away from us every year since he turned thirteen. But since the split, he seems to have moved away even more, and right now he can barely look at me. And it hurts like hell.

Motherly guilt weighs heavy on my heart as I think about both my kids, but Ruby is more of an immediate concern. She's struggling, having nightmares, and I should have spotted this and seen beyond her jokey facade. My daughter's hiding her pain and fear because she doesn't want to worry me. Our children protect us as much as we believe we're protecting them. But in the end, we all hurt.

Maybe it is just a coincidence that she had a nightmare that someone was looking into her upstairs bedroom window? As Josh said, she probably opened it herself while half asleep. I know if Jason was here he'd dismiss this as me being 'fussy', but a tiny part of me almost wishes he was here, so he could tell me I'm imagining everything.

Am I? Ruby used to sleepwalk when she was younger, so maybe the stress is bringing it back? But it's been years . . . *did* she sleepwalk and open the window? I can't quiet the little voice whispering *No, she didn't.*

Josh has now left, and while Ruby's still upstairs, I need to put my mind at rest. So I dash out through the side door to see if the ladder is where I left it.

I run around the side of the house, desperate to see the ladder leaning against the wall where I left it yesterday. My stomach drops. *It isn't there.* And with my heart in my mouth, I walk slowly round to the back. And there it is. Lying on the patio. Right under Ruby's bedroom window.

It's even been extended. I didn't extend it, hadn't needed to; I only used it to reach the ground-floor bathroom window to clean the frame. And no one else would use the ladder apart from Jason and he wasn't here. I collapse the ladder and take it straight to the shed. I'll know where it is, and from now on, I'll definitely know if it's moved.

I go back inside and call upstairs to Ruby, who eventually emerges.

'I put more concealer under my eyes. Do I still look tired?'

'No, you look good,' I soothe, popping another piece of bread in to toast. 'You're not worried about anything, are you?'

'Nope, I'm fine,' she says sulkily while pouring herself a glass of water.

I can't leave it there though. 'Are you sleeping okay?'

She gives a huge sigh. 'Mum, I'm *fine*,' she says through gritted teeth. 'Apart from the fact I'm late for school!'

We grab our stuff and I drive her to school, letting her eat her toast in the car, which is so unlike me. On the way we don't talk much, and once there, she disappears into the grey phalanx of uniforms trooping reluctantly into the building. Perhaps she'll come to me when she wants to talk. *Or not.*

An hour later, I'm trying to push my maternal concerns away to make room for professional ones as I drive through a bright blue day of sunshine and bluster towards Daniel's home. It's high on the cliffs, and just glimpsing it from a distance I realise Google Earth never prepared me for the sheer vastness and beauty of the place. I drive on, negotiating the steep path towards the huge, white mansion, and have to park up and sit for a moment, taking it all in.

I gaze up at the smooth, whitewashed facade glowing against brilliant blue skies. Enormous floor-to-ceiling windows look out on to the sea, along with several wide terraces at different levels. Sleek glass balustrades surround the terraces, enhancing the clean, modern silhouette. It's breathtaking. How can I possibly make the inside as stunning as the outside?

I'm extremely nervous – a lot rides on this. It could be the making of Sundrenched Interiors, and my ticket to ultimate freedom from Jason . . . but still the temptation to turn around is strong. After all, I could just go home and tell Jason I'm giving him one more chance, and despite Mum living nearby, I wouldn't have to live in two places. More to the point, I wouldn't have to torture myself with doubts that I'm not good enough to get this job. Instead I could fall back on Jason's salary, concentrate on the kids' welfare and live an easier life. Ruby would stop having nightmares, I'd be there for Josh's last few months at home before uni . . . and as I list the pros of keeping the status quo, however unhappy I am, I wonder if I should just surrender. Should I allow myself to fall back into that easier life? But then I think about my husband's careless affairs, his lack of respect or love for me, and how I now feel nothing for him. And I know I can't take another wretched day of our pretend-perfect life.

Climbing from the car, the fresh, salty air calms me, and Daniel Prescott's Xanadu fills me with hope and inspiration. My business is beginning to bloom, and I have a waiting list of clients – but *this* is what I trained for; it's the dream of every interior designer to be given a project like Silvercliff. Anticipation and fear thrum through me. This feels like one of those moments in life where things are about to change. I just hope it's true.

I approach the huge front door, ring the bell and the door opens slowly. I'm shocked to see a uniformed maid standing there, and when I give her my name, she says, 'Ah yes, Mr Prescott is waiting for you.'

She escorts me down a long hallway into the most beautiful sitting room I've ever seen: pure, understated elegance with pale walls, polished oak floors and cream linen armchairs. There's a high stone fireplace in pale French limestone as a focus, and the biggest window that opens out on to acres of lush garden, and the sea beyond. But I'm disappointed. The room's already been designed, and by someone who knows exactly what they're doing. It's perfect. So why am I here?

The maid gestures for me to take a seat, and within seconds Daniel sweeps into the room.

'Good morning, and welcome to Silvercliff,' he says in those familiar, plummy tones.

'A beautiful name for a beautiful house,' I say, standing up to greet him. For a second neither of us seems quite sure whether to shake hands or hug. But after a slight hesitation, he gathers me up in a bear hug and kisses both cheeks. Then he lets me go, grabs one of my hands and stands back, admiringly.

'You're as lovely as I remember, Alice.'

'And you're very kind, but I have a few more wrinkles I'm afraid.'

'You don't look a day over seventeen,' he says with a sigh. I roll my eyes at this, and he gestures for me to sit back down on the sofa, where he joins me.

'How's your mother?' he asks, like he last saw me yesterday.

'She's er . . . fine.'

'I remember her, from St Michael's. Such a great teacher.'

'Oh, of course yes.' I flush slightly. Mum taught at my school for a while, which was pretty mortifying as a teenager.

'So, I'm excited to hear all about you, and your life,' he starts, like we're on a first date. Again the quiet voice, suggesting secrets, the eye contact hinting at past intimacy that doesn't feel quite right now we're older. 'You have two kiddies?'

I nod. I don't remember telling him I have children, but perhaps I mentioned it in the phone call.

'So . . . I'm guessing there's a husband – or partner?' he asks.

I hesitate for a moment. Being estranged is new for me. 'Yes . . . I'm married. Well, I was . . . we're going through a separation,' I add.

'Oh, I'm sorry to hear that.' He turns his mouth down to create the illusion of sadness, but I'm not sure I believe him. 'Was there someone else?' he asks, taking me by surprise.

I'd forgotten Daniel sometimes had no filter. Clearly he hasn't changed, but I'm not offended.

'No, no we just . . . things fizzled out,' I try, not ready to discuss the details. 'But enough about me, let's talk about this beautiful house,' I say, feeling uncomfortable talking about Jason. I'd rather forget him when possible.

Daniel seems to be scrutinising me, like he's looking for an answer.

'I think you're sad, Alice.'

I shrug, just like Josh does. 'Not sad. A little unsure about the future, but I'm optimistic. I'm sure there's something wonderful waiting for me on the horizon.'

'Good for you.' He smiles warmly, keeping his eyes on mine for a moment too long. And I feel a stirring of something – something I haven't felt in a while. Attractive. I actually feel attractive. I like how he makes me feel. I always did.

'I have some sketches and ideas already. But looks like you've just finished this section of the house?'

He drags his eyes from mine, and looks around the room like he's never seen it before. 'I'm sure *you* could add something, Alice?'

'Okay,' I say slowly, but quite honestly, I doubt I can – it's already perfect. 'In the meantime, perhaps you'd show me around?' I ask, hoping the rest of the house is a wreck that needs my magic.

'Oh, of course,' he says, like he'd almost forgotten why I'm here. I follow him into the kitchen, where my heart sinks. 'It's stunning,' I gasp.

'Not bad, is it? It's a sort of homage to Georgian elegance with a modern culinary heart,' he says, apparently oblivious to the effect this might have on me.

Gazing at the high ceilings, sash windows, the original cornicing, the sweep of marble counters and vast oak island anchoring the bloody room, I'm quite devastated. And confused.

Why am I here?

Offering over-the-top descriptions of each amazing space we encounter, he guides me through the other rooms downstairs: all in the same vein, all appearing to have been recently completed – to an extremely high standard. This is weird. This house simply doesn't *need* an interior designer. But I *need* this job, so I keep smiling, hoping all will be revealed on the first floor.

'Shall we go upstairs?' I ask, staring in wonder at the floating staircase in front of us. Each tread seems to hover without visible support; it rises from nowhere and appears to vanish into the first floor.

'No. We don't need to go up there now.' Smiling, he gently manoeuvres me away and back into the kitchen.

'Daniel . . .' I hesitate. 'I don't want to talk myself out of a job, but I'm confused. Your home is stunning . . . and it looks like it's only recently been redecorated.'

He's staring at me intently, then he looks down, defeated. 'I should have known you'd guess. Of course you would, it's your job.' He wanders around the hallway like he's delivering a soliloquy. 'You're absolutely right of course. As soon as I moved in, just a few months ago, I immediately engaged an interior designer . . . a very good one.'

'So why do you need a designer now?'

'Because something happened here, and I need someone to erase it.'

8

Daniel and I are now in the sitting room, where the maid has left a tray of coffee and shortbread.

'I know this seems positively unhinged,' Daniel says, as he pours the coffee into two cups and hands me a cup and saucer.

'Homes hold memories,' I reply, wondering if he's referring to the death that happened here. But that was over twenty years ago, and he's only recently moved in.

Holding his cup in one hand he gestures around the room with the other. 'Homes are a silent witness to bad things, Alice.'

I feel a chill go through me. 'I agree, so much can happen within four walls, and after what went on here, I don't blame you for being concerned.'

'You *know* what happened?' His face is a picture of surprise, or is it horror?

'I . . . well, I googled and saw that about twenty years ago someone died here. They fell down the stairs, didn't they? But there were questions as to whether someone pushed them.'

'I wasn't referring to that,' he replies, his eyes suddenly dark, like he's remembering something.

'Oh, I'm sorry, then I'm a bit confused about *what* you actually want me to wipe clean here.'

His face seems to have completely shut down. 'I would rather not share it with you just yet, but something bad happened here, Alice, and if you're going to be the one to erase this, I'd prefer you came with an open mind.'

'Or a bunch of sage?' I say flippantly, trying to lighten his mood. 'Is this about evil spirits and ghosts and things? Because I'm a designer, not an exorcist.'

He smiles at this. 'You are funny Alice. You were always the cool and funny girl.' He smiles again. 'I was so fond of you.' He fixes me with his gaze. 'And I haven't forgotten that kiss.'

I feel myself blush.

'I also remember the two of us swimming in the sea at midnight, it was very romantic,' he adds.

'I remember that, it was freezing. Other people were there too though, weren't they?' I know this because it was New Year's Eve, we happened to be at the same party, but we weren't together. Daniel is remembering it differently. I was swimming with Jason that night, Daniel's kiss already a memory.

'You're right, we weren't alone, you were with him. But I still only had eyes for you,' he says, making me feel guilty after all these years.

'We were all very drunk,' I say, wondering if he liked me more than I realised. I always thought it was just a fumbled kiss on the bed of coats at his party. I really liked him, but at the time I didn't think he was interested in me.

'Why did you leave me for Jason Taylor?' he asks, unsmiling. His bluntness takes me by surprise.

It's like my whole teenage life is being reordered. Is it *me* who's misremembering?

'I'm . . . I didn't see it quite like that. We only kissed once, and after that we drifted apart, I didn't think you liked me, and when Jason asked me out . . . I said yes . . .' I smile awkwardly.

He holds up his hands apologetically. 'Sorry I didn't mean to make you feel uncomfortable. But you were wrong, I *did* like you, very much. That's why I went swimming that night.' He leans closer and says in that intimate voice, 'I wanted to get you alone . . .'

We stare into each other's eyes, and the world rewinds, until he turns away from me.

'But that bastard Jason Taylor beat me to it.'

I force myself to laugh, in an attempt to change the mood. I don't remember Daniel's anger; it makes me feel uncomfortable. Why is he still so angry after all these years? It doesn't make any sense.

'It was all so long ago, I'm sure neither of us understood what was happening,' I say, remembering him swimming with another girl. 'Anyway, so much for only having eyes for me,' I add in a teasing tone, 'I seem to remember you kissing Susie Pascoe in the sea that night.'

He smiles at this, his face turning a little pink, and I'm amused at his vulnerability. For all his silver-tongued sophistication, he's still that seventeen-year-old boy.

'You're right, but I was only with her because I was on the rebound from you,' he says with a wink.

Is he joking? Was all that about me leaving him for Jason just teasing? I remind myself that I'm here on business, not to discuss some teenage crush from twenty years ago.

'So, regarding the redesign, I'd love to know what you want me to erase? Have you been hosting seance suppers, or devil-worshipping soirées?' I ask, keeping the tone light.

He smiles, probably as relieved as I am to be off the topic of our tragic love affair that never was. 'I can see why you might think that, and I hate to be mysterious about it. But trust me, it isn't as dark as contacting the dead or worshipping the devil.'

'I'm glad to hear it. For a start you'd never get goat's blood out of that cream linen,' I joke.

'I disagree. In my experience Stain Devils always gets that pesky goat's blood off,' he chuckles, and we're back, both joking, bouncing off each other. This is the Daniel I remember – he was the friend I had a crush on, not the 'boyfriend' I dumped.

But turns out the dimples in his smile can still make me feel something I haven't felt since that kiss. And he's film-star handsome too, and as he offers me the plate of lavender shortbread he still reminds me of a young Hugh Grant, the deliciously wicked one from the first *Bridget Jones* film.

'I grow the lavender myself in the garden of my house in France,' he says as I take one.

I bite into the fragrant, buttery biscuit and imagine his lush second or third home somewhere like Provence. In my mind I see a table laid for dinner in the shade of an old olive tree, a bottle of wine in an ice bucket, and the air heavy with lavender and warmth. And I wonder how different my life might have been if I'd jumped into the sea with Daniel on that freezing New Year's Eve twenty years ago.

Over coffee, we talk through some ideas, and he seems impressed. But then that's Daniel, he's pretty positive and enthusiastic about everything, and I love his energy, it's so refreshing. 'I would love to work with you Alice . . .' he says, just as his phone buzzes. He pulls it from his trouser pocket, checks it, then stands up. 'Ugh, I need to deal with this, I'm sorry.'

I feel like I'm being dismissed, but then I guess he's a busy guy. 'It's fine,' I say, gathering my papers and files and standing up. 'Shall I leave these for you to look through?'

'That would be great, thank you. I'll walk you to your car.' He escorts me through the hallway and outside into the sunshine, where we stand looking out over the cliffs.

'It's the best view in the world,' he sighs, then turns to me. 'Thank you for coming today, it's been *so* lovely to see you again. I'll call you later in the week, perhaps we could run through some more ideas?'

'Oh . . . okay, great,' I say, unsure if I've got the job or not. 'Do you have any ideas about a schedule . . . hate to be pushy, it's just that I have a long waiting list.' I'm exaggerating, but still, I do have other clients to consider. I see his face drop slightly. I'm being pushy, and that might seem vulgar to him, and I don't want to put him off. 'But please, take your time, I can move things around as and when you decide . . .' My words tail off; I'm hoping he'll interrupt me with a starting date. But he just smiles.

'That's so kind, and thank you.'

He said he loves my ideas, he's raved over them – so what's he waiting for?

When he offers nothing more, I walk to the car, get in, give a little wave and pull slowly away. He waves back, but despite apparently being in a hurry to get off, he stays in my rear-view mirror far into the distance. I shouldn't be surprised – there was always something about Daniel that didn't quite add up. He had this ability to make you feel like you were the only person in the world, that you mattered, and it was like basking in warm sunshine. Until he suddenly took it away, and left you alone in the cold. It's hard to put my finger on, but I remember this same feeling after the teenage kiss that was everything but came to nothing.

My hands are gripping the wheel as I drive along the coast road, and despite the doubts – and my less-than-perfect memories of Daniel – I'm one of life's optimists and always hope for the best outcome. But that's why I stayed with Jason for so long: I believed I could make everything right, that if I loved harder, worked harder, and gave him everything he wanted, it would all work out. I don't want to go down the same road, either personally or professionally, but that optimism is kicking in like a class A drug, and my fingers tingle with excitement at the prospect of working in that beautiful house. I realise with elation and a tinge of fear that seeing Daniel again has sparked something in me that I thought was long dead.

◆ ◆ ◆

Over the next couple of days, I work on ideas for Silvercliff and enjoy my time with the kids. Things are getting better – no wandering ladders or scratchy bay trees, and no windows opening mysteriously in the middle of the night.

This morning I was up early cleaning the house for Jason's first night alone here with the kids, and after dropping them off at school I popped to the supermarket to restock the fridge. I bought a tonne of stuff: Ruby's favourite yoghurts, the cheese Josh likes, and cat food for Willow, whose raging appetite is equalled only by my son's. I even bought a couple of Jason's favourite beers and some snacks and sweets, because I want their time together to be positive, and happy; I want this nesting experiment to be a success. Even though it makes me sad to think of the children being home without me.

Before heading to Mum's, I call Martha from the coffee shop, I haven't spoken to her for a couple of days as I wanted to give my attention to the children. I haven't had a chance to tell her about how her posting on the alumni Facebook group led to me reconnecting with Daniel Prescott.

'Wow, if you get that gig you'll be home and dry,' she says.

'Yeah, I reckon he'd be fun to work for. He can be a bit intense, I'd forgotten that – but I think he has a sense of humour . . . hard to remember it was so long ago. But I like him, I always did.'

'Yeah, sounds like you're already smitten. You and him had a thing once, didn't you?'

'Once, literally. We kissed, it was nothing,' I add dismissively. I don't want Martha to think I have the hots for him, because I don't – well, perhaps a tiny bit, but I'm not sure he's the best antidote to Jason. He might be even worse.

When I tell Martha about Daniel wanting something 'erased' from the already perfectly designed house, it sounds even more crazy than I'd originally thought.

Her mouth is wide open, and she looks shocked and intrigued, and quite frustrated that I can't give her any clue as to what it is.

'But he must have hinted at something?'

'No, he just said something bad happened there.'

'I've gone all goose-bumpy. Be careful. If you do get the job, keep an eye out for the dead body.'

'You drama queen.'

'Yeah, scrub that – talking of bodies, Daniel probably still fancies you, and wants to see yours naked. What if next time you go, he invites you to work up a sweat in his master bedroom?'

I roll my eyes. 'He's charming, handsome, rich. I'm sure he has lots of beautiful and much younger women than me chasing him.'

'Yeah, but he might be looking for a change from young and beautiful,' she teases. 'Let's look at the facts. He invited you there to pitch a job that doesn't seem to exist. He said he'd seen your post on Facebook.' She gives an awkward smile. 'I reckon that charming, handsome and rich man might just have an ulterior motive. Lucky you!'

I chuckle at this. I can't help but wonder if she's right and Daniel Prescott does have an ulterior motive. I doubt it, but I'm extremely flattered if he does. On the other hand, perhaps he genuinely wants me to work on his home. What if there really is something in that house that disturbs him, that needs to be erased?

I feel a chill run through me as I think about what he said – *something bad happened here, Alice.*

9

Today, I'm going back home for four days, and I can't wait. I've only been away for three nights, but I've really missed the children, and my own bed. There have been positives. I've had ample time to work, but it's not easy because Mum's apartment is very small and there's not much space to lay out my mood boards and sketches and notes. Everything feels a bit cluttered, even the kitchen, where the cupboards are full of tins she'll never use if she lives to be a hundred years old. Books, bags of wool and old biscuit tins filled with her treasures sit in piles on the floor and all the surfaces, like mad half-finished games of Jenga. Then there's her collection of china dolls which she always kept in a cupboard with glass doors, so she could see them. I remember as a child I was scared of the way they'd stare out from the glass, their eyes watching me as I moved around the room, but about a year ago she took them all out of the cupboard and now they sit on any available space, even in the bathroom.

'Does Barbara have to sit by the loo, Mum, it's quite disconcerting,' I ask.

'Barbara can do as she likes, she lives here,' she jokes.

I guess I'll have to get used to being in Barbara's gaze. Dressed in full Victoriana, I find her rather stern, judgemental face quite intimidating in such an intimate setting.

I sigh. 'Mum, they're everywhere, it's like a creepy kindergarten in here, I'm convinced they all come to life when we're asleep.'

'Yes, you can hear them whispering, and their dresses rustling. I sometimes let them out to play,' she teases.

Over the past few nights, I've been trying to get used to sitting in bed with a book, with Tatiana, Mum's Russian doll from the Romanov reign, staring into my soul from the bedside table. As if this weren't bad enough, when I first arrived I sat on the sofa only to be stabbed in the thigh by an errant crochet hook. It hurt so much, I stood up too quickly and knocked over a cup of tea Mum had left on the floor, sending a river of milky old tea racing across the rug.

'What's been going on?' she asked, walking into the room like I'd had a wild party while she was in the kitchen. Even after I apologised and scrubbed at the carpet for ages, she didn't seem happy.

'I'll buy some carpet cleaner and get rid of it,' I offered, as Mum and the stain glared back at me.

'You'd better, Alice!' she snapped, like she was scolding a naughty child.

I was shocked at her reaction – she isn't usually an angry person; even when I was a child she rarely shouted. But perhaps it's my fault for invading her settled life with my own failed one?

Now, three days later, I'm relieved to be on my way back home. I love Mum, dearly, but we both need our space, and tonight I ache to get back to my study painted Schiaparelli Pink, lit by my feathery lampshade.

Pulling up outside the house for my second nesting 'shift', I couldn't be happier – and when I open the front door, I breathe a sigh of relief. I do a quick check of all the rooms, and everything seems fine. The kids' beds aren't made, but miracles will take a little longer. Meanwhile Jason has stripped our bed and put the used sheets in the washing machine – he hasn't turned it on, but again, that miracle will come I'm sure. The fridge is still pretty well stocked, which means they probably did at least one takeaway, but when I'm not here that's up to Jason.

It seems that this nesting experiment might just work. I miss the house and the kids, but I get to spend time with Mum, and if I need to be somewhere other than my office at home, like visiting a client, or buying materials, I don't have to rush back for the kids – well, for Ruby . . . Josh can look after himself.

I call Jason to check everything's been okay. 'Yeah, great,' he says. 'And I won't be working away as much from now on, so it means I can spend more time with them. It was fun.'

'Oh . . . you won't be going away as much then. Why is that?'

'No reason, I just . . .' He hesitates. 'Look I know it's against the rules, Alice, but you're welcome to come over when I'm there, to be together as a family.'

'Thanks, but let's just stick to what we agreed. I'll stay out of your time and you . . . stay away too. It's easier that way.'

I have to stay strong, Jason just wants to slip back into the old life, but I really don't.

'Okay, I just wanted to say it wouldn't be a problem if you did. Ruby misses you,' he says.

This plucks at my heart strings, as he knows it will. 'I miss them too. It'll take a bit of getting used to for all of us, especially the kids. How have you found Josh?'

'Fine. Why?'

'I don't know, I just wondered if, when he's home, he hangs out with you. He tends to spend a lot of time in his room when I'm here. We don't talk much.'

'He's seventeen, Alice! I *never* spoke to my mother between the ages of fifteen and twenty, except to ask what was for dinner,' he jokes. 'But yeah, he seems fine to me. In fact we're getting along better than we ever did when we all lived together,' he adds smugly. 'Who knew that this break-up would mean I'd become the favourite parent instead of you?'

I realise now, this is classic Jason – point scoring, competing instead of supporting, even with his own wife. He spent most of the kids' childhood rushing into the house after working late and waking them up, just because he wanted to see them. I know he adores the kids, and he genuinely did want to read them stories, or play with them. But they weren't his toys, and it wasn't good for them to be woken like that, and when I tried to object he'd call me a nag and say I was 'too uptight'.

'Alice,' he says, 'there's something I wanted to ask you . . .'

'What?'

'Well, what if one of us wants to *see* someone? What are your rules about them being at the house?'

I am immediately incensed. It's not just zero to sixty, it's zero to a billion degrees of abject fury and rage. I take a breath. 'Well, first of all, they aren't *my* rules, but surely anyone with a brain would know that it's too soon. Didn't you just say you're enjoying time with your kids, and now suddenly you want to bring someone back to the house? What the fuck, Jason?'

'Fine, if you don't want them to meet her . . .'

So he is still seeing Ellie. He obviously claimed it was over to keep his options open if I offered to return to the marriage, which would be convenient for him. Meanwhile, he'd keep the other woman on a string because as a narcissist he has to have his next 'supply' waiting. Now he knows I'm determined to end the marriage, he wants to move her in as his security blanket. Of all the manipulative . . . 'I just hope she isn't as unhinged as previous girlfriends and doesn't decide to visit us at home without an invite . . .' I hiss. 'Are you sure she doesn't drive a green Fiat?'

'No, she doesn't, and going around saying stuff like that – you're the one who sounds unhinged.'

I don't rise to this. He's done it all our lives and all he wants is for me to bite, and become hysterical, and he'll say 'told you you're unhinged'.

'No Jason, I can't believe you're even asking about bringing your new girlfriend into our children's lives. Let's sort this mess out before you add to it,' I snap. 'For the children's sake.'

'Are you jealous, Alice?' he asks calmly, in complete contrast to my anger. He does this deliberately so I'll spiral. But not anymore.

'Jealous?' I reply in a low voice, matching his calm. 'I haven't been jealous about you for years.'

He laughs. 'I don't believe you.'

I end the call, shaking my head at his arrogance, at his sheer audacity. Who does he think he is? When my phone rings again, I pick up straight away. 'Jason, I'm not fucking jealous, and if your sad little ego can't take it then you might need to find another intern with pert breasts to get you up again.'

The silence that greets me isn't surprising. He will, I'm sure, be shocked by what I've just said. The worm has turned and he really won't like that.

'Too much truth for you, Jason?' I say into the silence.

But there's nothing, no response. Just the faint sound of breathing. He's there. So why isn't he answering? Why isn't he fighting back?

'Did you hear me?' I say, now looking at the screen, surprised to see *No caller ID.*

'Do you think you're clever using your secret phone? Well, it never was a secret, I knew all along. Your spare phone for other women, mistresses, one-night stands, whoever you were stringing along.'

Silence, except for the faint breathing.

'If you're trying to scare me, Jason, it isn't working.' I hang up, and thunder crashes outside as I sit alone. It must have killed him not to say anything; he always has to have the last word. It's probably why he's such a good lawyer.

I wait for a minute to see if he's going to call back. But as the time ticks on a little worry sneaks up my spine. It *was* him, wasn't it? But what if it wasn't, and someone else is playing games with me?

10

I haven't heard from Jason since that weird heavy-breathing phone call the other night. I don't want to hear from him either because I might say something, and I don't want him to know how much it rattled me. If indeed it was Jason who called? But I'm trying not to think too deeply about it all – that way madness lies.

The rest of my time at home has gone okay, though Josh is still monosyllabic and spending all his time alone in his room. I feel like it must be me because he's obviously fine around Jason, but on a positive note, Ruby seems okay. Tonight I'm working on the ideas for Seacliff while both kids are in bed, but suddenly have this primal urge to check on them, so I head upstairs. The first thing I see is the closed door of Josh's bedroom. I know it's natural for him to want his privacy at seventeen, but he's seemed so closed off recently. It must be me he has the problem with, though it pains me to even think this. And since we told the kids we were divorcing, he's become even more detached from me. I'd hoped that on nights when it was just us three he might open up a little, laugh with Ruby and me about daft things like he used to. I'd thought he might join us to watch *the reality shows that* Ruby and I enjoy together and Jason says are 'rubbish!' I had a vague hope that it was Jason's disapproval that had kept Josh away from the sitting room. But being back in the house the past few nights, I feel like he's moved even further away. He barely spoke to Ruby and me when he wandered in at 7 p.m. after another late revision session. He didn't want dinner either, said he'd had a McDonald's – but I didn't bite. I feel like I need to pick my battles with Josh.

I walk past his bedroom door and try to hear if he's playing music or is on his computer. I guess I just want a sign of life, but whatever he's doing he's probably wearing earphones and in his own world. *All locked in.*

I turn away and move towards Ruby's room, and her open bedroom door. I wonder fleetingly if that's an age or gender thing? Is the difference between her and Josh that she's still too young to care about privacy, or does she have nothing to hide?

'Mum!' Ruby's voice is quiet but urgent, and something about this bothers me, so I immediately go to her.

'You okay, darling?' I ask brightly, but my heart jumps when I see her face. She's pale, her eyes half closed, and she's lying on her bed. 'What . . . Ruby, what is it?' I run towards her, alarmed.

'It's . . . I can't breathe . . . Mum.'

Now fizzing with panic, I immediately begin to open Ruby's bedside cabinet where we keep her inhaler. I see my hands frantically searching – hair scrunchies, discarded lip balm, an old eye mask shaped like a panda . . . but where's the fucking inhaler?

'I can't find it,' I hear myself say. 'You have more than one . . . Where's the other inhaler, Ruby?'

'At school . . . the one I have here is empty.' She's gasping now.

Fuck! I'd written it on the whiteboard and left the prescription out on the kitchen counter for Jason to collect after the changeover. I told Ruby *and* Josh to remind him. But right now, that doesn't matter – my daughter's wheezing and about to have an asthma attack. I speak as calmly as I can, take her dressing gown from the hook on the door, and help her into it while calling for Josh.

'Come on, darling, it's all fine,' I say in a forced calm voice. 'We just need to go to A&E, we can get an inhaler from there.'

As I manoeuvre her out of the room, I call Josh again, and as he hasn't responded by the time we reach the top of the stairs I bang loudly on his door. When he still doesn't answer, I push to open it, but it's locked. I rattle the handle vigorously. 'JOSH?' I yell.

'What the fuck?' I hear as the door is ripped open. I'm shocked, not only at the swearing but the anger in his voice – the expression on his face. And he's fully dressed, so he wasn't asleep in bed. *He chose to ignore me calling him.*

With my daughter gasping for breath at my side, now isn't the time to get into it with him. 'Ruby needs an inhaler. We're going to the hospital, you must come with us.'

'I don't need to come,' he says uncertainly, his anger ebbing as he glances anxiously at Ruby behind me.

'You *do*!'

'For fuck's sake, I'm old enough to be left on my own at night.'

'Josh, I know you're okay on your own, it isn't about that. I need your help – you can go into the hospital with your sister while I park the car. If you won't do it for me, do it for Ruby. . . she *needs* her inhaler.' I hear myself pleading, close to tears, but still he's staring at me, not moving. 'Josh, *please*! This is an emergency.'

In that moment, I see something in his eyes I've never seen before. But I don't have time to work out what it is. 'I'm not arguing with you, Josh, I don't have time and neither does Ruby, so do what you want.' Is my son really going to refuse to help his sister in a life-and-death situation?

I should have called an ambulance the minute I knew she was having an attack. I'm angry with myself, but the hospital's just down the road – it's only minutes away and we'd be almost there now if it weren't for Josh. I help Ruby down the stairs, my silent fury equalled only by fear for Ruby. Grabbing my car keys I open the front door, and in the light from the hall I'm horrified to see she's now white as a sheet, and the wheezing is much worse. I slam the front door shut. I'm so angry I don't care what Josh does.

We step out into the evening. It feels warmer out here than it does inside the house, and this heaviness won't help Ruby's breathing. The front garden is pitch-black, but the porch light helps us see where we're going as I guide Ruby to the car just a few feet away on the drive.

Once we're in the car, I turn on the ignition, and clutch the steering wheel like a lifebelt as we gently pull out through the gate. I'm just about to turn into the road when someone lands against the windscreen, both hands flat against the glass, their face yelling *Stop!*

I'm shaken, and Ruby screams raspily, but to my relief it's Josh.

'It's okay, love,' I say to her, reaching back to unlock the car door and let him in before moving into the road, where I put my foot down on the accelerator.

I glance at Ruby to check she's okay, and touch her knee, then check in the mirror to see my son. I can't see his face in the dark, but that's probably just as well. In this moment I'm furious with him.

Arriving at the hospital, I pull up near an ambulance at the main doors, and as both kids get out, I yell instructions: 'Go straight to the desk, don't wait – explain she's asthmatic, needs an inhaler.' He acknowledges this with a vague shrug which doesn't fill me with confidence, but does inspire me to park up very quickly.

The hospital is heaving, and I rush to the desk where a receptionist checks the computer and explains that Ruby is being seen as a priority, thank God. But the nurse can't tell me exactly where she is as there's been a computer glitch. After dashing around blindly I eventually find both kids in a cubicle with a nurse and doctor. Ruby's now had an inhaler, which has given immediate relief, and she's breathing much better already.

'Your daughter's fine, Mrs Taylor, but I'd like her to stay a couple of hours just to make sure,' the young doctor says. Her long dark hair is coiled in a bun, and her reassuring voice and the stethoscope around her neck fill me with calm.

After she and the nurse leave, Josh stands up. 'I'm getting a Coke, do you want a coffee?' he asks, unsmiling.

'Oh . . . that would be lovely, thanks.' I open my bag to get some change, but when I look up, he's gone.

'Ignore him,' Ruby says, obviously aware he's not happy about something.

'It was a bit stressful getting here. I reckon he's just a bit anxious.'

'No Mum, he's just a bit of a dick,' she replies, still reclined in the hospital bed but getting her colour back.

'Don't say "dick".'

She rolls her eyes.

'Do you know why he's being like this?'

She shakes her head. 'No idea and don't care. Sorry, but he's a total knob.'

'Ruby . . .' I say half-heartedly. In truth it's an absolute joy to hear her being rude about her brother. It means she's well again.

'Wish I'd brought my phone so I could tell Meghan where I am,' she says. 'Where's your phone, Mum, take a photo of me?' Within seconds, she's lying on the trolley making like a film star as I click away. We're both giggling when the curtain's whipped back and there stands Josh, with Jason. Neither of them is smiling.

11

'What . . . why are you here?' I ask, alarmed.

'Josh called – he said Ruby was in hospital.' Jason steps inside the cubicle.

'Hey Dad,' Ruby says, and she sounds so small again, not like the girl who was laughing and joking a few seconds ago.

'Are you okay, sweetie?' Jason goes to her, his hand touching her face, eyes searching for signs of pain.

She nods, all thoughts of a photo shoot for Meghan now abandoned in favour of Dad's attention. It's sweet, and I'm softening slightly, until he turns to me. 'You should have called me, Alice.'

I'm annoyed by the blame stitched silently into this remark. I'm also angry at the implication that I can't deal with an emergency without him, when I have been dealing with them the whole of our marriage. Alone.

'I didn't *need* to call you. Everything was under control.'

'That's not what Josh said.'

I look from Jason to Josh, who can't meet my eyes. *Betrayer.*

'Well as you can see, it's all fine. I'd have preferred that you called me first instead of dashing over here and making a wasted journey.'

The joke is, while he's been in big shiny offices and fancy hotel rooms advancing his career, I've been keeping our children alive on my own for years.

'I need to be told if there's a problem with one of my kids.' His voice is low, agitated.

'No one was keeping it from you. She couldn't breathe, I had to get her here quickly and didn't have time to call you. Obviously if it happens again, I'll call you first, regardless of her breathing difficulties.'

'Calm down, Alice, you know that's not what I'm saying.'

Without taking his eyes from mine, he reaches out and ruffles Josh's hair. I wait for my son to recoil as he has these past couple of days when I've gone anywhere near him, but he doesn't, and they both just stare at me. Has so much changed in just a few days?

I know why Jason's angry – he was hoping to waltz in here and be the saviour – but things have changed. In the past, as a young mum with two little ones, I was grateful to him for just showing up, as he was never around much for the difficult times. Consequently, he's always been the fond, distant father, turning up all calm and with instructions and advice like he's the cavalry coming to save us. But it's always after the emergency, when we've already saved ourselves. We've never needed him.

And here he is again, stepping in after the crisis is over, to tell me what I've done wrong and waiting for the applause, only this time *he* caused the crisis.

Wow! How did I never see this before?

'How did this happen Alice?' he asks. Jason is setting this up for a 'Mum's so ditsy she forgot to get Ruby's inhaler' narrative.

'Jason, you didn't get her inhaler,' I say calmly, and before he can argue I continue. 'I made a note on the whiteboard, and left the prescription on the kitchen counter.' I know this is a bit below the belt to say it in front of the kids, but he needs to be accountable for once in his life.

'I thought you had a spare inhaler, Ruby?' He turns to her, ignoring me because he has no comeback. He knows it's his fault, but he'll never take the blame.

'I do have another, I left it at school, my bad,' she replies, proving to be the only adult in the room.

'No, it's not *your* fault Ruby,' I say. 'Dad was supposed to collect it from the pharmacy.' He's about to cut in, but before he does, I add: 'From now on I'll order it online through the app. I'm sorry, darling, it won't happen again.' If her father won't apologise for this I will.

Despite thinking this whole nesting thing was working, that I'd have some respite and Jason would take the helm sometimes, nothing's changed. I still need to be on top of everything.

The next few minutes are spent in a tense atmosphere where Jason and I try not to make eye contact, but talk to the kids until Ruby's discharged. Leaving the hospital we all walk to my car together, and the kids say goodbye to Jason as I unlock the doors. But he's standing there, not moving, then leans towards the back window and gestures for Josh to wind it down. 'Do you guys fancy a restorative milkshake at McDonald's?'

Milkshakes? Josh is now seventeen. Jason hasn't moved on – the kids have grown up, but he hasn't.

'Jason, it's almost midnight, they've got school in the morning.' I hear the nag in my voice. God I hate myself when I'm around this man.

'Yeah, but you guys have had a horrible night. We could do milkshakes . . . or ice cream, you love the ice cream don't you, Ruby? My treat,' he offers. I'm surprised at the rush of approval from the kids, who are placating *him*.

This is how he does it. He targets the kids, and if I don't immediately agree and join in, then I'm the one spoiling everyone's fun. He's always done this. But I'm not allowing his coercive games to shape my parenting anymore, and I fight back. 'Josh ate McDonald's earlier and has his A levels in a couple of weeks, and the last thing Ruby needs after what just happened is a milkshake or ice cream. You are aware that anything very cold can contract and inflame the airways?'

It's my turn to shame him, because as the parent of an asthmatic child, how doesn't he know that? Once again, despite everything he said on the phone, this isn't about the kids, or even about Ruby's health. This is about him winning, about being the best parent and turning up at the last minute to buy treats. It's all about his approval rating.

Jason glares at me, then shrugs, switching from saviour to victim, and he gives the kids his sad face as they take in his version of what just happened.

'You're no fun, Mum,' Ruby says sulkily, while Josh glares at me with that new coldness in his eyes.

Our broken family tableau stands silent in the dark car park, and those old feelings of guilt overwhelm me. For a moment, I'm tempted to give in to the bloody milkshakes and ice cream and whatever else their father wants. But for me it would be a temporary patch-up, not a solution or a commitment, and it wouldn't be kind. I'd be giving false hope of a reconciliation to all three of them.

I start the car and move off, leaving Jason standing in the car park alone. I take no pleasure from this, and it hangs over me like a cloud as we drive home and past the McDonald's.

'Look guys, I know you wanted us all to go with Dad for ice cream, but please don't hate me for saying no.' I wait for a moan, even a 'pleeease' from Ruby. Neither respond, both obviously pissed off with me for being 'no fun'.

'I'm not a bad person,' I add, knowing that's not true. I am a bad person.

12

It's the day after the late-night hospital visit, and I'm still feeling angry and sad when Martha calls round for a coffee. I've had a busy morning, so I'm glad of the break.

'Have you heard from Daniel Prescott?' she asks as she walks in.

I shake my head. 'I think that might have gone away. It's been more than a week now.'

'Why don't you call him?'

I shrug, not even responding to this. There's so much going on, I can't take a rejection from Daniel Prescott – besides, after Ruby's asthma attack I've got things into perspective. I tell Martha all about it, and Josh's odd behaviour too.

'Alice, that's awful. Jason just sees you all as extensions of him, classic bloody narcissist. He sees you as the trophy wife and his kids are just trinkets, but you aren't baubles to show off along with the house. And he hates that you've "rebelled" and broken up with him. Jason doesn't want you for *you* – what he wants is to keep you all inside this place, so he can take you out and put you back when he wants to, like a child playing with a doll's house.'

'Ugh, that makes me feel weird. I've never seen it like that, but perhaps you're right.' I'm reminded of Mum's collection of china dolls and how she once kept them in the glass cabinet to admire and show to friends and visitors. Is that really all we are to him – is it all we ever were?

This is such a painfully true revelation, and I have to change the subject, so I start telling her about all the weird things that have been happening here: the shadow at the front door, the ladder at the window, Ruby's nightmares, the strange phone call that I'm beginning to think wasn't Jason at all.

'Oh love, you've had a rough couple of days. But I'm telling you now that mystery phone call was no mystery – it was definitely Jason.'

'I don't know, he's more direct. He likes to watch while he antagonises me, that's part of the fun. So why would he call me to heavy breathe down the phone . . . to make me think I'm going mad?'

'Yes, and sounds like it's working. He's trying to make you question everything you believe in, and a silent phone call is such a lazy cliché it *has* to be him. As for the shadow at the door, it probably was the bay tree – but to put your mind at rest why not get a doorbell camera fitted? My new boyfriend can fix you up, mates' rates.'

'Oh, I didn't realise Mike was a CCTV man?'

'No, Mike was a TV cameraman. Please keep up – I'm talking about the latest one, Ryan, who *installs* cameras.'

'Oh, yeah. Isn't Ryan the one you felt was coming on a bit too strong, wanted to see you all the time?'

'Yeah, bit clingy – I just wasn't ready, but I've reinstated him,' she giggles, with her usual flippancy around breaking men's hearts and not overthinking it. *I need to be more Martha.* 'Ryan's *very* good with his hands . . . and in bed he's—'

'Enough! Don't want to hear about Ryan's bedroom prowess. I'll only be jealous, I don't remember sex,' I joke.

'Yeah, well, shame the same can't be said for your husband.' She rolls her eyes disapprovingly. Like me, Martha's known Jason since our schooldays, and I really should've listened to her back then. But I didn't, and he swept me off my feet, promised me forever – but he got bored long before forever.

'Shall I call Ryan now and ask if he'll give you an estimate for the front door camera?'

'Just an estimate. Not sure I can afford it,' I say. 'But thinking about the weird stuff that happened, and the possibility that Jason's girlfriend might be stalking us, I think a camera's a no-brainer.'

Martha's already on it, pursing her lips as her long red fingernails conjure Ryan up on her phone.

'Ryan darling, my friend needs you to erect something in her doorway,' she says, a wicked smile playing across her lips as she winks at me. 'She's a woman alone and needs your immediate attention, just like me,' she giggles provocatively. I sip peppermint tea and watch her easy flirtation. I envy the fun she's having, and wonder if I'll ever be like that with anyone again.

Once Ryan's confirmed he'll pop over, the conversation shifts back.

'So, despite the shadows at the front door, and weird phone call, how's the nesting thing going?'

'Well, there are issues as I've said, but on the whole Jason seems to be coping without me.'

'Apart from the small matter of him forgetting to collect life-saving medication for your daughter?' she says sarcastically.

'Yeah, there are still some things he can't be trusted with. I naively thought he could be relied on to get something as vital as medication for one of his kids. I never for a moment doubted him on that – *big* mistake!'

'Yeah, well, he's another Disney Dad, always there for the fun and the milkshakes but can't do a trip to the pharmacy for asthma inhalers. Steve's the same, lets the kids down all the time, but then the one weekend he turns up and takes them to the cinema, they think he's a bloody rock star.' Martha rolls her eyes. She's been divorced about five years now, so is way ahead of me. 'So what's the story with Josh? Did he carry on being a truculent daddy's boy after the hospital drama?'

I nod. 'Jason's back here tomorrow for three nights. So, tonight's my last night, and I suggested we get a takeaway pizza this evening, which Ruby greeted with unbridled enthusiasm. But Josh just grunted, said he was going out, and headed off for school without even saying goodbye. I understand he doesn't want to spend the evening with his "lame" mother and sister, but why be so rude about it? I've tried to talk to him but . . .'

'Let me guess, he just grunts?'

I smile in recognition at this. 'Yeah, but I'm at the stage where even a grunt is a step in the right direction; I was grateful for the acknowledgement, even if it was only a noise.'

After she's gone, I put our cups in the dishwasher and start to clean the kitchen, so I take off my diamond ring and put it in the little dish by the sink. I scrub the kitchen, and realising I'm running late, set off to collect Ruby from school.

When I get to the school, there's no sign of Josh. I have to assume he's staying behind to revise, or perhaps going to a friend's. I remind myself that he's virtually an adult and I need to chill out, but then I also remind myself that his father's girlfriend is possibly stalking us all.

Ruby and I come home, watch TV together and chat, but it's now 6.30 p.m. and Josh still isn't home. Ruby's keen to order the promised pizza, and I've texted and called him on the pretext of pizza preference, but there's been no response. It's probably because it's me, so I ask Ruby to text him too and she leaves a couple of sweary voicemails which could be an issue if I have to report him missing to the police later. I don't approve of her X-rated insults, describing her brother in various phallic terms, but am prepared to let anything slide in the hope that he makes contact with one of us.

The thing is, I don't know what's going on. Is he ignoring us, or has something happened? Should I be worried, or angry?

'Let's just order a pepperoni for Josh. I'm sure he'll be in soon, ravenous.' I force a bright smile as my daughter rolls her eyes and adds a pepperoni on the app. She's oblivious to any potential danger, or even that he might choose not to come home. Right now, her pizza is paramount.

Meanwhile, I try to distract myself by cleaning the kitchen, to stop the nagging voice in my head by wiping down surfaces and putting things away. I want to leave the place nice for them all tomorrow, when I'm not here.

'Pizzas are two minutes away,' Ruby yells, thundering down the stairs, and I get a stabbing pain in my stomach realising it's now after 7 p.m. and Josh still isn't home, and hasn't responded to any of my texts.

We put our pizzas on plates and Josh's in the oven, and just as I go back to the sink to wash my hands I reach into the trinket dish to put my ring back on. I'm talking to Ruby and feeling around, but I can't find it, so move closer to look inside, thinking it must be stuck under the lip of the rim. But as I look, there is no ring. 'Ruby, have you seen my diamond ring?'

'Which one?' she asks, like I have several.

'The only one I have, the one Auntie Margaret, Nan's sister, left me.'

'No,' she replies between mouthfuls of pizza, her phone in her face. I abandon my search – it'll turn up, and it's time I joined my daughter.

I sit down and Ruby talks about how Meghan always has to decide what they do. 'It gets so stressful,' she complains, while I push around the pizza on my plate.

'Has Josh got back to you?' I ask, when she stops for breath.

'Nah,' she replies, unbothered, while I'm imagining all kinds of scenarios and wondering what the hell to do. I feel the old urge to call Jason, but he'll see it as a chance to arrive like a bloody knight in shining armour like he did at the hospital. He'll make me feel incompetent, and there's a good chance that Josh will then turn up and the two of them will both be judging me.

By 8 p.m. I'm seriously considering calling the police when I hear the front door open. My heart swells with relief and I rush into the hall, where Josh is closing the door behind him. I don't know whether to hug him or yell at him.

'Where the hell have you been?' Yes, I'm afraid the yelling wins.

He stops momentarily by the door, leans back on it, and I have the distinct feeling that he's wondering whether to stay or just turn around and leave. So I hold my breath; my fury will only exacerbate his mood and give him good reason to storm back out.

'We ordered you a pepperoni,' I offer, trying to soften my voice. 'I was worried about you, didn't you get our texts?'

'I've eaten already,' he says without looking at me.

We're standing in the hallway like strangers, and for the first time in my life I don't know what to say to my own son. He's on one foot then the other, looking longingly past me at his escape route up the stairs.

'I have homework.' He nods in the direction of his room, and I move aside so he can continue to walk through the hall and up to his bunker.

Once he's gone, I return to the kitchen where Ruby sits with an empty plate. 'Josh not having pizza?' she asks.

I shake my head. 'He says he's not hungry,' I murmur, almost to myself, but throwing it out there in case Ruby has any opinion on this. I feel so sad I might cry.

She looks at me, like she's wondering how to say something. 'He misses Dad, says he's outnumbered on the nights you're here.'

'Outnumbered?' This stings a little. 'That's an odd thing to say, why would he feel that? Do *you* feel outnumbered on the nights Dad's here?'

She smiles. 'Nah, but Josh just sees what he wants to see.'

'What do you mean?'

She shrugs. 'I dunno, he's angry about what's happened to our family, and I think he just wants someone to blame.'

She must see from my expression that this hurts, and that she's said too much, but she can't take it back. So she tries to qualify this, unintentionally hurting me even more.

'I don't think he *really* hates you, Mum, he just *thinks* he does.'

13

My precious four nights with my children haven't gone well. They included a late-night emergency in A&E and culminated in my daughter telling me my son hates me. I know we've struggled recently, and I thought it was just teenage stuff, but the fact he's told Ruby he hates me, that he's had that conversation, really hurts. He's seventeen and hoping to go to university in September, and I've been so worried about losing him when he goes – but have I lost him already?

'Has anyone seen Willow?' I asked the kids when they came downstairs this morning.

'Oh no, didn't she come in last night?' Ruby was very concerned.

'No, but she often doesn't come home on warm nights, doesn't she,' I offered, so she didn't worry too much. Losing Willow on top of everything else would be too much.

My daughter went out to the garden, checked Willow's favourite spots, and came in looking sad.

'She kept me awake the other night whining and scratching outside my room,' Josh said. 'I reckon there's a mouse in the attic.' He didn't seem too bothered that she hadn't come home, but after he'd eaten his toast, he went off without saying goodbye, and I heard him in the garden calling her name. Perhaps there's still hope for my lost child?

After dropping Ruby at school, I spent the morning preparing for my departure, leaving reminder notes for bin men, grocery shopping and after-school activities. Jason will hopefully do a guest appearance with the dishwasher and the vacuum, and will, at some point, squeeze in a visit to the supermarket, where he buys frivolous shit and flirts with the cashiers.

When I get to Mum's I call him, and he answers for once.

'Hey Jason, a couple of things,' I start. 'Can you keep your eye open for Willow. She didn't come home last night.'

I'm waiting for his usual reaction – 'she's a cat, they don't always get the memo about coming in at night' or something along those lines. However, it's quite the opposite. 'When did you last see her? Have you checked all her favourite spots?'

'Yes of course.'

'Did you look in the bin?'

'No . . . why would she be in there? She can't climb into the bin.'

'No, I know, but someone might have put her in there.'

'But our bins are down the side of our house. And to get into the garden they'd have to climb over the high gate because it's always locked. Why would *anyone* do that?'

'I was just . . .' He trails off and I feel my heart rate double. *Why is he even thinking that?*

'No, you weren't just anything . . . what do you think might have happened to Willow?'

'Nothing. For God's sake, Alice, I was merely suggesting places she might be.' Back to his reasonable 'you're being crazy paranoid again Alice' voice.

But he's deflecting. There's something he isn't telling me – which reminds me . . . 'The other night, when you and I were on the phone, did you call me back on a different phone?' I'm holding my breath, desperate for him to admit to it so I don't worry.

'What are you on this morning, Alice?'

'Someone called me after you and I were talking, they withheld their number.'

Silence. *Why isn't he reacting or even responding to this?*

'Jason, are you still there?'

'Yes, I'm still here, but seems to me I should be there – at the house. I'm not sure you should be alone with the kids.'

'Why, do you know something?'

'Yeah, you're losing it.'

'I'm not losing it.'

'I think you need to let me come back. You can't cope on your own.'

'No, we've talked about this, Jason. Our marriage is over, and ideally you'd respect my decision, let me move on and live independently with our children. But you won't do that, so our only option is to live this half-life in our family home, but I never thought there'd be safety implications. Shadows at the door, someone in the trees, a car following me, a stranger asking our children questions, Ruby's window being open at night, and now the cat's gone missing.' It's so bloody obvious – whoever Jason's seeing (and wants to introduce to our children) is the number one suspect. Once again this is all inconvenience caused by him and his wandering eye. 'I should be able to live alone with my kids and not be scared, so if you know or have any idea who might be doing this – you need to tell me, Jason.'

'I have no idea, I really don't . . . look, I have to go into a meeting.' He's talking to someone else. It's like he hasn't even heard me. He always does this: never takes me seriously, doesn't listen when I'm saying what he doesn't want to hear. It's ridiculous. He's with another woman, yet still he's suggesting he comes home. How could he imagine we'd live together and make it work? I turned a blind eye to it before. But now it's impossible.

He doesn't respect me. Not enough to listen. Not enough to stay faithful. I sigh.

'Okay, but before you go – one last thing, would you keep an eye out for my diamond ring, the one my auntie left me? I took it off and left it in the trinket bowl near the sink, but it's not there now. Perhaps it's fallen, but I've looked on the floor and can't see it anywhere, it's a proper diamond . . .'

'Sure you haven't moved it without realising?' *Always introducing the self-doubt.*

'No.'

'Okay, bye.'

'Jason?'

'Yeah.'

'Have a good time with the kids, and . . . Josh still seems a bit . . . angry with me . . . I don't understand him at the moment. If you could talk to him?'

Again, silence.

'Jason?'

He's gone. I climb from the car and go into Mum's. She greets me with a hug and puts the kettle on, and I have this fleeting feeling of safety, something I've always taken for granted. But being here with Mum makes me realise that I don't feel safe in my own home anymore.

I do some work while Mum potters, and later we have dinner and catch up on everything. I tell Mum about my time with the kids, but don't tell her about the phone call or Josh's odd behaviour because I don't want to worry her. But I do tell her about Jason turning up at A&E like he's the family saviour.

'But no one needed him, you were fine, you've always been so capable, Alice. It's insulting the way he treats you, like you can't do anything.'

'I know, but he's always done it, Mum. But until I can either buy the house off him or he moves out, I have no choice but to just put up with him.' I see the concern on her face, and quickly switch to a more positive perspective. 'It's not like he's horrible, and he and the kids are getting along better than ever. I think they prefer him being there to me, actually. I know Josh definitely does.'

'Well, he's a boy, and at his age he wants to spend time with his dad.' It's a simple and obvious statement, but it soothes me, cuts through my paranoia and overwrought thinking. I didn't understand when Ruby said he felt outnumbered. For me it isn't about gender – but for a teenage boy it is. And that's all it is. Josh doesn't hate me; it's like Mum says, at this point in his life he'd rather spend time with his father.

'You're right, Mum,' I say, grateful for her simple wisdom, 'Josh needs a male role model in his life, even at his age.'

'Yes, he's only twelve.'

'He's seventeen, Mum. Ruby's twelve.'

'Oh, I meant that *Ruby's* twelve. Bugger!' She bangs the heel of her hand on her forehead.

I laugh at her swearing. 'You're as bad as the kids, you're turning into a real potty mouth.'

'Am I?' she giggles.

'Yes, you never swear.'

'Oh I *do*. I just swear in silence, you don't know the half of it!' Her smile fades, and I suddenly see a sadness in her eyes that I can't identify.

'You okay, Mum?'

'Yes, I just wish I could wave a magic wand and make it all better for you, love.'

'I know you do, I do too, but the only way it would ever be all better is if it was me and the kids, living in the house, and Jason in another country,' I joke.

'Yes, is Siberia too near?' she says, and we both have a chuckle about the far-flung places we wish the company would send him to, permanently.

'He might as well be in Siberia,' I mutter. 'He's supposed to be making sure Josh is doing his revision, and keeping an eye on both of them, but Josh could be playing video games all night in his room for all Jason cares.' Then I smile. 'Ruby would say I was *lame* for even calling them video games.'

Mum laughs. '*Lame*. They have their own language these days, don't they? And everyone seems to use the F-word, it's appalling.'

'I know, I blame the internet. Josh has been on TikTok *and* YouTube since he was at least thirteen, and they're exposed to so much. I worry about him, especially with all this misogyny that's being pushed at the moment. No wonder he's unreachable.'

'Joshy? Why do you think he's unreachable?'

'Oh, his age, that's all it is,' I tell her, realising I need to be careful because she worries. 'Teenage hormones and confusion, so he lashes out at Mum – I did the same, didn't I?'

'I know, love.' She reaches out and touches my arm. 'You were a little bitch!'

'Mum, what a thing to say.' I'm surprised again at her using such a word.

'Oh, everyone says it these days, Alice. And Joshy's the worst, using swear words. He was here the other day and I heard him swearing down his phone.'

'He came to see you? He never said.'

'Yes, he was here last week, and the week before. He wasn't here long, came and went.'

'I'm glad he called in. I've been worrying about him for a while,' I admit. 'I'm waiting for you to say "I told you so", Mum,' I say, referring to Mum's doubts about nesting.

'Wouldn't dream of it. But if you ask me, it was always doomed to fail. It's *divorce*, and there's no way of dressing it up or hiding it in some pretend living arrangement. You aren't kidding anyone, you know.'

The word 'pretend' hits me – is that what we're doing, pretending? I stir uncomfortably in my seat.

'Remember, Alice, I've known you all your life, and I know when something isn't quite right with you. And this . . . this situation where you go into the house as he goes out – well, it's like a bloody cuckoo clock. Sorry, call me old-school, but I think it's *this* that's affecting Joshy, and Ruby will be next. You're not happy, you have no fixed abode, you're living out of a suitcase. It's hard to protect your children from divorce, but it's even harder to protect yourself.'

14

The next day, after spending the morning with some new clients, I stop at a coffee shop on the way back to Mum's to grab a sandwich when my phone rings, and since the silent heavy breather, I now always check who's calling before picking up.

'Daniel?' I feel a rush of excitement. *Have I got the job?*

I'm smiling confidently, like this might manifest positive news.

'Sorry it's taken me a while, Alice, I've been so busy – as I'm sure you have. But look, I love your work, and I'd like to see you and talk money.'

'Oh . . . great, of course.' This sounds promising. I reckon I'm home and dry. 'I would love to talk money. As an almost-single mother I'm keen to start as soon as I can on this project,' I say, keeping it light but hopefully making my point.

'I understand, it can't be easy, but be reassured, the fee we'll be looking at will support your new single life adequately. I may even put you on a retainer after the initial redo.'

Oh wow, this could work out even better than I imagined.

'Would you like to come for dinner the week after next, say Thursday evening? I'm travelling for business so it's the only night I'm available for a while.'

Damn. That's one of my nights at home with the children. Why does everything good come with a 'but'?

'That sounds great,' I reply, knowing that I cannot lose this opportunity, and I cross my fingers that Jason can swap with me on that Thursday evening.

'Great, so shall we say here at the house, about 8 p.m.?'

I'm surprised, I thought he might suggest we meet at a fancy restaurant. But then again, this is work – and it's all about the house.

I go back to Mum's feeling happier than I have for a while. Being with her reminds me of when I was young and ran home when things weren't working out – she always made me feel better. I guess some things never change?

'It's lovely to have dinner cooked for me,' I say, pouring us both a glass of red as we sit at her tiny dining table for two in the living room. 'By the way, I have a potential new client – Daniel Prescott, do you remember him?'

'The name rings a bell,' she murmurs. I wait while she sifts through the hundreds of names of the kids she once taught. Mum prides herself on remembering her pupils. He'll be in there somewhere.

'His family own Prescotts' Cornish Dream Holidays,' I say, to see if this unlocks anything.

'Oh yes, I remember *them* – old Prescott died a couple of years ago, I didn't shed any tears. That family built houses on protected coastal land, bulldozed habitats for rare birds, and seals . . . all kinds of wildlife and vegetation destroyed. All second homes for wealthy city types to leave them empty most of the year, turning up on high days and holidays, while locals were homeless.'

'I remember now, you took me on a protest. I must have been about Ruby's age, I carried a banner.' I smile at the memory of the home-made poster Mum made, *SECOND HOMES – FIRST-CLASS GREED* painted in urgent red.

'I've still got that poster somewhere.' She smiles. 'I wanted to push it up old Prescott's nose!'

'Daniel's different from his father.'

She shakes her head. 'Don't be fooled, love, like father like son. The Prescotts and their sort are all the same, selfish, careless people.'

I wasn't expecting Mum to be quite so angry about my new client. 'Well, Daniel seems kind . . . and I'm not getting selfish vibes. In fact he's invited me to have dinner Thursday week,' I offer, in an attempt to soften Mum's obvious hatred of the Prescott family.

But she doesn't respond, just starts playing with her mashed potato like a child.

'Daniel's house isn't a second home, Mum, it's—'

'Will the children be safe with Jason tonight?' she asks out of the blue, like she's forgotten all about the Prescotts.

'I . . . yes, of *course*.' I feel a rush of guilt and maternal longing sweep through me as I think about my kids.

'Will he cook for them?'

I'm still wondering how we got on to this from Daniel Prescott's evil property-developer heritage.

'Yes, before I left I bought the ingredients for bolognese.'

'Does he know how to *make* bolognese?'

God, Mum really hasn't caught up with the fusing of gender roles.

'Having a penis is not a contraindication to cooking . . . or cleaning, or anything else in the domestic realm,' I say, aware I sound like the teenager I used to be. 'Dad did a lot of the cooking at home when I was younger.'

'Did he? Well, I just hope it's okay,' she murmurs, presumably referring to the bolognese. 'If only he'd let you stay in the house like normal couples do when they break up. The woman stays with the children and the father gets himself a flat or something,' she adds, taking a forkful of lamb mince and carrots.

'I know, I wish we could do it that way too, but I guess a husband and father has the same rights as a mother, and Jason wants to be with the kids and to live in the house – we both do, just not together.'

'But you're their mum, *and* you did all the work on that house!'

'And it's in both our names.'

'Alice, has he threatened you again about telling social services?'

I put my fork down. My appetite is quickly fading. 'No. He wouldn't. Not now.'

'He said they'd take Joshy away from you.'

'That was a long time ago,' I say carefully. But both Mum and I know he only needed to threaten me once, and since then it's been implicit. Like a heavy chandelier, I feel its weight sway above me. And it doesn't have to fall, because the menace is in knowing it could, at any moment. At his will.

My appetite has died, but I force myself to finish my shepherd's pie. After supper, while Mum relaxes in the sitting room with the TV, I stack the dishwasher. I think about the house and how it doesn't feel like home anymore – just somewhere to stay where I can be with my children. And then my mind turns to Jason, and I feel a knot tighten low in my stomach; there's nothing now, just the echo of love curdled into unease, dread. It's startling how I wish I never had to see him again, or speak with him. Our conversations feel fake and forced, but I have to maintain that facade, and so does he. Jason and I will never be truly free from each other. We're caught, like fish in a net. Until death us do part.

After a couple of good days at Mum's, this morning things all took a bit of a turn, and as I drive back to the house I'm still feeling uneasy about it all.

I was up before her, and opening the living-room blinds I didn't see the bowl of cereal she'd left on the sill, and accidentally knocked it over. Milk and muesli went everywhere, and I quickly grabbed a cloth and dustpan and brush and tried to clear it up before she saw. But she soon wandered in from the bathroom to find me on all fours trying to pick up minuscule bits of muesli from carpet strands damp with milk.

'What have you done?' she gasped, like I'd just murdered someone and was trying to clear up the mess.

'It's only a bit of cereal, Mum,' I muttered, face down in the carpet. This was the second time in as many weeks I was cleaning up a mess on this rug. I hoped it would come out – the tea stain was barely there anymore.

'That's going to smell,' she huffed, pushing me out of the way and snatching the cloth from my hands.

'I'm so sorry.' I sat on the carpet like a child as she struggled to get down on her knees to attack the offending cereal carnage. 'I just didn't see the bowl there. I didn't *expect* it to be there,' I added, rather pointedly.

She frowned. 'I was watching the birds through the window.'

I was shocked by her outburst, as I have been by her swearing, and the way she loses her temper more than she used to. I've been wondering if it's her age, but driving home now, I'm trying to see this new situation through Mum's eyes. When you live on your own you can put your cereal bowl wherever the hell you like. You can put your china dolls all over the damned house, leave mini skyscrapers of books on the floor with full cups of tea. Because living alone means you don't have to alter your behaviour for others. No one else will come along and knock your bowl off the sill or accidentally kick your cup over, spilling warm, sugary tea all over your carpet. So when your grown-up daughter turns up with her daft ideas about a thing called 'nesting', and wants to play sleepovers, it's a bit much. And when that daughter gets in the way and her leg collides with your crochet hook, and she knocks over your tea and your cereal, staining the carpet in the process, who could blame *anyone* for swearing and losing their temper?

I arrive home looking forward to a few hours of quiet and alone time to work before the kids are home from school. I put my bags down in the hall and I'm immediately bothered by a heavy, oily smell of stale garlic emanating from down the hallway. It's not a good look for any potential clients I need to meet in my home office – who I scheduled to visit on my days at the house. So I spritz the hallway with Sea Salt room spray, and hope the bolognese was worth it.

But when I wander into the kitchen, I'm not prepared for the chaos waiting for me. My best plates and bowls, half-empty mugs and cutlery, are all piled in the sink and along the countertop. They must have used every single piece of crockery while I was away, and no one has cleaned up. Jam and Marmite are smeared on the kitchen counters, the bin is overflowing, and the stale-food smell has settled over the air like a film you can't wipe away.

I walk through the kitchen like a ghost in my own home. I can't believe my husband and kids would leave the place like this.

Then I notice a fragment of my favourite mug, the Emma Bridgewater one with *MUM* written on it that Josh and Ruby bought me years ago. It's lying on the floor, and as I pick it up, I check the overflowing bin to see if the rest of it has been put in there. It means a lot to me, and I might be able to glue it back together. I poke a sink plunger down there to sift through the rubbish – no sign of it. But as I stand up, something catches my eye on the windowsill. The remaining fragments of the mug. Not scattered, not carelessly dumped, but in a circle, each jagged piece placed to create a horrible mosaic. But what turns my blood cold is that the broken pieces of the mug that have been put back together now say *MUM.*

15

What the fuck! I slowly step back from the windowsill and bang into the kitchen island with a thud. I wish I could take my eyes off it, but I can't. Someone was here. Someone touched my things, *knew* the significance of that mug and what it meant to me. I'm scared and confused. Who would do that? Who on earth would take the broken pieces of my pottery mug and put them in a weird, ritualistic shape on my windowsill?

I take a photograph of the jagged pottery, not *wanting* to record it, but this is creepy, and the way things are going I might need proof this really happened. I hate to see it there on my phone, but I need to throw the mug fragments away, don't want the kids to see it. And I don't want to leave them there like an installation. Is this another game being played by Jason's girlfriend? If so, she broke in and I can therefore call the police. Or is this something entirely different, something I've been expecting – and the chickens have come home to roost?

I call Jason.

'Hey Alice, you okay?'

'No, not really, someone's been in the house, broken my mug and . . . have you given your girlfriend a key?'

'No, I told you it's over, she isn't even—'

'Well, someone's been in and there's no obvious sign of a break-in, apart from the fact that the kitchen is a total mess. Did she let herself in and trash the house? What the fuck, Jason?'

'Alice, I told you it's over.'

'And you expect me to believe that? You asked last week if you could invite someone over while you were here with the kids.'

'That was just . . . I was trying to make you jealous, get you to agree to be together again.'

God he makes me sick.

'So, what's all the fuss about a broken mug?' he asks, making me angry all over again.

I don't address the 'fuss' comment, just explain as calmly as I can how the mug was rearranged, and for a few seconds he's uncharacteristically quiet.

'That's weird, I don't understand.'

'Nor me, so if it isn't your girlfriend, or one of the women you've slept with – because let's face it there are so many – then what's going on? Did you notice anyone hanging around last night or this morning?'

'No. Well, I'm not sure . . . I left before the kids . . . I had to go early and left them to make breakfast and . . .'

'So you weren't here when they left for school?'

'Alice, don't start.'

'So you left them alone?'

'I had to get off for work early.'

'But you know how weird things have been around here. How could you leave them, Jason? Leave them on their own? Apart from anything they might have forgotten to lock the door and just gone to school?'

'I think, as always, you're overreacting.'

'What has to happen for you to take things seriously? Like today, someone has been in our house, they've broken my mug and arranged it . . .' Hearing myself say this makes me realise how crazy I sound.

'Don't be so dramatic, Willow climbs on to the counters all the time. She probably knocked it over.'

'Oh, she's come home?' Finally, some good news.

'No.'

'She's still missing then?'

'Yeah, we haven't seen her, I'm sure she's fine though.'

'But if she was back of course it would be Willow who knocked the mug over,' I say. 'She's always making shapes out of broken pottery with her paws – and she knows how to spell "Mum".'

'Alice, are you sure you didn't break the mug and arrange it yourself?'

'What the . . . why would I *do* that?'

'To drop someone else in it.'

'Your girlfriend?'

'Perhaps?'

'So you *are* protecting her. I'm going to call the police.'

'Wait . . . not yet.'

'Why?'

'You know why, Alice.'

His voice chills me, and the silence that follows chills me even more. I hang up and walk back into the kitchen, my head filled with the unspoken threat in my husband's voice. Just what would he do to keep me quiet – to keep his secrets?

A loud knocking on the door bangs through my head, and I'm suddenly jolted into the present. As always now, I walk cautiously to the front door, and despite it being the middle of the afternoon I'm apprehensive.

I don't open the door fully to the stranger on the doorstep.

'Hey, I'm Ryan.'

'I'm sorry, I . . .'

'I've come to fit your door cam. Martha called me – have I got the right house?' He's looking around the door frame.

'Sorry, sorry.' I open the door a little. He may be Martha's lover, but the days of inviting strangers into my home are over.

'Okay if I have a look around outside?'

He's probably early thirties, younger than I expected, wearing a tight white T-shirt and a tool belt. Ryan is straight out of central casting – all he needs is a shimmer of sweat and an ice-cold can of Diet Coke and women would be hanging out of windows to watch him. He's definitely one of Martha's.

I discreetly watch him from inside the house for the next fifteen minutes or so as he wanders past the windows making notes and looking up at the house.

Eventually he knocks on the front door and I open it, a little more fully this time. 'It's all done, Mrs Taylor.'

'Wow, that was quick,' I say. 'I wasn't expecting you to do it now, I thought you were just giving me an estimate?'

'Martha said it was a matter of life and death?'

'She would.' I smile.

'These new ones are easy to fit,' he says, 'only take minutes.'

But I wanted an estimate first, because Sundrenched Interiors is going well, but I don't actually have much money. 'Thanks,' I reply, a little grudgingly. 'How much . . . will it be?'

'I'll send you an invoice, but first let me go through it with you.'

'Oh . . .' My heart sinks. I don't have the time or the brain space for a TED Talk on cameras by Ryan, even if he is easy on the eye.

He walks me outside, asks for my laptop, and sits with me while I log in to the camera app. I can just about find and view the footage, and that's all I want, but he goes into so much technical detail, I switch off. I hear 'wide-angle lens' and '1080p HD video', which he assures me provides 'sweet, clear images, even from a distance'. Then: 'With this wide angle you can see out on to the road, and the sensors will tell you if someone's walking towards the house – even if they don't want you to know,' he says, pointing to the live feed excitedly.

'It covers half the street,' I exclaim, pulling my attention back.

'Told you, it's a good one.'

'How much is it?' I ask, dreading the answer.

'Four hundred,' he replies coolly. 'Mates' rates.'

Christ, all that money for a little box on the outside of the house. I feel a bit sick. If that's mates' rates, I dread to think what it would cost for people he doesn't consider to be friends. But I'm so jumpy, I'm sure it'll be worth it for peace of mind. I just hope Jason agrees to it, because if not I'll have to use money from the business, and being small and new there's always a cash flow problem.

Ryan's invoice is in a couple of hours later, along with various estimates, from my 'basic doorbell camera' to 'the full-on Fort Knox' – as he refers to the full bells-and-whistles version that probably costs thousands.

But it's the end of his text that makes my heart almost stop.

An exterior camera and extra security light around the back of the house would be advisable. Not sure if homeowner is aware, but the upstairs left window has been prised open recently.

16

'Has Willow come home yet?' Ruby asks when I collect her from school.

'I haven't seen her,' I offer, in what I hope is an optimistic tone. I'm really worried about what Ryan wrote. Someone has been trying to get into the house. I called an emergency locksmith before I left for school, and asked him to put a lock on Ruby's window and provide only two keys, one for me and one for Jason. I doubt Jason will agree to pay for extra cameras at the back of the house – he'll say I'm overreacting again – but I'll ask him, and if he won't pay towards it, I'll have to pay it all. I'm now feeling really exposed, and annoyed with myself for doubting my own instincts that something isn't right. But Jason taught me well to doubt my own instincts over the years he suffocated them with his lies. Thank God Martha called Ryan and we now know that this isn't just my imagination or overreaction.

'Mum, do you think Willow's dead?' Ruby's asking as we drive home. Her bottom lip is quivering, and I rush to reassure her.

'No, Willow's not dead,' I reply like it's the most ridiculous idea, but I'm worried about her. 'You know what a diva she is, I reckon she's at a cat health spa for a few days for some pampering and to get away from it all.'

My daughter smiles at this.

I can't ever say this out loud, but my biggest fear is that she bumped into Jason's girlfriend on a dark night. Then I remind myself that Willow's disappeared before, and it's a hard but fundamental truth that cats owe us nothing. And they sometimes walk away because they want to, without feeling the need for an explanation, a *thanks for all the fish* . . . or even a goodbye. Some days I wish I could be more cat.

'Was everything okay with Dad at the house?' I ask Ruby, wearing my happy-mum mask, trying not to show any concern about cats or kids or careless husbands. Josh hasn't responded to my text asking if he'd like a ride home, so I'm just letting that lie.

'Yeah, fine.' But she's not smiling.

'It's just that the kitchen was a bit of a mess, Ruby. Dad said he had to head out so couldn't stick around to clean up. But you and Josh should have cleaned up. You're both old enough to know that.'

'A mess? I didn't make it a mess,' she replies indignantly.

'Well, I know Josh is capable of chaos, but he didn't make *this* mess all on his own. No one washed the dishes or . . .' This isn't my primary concern, I'm not obsessed with washing-up, but I do want to know more about Jason leaving the kids alone.

'Dad did the dishes, I saw him do it. He doesn't make us do stuff like you do.'

Oh, so it's going to be like that.

'But Dad couldn't clean up this morning because he wasn't there, was he.' In an instant, the atmosphere changes. Out of the corner of my eye, I see Ruby's head turn to look at me. 'I know he wasn't there – it's okay, he told me,' I add.

'I didn't want to be on my own with Josh all night, he's so lame. And he had his friends over – that's not allowed without permission, is it?'

All night? What the hell? I feel like I've just been hit in the face. I had a feeling Jason wasn't being completely honest, but I had no idea he'd left the kids overnight – he told me he'd gone to work early this morning. I have so many questions I want to pull the car over and fire them at my daughter now. But obviously she'd clam up thinking it would cause a row.

'So what time did Dad go out last night?' I ask, lightly.

'About nine. He said I had to go to bed, but he let Josh stay up and watch TV with his knobby mates.'

'Ruby, just stop with the horrible words please,' I say more angrily than I mean. My fury is with Jason and hard to conceal; it's sharp and prickly and I want to kill him.

'Josh says far worse.'

'He isn't here. I'm talking to *you.*' I take a breath and ask, 'Were you okay, when Dad left? Josh wasn't horrible to you?'

'No more than usual. I just went to my room.'

This makes me sad. The whole point of nesting is to keep the family together in some form, but to leave a no doubt resentful seventeen-year-old and his friends to look after a twelve-year-old girl is out of order.

'So when Dad went out, was he going to work?'

'Yeah.'

He's such a liar! 'So why didn't he call me? I could have come over.' I get right back on it.

'I asked him to, because you'd come over and be with us, but he said it wouldn't be fair, that you needed some space. He said you'd told him not to call you, that you wanted time to yourself.' She turns to me. 'Mum, have we sucked you dry?'

'What? No, not at all, is that what Dad *told* you?' I ask, knowing the answer, gripping the steering wheel in rage.

'Yeah . . . but he wasn't being mean,' she adds. 'He said you'd told him you need the time and space to find out who you are.'

'Did he?' So he's using my own words out of context to make the kids feel like I'm abandoning them. Like somehow it's all my fault. *What the fuck?*

Once home, Ruby and I chat about other stuff, and later we have dinner and I try to put Jason from my head. By 9 p.m. Ruby's in bed. Josh wanders in later, pops his head round the door, looks disappointed to see me, and mumbles goodnight before I've even had the chance to ask him how he is. As much as I want to know, I can't face a conversation with him about his dad leaving them; it will only cause more problems between us. I feel at a loss, so try calling Jason again, hoping we can have a proper talk.

'Look, I'm sorry things weren't all spick and span this morning,' he starts before I can even say hello. 'I'm so sorry, Alice . . . I know how important these things are to you. And then there was your mug . . . anyone could have dropped it.'

There he goes again. His passive-aggressive apology for things not being spick and span is less about him fucking up and more to do with my problem of being a clean freak, and of overreacting to a broken mug.

'I'm not calling about the mess or the mug. Contrary to what you say to everyone, I'm not obsessed with cleanliness, and I'm not crazy.'

'Oh, come on . . .'

'You know there are certain safety issues around the house right now,' I say, moving on. 'And in spite of this, I've just found out that you didn't leave early this morning, you left at 9 p.m. last night – you left the kids here, alone all night.'

There's a moment's silence. 'Ruby I suppose?'

'It doesn't matter how I found out . . . we spoke earlier and you lied, so you know you're in the wrong.'

'For fuck's sake, Alice . . .' He pauses for a moment, then seems to change his approach. 'Okay, yes, I had to go and deal with something urgent at work.'

'*Urgent?* Jesus, what could be more urgent than our kids? This whole arrangement is about giving *you* time with the children. Your biggest issue with us splitting up and me staying in the house was that you wouldn't see them enough. That's why I go to Mum's, to give you that time, and then you leave them. I might as well be here with the kids while you live elsewhere.' I wait for his response, a faint glimmer of hope twinkling at the back of my mind.

'No way, I'm not doing that. I'm their father and—'

'And as their father, you should be looking after them, not disappearing off.'

I take a breath, then point out the dangers of leaving kids under eighteen alone in a house. 'And it's illegal,' I add.

'No, it isn't. It's not *advisable* to leave a child under twelve, but Josh is almost eighteen, he's very responsible and was happy for me to leave him in charge.'

'I bet he was! He could have all-night video games with his mates, drink beer, and be vile to his sister.'

'He wasn't vile to Ruby, was he?' Jason sounds horrified. I think it's dawning on him just how stupid it was to leave a seventeen-year-old boy in charge.

'I don't know, and Ruby wouldn't say if he was.'

'I was only about an hour away, in Exeter. A client was threatening to pull out of a huge investment. Larry said I was the only person who could get him back.'

I wish I'd had the pull that old Larry had during our marriage. I always said if my husband had to choose between me and his big, brash partner, he'd choose him.

'I should have called you. But I couldn't because you insisted that we had to respect the other's time with the kids.'

'That's not fair, you can't use that against me. In an emergency we have to talk to each other, for the kids' sake.'

'You mean like when Ruby was rushed to hospital with an asthma attack and you didn't bother to tell me?'

'Oh, don't use that against me – I had no time to call you, no opportunity. This isn't about scoring points, Jason, and I'm not being drawn into one of your arguments that go round and round in circles until I give in and you think you've won. All I'm going to say, is that if you ever need to leave the kids on your night, then call me, *tell* me. And telling the kids that they sucked me dry and I don't want contact when I'm not here is way below the belt.'

'I was just trying to help them understand the break-up . . .'

'Don't take me for an idiot. And do me a favour, let *me* be the one to explain *my* feelings to Josh and Ruby – it's not your place to do that.' I want to say a lot more, but for once I hold my tongue.

'Give me a chance. I'm trying to be better, Alice.'

'Really?' I say, looking around at the house I've had to clean, again. He just wants to manipulate everything for his own agenda, and is now making out that he's working on himself, *trying to be better*. What a joke. I used to believe him when he said he'd change, that *it will never happen again*, but it did, again and again. And right now, he's playing me, and I don't know why but he's definitely up to something.

17

'Mum, I'm scared, I can hear noises.' Ruby's standing in the doorway of the living room, pale and obviously frightened.

'I'm sure it's nothing, darling. Shall I come up and check under the bed like I did when you were little?'

She smiles at this. 'Might be an idea.'

'What sort of noises did you hear?' I ask as we walk upstairs together.

'I dunno, like someone was moving around outside my door.'

'It could have been Josh going to the bathroom, or even plugging his phone in?' I offer. He has so much gaming equipment in his bedroom it's like NASA, which means he sometimes runs out of plug sockets and charges his phone on the landing.

'I heard a scratching too.'

'Really? Did it sound like a cat? Might be Willow?'

She looks at me hopefully. 'Do you think so? Before she went missing she was hanging around outside my door and meowing a lot, I think she was scratching the carpet too. She might be hiding in the house somewhere?'

'Yeah, might be.' I try to sound like this is an option. Ruby's face is so hopeful I have to go along with it. I love Willow too, but I have a horrible feeling we'll never see her again. She's been missing for a few days now, and my mind keeps returning to the idea that a former – or current – mistress of Jason's has been bunny-boiling, *Fatal Attraction*-style, with poor Willow. God, I hope not.

Once in Ruby's room, I try to keep everything light and amusing, like this is nothing, while feeling pretty on edge. I get down on my knees and dutifully check under the bed maintaining a smile with my heart in my mouth, and trust me it's not easy to smile when your mouth is full. The logical side of my brain tells me there's no one under her bed, but the crazy part of me lifts the cover and sees eyes looking back at me in the darkness.

'No, there's nothing there,' I say, as relieved as my daughter, who now tentatively climbs back into bed.

'Are you sure, Mum?'

'Absolutely.' I sit next to her on the bed. 'Want me to stay until you're asleep?'

She nods and moves down under the covers. 'I can't go to sleep on my own.'

'You aren't worried about anything are you?' I ask, stroking her hair.

'No, but I can't sleep because Josh is always on his phone at night.'

'Is he?' This surprises me. 'I thought he was revising, or gaming?'

She shakes her head. 'Last night he was on the phone for ages, having this weird conversation with a girl . . .'

Fear is crawling across the back of my neck. 'A girl?'

'I don't know, the voice sounded female, but it was hard to tell? I don't think it was a man's voice, and he wasn't talking to one of his friends – he laughs and swears when he's talking to them.'

'What was he saying?' I ask calmly, my flesh tingling like it's about to set alight.

'I couldn't hear actual words, but he seemed upset. I thought he was saying "NO . . . No" really loud, and then . . . I heard him crying.'

What the hell?

'Did you ask him about it?'

'No . . . I wouldn't.' She sits up. 'Mum, please don't tell him I told you, will you?'

'No . . . no, of course not,' I say, hiding my distress. 'Do you think he might have a girlfriend we don't know about?'

She shakes her head grimly. 'No way.'

'Why not?'

She curls her lip. 'Have you seen him?'

'Don't be mean. You'll let me know if you think Josh is upset . . . if you hear him crying again, won't you?'

'Yeah, yeah,' she murmurs, already dropping off to sleep. I sit with her awhile, comfortable now that there are no strange noises and reminding myself this is an old house, and it does like to moan and groan like anything old. After a while I leave her with the lamp on, and walk across the landing to Josh's room. I know this could be a mistake, but I'm floundering here, and I really don't know how to handle this. I have to make a pilgrimage into the dark hormonal cave, so I take a deep breath and knock firmly on the door.

I wait, and wait, but there's no response, so I knock a second time and then hear him moving. Well, I hear *something* moving, and it sounds like the dragging of a chest of drawers. My chest tightens. *Has he barricaded himself inside his bedroom?* I'm horrified to hear my son manoeuvring a huge piece of furniture away from the door that he's shut to keep me out. I understand a teenager wanting their privacy, but I would never walk in without knocking, so why does he feel the need to use furniture to keep me, and presumably Ruby, out. What is he hiding? And who is he talking to on the phone who is making him cry?

The door opens suddenly and I'm greeted with a face that's pink with rage; I've never seen him so angry, and it's all directed at me. *All I did was knock on his bedroom door.*

'What is going on with you?' I say quietly, trying to quell my own fear and anger rising at this outburst.

He takes a breath, and even in the darkness I see his eyes, cold and staring – he's almost smirking – while I stand at the threshold like a guest.

'What's it to you?'

'Josh, talk to me.'

'Why?'

'Because I'm scared, I don't understand you anymore. You don't talk to me, you won't even look at me . . . and I don't know what I've done for you to hate me so much.'

He doesn't argue, just stares at me. 'You're really unhinged, you know?'

This is a blow, but I won't be knocked down. 'Is that what Dad told you, Josh? That Mum's unhinged?'

I hate myself for saying this, I've never involved the kids in our marriage issues, but he's almost eighteen and he's beginning to sound like Jason. Actually, he's worse than Jason, because Josh is just repeating what his father said to him, with no filter. But Jason's experienced enough in this kind of abuse to cover it in a veil of caring, and would tell me I was unhinged by suggesting I get some 'help'. But now I know there's nothing wrong with me, there never was. The only *help* I needed was to be away from my husband.

'Is something upsetting you, Josh?' I ask. 'Has something happened at school, or is it me and Dad? Is it a girl . . . has a girl upset you? Tell me why you're so angry. Talk to me, Josh.'

'You? Talk to *you*? *But you're* the problem.' He steps forward, and I instinctively step back. 'You broke up with Dad, and make him live somewhere else while you get on with your "career".' He lifts his hands, holding his fingers like speech marks.

'Josh, you're being unreasonable. I haven't made your dad do anything he doesn't want to do. I know it's hard to understand,' I say gently, 'but we just don't love each other anymore and—'

'You don't care about me or Dad. All you care about is *her*.'

'Ruby, you mean? Oh, Josh no, please don't say that, don't even think it.'

'Well, I do, because it's true, and you made us all live like this because all you care about is this house and Ruby. You hate Dad and you hate me.'

He continues to stand in the dark doorway, glaring at me defiantly.

'It's just not true. I . . . I love you.'

'So why have you moved Dad out, and why do you stay at Nan's now instead of being here with us?'

'I thought it was the answer, the best way of keeping us *all* together.'

He gives this weird, hollow laugh that slices me in two. I don't know him, he's not my son, he's an angry stranger in my home.

'You're not living separately because you want to keep us all together . . . you're lying. This is your plan so Dad loses everything, and you keep the house for yourself.'

18

I don't know how to explain to Josh that he's got this all wrong. Over the next couple of days I try, but he doesn't want to listen, and spends his time at home locked in his room. I'm almost relieved to leave the house after four nights, and head for Mum's.

Later, over dinner, I tell Mum about the encounter with Josh, and she suggests I give him some space. 'Just leave him, love, he's a bright boy, he'll soon realise he's being manipulated by that . . . that . . . ooh, he makes me so angry. I never liked Jason. Even on your wedding day I told you then it wasn't too late to back out.'

I smile, feeling wistful and regretful. 'I remember, and I wish I'd listened to you then. I'm beginning to think I should've listened to you about the nesting too.'

'Well, it's all a bit wishy-washy if you ask me – you're in or you're out, and as painful as it is, you have to just rip off the plaster.'

'You're right of course, and I wish I had . . . ironically I didn't want to hurt the kids, but I'm beginning to think it's actually more harmful. It impacts them both. There's Josh's attitude, and also Ruby's so young, she still needs us to be there for her, but he doesn't seem to consider the kids' safety. Last week it was our turn to collect Ruby and Meghan from gymnastics. Meghan's mum and I have worked out a schedule between us. I had no idea, but today I bumped into Yvonne, that's Meghan's mum, who asked me if everything was okay because on one of Jason's nights, Meghan had texted her to say no one had picked them up. So Yvonne called him and he'd forgotten! I was so embarrassed. I explained that I'd left notes, and it was on the calendar and the whiteboard. I don't know how he forgot.'

'He was probably with one of his fancy women.'

'Who knows where he was? He hasn't told me about it, and neither has Ruby. She wouldn't want to cause any trouble between us, or piss him off I suppose. I haven't seen Ruby since I saw Yvonne, and I imagine it was quite upsetting, so I won't mention it to her, but I'll mention it to *him*.'

'You should! Fancy forgetting his own daughter.'

'I know. When I think what might have happened, leaving two twelve-year-old girls to stand outside waiting for their lift. It doesn't bear thinking about.'

Mum flushes with anger. 'I can't believe it. Fancy leaving two little girls in the dark.' She's shaking her head.

'I know, it's so upsetting. I know as a husband he's a cheat and a liar, but I always thought he would care for our kids, but I don't even trust him to do that anymore. Today I walked out of there and it felt like I was leaving part of me behind.'

'I'm sure it will all be fine, love, you just have to be strong, and you are.'

After dinner, I make coffee in the kitchen, leaving Mum to watch *Coronation Street* in the living room. 'Shall we have biscuits?' I suggest. I brought Jaffa cakes, they're her favourite, and without waiting for her to answer me I put some on a plate. I *know* she'll say yes. While I'm waiting for the kettle to boil, my eye catches on the three ceramic dolls that sit on the kitchen windowsill. Betty, Sally and Boo have been turned around to face the window, as if they're watching, waiting for something. Or someone. Unease creeps over me – Mum must have done this, but what does it mean? The

Coronation Street theme tune, the sound of my childhood, plays in the other room. I'm intrigued and a little uneasy as to why Mum would do this. But I won't ask her about her dolls just yet; I'll let her enjoy her soap and relax. Perhaps there's a perfectly reasonable explanation? But for the life of me I can't think what.

Suddenly, a blood-curdling scream cuts through everything going on in my head. *Mum!* I dash into the living room, the TV blaring – someone's accusing someone else of cheating, it's loud and shouty. But Mum isn't there. I realise now that her screams are coming from the bathroom. I run to her, and in the two or three seconds it takes, so much horror goes through my head. But what I find in that bathroom goes far beyond anything my imagination can cope with.

I push open the door, and in the noise and confusion I can't pin down what's happening. Mum's naked, and screaming, but lying on the floor, she's sliding around in . . . blood? 'Oh God! Mum what's happened? Did you fall? You should have told me you were having a shower.' I'm now on the floor trying to help her, trying to see where the blood's coming from and how bad this is. 'Mum, tell me what happened?' I say again, more firmly, and more calmly this time. And she stops screaming, but she isn't looking at me, her face is pure terror, and she's looking behind me, and pointing her shaking finger. *Is someone standing behind me?*

In that instant I'm too scared to turn around. But I have to, and slowly my eyes move from her face, contorted with fear, her silence far scarier than her screams. I hold her hand to anchor us both, and turn to where she's pointing, dread flooding my veins. I hold my breath. But there's nothing there. Nothing. Just the open door leading into the dark hallway.

I turn back to Mum, who makes an almost inaudible whimper as she continues to look past me. I'm so confused, why is she so frightened? I'm aware of blood unfurling in the running water, the shower head abandoned but still spurting on to the floor, thin red ribbons unravelling into it before dissolving, turning the water a sickly red.

I step into the shower and turn it off, while watching the crumpled, naked human heap on the floor. My mum. She must be in shock, that's why she can't speak. I need to call for an ambulance, but first I step from the shower, and bend down to see her injuries. I reach out to her, and immediately she recoils, bringing her knees to her chest protectively. I can see now that the blood seems to be coming from her feet and legs. I look closely, wiping with my bare hands what look like scratch marks. She whimpers as if I'm hurting her.

'You have some cuts on your leg,' I say, confused, trying to work out what they are, but now she's pointing at the door again.

'Mum, there's nothing there,' I say tearfully now. I turn again, just to make certain there's no one behind the door. 'There's no one here.' I open the door wide to reassure her.

But her stare is fixed. And she doesn't look like Mum. It's as if someone else has taken over her body; her eyes are dead, unreachable. My blood runs cold. My lovely mum, a stranger.

But then I hear a noise in the apartment. *Was that the front door closing?*

I quickly wrap a towel around her. 'I'm just going to get some cloths to clean your wounds, I'll see if we have any bandages too. Just stay there,' I say gently, and walk through the apartment. Nothing. No one. Did I imagine the door closing?

I go back into the bathroom, where Mum is now sitting up, but still seems confused and detached. I suddenly see what caused the accident.

'Barbara fell from the shelf, Mum. I think you must have stepped on her and fallen.' The doll is made of china, and when it fell and smashed, the jagged pieces went all over the floor, and that's what caused Mum's injuries.

'Mum, you've cut yourself, haven't you? Is that what happened?' I ask calmly.

She nods. 'Yes, I fancied a quick shower, but stepped in, turned it on, and slipped.'

I sigh with relief. She's back again, the staring and pointing must have been shock, and there's now an explanation for all the blood.

'Come on, let's get you up. Can't believe you just decided to have an impromptu shower!' I joke.

'I was cold, thought it would warm me up.'

'But you were in the middle of watching *Coronation Street*. It's over now.'

'Is it? Oh dear.'

'You scared me to death. I thought someone had been in and hurt you . . .'

She chuckles at this. 'Oh you, you're always the prophet of doom, Alice,' she says, like nothing has happened and I'm being overly dramatic.

I reach under her arms to lift her up, surprised at how light and fragile she is. I help her into the towelling robe that hangs on the bathroom door, and as I hold Mum's frail bones, I consider the broken doll on the floor. Mum's always been such a strong person. I lean on *her*, I always have. But she's been changing, and with everything going on in my life, I hadn't noticed. I feel ashamed of my lack of care as I walk her into her bedroom.

'Shall I call an ambulance, Mum?'

'You'll do no such thing.' She's back to normal, which includes being stubborn.

'You've had a fall, I think you should see a doctor.'

'And I think you should bugger off.'

I'm surprised by her outburst, and as I help her get dressed, I try to rationalise her behaviour. Perhaps it's down to shock, but she was sharp and shouty over the spilled tea and me spilling the cereal bowl. It just isn't like Mum to react like that, and when I think about the confusion and mood swings a part of me knows I'm in denial.

'Would you like to have a lie-down, take a nap?'

'Take a nap? It's only eight o'clock, I'm not dead yet,' she snaps.

I decide then to make an appointment with her GP, because something isn't right. It's like a *Freaky Friday* role reversal: I've woken up, and I'm suddenly the adult and Mum's the truculent child. I have to reframe our relationship, take charge and stop leaning on her. I've probably told her too much about the break-up and Jason's behaviour, and like any good mother, she's angry and worried about me and the children. The split may even have been the catalyst for whatever it is she's suffering from. I just hope I can get her some help before it gets any worse.

She insists on coming back into the sitting room, so I settle her on to the couch, and she picks up her crochet hook. 'I'm making a hat for Josh,' she says, like she wasn't in a shower scene reminiscent of *Psycho* just minutes ago. Then she reaches into her bag and brings out some knotty textured yarn in bright red. I want to remind her that Josh is almost eighteen years old. But how can I? If and when she finishes what looks like a strange bucket hat, I will ask Josh to be grateful and gracious if she gives it to him.

She puts down the crochet hook for a moment. 'Is *The Shore* on tonight?'

I pick up the remote and check on the TV guide on-screen. 'Yes, it's on later.'

'Shall we watch it together?'

'I'd love to,' I say. 'Jason doesn't approve of soaps, or reality shows, he only watches sport. God I'm glad I don't have to suffer another night of balls on the TV.'

'I'm glad you don't have to suffer another night of *him*. Womaniser, that's what he is,' she sniffs, with a judgemental purse of the lips. This usually irritates me, but tonight it reassures me that she's okay and recovered from her fall. 'Do you know anything about the woman he had the affair with?'

'No. I've deliberately avoided asking him questions, I don't want to know.' I think about him asking if he could bring someone back to the house, and I imagine him introducing her to the children. Then my mind comes up with terrifying scenarios, like her stealing my kids, or harming them. It's irrational but I get really dark and I visualise her glittering eyes, staring at the kitchen knives.

'Now, how about a nice cup of hot, sugary tea? I have biscuits too . . . your favourite?' I say, dragging myself away from my real-life *Fatal Attraction* nightmare.

'Ooh, Jaffa Cakes?'

I smile indulgently before heading back into the kitchen to reboil the kettle. Mum turns up the volume on the TV, and my eyes return to the window that looks out on to the garden, feeling relieved and settled for now. Until I glance over at the window, where Betty, Sally and Boo are still sitting. Only now they aren't looking through the window. They've been turned around and three pairs of eyes are staring at me.

19

The day after Mum's fall in the shower, I made an appointment with her GP, and the earliest one I could get was in more than a week's time. I just hope Mum agrees to let me go in with her, because I need to talk to the GP about Mum's mood swings.

And today I'm leaving Mum, Betty and the other mean-girl dolls (and those vicious crochet hooks). I'm going home. It's almost our fourth swap week and I'm beginning to wonder how long I can do this. I look forward to being there with the kids, but seem to spend the first night feeling slightly disoriented. Only to get used to it, and then it's time to go again – and I'm only with the kids three nights this week, because on Thursday Jason's coming back to cover for dinner with Daniel.

I give Mum a hug before I leave. She seems quiet this morning, but okay in herself.

'Now, take care and call me if there's anything you're worried about,' I say before I go.

She looks at me with a concerned expression.

'Is there something, Mum?'

She nods. 'Alice, don't let Jason leave Ruby waiting in the dark again, will you?'

'No, I won't.' I wish I'd never told her that he forgot to pick her up – the way she is at the moment it will probably play on her mind, but I don't know if that's a problem, or just Mum. She's always been close to the kids, and living nearby she has always been there for them. Perhaps as she's getting older she feels impotent when it comes to protecting them? I understand that; I feel the same on the nights they're with Jason. Now we're almost a month into this whole nesting experiment and being away from them makes me anxious.

I arrive back home, and on opening the front door I breathe in. To my deep joy, there's no heavy garlic smell in the hallway when I walk in, which bodes well for the rest of the house. Then I pop my head around the kitchen door – which isn't quite as I'd left it, but an improvement on last time.

But the sitting room is a different story. My heart sinks to see my lovely cushions on the floor, and the silk and wool throw's been slung in a corner. Josh's open laptop lies on the windowsill, earphones and wires sprouting from the back and sides. I march into the room and move the laptop from the window – 'Talk about *inviting* a bloody break-in,' I murmur. Anger is now fighting with anxiety as I move across the room. I want to cry, *why, why?*

It isn't just the mess, it's the fact it's been left like this to hurt me. I feel violated, standing in the middle of the chaos, clutching the laptop to my chest, wires looping from me like arteries. I see empty crisp bags now staring at me from between the cushions, and with the laptop now under my arm, I pick them up, along with upturned beer bottles that someone's piled behind the sofa. 'What the hell?' I murmur, knowing now that this is Josh. It must be. One of the bottles lies on its side; it's been left overnight to bleed across the cream carpet, leaving a dark bruise on the pale weave.

On high alert, I move through the room scanning for clues. Am I imagining the woody tang of stale weed in the air? The cushions have been flattened, as if someone's been lying on them. Or standing on them with boots on. I imagine Josh and his friends lounging around here chatting, laughing lazily like cool boys do. His friends have always been welcomed, fed and watered, offered sleepovers and lifts to venues and a few quid to buy a drink. But this is different – they would never have been allowed to smoke and drink in the house, nor would they have behaved in such a destructive, uncaring way. I know these boys, and what's more I know their mothers, and they would be horrified to think their sons were coming here and being allowed to behave like this. What's changed? Have hormones kicked in and altered them forever? Their voices are now broken, but their hearts remain intact – at least I think so.

Martha rings.

'Oh, I thought you were Jason.' I must sound disappointed because she says, 'Since when would you rather talk to your estranged adulterous husband than your best friend?'

'Sorry, I wanted to ask him what the hell's been going on while I was away.' I plonk myself down on the sofa, abandoning the clean-up for a moment to tell her about it.

'Not again? Is it a rubbish tip?'

'Yeah. Just like before, it feels like we've been burgled.' I describe the carnage and, being Martha, she tries to make me feel better.

'To be honest, I'd be more concerned if mine *didn't* leave cushions on the floor and hurl beer all over the carpet. What's the rest of the house like?'

'I haven't had the chance to look yet,' I say, heading into the hallway and up the stairs.

I go straight to Josh's bedroom. 'As I expected, the theme continues,' I announce, observing the chocolate wrappers, and spilled Coke on the bedlinen. Then I look under his bed to see Coke cans and a couple of screwed-up, empty cigarette boxes. 'It smells of nicotine, vinegar and hate,' I murmur, getting to my feet, trying not to see the dirty clothes in heaps all around the room and floor.

'He's never been tidy, but this feels deliberate, like he's making a point.'

'Taking the piss you mean.'

'Yeah, I'm so angry, I can't believe the kids and Jason would disrespect our home like this.'

'Hey, they're just kids, and if you're not around to remind them, then they're bound to just be . . . kids.'

'That's the issue – I'm not around, but Jason is, and knowing him, he was probably the ringleader.'

'Before you say anything to the kids, have a word with him first then? I feel a bit guilty as I was the one who suggested this "nesting" thing – but I'm not sure it's for you guys.'

'Not if it means coming home to this every time, it isn't. The whole point for me is that Jason gets to share the domestic workload, but now I have to spend the next couple of hours cleaning. I was hoping to work this afternoon before the kids come home.'

'Then there's all the weird shit that's been going on.' She pauses. 'I was thinking, what if Jason's girlfriend wants your kids and it was her who broke into the house and did that with your "Mum" mug? Like she's making a comment about you being a bad mother or something?'

'Look, I'm as keen as you to create a bonkers true-crime narrative, but even I think that's a stretch. I mean, for a grown woman to go to that trouble to arrange a bit of pottery? Nah. It's probably Jason still trying to make me crazy.'

'What about that woman driving around in the green Fiat?'

'Yeah, we haven't seen anything of her for a while, and I have wondered if she's behind it all. But even if she's this Ellie, or a random woman he's seeing, she's got what she wants – Jason. So why would she be interested in me and the kids?'

'Checking out the competition? You said the woman in the coffee shop was quizzing the kids, then the car turns up at school . . . Whoever she is, she sounds like a total bunny boiler. Be careful, Alice.'

I feel a chill run through me. 'Don't say that, I'm on my own here tonight, remember? Anyway, Jason said he doesn't know anyone who drives a Fiat.'

'Yeah, well, as you said, he's a *massive* liar. And, he's hardly going to say "Green Fiat? Yes, that's my honey" – is he?'

I smile at this.

'You could find out if green-Fiat woman is this Ellie character. What's her surname? Check her out online, and see if it was her at the coffee shop. I mean most people are on Instagram or . . .'

'I didn't see her at the coffee shop, so I don't know what I'm looking for.'

'But you must have googled Ellie, or checked out her social media?'

'No,' I say firmly, 'because I don't know her surname. All I know is her name's Ellie and she worked with him.'

'What? Who even are you, Alice?'

'I'm trying to save myself and stay sane. I haven't even searched on his company website for her, because that way madness lies. I would be obsessively matching up dates on her Instagram and see photos of them having a romantic dinner when he told me he was working late. There's no point in me going over it all like some sadomasochistic wife, because that's not who I am anymore.'

'Yeah, I get that, but still – it would be useful to know who she is, what she looks like, if it's her that's stalking you . . .'

'I sometimes wonder if it's in my imagination,' I say.

'No! This isn't you, Alice, it's him. He's made you doubt yourself from the moment he met you. He chased you and chased you, and when he got you . . . well, the fun went out of the game for him. He was always looking for the next one . . . and in the meantime he kept you in that house, and lied to you, while all the time he was making you think you were a little bit cuckoo. But you're not!'

I appreciate her reminding me that I'm not mad. But equally, until I can prove that someone is responsible for the creepy stuff that's been happening, I have to consider the fact that I might be imagining them. I know I'm not crazy, but I can be suggestible, and if I'm feeling edgy a creaking floorboard is a potential serial killer coming up the stairs.

I'm also now worried about Mum, and I just want to move her in here and lock me, Mum and the kids inside. But I'm not sure I'd feel safe even then, because I don't know who my son is anymore. Josh could be the one who's doing these things, and he's *inside* the house.

20

I'm waiting in the car outside school and have about five minutes before Ruby's out, so I call Jason. Who amazingly picks up after the first ring. It's becoming a bizarre pattern ever since we separated. Considering my past relationship with his voicemail, maybe I should've done this years ago?

'Jason, what the hell happened while I was away – again?' My words are spiky and cross, and I know this won't end well.

'Look, the kids got a bit carried away. Josh had some friends round, and by the time they left he was really tired. It's my fault, I told him I'd deal with it, but I didn't have time.'

'You shouldn't be cleaning up after them anyway, they'll never learn.'

'I hardly think Josh needs to learn to tidy a room. He's an A student, one day he'll have staff to do that,' he chuckles.

'I'm sorry, I don't think it's funny to let Josh think it's okay to behave like an entitled brat.'

'For fuck's sake, Alice, I was joking. If it really upsets you, I can come round now and tidy up, would you like that?'

'No, I wouldn't. I've done it.'

'Then why are you still banging on about it?'

I take a breath. 'I'm *banging on* because you letting Josh think you'll just clear up after him is not good parenting.'

'Oh, and insisting we split just because I left a jokey voice note for some woman? Is that "good parenting"?'

'A jokey voice note? You *told* me you were having an affair with her. You confessed, you idiot.'

'Yeah, but I also said it was meaningless.'

'To you maybe, but not to me – or her probably. You really are a psycho, and I don't want to even discuss it anymore, there are more important things we need to talk about. Like we need a security light and camera on the back of the house. I can get the same guy who did the front doorbell camera.'

'Fine, fine,' he says, sounding worried. I'm relieved because I expected him to refuse to contribute and say I was imagining this. But he agreed to the emergency locksmith last week after Ryan said Ruby's window had been prised open. Mind you, I had to exaggerate and tell Jason the security guy had said there'd been several attempted break-ins around the house.

'We also need to call the police about Ruby's window being broken into, but I don't want to do it in front of Ruby, she's about to get into the car. Would you mind calling them? If they come round in the daytime tomorrow when the kids are out that would be great.'

'Okay, okay, I'll see what I can do.'

That's not going to happen. I can tell by his voice he has no intention of calling the police. I'll do it myself. 'I know I've been on my own many times when you worked away, but this feels different, Jason.'

'Well, you can say what you like about being an independent woman, but you're more vulnerable without me there – fact.'

How do I hate him? Let me count the ways.

'Look Alice, I know the marriage is over, but we could just go back to living in the same house with our kids like normal people.

I'd be around more and you wouldn't be alone at night. We don't have to sleep together or—'

'No.'

'Why?'

'Because I'd rather be alone and terrified than live with you.' And there it is: the truth.

He doesn't respond. He can't handle receiving any kind of pushback.

In the past I've been cautious, scared that he might try to take the children – after all, he's a twisted man, and an even more twisted lawyer. And Jason always gets what he wants.

'Are you still okay for Thursday evening?' I ask, dragging myself from the past. 'I'm having dinner with that new client?'

'Yeah, sure.' He's not remotely interested, as usual. And it's just as well because I've decided not to tell him yet who my big new client is. I worry that if he knows he might, out of spite, suddenly be unavailable to cover my night at the house with the kids. Or worse – I wouldn't put it past him to sabotage my chances, knowing the fee for working on a house like that will kickstart my financial independence and everything he fears. So, for now, I'm keeping schtum, but look forward very much to telling him everything very soon.

I end the call, knowing that I've been kidding myself. Jason and I can't be friends, there's too much bad blood between us, but we can't truly split up either. My business might tick along with the small jobs – but that's the problem, they're small. I'm desperate for that breakout project, to give me back my freedom.

Jason will be horrified that Daniel has a more beautiful place than his. He grew to love the house as much as I do – he sees it as a symbol of his success, his money, the facade of his perfect life with the perfect family. That's the only reason he wants everything to stay the same, so he can continue to live this shiny, beautiful lie of a life. I was part of that lie, and we've both always been careful not to rock the boat too much and keep that lie intact. And now, my biggest fear is that Jason's never going to let all that go. My dream of divorce and freedom from him could be a dream too far, because he'll do everything and anything to make this separation – this nesting trial – a nightmare, and for me there'll be no way out.

21

Daniel suggested I come for dinner at Silvercliff at 8 p.m. But I'm on track to arrive at 7.23 p.m. because I was worried about being late, so set out far too early. I feel it would be rather gauche to knock on the door before eight, and want to time it for about five past – not too keen, but not too late either.

So I'm now sitting in the car a couple of miles away, watching the beginnings of a pink sunset. The fading blue sky is smeared with melting strawberry ice cream, which minute by minute is turning into a deep sorbet. It's inspired me to add more shades of pink to the sunset concept in my pitch, and by the time I pull up at the house I'm buzzing with even more ideas. I'm also buzzing with nerves, and when the door is opened by Daniel himself, I'm a little surprised.

'No staff tonight?' I ask.

'Alice, you look gorgeous,' he says, not answering my question.

I'm trying to impress in a new pink kimono and headband, looking like I've just stepped out of an F. Scott Fitzgerald novel. Instead of flapper pearls though, I'm clutching my iPhone and a notebook. He guides me into the sitting room, and I can feel his eyes on me.

'And that kimono? Wow! It takes me right back to the South of France in the thirties. Pure old-money Riviera chic.'

'Yeah? I'll take that. I ordered it online after three glasses of prosecco.'

He laughs, and I feel witty and beautiful. I'm neither.

I sit on one of the pale sofas, so soft and comfortable, like climbing into a warm bath. I can feel the stress and worry floating off me, a dark cloud heading out over the cliffs, leaving me in peace.

Without asking, Daniel makes me a gin and tonic, with ice shaped like fruit segments, and a spritz of fresh lime. He does this with such exuberance and charm, reminding me of a young Richard E. Grant.

'So, have you had any more thoughts about the project?' I ask, as he hands me the cold, heavy glass. I'm aware I might be being a little pushy, but I have to be.

'Yes, I love your ideas, and I'm desperate to work with you, but I just need to check with someone first.' He sits down next to me, and the aroma of his expensive aftershave mingles with the zest of gin, creating quite a heady cocktail.

'Okay.' I give him a big smile to cover my deep disappointment, and wonder who he needs to 'check with' as he clinks his glass against mine. Perhaps it's another designer. Do *I have competition?* He knows I can do the job, but perhaps someone else has done a better pitch?

Okay, so he loves my ideas, but if I'm competing with another designer, I'll have to offer a little more. So I need to step up my game and let Daniel see how much fun it would be having me around on this project.

'You smell delicious. Sea salt and citrus – takes me back to a warm night in Positano. He was Italian, and drank limoncello like it was holy water,' I joke.

'Ah Alice, youth and bad decisions. I remember it well.' I chuckle at this. 'Your talk of young Italians on the Amalfi Coast has made me long for the Mediterranean. Can you design a house that conjures a Positano sunset? You know, waves tickling the shore, terraces bursting with lemons, the fragrance teasing your memory like a mischievous old lover.'

This makes me laugh out loud. 'That's the cheesiest thing I've ever heard.'

I'm laughing and joking but starting to panic slightly. I came here tonight thinking it was a slam dunk, that I'd got the job . . . so what's going on?

I have to drive back tonight, so ease up on my half-drunk gin and place it on the coffee table. I'm wondering if he's given his staff the night off, and if so, who's cooking dinner? I hear a noise from above, like someone walking around upstairs, but Daniel seems oblivious and just keeps talking. Then whoever it is decides to make an entrance. It's probably the stern housekeeper I met last time.

'Baby, where are you?' a woman's voice calls from upstairs. Presumably this isn't the housekeeper?

'I'm here, babe,' he calls. Then he looks at me and gives a little wink. 'Darling, come and meet Alice.'

I'm shocked, and I have to say, a tad disappointed. Does Daniel have a girlfriend?

I see her feet first. She's barefoot, with glossy scarlet toenails. I wait forever to see the rest of her as she walks down the floating stairs, one by one, like every step is choreographed. All I see for a while is long pale lemon silk, swishing every now and then, allowing a tantalising glimpse of long brown legs and those scarlet toes.

Daniel's now joined her on the stairs, gently taking her arm and virtually carrying her down, step by step.

And suddenly, she's in my vision. Those great legs have a body to match, and now a face, a very pretty face. But what really takes my breath away is the huge bump now visible under the swishing yellow silk. *She's pregnant!*

22

'Hello.' The woman's voice is soft and babyish. This is all so unexpected, it takes me a moment to respond. I thought he lived here alone, and tonight was just the two of us discussing the house design and celebrating the project. If I'm honest, due to his flirtatiousness, I was also under the impression that Daniel might want to rekindle something. How stupid that I would even think he might be interested. Of course Daniel Prescott has made a life for himself – he's with a beautiful woman, and they're expecting a baby.

I smile at her and she smiles back, a warm, open smile – but there's something really familiar about it. Was she at school with Daniel and me? I just feel like I know her – perhaps she's just local and I've seen her around? Then it hits me who she is. 'Maddie Lavender?' I blurt out, before Daniel has a chance to introduce us.

She smiles and flicks her honey-blonde hair self-consciously. No wonder I thought she looked familiar. Maddie Lavender is my age and she's been on TV since she was a child, living her life in the full public glare from about fourteen.

'I feel like I've known you forever,' I say, fangirling and suppressing my urge to ask for a selfie, 'and I guess that's because I have. I've grown up with Maddie Lavender,' I add, aware I'm now gushing.

She's beaming. 'Welcome to Silvercliff.' She steps forward, reaching out for a hug and I reciprocate. We try to embrace, but her tummy is in the way, and we both chuckle at this to ease the awkwardness.

'Well, congratulations you two,' I say, hugging Daniel too. I'm genuinely happy for him – she seems lovely, and the way he looks at her it's clear he's in love. I'm pretty starstruck, but now I'm over the initial shock, I can't help but wonder why he didn't mention her, or at least tell me he was expecting a child with his partner?

'Alice, come through to the kitchen,' she says, taking my arm. 'Mary has left us a simple supper.'

My suppers are pretty simple every night, and I was hoping for something special this evening. I'd read in a local magazine that Daniel is a great cook, and imagined all kinds of exciting things for dinner, but on entering the kitchen I realise one woman's simple supper is another's sumptuous feast! No beans on toast here. The table hasn't been laid, it's been landscaped – just an array of charcuterie boards, an acre of salads, luscious dressings, home-baked sourdough bread, and a mountain of fruit piled so high it seemed to defy gravity.

'This *simple supper* is like a wedding buffet,' I say, as we walk round the huge kitchen island, taking whatever we fancy.

'Nothing is too much for Maddie.' Daniel smiles at her as she takes a stick of celery and puts it to her lips. If my kids were here now they'd say 'get a room'. I avert my eyes and study the white ribbons of fat in the *prosciutto di Parma*, thinking *this got hot quickly*. Eventually I look up; she's still smouldering, he's salivating, and I doubt it's the *jamón Ibérico* that's making him moist. I smile to myself as I imagine the retelling of this to Martha.

I fill my plate and follow Maddie to the round kitchen table, where she puts down her food, a fig and a few leaves, and I put down mine – a pig and a few loaves. I thought I was on safe ground as pregnant women eat for two, but clearly Maddie hasn't got the memo.

Daniel produces a bottle of wine, but as I'm driving and Maddie's pregnant, he's the only one drinking. I can see by the label it's an expensive red. I wonder if they eat and drink like this every night?

'This is lovely,' I say, hoping they haven't clocked my greed.

'You enjoy these kinds of suppers, don't you, darling?' he says to Maddie as she takes minuscule bites of her fig. 'This kitchen is perfect for romantic little nibbles, isn't it?'

She just ignores him. She's being quite rude, but he seems oblivious. 'I have to say, darling, I haven't been strictly honest with you about this evening,' he starts. She looks up from her fig with an alarmed expression. I'm feeling pretty uneasy myself.

'You mean you lied about Alice?' She's holding the fig between two fingers, and looking from him to me and back. She seems suddenly anxious about what he's about to say.

He smiles, then takes a long sip of wine, savouring the mouthful. We're now both on tenterhooks waiting for him to speak.

He takes his time lathering salt-crystal butter on his slice of wild fig and walnut sourdough. 'Alice is . . . well, she's an interior designer . . . a fabulous interior designer,' he adds, biting into the bread, watching us both.

'Oh?' She turns to look at me, obviously surprised. *Who the hell did she think I was?*

Things are getting a bit weird. He clearly hasn't told her he's asked me to work on a proposal for the house. What if she's already chosen the other designer and Daniel only invited me here tonight as a palliative to spare my feelings? I've given up a night at home with my children. I hope I'm not wasting my time, but I refuse to give up, so I push on because I *need* this job.

'You're a designer, Alice?' she asks enquiringly, but I see something else in her eyes. Is it doubt? Fear?

'Yes, I'm working on . . . designs for . . . this.' I gesture around me to indicate this house.

The mood in the room has switched, like a dark veil just landed on the table. I know it's not in my interest to change the subject, but it feels so odd, so tense, I have to just dive in. 'When's the baby due?' I ask, rather clumsily.

'In six weeks,' she answers without a smile.

'Gosh, how wonderful, are you excited?'

'I'm nervous.' Her gaze flickers quickly to Daniel then back to her plate.

'Oh, there's nothing to be nervous about. Do you have plans for the nursery?' I say, feigning brightness, which isn't easy in this atmosphere.

Maddie doesn't flinch, just keeps gazing downwards. The silence is deafening, until Daniel says, 'I think we'll wait and see about the nursery, don't you, darling?'

She doesn't look at him, but I see a slight shrug of the shoulders. *What is going on here?*

Neither of them is making any attempt to speak, even Daniel is silent, and it's so agonising I try to keep talking.

'I have two children,' I offer into the emptiness. 'They're seventeen and twelve, and they make me so happy, they really do. You forget all about the morning sickness and the labour. Just holding that baby in your arms erases all that.'

'It's Josh and Ruby, right?' Daniel steps in to rescue me.

I smile, grateful for the save, and touched that he remembered.

Unexpectedly bouncing back, Daniel turns to Maddie. 'I used to play cricket with Alice's husband, Jason. And Alice and I were in the same class at school, and later we became . . . friends,' he adds, obviously stopping himself from hinting at anything more, but it's so obvious I wonder if it's deliberate.

He gives a half-smile, and I see a glance pass between them. Her eyes drop, like something sharp has stung her, but it's so subtle that I wonder if I imagined it.

While making stupid small talk I'm trying to work out what's going on here – it's pretty unfathomable. Does she feel excluded by Daniel's and my old friendship? Even the most beautiful and successful women in the world can have low self-esteem, and see other women as a threat, even when they aren't. Being with Jason, I was on constant alert and I would hate for another woman to feel like that because of me. So in an attempt to reassure Maddie, I turn to her and continue my benign baby chatter.

'So, a first baby, you must be buying lots of lovely things?' I sound so superficial, but I don't know what else to say – and this is Maddie Lavender!

She doesn't look at me; her head's down, and she's just staring at her half-eaten fig. She's given up even trying, and I'm drowning here.

'Yes, she's spending a fortune on all kinds of things, aren't you, darling?' Daniel steps in to save me again. He's chuckling at this and I smile politely, but she seems to be miles away. It's as if a cloud has covered the sun, but I have to resurrect the evening. If I don't, this could all end in nothing for me.

'I imagine it's cold here in the winter?' It's pitiful, but I'm socially exhausted and it's all I can come up with to try to pierce the surface tension. I turn to her, about to say something really pointless, but it's greeted by the scraping of Maddie's chair as she stands up, and turns to me.

'I'm sorry, Alice, I'm not feeling very well. I'm afraid I need to go and lie down. It was lovely to meet you.'

I feel dismissed, but move to stand, to hug her, to thank her for supper and for having me, but despite her rather lumbering pregnancy, she's already left the room.

The relief is palpable, as if the room breathed out the moment she left.

I pull my chair back under the table, opposite Daniel. 'I haven't upset her . . . have I?' I ask him.

His smile is warm, and he tilts his head to one side. 'Oh Alice, you're so sweet,' he sighs. 'No, it was nothing you said. There are a lot of . . . complications.'

I sigh. 'Good, she's lovely, I imagine she's just tired and exhausted from the pregnancy?' I offer, hoping he'll tell me what that was about.

But he's just staring at me, smiling. 'I never forgot you, you know. You are one of those people who come along once in a lifetime,' he says. 'You were beautiful, still are – and whenever I think of you, I hear your laughter, and the jangling of all those bracelets you wore. You used to use your hands a lot too back then – so expressive, a constant explosion of ideas.'

I listen to him, and in that moment I remember her, that girl, the laughter, the bracelets.

'We laughed a lot back then, and I loved those bracelets, I had so many.' I wonder when I stopped wearing jangly bracelets, and when did I stop laughing?

'And I always remember, there was that one piece of hair, that was caught by the sun,' he's saying – and reaching up, he touches my cheek with the back of his hand. 'If you look closely enough, it's still there, more golden than the rest.' He holds my hair in his fingers as if it were silk. I feel the heat rising in my face, and he gazes at me, in a way no one's gazed at me for a long time. I know it was only a kiss to me, but it feels like it meant more to him – which has surprised me, but it's flattering.

I'm sixteen again, with my life before me, an open horizon, so many possibilities to embrace. I look at his lips, and remember the awkward but urgent kiss of those years gone by. And for a moment, just a moment, time stands still, and the world stops. I hear nothing and see nothing. Except him, the faint jangle of bracelets. And who we once were.

Then suddenly the tension breaks, and the film in my head fast-forwards to now, as the past and the sound of those discordant bracelets fade.

'I'd better go,' I say. 'I think Maddie might need you.'

'You think so?' He curves his lips into a smile that holds no warmth.

'Would you like to talk about it?' I offer, intrigued.

He shakes his head. 'If I told you, Alice, you'd never believe me.'

23

I leave Daniel's without anything decided on the design project. It's frustrating, but I could hardly talk business after Maddie left. I drive straight to Martha's where I've arranged to stay tonight, and try to work out what the hell is going on between 'the couple with everything'. Was she genuinely feeling ill, or was she angry about something? I'm still surprised that he has a partner, and amazed that he never mentioned they're expecting a baby.

I am a little disappointed that Daniel's taken, because it was nice to flirt and I enjoyed the attention. I was mistaken to think that he'd ever be interested in me now, but it gave me an escape if only in my head. Now I know he's with someone, I can't think of him that way. But I like him, and hope we can be friends – if Maddie will allow it.

Perhaps Daniel was the one that got away? If I'd pursued him back then, my life might have been very different. But I thought he wasn't into me, and along came the edgy, sexy, ambitious Jason – who made it clear he did want me, and he always got what he wanted. Scary how our choices at seventeen can impact the rest of our lives. At seventeen I went for the sexy, ambitious one – and lived to regret it.

Jason's at the house with the kids, and I wasn't sure what time I'd be leaving Silvercliff, and didn't want to wake Mum, or confuse her, by going back to her apartment late, so Martha had offered to let me stay. It was kind of her, but she was also desperate for an update on the dinner with Daniel.

'Don't make me wait . . . did you get the job? Did you sleep with him?' Martha jokes as she opens the front door. At least I think she's joking.

'Where do I start?' I follow her into her kitchen where I know there'll be little bowls of savoury nibbles and something pink chilling in the fridge. Martha always knows how to make you feel welcome.

'So, what happened?' she says, pouring me a drink.

'I'm trying to process it all.'

'Start at the beginning.'

'I would if I could but it was . . . just weird.'

'I'm not surprised, Daniel always was a bit bonkers,' she chuckles.

'It wasn't Daniel so much.' I take a cocktail stick and prick a big shiny green olive, and run through the evening. I start with the drinks and the flirty banter between me and him, and then Maddie's entrance.

'Whaaat? No, no . . . you're winding me up. You mean Maddie Lavender from *The Shore*? NO!' Martha's genuinely shocked. And when I add that she's having Daniel's baby, she screams. 'Oh my God! Mike, the cameraman who I dated, he worked on *The Shore*, I remember him saying she was a bit of a diva.'

'I reckon he's right.'

'I'm trying to remember if he told me anything else juicy about Maddie Lavender, he's such a gossip. Easy on the eye too. Wonder if he's still working on that programme?'

'Probably, that's a job for life. It's been going for at least twenty years or more, part of our culture. Mum's always loved it – *The Shore* and *Coronation Street*.'

'Yeah, "Corrie by the Sea",' she laughs. 'Maddie Lavender's not a great actress, let's face it. She only got the part because she was young and pretty in a bikini.'

'She's still pretty, but I doubt she's wearing bikinis at the moment being pregnant.'

'I wondered why she hasn't been on *The Shore* for a while, not for a long time come to think of it. That must be why.'

'They'll have written her out until she has the baby I imagine. The storyline's probably sent her to work abroad or something. Mum will know, she watches all the soaps.'

'So, old Daniel the star shagger, eh? That wasn't on my bingo card. I haven't seen anything in the papers about him being with her.'

'Nor me, but I reckon they've just agreed to keep their relationship secret, they don't want the press crawling over their property, especially as she's pregnant. Thing is, they're so private, looks like they don't even tell each other much.' I smile. 'He hadn't told her who I was, or why I was there.'

'Yeah, it's all a bit odd. You'd think he'd tell her exactly who's in her home. Being in the public eye she's probably paranoid.'

'Yeah, I could have been a stalker.'

'I reckon Daniel's more of a stalker. I bet he bought that house on the pretext of "keeping her safe", but all the time he's just keeping her to himself.' She shudders.

'No, honestly Martha, he's okay. At school everyone said he was a bit weird, but he's not, just eccentric perhaps. But I think Maddie Lavender might be a bit of a diva.'

'I can imagine that.'

'Mmm, it's a weird dynamic. He seemed to be trying to please her . . . but she suddenly went cold and stomped off, like a child. He's probably had his head turned with her looks and her celebrity, but I'm not sure about the dynamic between them. She seems unhappy, but how could anyone be sad living in a house like that with a man like Daniel, who probably gives her everything her heart desires?'

'Yeah, at school everyone envied him, his family were so rich. They lived in that big house, he always wore designer clothes, and had the latest gadgets. He was a schoolboy with a Rolex, for goodness' sake!' She's shaking her head, still in disbelief after twenty-odd years. 'But I don't think his life was as great as we thought. Do you remember that time his dad was called into school? Daniel was in trouble, can't even remember what it was for, something really minor, but old Crocket the headmaster called his dad about it.'

She takes a sip of her wine, and continues. 'His dad turned up in a fancy car, parked it right in the middle of the car park, and started screaming at Daniel.'

'God I'd forgotten all about that, I didn't see any of it myself, but the rumour was that Daniel was so terrified, he wet himself,' I add, reaching for my drink. 'I think when someone's downtrodden like that as a child, they go looking for the same weird dynamic in their adult relationships. I hope Maddie's not mean to him like his dad was.'

'I reckon she needs him far more than he needs her, Alice. He's a multi-millionaire, and she's an ageing Z-lister.'

'Ageing? She's almost thirty-eight, around the same age as us.'

'That's her showbiz age, she'll be at least forty.'

'Oh my God, what an old crone,' I say in mock horror.

'You may laugh, but in her world anything older than thirty-five is past it,' Martha points out. 'Let's face it, there are lots of younger, thinner, blonder actresses sashaying around *The Shore* in tiny bikinis – she's yesterday's news. And after that baby, her breasts will be down to her knees and she'll need a corset!'

'Hey what happened to women supporting women?' I laugh. 'She's beautiful, age and body size has nothing to do with that. What's your beef with Maddie Lavender anyway?'

Martha frowns sulkily, taking a generous sip of her wine. 'Every boyfriend I ever had seemed to fantasise about her. I couldn't compete. She's always been the other woman in my life.'

'Fair enough, your unbridled hatred is justified,' I joke. 'But it won't do my business any harm to have Maddie Lavender as a client.'

Martha warms to that idea. 'Oooh, yes, and I'll do the PR. I can already see her wrapped in designer silks, leaning against the sparkly white backdrop of the wall, the morning sun pouring on to the scene like honey. A double-page Sunday magazine: *Maddie chose Cornish up-and-coming designer Alice Taylor of Sundrenched Interiors to decorate her fabulous home . . .*'

24

I've just had breakfast with Martha and I'm now heading to Mum's for the next three nights, and for the first time in this nesting trial period, I'm keen to check on the kids. It feels like I've let things slide enough, so I call Jason from the car.

'Yeah, they're both fine, went off to school . . .'

'Did you drop them off?'

'No, they can walk themselves. You're too paranoid, you're making them lazy, Alice. And yes, Ruby has an inhaler and Josh revised.'

I have to hope he's right and they're fine, otherwise I'm going to drive myself mad, but something sounds off with him, and it's not the usual backdrop of a busy office . . . ?

I press my phone closer to my ear. 'Are you in the office?'

'No, I'm at the house, working from home today, dealing with an injunction – messy work.'

I try to take the sting out of my voice. 'Ugh, can't be much fun.' I'm keen to ask more about the kids; I miss them and need colourful anecdotes and quotes. Jason isn't the one to provide any colour, but I hope for crumbs, and ask again. 'So, are the kids okay?'

'Yes, I told you,' he answers abruptly. It's a sore point because I know he feels like I don't trust him, and he's right.

'Don't forget to let me know if you are called away. I'm only at Mum's for the next few nights and can come over.'

'Yeah. You've made your point on that. Actually, I've asked if I can have a more home-based role from now on, it makes sense with the living arrangements.'

This is interesting, and a little worrying. Does he want to be around even more for the kids? I like that his nights at the house have landed on weekends so far. I don't have to worry about him getting them up for school, or making sure they're home, but if he doesn't have to be in the office or away, then he'd be involved in more everyday stuff. Having seen how unreliable he has become, I'm not sure I trust him with that.

'So, thanks for calling . . .' he starts.

Oh no, you're not getting rid of me that quickly. He never asks about me, or what's going on in my professional life, and I have this urge to tell him all about Daniel Prescott's job offer. I also want to really rub it in and describe Daniel's perfect life, omitting anything that seems less than perfect . . . or outright weird.

'Thanks for staying over last night for me, I had a great dinner meeting,' I rush in, before he can even think about putting down the phone.

'Good, good.'

'Yeah, not sure if I mentioned, the client is Daniel Prescott.'

Silence, followed by: 'You know he can't be trusted, Alice, he's a liar and a—'

'Well, he's offered me a great fee, and I'm just working out if I can fit him in with the other work,' I lie. I don't want him to know it isn't absolutely confirmed yet.

'Big mistake.'

'Really?' I want to laugh out loud at his obvious disapproval. *How did I live with this guy, why did I ever love him?*

'The man's an idiot,' he spits.

I swallow a laugh. 'I like him. He said you both played on the same cricket team. And you know he went to our school for a while, and I went out with him,' I add. I'm exaggerating, of course, but I just want him to think there were other boys in my life before him.

'Yes I've *heard* of him, but I wouldn't call him a friend. He's just some loser.'

'And how are we defining "loser" this week? Just asking, because he's in a relationship with a beautiful actress, lives in an ocean-front house worth upwards of three million and they have a baby on the way. Loser? *Really?*'

I hear his heavy sigh; he's obviously hating this news. 'Did you call for any other reason than to brag about someone you might work for?'

I'm building up to this. If he's pissed off that Daniel's done well, he's going to be even more pissed off when I tell him the next bit.

'You'll never guess who his girlfriend is?'

'Amaze me,' he monotones.

'Maddie Lavender.'

'Who?'

'Now I *know* you're jealous. Who hasn't heard of Maddie Lavender? She's Lucy in *The Shore*, not like you to miss a pretty face. And you know exactly who she is, we watched her in that drama a couple of years ago, the one about the woman who killed her husband by putting anti-freeze in his quiche Lorraine. You fancied her . . . but then again is there a woman with a pulse that you don't fancy?' I add, unable to resist a little dig.

'I don't remember. I don't think I've ever heard of her, but I have heard of Daniel Prescott, and trust me, trouble always follows him.'

'Is this about Daniel Prescott, or is it because you're scared I'm finally making a real success of my business, building a new life for myself?'

I hear him scoff. 'Don't be stupid. You don't know what you're getting yourself into, Alice.'

'I know exactly what I'm—'

'Look, ask yourself this . . . if Daniel Prescott is so rich, and can have anything he wants, then why is he asking *you* to design the interior of his multimillion-pound home?'

I'm taken aback. 'Wow!'

'Oh, stop with the drama, I'm not criticising your work, but think about it – he's got all this money, he could hire the *very* best . . .'

'You're digging yourself an even bigger hole, Jason,' I warn.

'Well, it's true. He could employ a really famous designer, top of their game, and you're not exactly . . .' He's searching for the name of an interior designer, but not being familiar with his wife's profession, he can't think of one.

'Kelly Hoppen?' I suggest, wanting to hear him go on to justify his belittling comment about my work.

'Yes, a professional with other celebrity clients, people who mix in the same circles, not some local woman with a small business.'

And there it is – *that's* how he sees me, it's how he's always seen me. *Some local woman.* I'm a nothing in his book. From the moment we were married, I became a wife and mother, *some local woman*, who stayed home to look after the children, whose career wasn't big enough to justify leaving the house. Last night, Daniel told me how he never forgot me, how he remembered my laugh and my jangly bracelets – he said I was an 'explosion' of ideas. Jason knew that same girl back then, but he saw someone different: he saw someone he could manipulate, who might be useful to him. I was invisible to my husband then, and continued to stay invisible until I ended it – and now I feel like I'm re-emerging as the me I was before him. I'm growing in confidence, my horizons are opening, and I'm excited for the future for the first time in forever.

I haven't spoken for a while, and Jason knows he's pissed me off and sighs down the phone. I resist the urge to rest my head against the steering wheel as he puts on his 'reasonable' voice. 'Alice, why don't we stop all this nonsense. I don't want this *arrangement*, and I don't want this divorce, because either way the children suffer. They are suffering now.'

'You don't want this "nonsense" because it's inconvenient. To you. You want things back to normal; you only love our house as a status symbol, and the wife and two perfect kids give you an air of respectability that quite frankly you don't deserve. Do your partners know you were having an affair with someone you worked with? And it wasn't the first time. It's not a good look is it, and without me standing by you, there's no cover, nowhere to hide. You can't carry on living your big life because the perfect family aren't waiting for you in your perfect home anymore as a perfect smokescreen.'

I'm so angry I have to stop for breath and allow my blood pressure to drop a little. Adrenalin is raging through my body and I'm just glad he's on the phone and isn't here with me, because I'd be tempted to punch him. Hard.

'You paint such an awful picture of our life, but you were happy to live it.'

'I *endured* it, Jason, and you know why.'

We both stay silent. It's so painful that neither of us have talked about it for years, yet like a buzzing housefly it hovers between us.

I hang up and hurl my phone on to the passenger seat. I can't believe he'd be so negative, so bloody dismissive of what I'm doing. He's absolutely seething with jealousy, and can't get past it to even say 'well done'. Instead he just spouts poison about Daniel and pretends he doesn't even know who Maddie Lavender is, when he so obviously does. Which makes me wonder if he lied about not knowing a woman who drives a mint-green Fiat too?

25

I wake up to a text from Daniel, and it feels like such a gift. He's confirming the commission – asking me for high-end finishes, bespoke furniture, full design and project management. The fee works out at more than a hundred thousand for everything: my talent, my time and all the physical work involved. It's my route to freedom. With a couple of loans and some extra work, I can buy myself out of this marriage.

He's asking me to send over the official pitch and contract for him to sign, and is asking for the plans asap. It's a done deal. I'm elated, and I leap out of bed and want to dance around Mum's apartment singing at the top of my voice, but I resist. I don't want to alarm Mum. So I sit on the bed with my laptop and send all the paperwork over to Daniel to sign.

Today is going to be the beginning of the rest of my life. My second chapter is about to start, and I can't wait.

Mum's been out to her coffee club, and arrives home just before lunch.

'Guess whose house I'm going to be working on, Mum?'

She looks at me vaguely. 'I don't know. Should I?' She looks worried, like I've told her and she's forgotten.

'Remember I was talking to Daniel Prescott about working on his house?'

She smiles.

'I told you I went for dinner and . . . remember, Maddie Lavender showed up?'

'Maddie who, love? Did you go to school with her?' Oh no. I cling to the hope that Mum's hearing is playing up.

'Lavender . . . Maddie Lavender, she plays Lucy in *The Shore*.' I'm waiting for it to dawn on her.

'Lucy?'

'Maddie is the *actress's* name, Mum. Lucy is the character she plays.' For a moment I wonder if I'm going mad, until she suddenly seems to realise what I'm saying.

'Oh, of course, I know who she is. Yes . . . I remember.'

I'm not convinced. 'So what do you think?'

'Can I come and see her, will you sneak me into the house?' She recovers well, but I can tell already that Mum's not quite with it today. I hope it's just tiredness, or something minor like a mineral deficiency, and when we go to the GP they can give her something. The appointment is in a couple of days. 'I'd love to sneak you in, but we'll see. She's lovely, just as pretty as she is on the show.'

'So her name's Maddie?'

'Yeah, the girl that plays Lucy, her real-life name is Maddie. It's confusing, I know.' I over-explain this because I need to be clear, I'm desperate for her to understand.

'I'll get you her autograph when I start working there,' I offer, looking into her face for clues, but what to look for?

'Autograph! That would be lovely, yes – I'd like that.' Mum smiles and then pulls out the red bucket-hat construction that she's crocheting for Josh.

'That girl . . . she was here you know,' she says, working the yarn around the hook, red wool spilling across her lap.

'What girl? Maddie Lavender?'

'No, the girl who'd been abroad . . . she lived somewhere sunny.'

'I'm not sure who you mean, Mum . . . ?'

'When she knocked on the door, I thought I knew her. I didn't. She said there's a family resemblance.'

She's scaring me, and now, without a shadow of a doubt I know there is something wrong with Mum.

'Who did she resemble, this woman?' I ask carefully.

'She had a lovely tan, hint of an accent too – I think she must have been from abroad. Your dad and I had a lovely holiday there once.'

'What was her name, Mum?'

What the hell?

'How do I know!' she snaps, agitated now. But I don't understand what she's telling me. 'She was here yesterday. She brought lemon cake. It was very nice . . . you must remember her, she knows you.'

'She did? What was her name? Did she tell you?'

'Gabriel . . . like the Angel Gabriel . . . something like that.'

My whole world shifts as she lifts her face and stares ahead. Something is definitely wrong. She's delusional – she thinks the Angel Gabriel brought her lemon cake.

'What else did she say?'

'I can't think.' She clenches her fist in frustration and shakes her head. 'Was she a friend of Jason's?' It's as if she's talking to herself. 'I never liked him – don't think she did either.'

My mind is still scrabbling for answers, but the more I hear, the less I know.

'She brought lemon cake, baked it herself she said – kept asking lots of questions about *him*. I didn't *tell* her anything, Alice.'

She's repeating herself – she's confused. This is terrifying. But her strong belief that this woman was here bothers me. Is Mum delusional, or is she mixing her memories with something real? The fact she says this woman is a friend of Jason worries me the most.

Was Ellie here? Or was it someone else asking questions about Jason and me and the kids? My blood runs cold.

'This woman who came to see you yesterday, she wasn't a police officer . . . was she, Mum?'

She looks at me. 'Who?'

Her eyes are a mixture of fear and confusion. I'm ashamed because I'm hoping this is Mum's failing memory and not a real event. Because as awful as the prospect of dementia might be, the alternative, that this woman was a police officer, is far too scary to contemplate. If what Mum is saying is real, then whoever her visitor was yesterday, they know something about what happened all those years ago – and they've set out to find Jason . . . and then it might be me, and then . . . the children.

'I'll make you a nice cup of tea, Mum,' I say. Tea is the curer of all ills in our family, and even now there's a tiny part of me that hopes it will give her some clarity. I wander into the kitchen, trying to stay calm, reminding myself that we've got the appointment with her GP. I'll get some answers there and Mum will get the help she needs.

I open the cupboard to take out the tin she keeps her teabags in, and just behind it I see something wrapped in tin foil. I pull it out, and open the foil slowly. Citrus hits the back of my throat. Inside the foil is a fresh, home-made lemon cake.

26

I really thought Mum had lost it, but then finding the lemon cake in the kitchen made me think someone had paid her a visit. Mum may have just been confused about someone turning up from the past – she mentioned family resemblance, so could it be a long-lost relative? I asked her again where the lemon cake had come from, assuming she'd forgotten or she'd say 'Marjorie dropped it in'. But she didn't; she stared at me, and replied impatiently, 'I told you Alice, that woman who came to see me, the one from abroad . . . she brought it over.'

Later, I called Jason, and left a message. I had to tell him what Mum had said to see if he could shed any light on it.

It's a couple of days after Mum told me about the visitor, and I'm taking her for the appointment to see Dr Manjit, her GP. I discreetly explain to him what is happening, with Mum there, tutting at my side and saying I'm 'exaggerating'.

'You've done the right thing bringing Mum in, Mrs Taylor,' the doctor says kindly. 'These things can be difficult to notice when you're close to someone. Forgetfulness can have all sorts of causes. It could be something as simple as low vitamin levels or a thyroid issue.'

'Oh, that's what I thought, it's not like her . . . and most of the time you're fine, aren't you, Mum?' I say, hoping this isn't frightening her.

'Yes, I'm fine, I don't know why you're talking like I'm not in the room,' she snaps.

Dr Manjit leans in. 'Liz, we've known each other a while. I know you're fine, but your daughter's worried,' he says. 'So, I'd like to do some blood tests and check your memory, just to put your daughter's mind at rest, okay?' He gives me an almost imperceptible wink and starts straight away. 'I'll ask a few questions and do a short memory test here, and we can refer you to the clinic if we need to. Does that sound alright?' he asks gently.

I know for a fact if I'd so much as mentioned a memory test she'd have bitten my head off, but Mum loves Dr Manjit, and happily plays his memory game.

Later, while the nurse is doing Mum's blood tests, I ask if I can have a word with Dr Manjit alone.

I tell him about what has been happening – the confusion over the woman who visited her with lemon cake, the way she moves her dolls around. 'She was joking about how she sometimes lets them out to play – but now I wonder if she was joking? Has she started to see them as real – does she think her dolls are alive?' I add. 'And then there's the way she leaves bowls and cups around the apartment like she's forgotten them, and she's irrationally angry when I've accidentally knocked them over. It's just so out of character.' I go on to tell him about the cereal and the cup of tea, and, hearing my own words out loud, now see these things in a different light.

He listens carefully, nodding his head slowly, and when I've finished, he says, 'At this stage, Mrs Taylor, I can't give you anything definitive. We need the full range of test results to have everything confirmed, and an MRI scan will provide the most definitive physical evidence.' He pauses. I suppose he's bracing himself to give me the news I know is coming, and I wait for the punch. 'In my experience,' he says, 'from what you've told me, and the memory test I just gave your mum, I suspect we're in the early stages of dementia.'

I want to be sick.

'However,' he continues, 'what concerns me is that her change in behaviour seems to have happened quite suddenly, and dementia usually takes years to develop. So my guess at this stage is that we're probably looking at vascular dementia, this is a series of mini-strokes, which can accelerate the condition. In my opinion, this would account for the rather sudden changes in your mum's behaviour.' He adds this final sentence softly, knowing how hard it will land.

I've known this in my heart, but it's completely different hearing it from a doctor.

'It's difficult at this early stage to say how this will progress, and the tests may give us an indication, but in the meantime just try and behave as you normally would around her. This disease is different for everyone. In some patients it can manifest in confusion and impulsive behaviour, and the sudden, uncharacteristic responses you describe.'

I'm horrified; I feel so lost. 'How can I help her, what should I do?'

'For now, let's not frighten her with any unconfirmed diagnosis, and try not to react negatively or shame any strange behaviours, as long as they aren't endangering herself or others.'

Then he tells me he'll arrange a scan and, once we have the results and diagnosis, a treatment plan will be put in place.

I arrive back home, scared for Mum but looking forward to seeing the children. I feel beleaguered and uncertain after talking to Dr Manjit, and don't feel strong enough yet to take on anything else. I'm just hoping things are better than they have been on my previous returns. I don't want to even consider the horrible implications of a dementia diagnosis for my mum and how that will affect her and how I will cope with becoming her carer when I've just become a single parent. How will that impact on the kids, too?

Hoping to be able to relax in the sanctuary of home, my heart sinks as I walk into a kitchen littered with takeaway cartons, and the chicken fillets I left in the fridge are now past their use-by date. There's no milk or coffee, no bread, and the bin is overflowing again. I was hoping to work on my designs for Silvercliff today, but now I'll have to spend at least a couple of hours cleaning and shopping. Again. Why do they do this?

I start with the kitchen bin, pulling out the bin liner of stickiness and grease, and glass bottles. Jason hasn't even recycled, just thrown everything in together. I take out the bottles, one by one. They're all identical, all whisky, and all the very expensive brands that Jason insists on. I once asked him what was so special that he spent a week's salary on a bottle of the stuff.

'It just gives me a hit, a smoky caramel aftertaste that I don't get with other whiskies.'

It's always been his favourite tipple, but three bottles? He's been here four nights – has he really drunk three bottles of profanely priced whisky in four nights? I don't know what horrifies me most, that he's severely abusing his body or his bank balance. *Glad he hasn't had to compromise on his little luxuries*, I think, dropping the bottles into the recycling bin.

I attempt to pull the bag from the bin, but groan under the weight of several days of domestic eating and wiping-up and *ugh*. It's so heavy, I have to drag the rubbish through the back door to where the bins live. The bin men came today and took the rubbish, so I'm expecting a clean, empty bin, but as I lift the lid, I'm met by a foul stench. The bin is full, and the thick odour, warm and sour, hits me in the face, the smell of death and decay filling my nostrils and hanging in the sultry air.

Fucking hell, he didn't put the bins out! I left him a note telling him the bin men come today, and texted him too because it's so hot. There's a week's worth of rubbish here – it's already turning toxic and now it will have to sit for another whole week. In searing temperatures.

I gaze down into the open bin, and to my horror, the rubbish inside is *moving*. I gasp as it takes a minute for me to realise what I'm seeing. And when I do, I hear my own voice, whimpering in horror. Maggots. A living, moving tsunami of glistening white bodies. And now I've opened the lid, they're moving out, spilling over the rim in clumps, tumbling out like overcooked rice, landing on the scorched paving. I instantly drop the bag on the ground and slam down the lid, but despite the lid only being open for seconds, it seems thousands have already escaped. They are now moving as one across the patio. Recoiling, I move away but some of the maggots are on my bare arms, and falling down my summer dress.

I shake them off, squealing with horror, and run back into the kitchen, straight to the cupboard where I keep all the cleaning materials. I rip open the doors, and take out the bleach and disinfectant and anything else I can find and fill a bucket with hot water, then I open up the bottles. The bleach is empty, so I open the disinfectant. That's empty too. The sink cleaner, floor cleaner, and even the dishwasher fluid. All have been used and put back in the cupboard empty. Jason never cleans, so why would he do this? Is he trying to mess with my head?

I don't have time to think about it, I just channel my anger into energy to get rid of the army of white that's now crawling all over the back garden. Tears fill my eyes as I boil a kettle, and dig out an old one I stashed away in the kitchen cupboard so I can double the boiling water. Stepping outside with the bucket full of scalding water, I'm driven by my instinct to kill. And so I begin what feels like an impossible fight, with a bucket of boiling water and a plague of writhing maggots.

About an hour later, I emerge feeling fragile and battle-worn. But I did it, without a fuss – okay a little drama, perhaps? I run upstairs to take a quick shower, and run into the small en-suite, desperate to stand under hot water and scrub myself clean. But as I open the door I'm met with a complete mess.

Half-open aftershave bottles, toothpaste smudges, a dripping razor and several used, wet towels. Jason's clutter is spread everywhere, the shower hasn't been cleaned, his hairs are in the plughole, the aftermath of soap lies in the corners, and an empty bottle of my expensive shampoo is on the floor. It all feels like a deliberate act of sabotage. And after my fight outside with the maggot army, this is another battle I didn't sign up for. I pick up his T-shirt and towels, and put them in the laundry hamper. Why does he do this? It's claustrophobic, suffocating – as though the bathroom has shrunk around me. I know it's petty, the rage pulsing in my temples is out of proportion to what's happening, but this is my space and he's ruined it. The bathroom is damp, like he's only just left. I feel like he's still here, and my skin crawls.

I have to scrub this clean, wash him away, so I open the cabinet to take out the shower cleaner and . . . guess what? Yep, that's empty too. This is fucking war! I scrub the shower with his cheap shampoo, then scrub myself clean and somehow, through my red mist, I get dressed. Then I go downstairs and check the fridge. I bought plenty of food for the week, but there's nothing left. I also bought a bottle of Martha's favourite pink wine that was on offer last week. I definitely put that in the fridge, and it's gone. I can't find it anywhere. So I drive to the supermarket, buy food, replace the cleaning fluids and bleach, and pay more for the rosé, because it's not on offer anymore. I have an hour and a half to get everything on the list, pay for it, put it in the fridge, then go and collect Ruby. The car's hot, and my forehead drips sweat as I drive back home, empty all the bags, put the food and pink wine in the fridge and then put a wash on. I scrub the kitchen until it sparkles, along with the downstairs toilet. I'm on all fours, wiping the toilet, and I suddenly stop and see myself in the mirror, resentment building, stress eating into my veins – I look at my sweaty face and heat-frazzled hair. And all I can think is *why?* In what world did I ever think this nesting thing could work? I'm trying to end my marriage, build a new business, my mum's showing signs of dementia, my husband's being uncooperative while pretending to be on board, and my son hates me.

I take the just-bought shower cleaner upstairs to clean the en-suite shower after I used it earlier, but when I get up there and see all his stuff lying around, I think *fuck you.* So instead of cleaning the shower properly, I empty his bottle of aftershave down the plughole, and recoil at the pungent scent of Jason. Then I open the bottle of cleaning fluid, and pour it into the empty bottle. Enjoying the acrid stench of toilet cleaner filling the air, I wonder if this will make women swoon when he wears it? I giggle at the thought of him splashing it on all over, before heading downstairs to dig out his one remaining bottle of fancy whisky. When I find it, the bottle's already open, with just a few shots drunk, so plenty left for me to spoil – good! My 'recipe' for ruining his precious liquor is to add several large tablespoons of salt, and a good dash of cumin. But I'm not quite finished, and, feeling like a deranged Gordon Ramsay, I do a final flourish of garlic powder.

The idea of ruining Jason's many avenues of pleasure gives me more joy than it probably should, and is more restorative than a day at the spa. What I'm doing is nothing compared to what my husband's done to me, but in my own way I'm taking back control. It's revenge on a small scale – for now.

Pulling up to the school I'm feeling so much better, like I have some agency. I'm not the victim, I can fight back in my own quiet way. I feel almost happy – until I see the back of the mint-green Fiat leaving the school car park.

27

I'm still feeling a little shaken having seen the Fiat at school. I ask Ruby if she knows who it was. 'Is it a teacher?'

'I dunno,' she shrugs.

'One of the parents?'

'It's just a car, it could be anyone's. Mum, chill, seriously.'

I don't mention it again, but it unnerves me, and I'm relieved to hear Josh coming in about an hour after we get home. I make dinner for the kids and call upstairs for Josh, but when he comes down to the kitchen he barely speaks to me. I ask about his day, but he just mutters something about 'revision' and disappears upstairs with his dinner on a tray.

About 7 p.m., Meghan's mum arrives at the house to pick Ruby up. She's driving the girls to gymnastics tonight. Still feeling bad about Jason forgetting to pick them up recently when it was our turn, I walk to the car with Ruby and thank Yvonne. Ruby clambers into the back of their car with Meghan and I wave them off. Then I go upstairs to my room, put on a little make-up, and try and cool down before Martha arrives about eight.

'Babe,' she says as she plonks down her bag and takes a stool at the kitchen island. 'I'm exhausted with this fucking heat!' Her hair is frizzy, her forehead shining. 'Good news about the Daniel

Prescott job?' she says. I left a message on her phone to tell her the fee we've agreed on and everything.

'It's such a relief, Martha,' I say. 'I'm just waiting for him to sign and send the contract back. He's so bonkers, God knows when that'll happen.'

'Yeah, well, these rich people think we've all got trust funds to live off. He doesn't realise you need that money asap.'

She takes a bottle of wine from her bag and slides it across the island towards me. 'I just bought it from the off-licence, it needs chilling.'

I thank her and open the fridge to pop it in and reach for the one I bought earlier that's been chilling in there all afternoon.

'I could swear I put the bottle in the door.' I'm moving stuff around the fridge. 'Perhaps I laid it down in the salad cooler?' I pull out the drawer. I then look on the kitchen counter – did I forget to put it in the fridge, and it's been languishing in the warm air all this time? 'Bloody hell, where is it?'

'What?'

'The rosé wine I bought this afternoon. I distinctly remember putting it in the fridge door.' I see it so clearly in my mind's eye.

'Don't worry, I can wait, that one will chill soon enough.'

'That's not the point, Martha, I *need* to find it.' I open the fridge again, returning to the door, like it's hiding behind the milk, crouching behind the orange juice. 'I definitely put it in,' I'm saying, my head in the fridge, and then, without warning, I burst into tears.

Martha gets off her stool and walks over to hug me. 'This isn't about a bottle of wine, is it?'

'No, there's just too much going on,' I tell her about the bins, and the maggots, and she recoils as I describe the way they moved, and how the place was a mess, and how Jason hadn't cleaned the shower and had left his stuff everywhere.

'God forbid I would ever defend Jason, but maggots? Even he wouldn't let things get that bad, would he? He can be untidy but he's not a total slut – he always hands me a coaster to put my cup on when I'm here.'

'Yeah, he does that because he likes everything to look nice. This house is his showroom too.'

'Yeah, the perfect house, the perfect abode for the perfect husband and father. He has to be successful at everything, doesn't he? So why would he let the bins get so bad?'

I shrug. 'Sabotage? Alcohol?' Then I tell her about the whisky bottles.

'Wow! Drinking whisky by the bottle? He's lost it. I mean he wasn't exactly an Adonis, but he looked after himself, watched what he ate, and I don't remember him being a big drinker?'

'No, he'd have a bottle of wine with me sometimes, a few beers, but rarely drank spirits.' I get up and, taking Martha's wine from the fridge, pour us both a drink. 'This wine's still warm, but I need it.'

'Me too.' She takes the glass gratefully.

'Yeah, I was shocked to realise how much whisky he's been drinking. Expensive stuff too.' I sit back down, and take a sip. 'But I guess he can afford to drink whisky every night. He contributes nothing to the food bills – I'm paying for everything that everyone eats and drinks, several times over. Obviously I spend on the kids, but when he's earning about five times what I earn I do object to buying his milk and cereal.'

'Well don't!!!'

'I buy it for the kids. It would seem petty to ask him not to eat or drink stuff in the fridge.'

'What about household bills?'

'We split them all now. I just pay my half into his bank and he pays it – it's not ideal but this is all temporary. I just need to give him his half of the house and he can do what he likes.'

'Sounds like he's doing that already. I mean, jeez, almost a bottle of whisky a day? How is he even functioning? Unless of course his new girlfriend is drinking it?'

'I hope not, because that would mean she's drinking it here, the bottles were in the bin . . . Talking about Jason's girlfriend, I saw the Fiat today, at the school.'

Martha looks horrified. 'No . . . what the hell? Are you sure it's the same car you saw before, the one from the coffee shop?'

'I didn't see the registration number that day, but it's a bit of a coincidence.'

'Wow, it's been quite a day, hasn't it? No wonder you nearly lost it when you couldn't find the wine.'

'But I know I put it in the fridge.' I lean forward, and say in a low voice, because he's upstairs, 'I've been thinking about it – and the only person that could have taken it is Josh.'

Martha is staring at me, her eyes wide, and I turn to see him standing in the doorway. He must have been listening in the hall. In the dark.

'What have I done now?' he says quietly.

'Hey Josh,' Martha says, but he ignores her – he's glaring at me, his eyes unblinking and his face expressionless. He walks into the kitchen like he's in a trance, and my stomach drops. 'What were you saying?' His voice is low, broken and deep, but still clinging to the last echoes of the child he used to be.

I need to show him strength, not weakness, so I try to be assertive and firm without being angry or emotional.

'Okay Josh, I'm going to be honest with you.' I look up at the familiar smirk that appears whenever I speak. 'I left a bottle of wine in the fridge last week, and today it wasn't here. I wasn't going to say anything, and I just replaced it today with a new one and put it in the fridge this afternoon. Now that's gone. And there's only been you and me in the house.'

His face opens up as he realises what I'm saying. 'So now I'm stealing your sad wine?' The quiver in his voice betrays his outrage, but also his hurt – and I'm actually relieved to see he still has the capacity to feel anything but anger.

'I'm not saying you *stole* it, you may have seen it, had a drink then thought I might be pissed off with you, so hid it or drank the rest. Is that what happened, Josh?' I offer, desperately hoping he'll grab this alibi.

His face is dark, blank.

'It isn't about the wine, Josh, it's about you taking it without asking, or even telling me – twice! And if you *are* drinking a whole bottle at a time, we need to talk. Is this because your dad's started drinking?'

He offers me nothing but his silent, male rage; but as a mother, I know if I look hard enough, I can see the boy. And he's still in there, on the verge of crying, the dimpled chin and eyes heavy with unshed tears.

But the boy doesn't stay long, his breaking voice suddenly filling the air. 'I haven't touched your *fucking* wine!'

The power of his anger scares me. I feel his fury building, coming to the surface, a volcanic eruption of hate and resentment. He's kept his feelings down for so long, but now he's cracking wide open.

Neither of us move, our eyes are locked. I hold my breath and slowly, cautiously, reach my hand out. The air is tight.

Martha shifts in her seat. 'Josh,' she croaks from behind him.

In that moment, I remember her joy when she first saw him, our chubby baby boy, and the past overwhelms me. She gave him a gift, his own fire engine to drive. He was three and beside himself.

'Sorry I didn't see him sooner, as a baby,' she said, after her world travels with an unsuitable boy.

'It's fine,' I said, 'you're here now.' She was suntanned, smiling, so happy for Jason and me. But my best friend had no idea. I couldn't tell her then, and I can't tell her now.

28

Josh's fingers dig into his temples as if he's trying to hold himself together. His breath is now in shallow gasps, and a low rumble of sobs emerges from him, muffled against his palms. He's trying to stifle his pain, but it's wrapped around him like a python, tighter and tighter. My son was already hurting, but I've hurt him more. I don't know how to soothe him, to say I'm sorry. I don't care about a missing bottle of wine. I just care about *him*.

I tentatively reach out my hand again. But as the tips of my fingers touch his arm, he shakes me off vigorously, and runs from the kitchen. And as his feet thunder up the stairs to his sanctuary, I know I messed up, and this time I'm not sure he'll come back.

'Fuck!' Martha groans. 'What's going on, Alice? The last time I saw Josh he was teasing Ruby and joking about you being menopausal, which of course you aren't,' she adds, not wanting any more tears. 'What on earth is happening with him?'

'I wish I knew. He's changed so much in such a short time.' I shake my head, the weight of guilt pressing into my bones.

Martha pours us both some more wine, and says, 'It's all connected to his parents splitting up, and it's not you . . . you're there for both your kids. But Jason's to blame for this, he's angry and resentful towards you, and he's passing it on to your son.'

'I know, and this nesting thing is making everything so much worse. I have no idea what's going on when I'm not around, and . . .' I get up from my seat and check the hall before closing the door. 'You're probably right, Jason's a big influence on Josh. It might explain why he's become aggressive. He's paranoid, and oversensitive too.'

'I've never seen him like that, especially with you.' She shakes her head sadly.

'I'm really worried about him, Martha, and the irony is, the main reason for this *arrangement* was to make the children feel secure, and stable. But it seems to be having the opposite effect on Josh.'

'And Ruby?'

'I think she's just caught in the middle, between me and Josh, and me and Jason. You know Ruby, always the peacemaker, the mediator. But I know she's worried, she told me she heard Josh on the phone to a girl, and from what she said they were arguing. She said his voice was raised, and he was crying.'

'Who's the girl . . . does he have a girlfriend?'

I shrug. 'I've no idea, he doesn't talk to me anymore. I really hope he does have someone, he needs some support, but if she's making him cry . . .' My throat tightens at the thought of some girl hurting him.

'Did Ruby know why he was crying?'

'No, or if she did, she wasn't saying. She made me promise not to tell him she'd told me.'

'Do you think she's scared of what he'd do if he found out she'd snitched?'

'God, I don't know.' I'm shaking my head. I hadn't considered that Ruby could be *scared* of her brother. 'Jesus, Martha, what have I done to my kids?'

'Nothing, this isn't all you . . .' She looks up from her glass, reaches her hand out to mine.

'I made an emotional decision. I wanted my children and my house to stay together, for their sake . . . but also mine. This house was everything – my past, my future, my sanctuary. I'd put so much time and love into it, I couldn't bear the thought of anyone else living here. But from the minute we started this "social experiment" it stopped feeling like home.'

'That's so sad. A house *should* be a home.'

'Yeah, but it isn't anymore and I need to start prioritising the people, not the things. It doesn't matter how beautiful this place is. If my kids are sad, it's meaningless.'

'It's true what they say – you're only as happy as your saddest child,' she sighs.

'So true,' I murmur, still going over that awful encounter with my son.

'Every age is tough, but teenagers . . . I dread it.' She wafts her hand on her face to cool down. Martha's kids are both younger than Josh, and she has yet to experience the challenges of the teen years. 'Have you talked to Jason about Josh?'

'Tried to, but he just saw it as an opportunity to say he's now the favourite parent.'

'Ugh, classic Jason.'

'He's as unfathomable as ever, says he isn't seeing anyone, then hints there is someone. I reckon he's just never stopped seeing Ellie but wants to keep his options open.'

'Wonder whose bed he's sleeping in?'

'No idea, and don't care. I just want him to look after the kids when I'm not here, instead of abandoning them to "work".'

'Mmm, such a liar. Is he living with this Ellie woman?'

'Probably. He told me he's staying with his old friend Olly, but he isn't. I saw Olly the other day and he said he hasn't seen Jason for weeks. Thing is, I hope he is staying with that Ellie, because I feel like we're still living together. There's this horrible intimacy of sleeping in the same bed, even if it is a different night. All his stuff's hanging about, his clothes are in the wardrobe, his books lying by the bed, and this is my first night back and he hasn't changed the sheets.'

'Ugh, that's revolting. And in this heat? Gross.'

'It sounds mad, but every time I come back it's like he's left more of his stuff around, and at the same time, taken more of mine. It's like he's moving back in, inch by inch, taking over the space, drinking my drink, eating my food, and every time I walk in it's like he's getting closer and closer, trying to swallow me back into the house, into his life.'

'That's creepy.' She shudders.

'It is. It's also bloody infuriating because he's using my stuff now. He didn't do that the first few times, but he's encroaching, stepping further in – and I come back to empty bottles and jars, empty toilet rolls, used cotton wool. He's been washing his hair with my good shampoo . . .'

'Not the fucking Olaplex?'

'Yep! And last week there was nothing left of the Crème de la Mer that Mum bought me for my birthday.'

'No. Oh my God!' Her hand flies up to her mouth. 'That stuff costs a fortune. What the hell is he using it for?'

'He said he'd used it for dry patches on his bloody elbows and knees.'

'Fuck that! He could let my kids have screen time 24/7 and smoke weed until dawn, but touch my Crème de la Mer and you're touching my soul. Hope you told him to buy you another?'

'I wanted to kill him. But I stayed calm, because I'm convinced he's getting a kick out of winding me up.'

'Bastard! He can't accept it's over, yet he's the one with someone else, and he's just getting off on stressing you out so you'll go back to how you were.'

'He's used to having me at home, and another woman on the go at work, or the gym or somewhere – and that's what he wants again. He doesn't want me.'

'Perhaps he wants the house?' Martha suggests after a brief silence blooms between us.

'That's what worries me,' I murmur.

'Be careful, Alice,' she says. 'We all know if he wants something, he'll do anything to get it. And if Jason wants this house there's only one thing stopping him. You.'

29

Martha's energy fills every space, her anger over face cream as vigorous and damning as her rage over Jason's affairs. And after she's gone the silence hits. It's now just me and the house. Josh is locked in his room, and Ruby's at Meghan's. I feel vulnerable and exposed in the kitchen with the floor-to-ceiling glass looking out on to a very dark garden, so I turn off the lights, check the doors and go upstairs to bed.

As I pass Josh's door, I'm tempted to knock, ask if we can talk, but that went badly last time. I check my watch – it's almost midnight, he's probably asleep. I need to give him space.

I go to my bedroom, leaving the door open as always, a hangover from my kids' younger days when they'd call for me in the night, or run into our room scared after a nightmare.

I used to sleep well, but since the split life feels stressful, and being here makes me anxious. So I open a book, in the hope that my mind will drift and sleep will come. But a sound somewhere in the house alerts me, and I lift my head from the page. My eyes go to the dressing table, *my* dressing table, where I've laid out my perfume, moisturiser and gold make-up bag for my stay. Something doesn't look quite right, and I get out of bed to check. My lipstick and mascara lie on the dresser, but I know for a fact I put them away in my make-up bag. Earlier tonight, before Martha arrived, I was so hot and sweaty, I took my second shower of the day, applied some make-up, and remember putting the mascara and lipstick back in the bag because the zip's faulty and I struggled.

But now they both sit on the dressing table, defiantly. I sit down and look more closely at what's on the dresser – nothing missing, nothing extra, but things have been moved, and as I reach for them, I happen to glance into the mirror. And behind me, blurred in the half-dark, something or someone moves, and then slips out through my bedroom door.

I'm frozen to the spot, waiting for my brain to catch up. Every instinct screams at me to bolt for the door, to check the stairs, but my legs won't move. I can't leave the bedroom.

I hold myself rigid, and wait for the creak on the stairs. My heart thumps in the darkness, waiting. But there's nothing. The only other person in the house is Josh. Was it him?

I step out on to the dark landing. Nothing. No one. I turn on the flashlight on my phone and, without knocking on Josh's door, I push hard to open it. Tonight there's no chest of drawers to keep me out, and I creep in, pointing the flashlight straight at his bed. At first I can't see properly, but as the light hits him, relief floods through me. *He's sleeping.* I move closer to check he's breathing. When he was little, I did this every night, tiptoeing around his cot, and later his little bed, to check he was alive and no one had taken him in the night.

Tonight, I watch him, as I watched him then, knowing he doesn't understand why I love him, and sometimes I think he doesn't even believe I love him. But in spite of what happened, I do. Then I leave, closing the door behind me.

Perhaps I'm mistaken, and there are only two hearts beating in the house tonight after all? Still, I don't feel ready to check downstairs, so I go back to my bedroom, where Jason's jacket hangs on the door – another reminder that he'll always be here. Was that what I saw, and mistook for someone in my room? I don't think so, but I was looking into a mirror, and it's possible my eyes played tricks in the dark. Isn't it?

I sit on the edge of the bed telling myself there's no one else in the house. But I'm so desperate to believe this that I convince myself I'm being silly, something Jason always did so well. I don't even need him to gaslight me anymore, I can do it too – true independence. I smile to myself.

Then, just as I climb back into bed, I definitely hear something downstairs – just a movement, a rustle. All my senses are slammed back on high alert. My heart's pounding and my flesh is raw and tender. I move to the edge of the bed, trying to comprehend the sound. Now I have to do something, so I dash to the top of the stairs, phone in hand and shout, 'I'm calling the police!'

A blanket of silence lands on the house. Whoever was making the sound has stopped. Please God, have I scared them off? I'm looking down into the hallway when I see something move, and immediately point my phone's flashlight down. Another sound. And the flashlight catches the movement. Is it a rat? I'd prefer it to a burglar, but still it freaks me out, and given the maggots it could easily be their accomplices in the feast of rotting bins.

Then I catch the movement again with my flashlight, and hear a little miaow coming from the bottom of the stairs.

'Willow?' I call hopefully, and dash downstairs to find my lost furry baby. Being a cat, she doesn't do drama, or reunions, or kisses, but I do enough for both of us as I scoop her up and cuddle her, burying my face in her soft, downy fur.

'Where've you been, baby?' I'm almost in tears with relief that she's home, but also that it's her and not an intruder.

She's been missing for more than two weeks, but on closer inspection, wherever she's been she hasn't starved. In fact she feels heavier, and looks very well: her fur is shiny and she's calm and is now purring in my arms.

Before heading into the kitchen to feed her, I double-check the front door is locked. I then check the windows, the bifold doors and the back door, as Willow joins me in my nocturnal safety patrol, and we establish that the house is secure. No one got in, and therefore no one got out.

'I need to get a grip Willow.' At this she miaows again, and as I look down at her, something hits me.

If all the doors and windows are locked, and we have no cat flap, how did Willow get into the house?

30

Thinking about it, the noise I heard earlier was heavier than a cat, and coupled with the shadow in the mirror, I'm still concerned. *Did someone let Willow in as they left?*

Her miaowing is now quite persistent, so before I do anything else, I feed her. Then I make myself a cup of tea, grab the laptop and log on to the door camera. I'm terrified in case I see something disturbing, but equally I'm the only grown-up here and I need to face whatever it is. And if it's something, I'll call the police; if it's nothing, I'll be able to go to bed and sleep soundly.

The footage starts first thing this morning, at the front of the house. I don't need to see the day, so now and then I speed it up, but then I rewind, worried I've missed something. But there is nothing so far and the picture's really clear and records every single second faithfully.

I continue to watch the morning's activity, or lack of it. And I can't help but wonder if Jason's been playing tricks, or if it's Josh? I think in an ideal world my husband and kids would choose to have everything back to how it was. I feel terrible that I'm the only one that doesn't.

It's taken me almost an hour to watch four hours of nothing. Am I obsessing too much? If I'm going to stay awake all night staring at this, I might as well work on some designs. I should be channelling my energy into Daniel's house, not scrutinising CCTV, seeing every little thing as a threat or a sinister game. Is there anything that's happened tonight that's genuinely odd or can't be explained?

There was the wine, that was weird, and then my mascara and lipstick – they'd definitely been moved. Josh wouldn't do that, and Jason wouldn't even *see* them; he only sees what's relevant to him. I gaze into the screen absently, not really expecting to see anything but the day grow darker. I see myself dashing out to pick up Ruby, then Mum walked round at about 4 p.m. She's clutching Natasha, one of her dolls – not sure why, she doesn't usually take her dolls out. A worm of anxiety wriggles into my brain and settles there, and I think about what the doctor said when I told him about her dolls being moved around the apartment. *Try not to react negatively or shame any strange behaviours, as long as they aren't endangering herself or others.*

I watch her on camera now. But despite my fear for Mum that sits permanently in my gut, I can't help but smile watching her fix her hair on the step for the camera before she goes inside. 'I put my lipstick on especially,' she says, into the camera, then stands by the bay tree posing. She is convinced the camera takes still pictures, and can't quite get her head around the fact it's a video. This is more likely to be because she doesn't understand the technology rather than any condition she may be suffering from.

I smile to myself – whatever makes her happy. She stayed for about half an hour, she must have cleaned, but I didn't notice because I'd already done the cleaning. I wonder fleetingly if Mum moved the wine, but why would she? Mum doesn't even drink, and wouldn't dream of taking anything from my fridge.

I watch her leave, and she waves to the camera again, and blows a kiss, which makes me smile again.

I'm now at the point where Ruby goes off in Meghan's mum's car, and I wave them off. That'll be just before I took a shower and got ready for Martha to arrive. Worryingly, it's at this time, 7.27 p.m., the icon of a person's silhouette appears to show human-triggered movement. My stomach dips: someone is close. Dreading what I might see, I immediately zoom in, but there's no one visible on-screen. Perhaps they're just passing, or watching . . . or whoever it is knows there's a wide-angled camera. *And* knows how to avoid it. Did Jason pop back to the house, pick up the wine and move my stuff around on the dressing table in our bedroom while I was having a shower? Jason is annoying, selfish and vain, but he's not a psycho! Then I think about some of the things he did when he was younger and I question this. Did he change, or does he just cover it better now?

Or do I need to accept that I'm living in some Gothic horror novel where the husband commits the wife to a sanitorium to gain control of the house and the kids? This is real life, and I really have to face the fact that it's probably my son who has the problem with me – not my husband. But it's so painful, I can't deal with it now, and so, pushing it away, I return to the screen, and fast-forward to 8.10 p.m. Martha's now at the doorstep, and I answer the door. She comes in, and after that, there's no front-door action until she leaves at 10.53 p.m.

I'm seated precariously on the high stool when Willow jumps on to my lap and pushes her head under my hand to be stroked. I almost fall off the stool, but try to keep my eyes on the screen, wondering if I'm wasting my time, when I see a car drive past. It's 11.03 p.m. and dark, so hard to see, so I zoom in and slow down the camera speed; I can just about make out a light-coloured Fiat driving slowly past my house.

I watch again and again. Slow, fast, rewind, zoom – damn, I can't see a registration number. This isn't the only Fiat in the area, so I can't be a hundred per cent sure, but a few minutes after the car passes the house, the sensors pick up movement, because the camera starts recording again. I look closer, the zoom now at maximum, my face close to the screen. It's almost impossible to differentiate anything in the tangled silhouettes of the trees, half shrouded in shadowy branches. But as I look, a wild, creeping sensation crawls along the back of my neck.

'What the fuck?' I hear my own voice in a whisper. *Someone is standing between the trees at the front of the house.*

Despite the oppressive heat, I shiver as if exposed to cold air. The stillness on the screen and around me now is terrifying. No movement, no sound, just the pulse of heat throbbing in my head.

I try to see more by brightening the screen, slowing it down and zooming in and out. I still can't make out a face. Is my mind playing tricks again? Am I being fooled for the second time tonight by shadows showing up as human?

I can't look away, and as I watch, whatever is in the trees emerges slowly. With a stinging slap, I know my mind isn't playing tricks. I can't see who it is, but this is someone, and they are real. Too real.

I glance at the time on screen. Ten p.m. I'm looking at life from three hours ago. Martha and I drinking wine *inside.* Someone watching us *outside.* Then it hits me: the direction they were looking was towards Josh's bedroom window. Even if you didn't know it was his room, you'd guess from the football and gaming stickers on the window. *It was Josh they were watching.* The idea lodges in my throat like a stone, dry and uncomfortable, and the very thought of this . . . I can't bear it. *What if they're still outside?* I close my laptop and walk to the front room, then look through the window, my skin alive with heat and goose-bumps. I stand in the window defiant, outstaring the darkness. The primitive side of my brain flickers, *threat, move, hide* – but how can I?

After staring for a long time, I see nothing from the window and return to the dark kitchen. I feel scared but listless not knowing what to do. I call Jason and leave a message: 'I'm worried, someone's been hanging around. I can't say for sure, but I'm calling the police. I know you said you'd do it a few days ago, but obviously you didn't!'

So I call the police, and say I think someone's watching my house, and the woman on the phone asks if I know who it is. I tell her I don't – 'I just thought I saw someone on my door camera.'

She takes my name and address and says, 'Okay, stay in the house, don't try to confront them. Can you describe the person, male or female? I'm sending someone over to your address now.'

'Oh . . . no, they've gone, they aren't here now. This is from footage earlier this evening,' I say, feeling rather foolish.

I can tell by her response she thinks I'm a lunatic, and asks me to confirm there's no one there now.

'No . . . I'm looking out of the window and there's no one,' I say.

'Okay, we'll still send an officer, but it won't be immediate as it's not an emergency.' In other words, *you're a time-waster and I'm not putting up with your shit.* Which I think is probably fair enough, and if nothing else it puts things into perspective for me. Someone may have been watching, but I need to look properly, probably tomorrow, when I'm not so tired and jumpy.

I know I suffer from anxiety, and I might need to go back on the medication. It began when I became a mother for the first time – I had therapy and medication for a couple of years, and though I probably worry too much about the children, I have good reason. My fear is real, and triggered by what happened years ago, but I've tried not to let it ruin my life. I thought I'd accepted that what happened lived dormant inside me, but since the split it's made itself known. It walks beside me, climbs into bed with me at night, and sits in the back seat of my car, watching, waiting.

I'm suddenly struck by a thought. The car that drove past just minutes before. Did it park a little way down the road, behind a tree? All the time I've assumed that whoever's in the Fiat, who talked to the kids, turning up at school and driving around night, is connected to Jason. I still wonder if it's Ellie, his current girlfriend as far as I know, trying to find out about us, or scare me. Is she doing this on Jason's instructions and they're planning to erase me from the picture? I *know* Jason could do that if he had to, and Martha sees that too.

Her warning echoes in my head: *If Jason wants this house there's only one thing stopping him. You.*

31

I wake in the morning with an undercurrent of fear, low and constant like the humming of the fridge. It vibrates through the floor and up into my bones. What does it all mean? I waited up until about three this morning as I wasn't sure if the police would turn up. The woman on the phone didn't give me a time – as I feared, she obviously thought I was a time waster.

I get up, go downstairs, make coffee and call Josh. Ruby's already texted to say she had fun at gymnastics and they stayed up until 1 a.m. at Meghan's. I'll collect her from school later, tired and grumpy by then, I'm sure.

Josh emerges a few minutes later, so I'll call the police when he's gone. I don't want to add to his concerns.

'You look tired, were you up late last night?' I ask. It isn't meant as a criticism or judgement, I'm just wondering if he heard or saw anything, but don't want to alarm him.

He mumbles something while grabbing the orange juice from the fridge and drinking it from the carton. He's never done that before, I bet Jason lets him. I want to say something but think better of it. *Pick your battles.*

'Josh?'

He turns, the scowl on his face even less inviting than usual.

'Sorry about last night. I just . . . there was no one here but you and me, and when the wine went – what else was I to think?'

He shrugs while moving slowly to the door, his back to me.

'I'm sorry if I got it wrong Josh. *Really* sorry.'

He mumbles something from the hallway, and before I can ask him to repeat it, the front door slams. He's gone. I'm frustrated and sad. We've always had a good relationship, even through his teens – until now.

I drink my coffee, eyes blurred with tears. From the very beginning, I did everything wrong with Josh, and now I need to make it right. Tonight I'll try to talk to him, and instead of dwelling on the past, I'll look forward, and be better.

Yesterday was hell. I barely slept last night and I'm still coming down from all the drama. I leave three messages with Jason, who has gone from answering every call promptly to sending me to voicemail, and I call the police, telling them it's 'urgent' and 'my kids might be in danger'.

I receive an automated call-back, to say they've received my call. So that is a great comfort. And now I can devote the morning to work which desperately needs my attention, but just as I open my laptop, the doorbell rings. I assume it's Mum with one of her doll children, but my new paranoia doesn't allow me to take a chance, and I check the camera first. '*Fuck*,' I murmur under my breath. It's Daniel, and I think Maddie's with him.

My biggest clients are now on my doorstep. I'm not in the mood, and nor is the house. Despite the extensive cleaning, washing and vacuuming, I'm still finding crumbs and spills and empty bottles in the strangest of places. Only ten minutes ago I discovered an empty beer bottle behind the TV. That has to be Josh.

I don't even have time to spritz room mist everywhere, and as I open the door, I realise I'm in my big old T-shirt and jogging bottoms. I try to compensate for this by greeting the couple with a big, open smile.

'Hello you two,' I beam, like they are the best surprise I've had in months.

'Hello you!' Daniel lunges in for a bear hug, and after extricating myself from him, I turn to Maddie, going in with the same enthusiasm. I grip her warmly like my oldest friend, but her response is limp, and as we pull apart I can see by her face she doesn't want to be here. I want to ask why they've turned up unannounced on my doorstep without calling first, but of course I can't, that would seem rude. Besides, they might be here to deliver the contract for the work I sent to him on email. I used document-signing software, but perhaps he wants to deliver it by hand and drink champagne to celebrate? I'd be up for that, so I keep the perma-smile going and invite them in.

'This is charming,' Daniel says, as he strolls down the hallway.

Damn. He isn't carrying any documents.

'Come into the kitchen, you'll have to forgive me, the place is . . .' I turn around to see him opening the door to the sitting room and peeping in. Aware it may still harbour the faint stench of smoke and weed, I hurry him along. 'This way,' I say, gesturing with a big sweeping motion, as Maddie, head down, walks past me into the kitchen. It's as if she's walking *through* me.

I suggest we sit nearby on the sofa in the kitchen, not the breakfast bar stools, as Maddie looks like she's about to give birth at any moment. While I help her sit down, Daniel is making loud noises of approval regarding the layout, and I'm slightly horrified to hear more doors opening and closing. I just hope he doesn't wander into the utility, where all the dirty washing I found yesterday is still overflowing in the basket.

I move my focus to making coffee, and try not to think about Daniel Prescott poking around in the broom cupboard, otherwise known as the family dumping ground.

Feeling quite exposed by this horrible surprise, I try to fake normal, and take out the cafetière to make proper coffee. I doubt Daniel's palate could tolerate instant; he'd probably pass out.

Perhaps he's left the signed contract in the car and just wants a look round before he gives it to me?

I glance over at Maddie, who looks gorgeous; she's wearing a white linen dress, her tummy is huge, and her face is prettier in pregnancy softness than when she's on-screen. She wears little make-up today, just a slick of lip colour, she seems to have naturally long lashes, and her skin is pale gold porcelain. And while my hair clings to my hot, damp forehead and my upper lip drips salty sweat, Maddie shimmers like a golden goddess. She sits on the sofa, like royalty, surveying everyone in silence. This is slightly unnerving, but she is very pregnant and probably tired.

'I won't offer you and the baby coffee,' I joke. 'What about some iced tea?'

She shakes her head, unsmiling. 'Water's fine.'

'How are you, Maddie?' I try. 'I had a summer baby too. This heat isn't much fun, is it?'

At first she doesn't answer, then lifts her head and gives a quick, sideways glance towards the door. Her expression is sulky – she reminds me of a spoiled child. I suppose she's used to people fawning over her, as I guess I am now. But even though I try to reach out to her, she's deliberately not engaging with me.

'It's been so hot, hasn't it?' I continue. I wish I could say I'm doing this out of kindness, but she's so rude, if she was anyone else I might be rude back and ignore her. But this is difficult, she's Daniel's partner, and I'm waiting for him to sign on the dotted line with this project. I've got the feeling that, for some reason, she doesn't like me – and if that's true, she won't want me working at the house and might try to change his mind.

'Yes, it's . . . too hot,' she murmurs, and finally looks up and meets my eyes, and by the light of the window I can see she's been crying.

I'm not sure if I should even acknowledge this, but I have to. 'Would you like a tissue . . . or should I get Daniel?'

She shakes her head slowly then, still unsmiling, she lifts her head, her chin jutting out slightly, and finally makes direct eye contact. 'You don't know why he's brought me here, do you?'

32

Maddie and I are staring at each other. I'm holding my breath waiting for her to tell me why Daniel's brought her here. But before she can say anything else, he comes bounding in.

'What an amazing kitchen,' he exclaims, then turns to her. 'Isn't it, baby?'

He doesn't wait for her reaction, or even look at her; he's already turned away and is now wandering towards the glass doors that lead into the garden. God knows what's going on between them, but it just feels off. Meanwhile, I need to know what they're doing here.

'So, it's lovely to see you both, to what do I owe the pleasure?' I say, finally working out a polite way of saying *are you here with the signed contract?*

'Oh . . . I'm so sorry, we should probably have let you know.' Daniel turns back to me, in apparent horror at his social faux pas. 'We happened to be passing and thought you'd be pleased to see us. My apologies, Alice . . .'

Happened to be passing?

'Oh, please don't apologise. I'm *delighted* to see you . . . both.' I look over at Maddie, who's making no eye contact. 'If I'd known, I'd have done a spring clean and made brunch. But as it is, I don't even have any biscuits to offer you with the coffee.'

'Oh my goodness, we don't need biscuits. It's just lovely to see you and your beautiful home,' he replies, wandering back towards the island where I'm standing. He sits on one of the breakfast stools opposite me, like he's at a bar and I'm the bartender.

'The thing is, life is slightly chaotic at the moment. I don't stay here full-time – as I explained Jason and I are . . . parting,' I say, not wanting to sound dramatic. 'So we're nesting, it's where you share the house and the children, taking turns.'

He and Maddie both look at me expectantly, like there's more to tell. But there isn't, so Daniel takes up the slack. 'Did you hear that, Maddie? They're nesting.'

She shrugs, and I'm reminded of Josh on a bad day.

'It seemed like a good idea at the time, but for me it's just made life harder.' I smile, trying to make light of the hellish situation. 'I mean, how many times can a girl forget her toothbrush?'

Daniel laughs heartily at this. 'You need to buy another one and have one at each abode!'

'I do, and I have. But it took me a while to work that one out,' I chuckle. 'It's like moving house, albeit on a small scale – every single week. It's really quite stressful,' I add honestly. I don't get into Jason's selfish behaviour, but if this was an evening and I'd had a couple of wines, Daniel and Maddie would get the lot, whether they wanted it or not.

But Daniel isn't really listening, so it's as well I'm sober and restrained. He can't seem to keep still, he's down off the stool and now wandering back towards the bifold glass doors. 'That garden, just beautiful,' he exclaims.

'Compared to your acres it's a tiny little square,' I smile. Compared to his lush, cliff-edge acreage this is a small, unremarkable square of lawn; so why is he making such a fuss? And why is Maddie looking at him with what looks like murder in her eyes?

I watch as I pour her a glass of water while the coffee brews.

'Mind if I go outside and have a look? It's very warm in here.' He wafts himself.

I'm loathe to unlock the doors even in this heat, still fearful after last night. But it's daytime and I'm not alone, so I take the remote control from the cupboard and open the doors.

'Wow, wow, wow!' he's saying, his voice fading as he walks through the slowly opening doors and out on to the lawn, like an actor walking on stage.

Holding Maddie's water, I see my chance and walk quickly over to her. As I hand her the glass, I check behind me to see he's still in the garden. 'What did you mean before, when you said I don't know why he's brought you here?'

She looks up, suddenly engaged, about to say something, then pauses. I almost drop the glass when I hear his voice behind us.

'Now, now, ladies, did your mothers never tell you it's rude to whisper?'

'And did yours never tell you it's rude to eavesdrop?' I hear myself say.

His smile drops for a moment, and he looks sad, like I've just told him off. I instantly regret opening my mouth. I was just so frustrated that he'd appeared again before Maddie could speak, and now I want him to go back outside so we can talk. There is obviously something eating at her, and I want to know what it is, but it's as if he knew she was going to tell me something, and stopped her.

I hope I haven't offended him – after all, it's Maddie who's being cold and uncommunicative, he's just trying to lighten the mood. It's actually the same as the night we had dinner together: he's trying to cajole and she's pulling away and behaving like a moody teenager. I go back to the island and pour two coffees for him and me, and he takes his stool again and makes small talk for a while. He's facing me, with his back to his wife, but I can see her glowering behind him in the background. She must feel excluded, so I try once more to reach out.

'Maddie, are you okay? Can I get you something?'

She shakes her head without even looking at me.

'Alice, would it be impolite of me to ask if you'd give me the tour?' Daniel asks. 'I love this place and what you've done to it. Can I see the bedrooms?'

I look at him, puzzled, and pause for a moment. What is he playing at? His partner is obviously upset about something, and yet he seems to be deliberately ignoring her, and it's hardly appropriate that he and I go upstairs leaving her here sulking. Also, I'm not exactly thrilled at the prospect of taking my new client upstairs, given that Josh's room will no doubt resemble a crack den. But I have no choice, don't want him to think the upstairs is so bad he can't see it. 'Er . . . of course, but my son's bedroom is out of bounds – for your own safety,' I add as a little joke.

He laughs at this, then reaches out his hand, touching my bare arm. 'You are so funny, Alice, you're the whole package. I'll never know why your husband strayed.'

'It was my decision to part. I wasn't aware his affair was common knowledge,' I say.

'Oh, forgive me, that was terribly indiscreet. I thought it was you who told me?'

I bristle a little, but try to keep up the appearance of ease. 'No, I never discuss it. I hope whoever told you didn't tell anyone else. We're trying to make this easy for the children, and people gossip, and of course there's social media . . .'

'Of course, don't want the kiddies finding out.' He turns to Maddie. 'Baby, as new parents we really should think about the impact of social media, especially as you're in the public eye.'

She slowly rolls her eyes, like he's stating the bloody obvious, which I guess he is.

And she's now staring at Daniel with barely concealed hate. I suppose him mentioning Jason's indiscretions implies an intimacy our friendship really doesn't have, but Maddie doesn't know that and probably feels excluded. I think I realise what's going on here. Maddie's pregnant, feeling unattractive and insecure, and in his desire to be nice to me, Daniel's being a little insensitive to Maddie.

'Come on then, let's go and see the upstairs,' he's saying to me.

'We can't leave Maddie. Are you joining us?' I ask, with a smile.

'Yes, do you want to see Alice's bedroom, darling?' Daniel offers unnecessarily.

She shakes her head vigorously. 'I'm fine, really not bothered,' she mutters.

'Okay then, let's go,' Daniel's calling from the hallway, clearly happier with just the two of us. 'I'm excited about working with you,' he says as we mount the stairs. I glance behind me through into the kitchen. Maddie's now on her phone, but she looks up, catches my eye, and glares at me. Her brow is furrowed; she's angry and sulky and, suddenly, for me everything tilts. I assumed Maddie's awkwardness today was due to something between her and Daniel – after all it's clear she doesn't want to be here. But I now think it's because of me. She's misconstrued mine and Daniel's jokey, friendly banter, and I think she's just plain jealous.

She was pleasant the night I went for dinner – until she wasn't. Martha said she thought Maddie might think Daniel and I had something going on and she was jealous, but I didn't believe it. Maddie Lavender, jealous of me? I would never have thought someone like her would have any insecurities, but people surprise you.

'Is Maddie okay?' I ask Daniel, once we're upstairs.

He takes a breath, and pauses, like he's trying to break some bad news to me. 'Don't be fooled Alice, Maddie isn't who you think she is . . .'

33

'What do you mean, that Maddie isn't who I think she is?' I ask Daniel, who's now heading into my bedroom.

'What? Oh . . . not now, I'll explain another time.' He leans in and mouths, 'She's probably listening.'

I don't want to cause any more problems for them, so as much as I'd like to press him on this, I don't. I just go along with him as he marches around my bedroom like a crazed estate agent, fingering the curtains, caressing the iron bedstead.

'It's a symphony in green and I love it,' he says, then points at the bedroom's feature wall and walks towards it. 'And *this*' – he leans against the wall – 'is the most beautiful shade of green. It speaks to me.'

'What does it say?' I ask with a smile.

'It says . . .' He pauses for thought. 'It says English garden after the rain.'

'You should write my advertising copy, Daniel. You have a way with words.'

'It would be my pleasure.'

'I'm imagining how you'd describe my son Josh's room if I ever allowed you to see it, which I can't. You'd fire me straight away if you saw that horrible mess . . . he's a teenager.'

He laughs at this. 'Ah I see. Well, I'm sure the state of his bedroom is only to be expected. I'm the tidiest person there is – in fact Maddie says I have issues.' He pulls an awkward face. 'But I was a total mess as a teen. My mother despaired.'

'Okay, so there's hope for Josh yet?'

Daniel's warmth and openness almost tempts me to tell him that Josh's messy room isn't all that concerns me. But now probably isn't the time for me to start sharing my personal and family worries with Daniel. After all, he is my client.

'And what's this interior genius?' he's saying, his hand stroking the freshly painted window frame. 'This grey-green paint has the kind of studied neglect that can only happen after hours of artisanal sanding. Am I right?'

'I wouldn't say that,' I reply, puzzled. I walk over to where he's standing, and to my horror, the beautiful, grey-green Farrow and Ball paint on the window frame looks like it's been deliberately scratched. Like someone's taken a blunt knife and scraped, and scraped. It feels like an injury.

'Nothing happens by chance with your work, does it, Alice? It's all curated, but not in an obvious way.'

'*Never* obvious,' I murmur, trying to hide my surprise. Does Daniel really think it's meant to be like this or is he simply being polite? I look more closely at the damage. Has someone deliberately done this, and if so, why? Did someone take the trouble to climb a ladder and wrench open the window just to wreck the frame? Or was it someone on the inside?

'Yes, I've worked hard on this effect,' I say vaguely. I can't tell him the truth – I'm not even sure what the truth is. Besides, I'm Daniel's interior designer, he needs to believe I know what I'm doing.

'Alice?'

'Yes?' Is he about to challenge me on the shabby-chic window – is this where I lose the contract that's going to change my life?

'Can I ask you. Is it Mizzle?'

'I'm sorry?'

'Mizzle . . . the Farrow and Ball shade. Named after that delicate drizzle that blurs the line between fog and rain. I'm probably quoting straight from the paint catalogue here.'

Of course! I breathe out. 'Yes, *that's* it – gosh you know your paints. You are a man after my own heart.'

'Did your husband enjoy sleeping with this colour?' he asks, which is a bit odd.

'No, I'm afraid Jason doesn't get the Farrow and Ball thing – well, he isn't interested in interior design.'

'What a shame you couldn't share your passion.'

'Yeah, Jason was horrified at the cost, but sometimes you have to pay for perfection.'

'Perfection is always pricey, but then again, so is truffle oil and therapy – and frankly, *this* is both,' he says, gazing at the walls.

'Truffle oil and therapy, what a great name for a paint colour.'

'Oh yes. Alice, let's start our own paint company. It would be great fun.'

He makes me smile, and I think again about how different life might have been with a man like Daniel. Every day would be entertaining – I'd feed off his enthusiasm, and we'd probably have a string of design businesses and a handful of children in that beautiful house by the sea. From what I've seen, Maddie really doesn't appreciate what she has – which reminds me, she's probably not happy that we're up here alone together.

'We've been up here a while,' I say, dragging myself away from the ridiculous daydreams. I'm feeling a little uneasy about being alone up here with him while his pregnant partner sits downstairs, hearing our laughter and probably seething. I don't want to antagonise her any more than we have already.

'Yes, of course.' He gestures for me to go on ahead, but as I get to the top of the stairs he's still in the doorway of my bedroom.

'Alice, I hate to be indelicate,' he says, 'but I'm in rather urgent need of your bathroom.' He glances at the en-suite.

'You can use the family bathroom if you like?' It feels slightly inappropriate for him to be in my private bathroom.

'No, I'll be fine in here,' he says, and disappears back into the room. I stand on the landing awkwardly. 'Shall I wait for you?' I call.

'No, no, I can find my way downstairs,' he calls back.

'Oh, okay, I'll leave you to it,' I say, uncertain about leaving him in my bedroom and the en-suite. But after a morning of his madness I'm beginning to think that perhaps this is what they do in 'old money' circles, and I'm probably gauche to even think about allocating a family bathroom for guests.

I'm still pondering this, and hoping he doesn't nosey around too much, as I walk into the kitchen, where Maddie's getting herself another glass of water. She's still stiff and awkward around me, and as we're alone I'm about to ask her again what she meant earlier about Daniel's reason for coming here. But before I can say anything, the doorbell chimes. I rush into the hall, and it's Martha, so I let her in.

'Sorry sweetie, I was passing, and wanted to see if you were okay. I felt guilty last night, like I should have stayed with you.' She's walking through the hallway and into the kitchen before I can tell her who's here.

'Oh!' she exclaims, as I walk in. 'I saw the Porsche in your drive, thought you'd won the lottery . . .' Then she sees Maddie and is genuinely surprised. 'I'm so sorry, how rude of me to . . .'

'Don't be silly,' I say and introduce her to Maddie.

'Lucy!' she says, clearly starstruck. But Maddie looks even more uncomfortable now, and I get it because Martha can be a bit much and is behaving like a superfan. Any second now I'm expecting her to whip out her phone and demand a selfie with Maddie.

'Hey Martha.' She throws this greeting in her direction, picks up her straw bag and moves across the room. 'Alice – thanks for the water, but I'm not feeling too good, I'm going to wait in the car for Daniel.'

'No, it's even hotter out there,' I say, following her down the hall to see her out.

'It's fine, we have air-con in the car,' she replies as I open the front door for her. I'm dying to ask her again what she meant, but she doesn't even say goodbye, just walks quickly to the Porsche sitting on our drive, and climbs in.

I walk back into the house wondering what the hell just happened. Maddie made it clear she didn't want to be here, but what was it that made her suddenly storm off like that?

34

'What the actual fuuu . . .' Martha's squealing as I walk back into the kitchen. 'That was so rude, the way she just went off like that.'

'She's been weird ever since they got here, but something seemed to escalate. Just before you arrived, I was showing Daniel upstairs. She was invited, but chose not to join us. She may have heard us laughing and it annoyed her. Perhaps she's jealous?'

'Oh, trust me, she is.' Martha throws her bag on the counter, and I feel like a bartender again. She's looking at me, and smiling that smile I know so well.

I start to salivate. 'Do you know something? Oh my God, you know something don't you?'

She just keeps smiling.

'Martha, what?'

'Remember I was talking about Mike, the cameraman who works on *The Shore*?'

'Oh yes . . .'

'Well, did he have some juicy gossip for me. Alice, you won't believe what he was telling me about Maddie Lavender.'

Through the doorway, I can see Daniel walking slowly down the stairs, like he might be listening.

'She's the loveliest, isn't she?' I'm saying.

'Oh yeah, the loveliest.' Martha's rolling her eyes, assuming I'm being sarcastic.

'Daniel, you remember Martha from school, don't you?' I call through, and he moves up a gear and almost marches into the room.

'You haven't changed a bit,' he starts with his usual charm. Martha almost falls off her stool as he gathers her into a bear hug.

'Maddie wasn't feeling well, she's waiting for you in the car,' I say, as Martha extricates herself from Daniel.

'Oh, I'd better not keep her, it's no fun for a lady with a baby in this heat.' He smiles, giving me a hug and a peck on the cheek. I see him off at the door.

'I'll call tomorrow. We have lots to discuss,' he says.

'Yes, and the sooner I can start the better,' I reply, still hoping he'll suddenly produce the contract, but it's not delicate to talk business on the doorstep with others around. I'll email him later, as I need the contract signed. I'm holding up other clients waiting for it.

'Absolutely.' He smiles, then as he's walking away, he stops, and strolls back towards me on the doorstep. 'You're a lovely woman, Alice. Don't waste any more time on a man who doesn't love you.'

He doesn't wait for my response, which is probably just as well because I don't have one. I close the front door and watch him through the stained glass as he walks down our gravel path to his very fancy sports car, climbing in and zooming off.

Martha's flopped on the sofa in the kitchen when I walk back in. I tell her what he just said.

'He's coming on to you,' she says firmly.

'I hope he wasn't. I don't like to think of Daniel Prescott being unfaithful to his partner. He's better than that, even if she is a nightmare. And he said this really odd thing . . . that she isn't who I think she is.'

'And I have it from a very reliable source that she isn't who anyone thinks she is – and she's a total, total nightmare.'

'Is this from Mike the cameraman?'

'Yes, he's seen it all and knows the full story.'

'So – start at the beginning.' I'm so intrigued.

Martha smiles and leans towards me across the kitchen island. 'So Mike says on set she can be a diva, but he says she gets away with a lot because she's flirty and seductive. He described her as a bit of a minx.'

'Yeah, she's a beautiful woman, I don't blame her. Look at her here.' I've googled her on my phone and come up with some photos. '*Maddie Lavender from* The Shore *in a stunning designer gown. She wore her caramel highlighted tresses down.*'

'Caramel highlighted tresses? What the fuck.' She takes the phone from me, and reads out loud from her Wiki page. 'Madelyn Eleanor Rose Lavender – what a mouthful. Born 21 August 1988, landed her first TV acting role at the age of seven, and went on to make a name for herself as "everyone's favourite lifeguard" on Cornwall-based TV soap *The Shore* . . . Anyway, I digress – Mike says she starts seeing this scriptwriter who works on *The Shore*, and about two years ago, they move in together, and surprise, surprise, she gets some really big and juicy storylines . . .'

'I remember, she went from being terminally ill to a blushing bride, then she almost drowned in the sea, and . . .'

'Oh, Alice, I was there when she was resuscitated on the beach by that big hunky lifeguard. I may have been on my sofa at home, but like everyone else watching that night – I felt every breath he forced into her lungs.'

'I think Mum did too. She talked about that scene for some time.'

'Yeah, I bet Liz loved it,' she chuckles. 'So, life's good, she's got the man of her dreams, the storylines of her dreams and is apparently living her best life. But Mike said everyone on set knows she has trust issues and Maddie Lavender is *massively* possessive of every man she's ever had a relationship with. Mike says they can't go to the toilet without her following them, demanding to know where they've been. And he says some of the rows she's had accusing them of going off with other women, and attacking the other women verbally – just unhinged.'

'Oh, that's awful. I mean it's as bad for her as it is for them. I feel sorry for her now. That's why she's like she is. She can't rest, she can never be happy – I wonder if she's had therapy?'

'Er, yeah, Alice, we're not here to try and cure her, we're here to enjoy the drama, so less agony aunt and more OMG please!'

'Sorry.'

'It's no fun when you're kind and caring. I need more *mean girl* energy for this scenario.'

'Fair enough.'

'So anyway, because of Miss Lavender's "trust issues",' she says, using her fingers to indicate speech marks, 'she doesn't keep a man for very long. And . . . apparently her management team then have to step in with the super-injunctions and chequebooks to stop these guys talking. Mike says her insane possessiveness is known on set, but whenever a new man joins the team, she has him scrubbed and sent to her tent – I mean not literally, but you get the picture.'

'Wow!'

'There's more, and anyway – when this scriptwriter decided he couldn't handle any more and wanted to end things, she kicked off. Not only did she turn up at his home, yelling profanities at his window, she broke into his flat and threatened him with a knife!'

'NO!'

'So, as always, the management team were dispatched to make it all better, but this guy wasn't going to go quietly, so she had to get lawyers involved – and by now, the senior management on *The Shore* were aware of what happened. And that's why she's not on air at the moment, because this scriptwriter is threatening to go to the police, the press and anyone who'll listen. And her management and her lawyers are having problems shutting him up.'

'Bloody hell, her career is over,' I sigh. 'But where does Daniel fit in? I think he said they've been together a year?'

'Yeah, Mike knew about Daniel. He said that she needed a port in a storm, and he was just another nice guy who got roped in. Mike says she hasn't been faithful to him, treats him like dirt, but he pays for everything. And if things go wrong for her legally and she ends up in court, she'll need someone to pay those bills and to come home to after a stretch in the clink.'

'This is a bigger story than any she's ever had on *The Shore*.'

'Isn't it? Mike mentioned some of the things she's done, like threatening to kill herself, kill her boyfriends, kill their girlfriends! He said he could write a book.'

'But her management team would sit on him?'

She laughs. 'Yeah, something like that.'

'It all adds up though – the way she behaved today, it was bad enough for her that I was engaging with Daniel, but when you arrived she saw you as a threat too. She was probably worried that he'd run off with you. That's the tragedy – the way she behaves means she can't keep a partner, but because she can't keep a partner, she behaves like she does. It's a never-ending circle.'

'Yeah, but it's also bloody juicy!'

I have to agree, but I do feel very sorry for this poor woman who's tormented by her own insecurities. I wonder if she really does see me as a threat to her relationship with Daniel, and if so that's going to make things very difficult.

'I'm just amazed she's got away with it for so long. Mike says she can be really sweet, but on set the minute anything goes wrong, she turns into someone else. And when the girl that plays Melanie started to get good storylines, Maddie accused her of having an affair with the scriptwriter. She started making abusive phone calls late at night to the poor girl, she even threatened her kids!'

That's when I sit up and really listen. 'She threatened her kids?'

35

'Okay, Maddie clearly has issues, and I feel for her, but I'm scared, Martha. What if she starts targeting the kids? I'm already paranoid about the woman in the green Fiat.'

'She's a bit unhinged, but I reckon she's more concerned about what you're doing with her boyfriend. Daniel's rich and good-looking and she's having his baby. I remember being a bit possessive of Steve when I was pregnant. No, I think you're the one who needs to watch out.'

'Great! So we now have a convicted stalker in our midst! And she might be after me. As if I haven't got enough to worry about with Mum.'

'Yeah, how is she?'

'Great in herself, quite happy on the whole, but I haven't told her what the GP said. I'm not sure she needs to ever know.'

'Yeah, kinder to let her carry on being her – until she isn't.'

'It's just so sad, isn't it? When you think we go through all this life, all the stress and fighting and fun, and we all end up in the same place at the end.'

'Yeah, but try and be positive, your mum's close by and you can look after her. And I'm sure old Liz still has some lucid years left.'

'Let's hope so . . . oh, I just remembered – as if I could forget. I haven't even had a chance to tell you about last night.' I go on to explain about the noises coming from downstairs, and Willow turning up, and how I saw someone on the door cam footage.

'Someone was watching us from the front garden?' she asks, horrified.

I nod. 'Watching from the trees, and now I'm thinking it might have been *Maddie*!'

She raises an eyebrow. 'Checking up, thinking Daniel might be here?'

'Yeah or just waiting with a kitchen knife to end me?'

'Not dramatic at all,' she says sarcastically, then her eyes open wide like she's just thought of something. 'But what if . . . what if?'

'What?'

'What if it wasn't Maddie, but Daniel lurking in the trees?' She's gone full Agatha Christie now. And if I wasn't so creeped out by the conversation, I'd find this hilarious.

'Why would Daniel Prescott be hiding in *my* garden at night?'

'Because he's got the hots for you?'

'That's a stretch on many levels.'

'I couldn't help but notice he seemed to be very handsy around you – his arm slipped easily around your waist. At one point he looked like he was nuzzling your hair.'

'He was kissing my cheek when he left, that's all, he's an affectionate person. Makes a change from Jason who was only affectionate with women who weren't his wife.'

'Yeah, well, you're desperate for any kind of male attention because you were starved of it while your husband was spreading it around town.'

'I think his reach went further than Looe.'

'No doubt.' She pauses. 'But you should be a bit careful around Daniel. Don't give him any inclination that you're interested.'

'I'm not, it's just a friendship – and hopefully a working friendship sometime soon.'

'Yeah, I suppose you have to be nice to him if he's paying you,' she says, like it makes sense. 'Come to think of it, he was a bit creepy at school. Do you remember Natalie Fraser saying he'd stolen her netball top, and when she asked him to give it back, he said he'd give her the money because he liked sleeping with it. Loved her smell apparently.'

'Ugh, a sweaty sports top? I thought he had more class than that. But Natalie . . .' I say, thinking back. 'Wait, she was such a liar!'

Martha shrugs. 'I believed her. Ooh, and Natalie's cat went missing soon after Daniel was caught sniffing her shirt.'

'No one had any proof. Cats go missing, like Willow did, and sometimes they come back, sometimes they don't. I felt sorry for Daniel, he was just misunderstood, and kids are cruel, I never believed them.'

'Mmm, I believed every word. Natalie was distraught about her cat, and he knew how much she loved that pussy.'

'Daniel is not a cat killer, or any other kind of killer. He doesn't have it in him – he's sweet.'

'Of course he is – he's sweet to you because he probably wants to sniff your netball shirt too. Ugh, I just made myself feel nauseous even saying that.'

'I'm not convinced, I still reckon the person watching us was Maddie.'

'Could be. But remember Daniel was the poor little rich boy who lost his mum young and was constantly put down by his dad. That's a freak show just waiting to happen.'

I shake my head. 'All he wants is someone to love. He's harmless.'

'Is this because Daniel's offering you a big fee, or because you fancy him?'

'Neither . . . I feel a bit sorry for him, to be honest. He's always so positive, and upbeat – and I get the feeling that he wants to please

Maddie, but doesn't know how to. If what Mike the cameraman says is true – he's wasting his time, she'll never be happy.'

'So true, and she can't rest, she has to be constantly checking up on whoever she's with. So come on, let's have a look at the footage, see if I can tell if it's her in the trees.'

'Good idea.' I grab my laptop while Martha pulls up her stool to get close to the screen.

'Give it to me,' she says, pulling the laptop towards her and clicking on the keyboard, her eyes scouring the screen.

'Can you see, in the trees?'

She slowly raises her head. 'There's nothing here, Alice.'

I'm slightly alarmed, but sure she's wrong. 'Yes, it is, it's definitely on there,' I drag my stool to sit next to her, and start winding through, then I rewind, then fast-forward. 'This is strange, I don't understand. It's just a blank screen,' I say, panic blooming in my chest.

'Perhaps you accidentally wiped it?' she suggests.

'No! Oh God, I don't believe this.' I'm still rewinding. 'There are twelve hours missing from the tape.' I look at her.

'These things happen, don't beat yourself up.'

'I can't believe I'm so stupid. I thought I knew what I was doing, but Jason always says I just jump in and make mistakes.'

'Whoa, that's enough of the self-gaslighting. Jason's done a good enough job on that without your help. Come on, Alice, you're only just starting to believe in yourself again. Don't stop now.'

She pulls the laptop in her direction and tries a few things, but still – nothing.

'This was my only proof that someone was here, watching, I even called the police and told them I had the footage.'

'Well, let's hope they don't turn up again – and if they do, then you'll have it next time. You just have to be a bit careful that this model wipes easily.'

'The police will turn up and now I have nothing. But there was definitely *someone* out there,' I add tearfully.

'As much as I hate the idea of anyone stalking you, I have to admit I would love it to be Maddie Lavender or whatever her name is, just for the drama. I mean if you're gonna get stalked, go big with a Z-list soap star . . . Only you, my darling,' she chuckles.

But I'm not laughing.

'Too soon?' she says, when I don't join in.

'Too soon.'

'Sorry, I was trying to make you laugh.'

'Read the room, bitch,' I joke.

'Fair play. So, my thoughts are this – yes it could be old Lavender knickers, but she looks like she's about to drop triplets any second, and can barely walk. I'm not convinced even a whacko like her would be able to stand out there for hours. I mean the weight on her pubic bone alone . . .'

'Yeah, I suppose you're right.'

'What about that woman in the Fiat?'

'That might be Maddie?' I suggest. 'I've seen that car drive past the house a lot recently, sometimes more than once a day. It could be her stalking me?'

'Driving a little Fiat? I don't think so. She will have made Daniel buy her a nice Porsche like his too, she wouldn't be seen dead in a Fiat.'

'If the woman in the Fiat isn't Maddie, then she could be Ellie?'

Martha pushes the laptop away slowly, while scrutinising me.

'Is there anyone else you can think of?'

I shake my head vigorously. *There is someone, but she's dead.*

Her face is tight; she wants to say something but can't, then gently touches my arm. 'I think you're right, but – keep an open mind.'

She's looking at me now, and suddenly my stomach dips.

'What?'

Her face is pained at this. 'I . . . hate to say it, but do you think it might have been Josh who was standing out in the garden last night?'

'No, he wouldn't . . .'

'I agree it's not like the Josh I know. But the Josh I saw last night *isn't* the one I know.'

'But it doesn't make sense.'

'Not to us, but it seems like he's been affected by the break-up, and it might be his way of getting you guys back together? If he scares you, then you might want Jason here to "keep you safe".'

'No. Besides, Josh was in his room, you watched him go upstairs.'

'Did you check his room? Do you know he *stayed* upstairs, Alice?'

No I don't.

'Look, I'm not saying this happened, but just think about it. If Josh wanted to scare you by standing in the front garden, he could have climbed through his bedroom window?'

'He couldn't jump down into the front garden, though.'

'No, but he's young and fit, he could easily clamber down the wall clinging to a water pipe or something – he's pretty fit, isn't he? He wouldn't have come downstairs and gone through the front door because we were here, and we'd see him, and besides, he knows there's a camera on the hallway.'

As hard as it is to imagine my son doing anything like that, Martha has a point.

'And he shuts his bedroom door,' I murmur. 'I assume he's in there with his earphones on. He knows I wouldn't burst in. I don't invade his privacy.'

She gives me a sympathetic smile. 'Perhaps you need to start invading his privacy, for his sake – and yours and Ruby's too.'

This is hard to hear.

'I was thinking, when Ryan puts the back garden camera and lights in, why not get him to install a few hidden cameras *inside* the house too?'

'Is that even legal?'

'I don't know, but it's your house, surely you can do whatever you like?'

'I can't do that to my own family, even Jason.'

She shrugs. 'It's your call, but just because it's your family doesn't mean you can trust them. Everyone lies, Alice, even the people we love. And – newsflash – our kids are the best liars of all.'

36

Later, when I'm alone, I think about what Martha said, but I know my son, and don't believe he would try to scare me to go back to his dad. But *someone* is trying to scare me, and my mind instantly flickers to the mint-green car turning up everywhere, and the woman asking my kids questions. I wonder again what she might want . . . or what she might *know*.

'Yoo hoo, only me!' I'm startled from my paranoia by Mum's face at the window.

I wave back, gesturing for her to go to the front door.

'I didn't want to set your camera off by knocking on the door,' she says as I open it and let her in.

'Mum, that's the point!' I say. 'You don't need to knock anyway, you have a key.'

She stands in the hall, looking a little guilty.

'You do have a key, don't you?'

She hesitates for a moment. 'I can't find it, Alice. I've looked everywhere.'

'Oh . . . I wonder where it can be?' I try to sound calm, remembering what Dr Manjit said about not reacting negatively or shaming any strange behaviours. But inside I'm screaming. A missing house key is the last thing I need right now.

Mum's current absent-mindedness makes her the perfect target for someone with bad intentions, and the idea of that person having a key to our house fills me with terror.

'Any idea where you might have lost it?' I ask, trying to sound calm while putting the kettle on to make a cup of tea for her.

'Lost what, love?'

'The key . . . the key for here.'

'Oh sorry, I was miles away – of course, yes. No. I mean I don't know where it is.' She's delving in her carrier bag, and produces a cake tin.

'I made a chocolate cake. Joshy's favourite.'

'Thanks Mum, that will cheer him up, he's been a bit . . .' I avoid anything too strong. '. . . low recently.'

'Oh no, well I'm sure my chocolate cake will perk him up.'

'Talking of cake, you know that woman who came to see you? Brought you lemon cake?'

'Did she? That was nice.'

'Yeah, do you remember her, you said she was from abroad?'

'Yes . . . that's right, she was from Spain.'

'Spain?' I drop the cup I'm holding, and it shatters all over the floor. I think of the mug fragments in a circle, the stolen wine, the phone calls, the lost diamond ring, the noises at night – and Mum lying in the shower, her doll smashed on the floor. I can't even remember what life was like before this.

I look up and Mum's hands are over her mouth at the sight of the broken cup.

'Gosh, I'm such a butter fingers,' I say, my hands shaking as I get the dustpan and brush and sweep the shards.

I'll need to get the locks changed. God knows when I'll get the chance to do that. It's now 2 p.m., and I've promised Daniel Prescott the final design proposal as soon as possible. I'm hoping by then he will have signed the contract, I'll tweak and complete the final plans and we're good to go. Meanwhile, I have other clients to consider too, and it's extra pressure on me, so to keep on schedule I need to finish the final proposal and send it to him by lunchtime tomorrow. Even if I had nothing else to do between now and then, I'd need to work until very late, but now I have to get Tom, the emergency locksmith back. Yes, we're on first-name terms as he's becoming a regular visitor.

The doorbell is now ringing – and so is my phone. I'm living with constant inner panic, and have no peace.

I pick up my phone and see Jason's name on the screen. I need to answer this, but . . . 'Mum, would you mind getting the door for me?' I ask, and she rushes off to answer it as I pick up.

'Jason, I've been leaving messages.' And I tell him quickly and quietly what I saw on the camera footage, and about the Fiat driving past.

'What the hell?' he's saying. 'But who would . . .'

'Exactly. Who?' Silence. So I continue. 'Jason, this has to be connected to you.'

'Don't be ridiculous,' he snaps.

I'm keeping my voice low so Mum doesn't hear my anguish, but she's now talking to someone at the door, so I need to go. 'If you really don't know who the woman in the green Fiat is, then we're in trouble.'

'What do you mean?'

'I think the woman who spoke to the kids in the coffee shop is the same woman who's driving the green car. And she's doing regular laps around this house like a shark scenting blood in the water. You must have seen the car when you've been staying here?'

'No, I haven't.'

'Well I have. I don't know who she is, but I'm worried that whoever it is she *knows* something.' I pause deliberately. 'Mum says a woman came to see her – a woman from *Spain*.'

'Fuck,' he mutters; like me he knows this could be significant. But before we can say anything else, Mum appears in the hallway as white as a sheet, flanked by two police officers.

'They say they've come to see you, Alice,' she croaks. Looking terrified.

'I've got to go, the police are here.'

'No. What the—'

I hang up and put on a smile.

'Oh yes, it's fine, Mum, don't worry, I'm not in trouble.' I give a mirthless chuckle. I feel absent, my mind all caught up with the woman from Spain.

'We did explain to your mum that you were expecting us,' the older one says.

'Of course. Please come through to the lounge.' I sweep them in and ask Mum if she'll make coffee, then while she's out of the room, I tell the officers very quickly about the footage. 'But that's now gone – I think I must have wiped it by accident,' I admit, and see a glance pass between them. 'But it isn't just that. There was a suspected break-in, stuff's gone missing, and our bedroom window frame's been scratched . . .' I can hear how weak and petty this sounds. Without going into the mess that is my life right now, I can't see how these two police officers can take my paltry list seriously.

I could explain about my marriage break-up, the nesting arrangement, my husband's girlfriend, that the figure only I saw on the wiped footage – *that I wiped* – might be a famous soap star stalking me. But it sounds like a cry for help, and if I told them, they'd be less likely to investigate and more likely to have me committed.

By the time Mum returns with a tray of coffee and biscuits, it's all over. They drink their coffee as we make small talk, the colour returns to Mum's face, and she starts making police jokes, which is as uncomfortable as it sounds. 'Anything you say may be taken down,' she's saying as they bid their goodbyes at the door.

'Nice girls!' she remarks as we go back into the house.

'They were,' I reply.

'Why were they here, Alice?' she asks.

'I, er . . . it's to do with my car, the tax ran out,' I reply desperately, scrambling for something.

'And they sent *two* officers out for that?'

There she is. Mum's back. Underneath the confusion she's still in there somewhere. 'Yes, but I think one of them was a trainee.'

I'm surprised how easily the lies slip from me. But then I've had years of practice.

My phone suddenly rings and I'm about to answer when I see it's Mum's doctors' surgery. Shit, that could be the blood test results. I feel sick. I can't take it here, in front of Mum, so I don't pick up.

'Your phone's ringing, Alice,' she says, like I haven't heard it.

'I know, Mum, but it isn't urgent, I'll deal with it later. Now I need to do some work, so I'll be in my office.' I gesture towards the little study just off the hall.

'Of course, love, you get off. Shall I collect Ruby and Josh from school for you?'

I can't let her drive herself, let alone with the kids.

'Did you drive here?'

'Yes, my car's outside so it won't be a problem.'

Oh no. 'Thanks, but I'll pick them up – come with me if you like?' I suggest, wanting to keep her close. And out of her car – given the potential diagnosis, I can't let her drive, which is a problem I have to deal with. 'It's only two-thirty. Ruby doesn't finish school until three-thirty, and Josh wasn't sure when he would finish today, so let's go together about three-fifteen? I'll drive,' I add quickly.

'But I like to be early. Don't want the little mites waiting and worrying.'

My six-foot son and sassy pre-teen daughter could never be described as little mites, except perhaps to their confused nana.

'We won't leave them waiting, Mum. You relax for an hour while I get some work done and we'll leave early,' I say to placate her.

She seems happy with this and toddles off to the kitchen, no doubt to cause mayhem with the dishwasher. She presses all the programmes at once, a regular trick of my mother's that causes it to lock and renders it unusable for twenty-four hours while it works out what the hell just happened. *My mother just happened*, I tell it in my more unhinged moments when I'm alone talking to white goods in the kitchen.

Finally, I lock myself in the office and turn on the much-needed fan. It's hot and stuffy and my head feels the same. I'm beginning to wonder if I can even do this. I take a deep breath and call the doctor back – I have power of attorney and Mum's written permission as her next of kin to talk to her GP.

Dr Manjit is as gentle as ever, without hiding anything. 'So Mrs Taylor, the blood tests were all normal, which means there's nothing physical like a thyroid problem or vitamin deficiency causing the memory issues.'

My heart sinks. I know what this means.

'But the memory assessment suggests your mum does have some problems consistent with early dementia, likely the early stages of Alzheimer's disease. The next step will be for the memory team to see her at Memory Assessment Service. They'll talk you through the diagnosis properly, discuss treatment options and support.'

'Okay.' My voice sounds quiet and scared.

'It's a lot to take in, isn't it?' he says gently. 'But there are medications that can help slow things down, and we'll make sure she has the right medical support in place.'

‘Thank you. It’s difficult to hear.’

He tries to reassure me, and I thank him. It isn’t a surprise, but still so difficult to comprehend.

I hang up and gaze out of the window. The gravel path to our drive gleams faintly under a dull, heavy sky, leading straight to the trees – tall, dark, and still. But then there is the shudder of leaves as a figure emerges from behind the trees and walks along the gravel towards the house. Oh no. *Not today, Satan.*

37

'Jason.' I groan audibly as he approaches.

'Oh . . . it's you!' I hear Mum's indignant tone as he lets himself into the house. I take a deep breath and stand up from my desk.

'Hey,' I say wearily as I walk into the hallway from my office, closing the door behind me. The irony is, I can close as many doors and drawers and lock as many cabinets as I like, but in a couple of days Jason will be back here and has access to everything. It's a horrible feeling.

'You said the police were here.' He's talking quickly, his face is flushed, and his eyes are darting around like an officer might be hiding in a cupboard.

'They've gone now. Why are you behaving like a wanted man? Calm down.'

He sighs with relief. 'Why did you call them in the first place?'

'Not now,' I say, glancing at Mum, who's standing nearby, folding some washing.

'I think now is as good a time as any. What the hell's been going on?'

At this Mum looks up, alarmed.

'*Nothing's* been going on, Jason.' I widen my eyes, hoping he'll stop, but either he doesn't see or doesn't care. There's a definite waft of toilet cleaner in the air; presumably he's continued to slap on the aftershave even after I added my own ingredient. This reminds me of the cumin- and garlic-laced whisky I left for him. I wonder idly what he thinks of my 'cocktail'.

'You said someone was out there last night.' Jason gestures towards the front garden.

'Is *that* why the police were here, Alice?' Mum's concerned voice, her head to one side. She's now talking to Natasha, her doll, which she presumably brought with her in her carrier bag. I see Jason do a double take.

I open the door of my office, almost push him in. 'No Mum, Jason's confused,' I say, closing the door behind him.

'Yes I am confused, why is your mum talking to her doll?'

I explain the situation and how I've literally just got the results from her tests.

'That's why I don't want to upset Mum. She thinks the police were here because of car tax.'

'Okay, I was just worried and . . . do we know who was outside?' he says, returning straight back to the situation most affecting him. He barely registers that my mum, a woman he's known for many years, first as a teacher, and then as his mother-in-law, has just received a devastating diagnosis.

'Do we have to do this now, Jason? The police have been informed, I don't need to go over it with you. I'm worried about my mum . . .'

His hard, fixed glare turns my stomach and stops me in my tracks. Now I see it – the same expression that was on my son's face. That quiet, burning rage. Jason's anger is more contained, more hidden, but that's because he's learned how to hide it.

'What did the police say when they saw the footage? Do they have any idea who . . . ?'

'No.' I don't tell him there is no footage, he'd tell me I was stupid and I can't expose myself to his ridicule or anger anymore, it's too destructive.

It feels hotter, more oppressive now he's in here, so I turn the fan up. But it blows the business documents off my desk and they flutter to his feet.

'And the woman that came to see your mum, are you sure she was from Spain?' He has an air of desperation about him.

'No, I never saw her, at first I thought Mum was just confused, but now I'm not so sure.' I stand up to get the papers, but he holds up his hand to stop me and bends down to pick them up off the floor.

'Your mum is confused though?' he says absently while studying each piece of paper as he slowly puts them back on the desk. One. By. One.

'Yes, Mum's confused. But it's a strange coincidence that the woman is from Spain . . .'

'Your mum knows I was there years ago though, she might just be mixing up her memories?'

'After what happened in Spain, a woman turns up asking questions years later – who is from Spain. Is that just a coincidence?' I ask.

He sighs deeply, frustration and fear in his eyes. 'How many times over the years have we talked about this? I told you, no one knew, she had no family.'

'You can't be absolutely sure. What if someone *looked* for her, and what if they're still looking for her? She may not have had family, but there might be *someone* . . . a distant cousin, a friend . . . someone who knew Sarah, and is suspicious about what happened to her.'

His brow is furrowed. 'We made the decision together a long time ago to accept it, and get on with our lives. Alice, we agreed to bury the past, but you're digging it all up.'

'You might be able to forget, to pretend it didn't happen, but it's haunted me. Now I'm worried someone's watching me and the kids, and possibly you too.'

'There's nothing we can do about it now. We chose this, Alice.'

I feel tears forming in my eyes, anger raging in my chest. 'No, Jason, YOU chose it.'

'You wanted it as much as I did, Alice.'

The fan in the corner clicks every few seconds, reminding us how useless it is in this thick, oppressive heat. As useless as we are. Sweat trickles down my back like a slow finger. And I think back to that night when he called.

It was before we were married, we were on a break – we were always breaking up, I guess I should have seen the signs then. But we were both so young. We'd met again at university, and one thing had led to another, until we were in a casual student relationship: lots of drinking, a sprinkle of recreational drugs, and some studying in between. To me it always felt a little one-sided, like I was more into him than he was me, but I was more resilient then, and had this crazy idea that if you loved someone enough they'd eventually love you back.

By the end of the final year, I discovered I was pregnant, and we were both devastated. That wasn't the plan, but I wanted to have the baby. When after a couple of months I lost the baby, we were both overwhelmed with relief and guilt. I had a breakdown, and had to step away from uni and from Jason and we broke up, but he continued with his studies. I soon started work and, after graduating, Jason went travelling through Europe, where he met up with a friend in Spain. I missed him so much, realised I still loved him and wrote to him to say that. I offered to meet up with him wherever he was in the world and *see what happens next?* I had this romantic vision of meeting by a mountain, a monument or a beach somewhere far away and falling into each other's arms. He eventually replied to say he was staying in Spain, had a place to live and a job in a bar, and perhaps I'd like to go out there later, when he was more settled, and then we could *see what happens next*?

After that I didn't hear from him for a long time, and I started to think that we probably weren't meant to be. Social media was in its infancy, and we followed each other on Facebook – I'd sometimes see a photo of him behind the bar in Spain, by the sea, up a mountain. And when I saw those photos, I knew I'd always love him, but after more than a year he still hadn't been in touch, and I thought that was it.

But then one night, nearly four years after he'd left for Spain, he suddenly called me out of the blue. 'I've been thinking about you,' he said. I'd never really stopped thinking about him, and was beyond flattered that he'd called me all the way from Spain just to hear my voice. To my twenty-something heart, his move to Europe in the wake of my miscarriage hadn't been cowardly, it had been adventurous. And despite living off his parents' cheques, being a bartender in Spain to me was exotic and sophisticated.

'Are you still single, or have you been snapped up?' he asked in that first phone call.

I was still single. I didn't tell him, but subconsciously I'd been waiting for him to come back to me. And when we started talking on the phone that night, Jason in Spain and me in London, we just slipped back into who we used to be. To me he was fascinating, worldly and funny, and we talked and talked for hours, and I knew what I'd suspected all along: I still loved him.

But towards the end of the conversation, he became distracted, and I heard a noise in the background.

'What's that? Sounds like a baby crying,' I said.

'It is. It's *my* baby,' he replied.

38

It transpired that the 'friend' Jason had met in Spain had become a lover, and within a few months of them being together, she was pregnant. According to Jason, he was still getting over our break-up and the miscarriage so had to have this baby. Looking back, I should have seen the warning signs. In the time we'd been apart, he'd moved on, and not only had he found a new partner but they'd had a child who was now three years old. When he'd called me that night and I heard his child crying, he was alone in the apartment with his son – his name was Michael.

'Where is his mother?' I asked.

'She's gone to score some drugs,' he said.

I was horrified. This didn't sound like the idyllic Spanish life I had imagined, so different from Facebook photos of him laughing with friends on a beach, beers held high in a melting sunset.

Jason explained that Sarah, his girlfriend, had an addiction problem, which he thought she'd conquered when pregnant. But after Michael was born, her days were spent in the bedroom, shutters closed, sleeping heavily, and her nights were spent in bars with friends who gave her drugs.

Jason cried when he told me Sarah had never really bonded with Michael from birth, and rarely responded to his cries as a baby. He soon realised that he couldn't leave her to care for their child, so had to give up his bar job and stay home. He described the nights spent alone trying to feed a crying baby with the shadow of his partner curled on the bed.

This was all so sad, but I was scared of falling for him again, and I rather naively explained this to him. I guess he knew I was vulnerable, and despite me asking him not to call me, he did. One night, during one of our long talks, as he fed Michael, Jason told me he loved me, and couldn't live without me. In that moment, I knew I felt the same, and from then on I agreed to everything. I've regretted that moment ever since.

I know now, that first night when he called me from Spain, he wasn't looking for *me*, he was looking for a mother for Michael. I was his way out of a difficult situation – he could extricate himself from a relationship that wasn't serving him, and I'd be waiting in the UK, a reliable rescue package. He knew I would provide the childcare and home comforts, and enable him to pursue his legal career back home.

But he also knew that Sarah wouldn't let him or her son go without a fight. Flawed women don't fit into his vision. My anxiety, my weaknesses, what he saw as my 'flaws', were manageable. But Sarah wore her flaws like a badge, for everyone to see, and her drug-taking was an obvious embarrassment to him. At the time I saw everything from his perspective, but now I realise, just like in our relationship – Jason was the problem. He once admitted to me that, when they first met, Sarah had never taken drugs, so what happened? Jason was what happened. Knowing him as I do now, having a partner who was knocked out on drugs was convenient for him. Jason hates having his 'freedom', i.e. access to other women, curtailed and I doubt very much he tried to help her. I'll be honest, there have been times in my marriage when I've considered having that extra glass of wine, curling up in a ball and forgetting the world. Finding out about other women, and his threats to take the children from me, have often made me long to escape into some kind of release. But I've always known that extra drink, or curling up into a ball, would be misrepresented by my lawyer husband and give him even more power over me. And I'm sure being with someone as manipulative as Jason helped send this poor young woman down the wrong path.

Like me, she was probably seduced by his facade – his looks, charm and intelligence cover up exactly what he is.

I was married to a man I didn't know – a stranger I didn't like – but by the time I realised that, we had two children and were locked into a house and mortgage. We were like a business – 'the perfect Taylors' – and Jason was scared of me leaving because he cared more about the optics than my happiness. He was obsessed with how we looked to the rest of the world, our beautiful home, his successful career and the kids' achievements.

He'd invite his bosses to our home, and I'd cook lavish dinners that at the time we could barely afford. But it paid off because the partners weren't only impressed by his brilliance as a lawyer, he also seemed to have this perfect home and family. Consequently, he was admired, trusted and promoted until one day he was made a partner in the law practice. But in the middle of all this was me, keeping the wheels on, and making it all happen, because I knew if I tried to leave, I risked losing the children.

We glare at each other now through the shimmering heat.

'You've already broken this family, and now you want to shatter us all to smithereens,' he spits.

'You broke us, not me. I can't live this lie anymore, Jason, I have to tell the truth, whatever the cost.'

He moves past me towards the door. 'You lived a very pretty lie in this fine house that I bankrolled. I don't recall you wanting to tell the truth then.'

'I agree, I lived in this gilded cage and never tried to fly away. Instead, I built my own prison, painting walls to cover the cracks, hanging pretty pictures over the parts of my life that were too painful to see. And even when we broke up, I was so desperate I was prepared to stay just a few nights a week rather than none at all. But now I know it's a half-life, a meaningless way to live, and I'm done. I'm finally ready to leave.'

'You'd never leave this house.' He's almost laughing at me. 'You said yourself it's like your third child, you love it more than anyone.'

'No, I love my children more than anyone – and I love my mum and my friends, and they are what make my life whole. I thought this house represented my freedom, my independence. But as you said, you "bankrolled" it. You used it to control me. Not anymore.'

'Okay, I'll call the estate agent first thing and put it on the market,' he smirks. By the flippant way he throws this in my direction, I know he isn't serious, he's calling my bluff.

'No, *I'll* call the estate agent,' I reply firmly, and I open my office door and gesture for him to leave.

'Okay, if that's what you want,' he replies, unsmiling, and I follow him down the hall to see him out.

But as we get to the door, he turns around. His demeanour has changed, he's covering his anger with a false smile. 'I need to get some of my clothes and stuff I left,' he says, walking back down the hall and heading up the stairs.

I feel tense about him being upstairs where my things are. By giving up the house, he knows he's lost, he has nothing over me anymore. No, that's not true – he has one thing, Josh. But it looks like I've already lost him. My perfect son, who I love so much, the little boy I met off the plane fourteen years ago, who from the moment he ran into my arms called me 'Mummy'. The bond was instant, like an electric shock of love, and from then on, that little stranger had my heart. He still does – and always will.

39

I stand at the bottom of the stairs trying to listen for Jason. I feel invaded, like I'm being ripped open. He isn't my husband anymore, we don't have an intimate life, and he has no right to go into my bedroom when I'm not there.

He could be going through my bag, looking at receipts, trying to find anything he can use against me, to get back control. I know him – he'll leaf through the notebooks on my bedside table, check the bathroom cabinet for medication, anything he can twist so I look like an unfit mother and he can take the children. All Jason wants is to win. And there are no depths to which my husband, the lawyer, won't plummet to be the winner.

I check my watch; he's been up there for seven minutes. I ache to march up those stairs and walk in on him, but now isn't the time to antagonise him.

I try to stay calm, knowing there's an end to this and I can get through it. Even if the move takes months, I've made up my mind, and it's going to happen. The very thought of calling the estate agent makes me feel liberated – truly, properly liberated. It's my first step towards freedom. I finally have wings.

I go into the kitchen and wait for him to come down, which he does, after almost nine minutes. It's a long time to grab a few clothes, and dread flops around in the pit of my stomach.

'Alice,' he says, wandering into the kitchen holding the shirt, 'I'm going now, but before I do I just want to say, think very seriously about what you do next.'

I take a deep breath and turn to face him. 'You too, Jason,' I say, maintaining eye contact. I know he still has the capability to ruin my life, but I can't let that push me under. I need to stand strong.

He makes a laughing sound but that's all it is, a sound. 'You always play the good girl, don't you Alice, but inside you're just as rotten as the rest of us. You knew Sarah died, but you didn't ask any questions. You were just glad she was out of the way.'

'You told me she'd killed herself, and that was enough. I didn't ask for details because it was distressing.'

'You wanted Michael. and once he was here, you'd never have let him go – it suited you as much as me for Sarah to be dead. You got the family you craved, then the daughter and the house. You aren't any better than I am.'

'I don't pretend to be. I'm ashamed that I didn't ask more questions, and horrified that when I did find out what happened, I stayed with you. I stayed and I lied for you. I never told a soul, because I didn't want to lose Josh, but this has become weird, Jason. You say she had no family, so who buried her, and where is she?'

He shakes his head.

Josh has always known I'm not his biological mother. We decided early on that we would tell him the truth – I insisted on it. He's grown up knowing she died when he was a baby, accepted it, and any questions he's had I've answered as truthfully as I can. His father, on the other hand, has always been vague, evasive even, and he's the only one who can answer some of Josh's questions, because I wasn't there. So, despite being a curious, intelligent child, Jason's attitude has made it difficult for Josh to discover who his mother was, and what really happened in their lives in Spain.

'Josh deserves to know more about his real mother,' I say. 'He's almost eighteen, he'll want to know about his heritage – go to her grave, look for her family, however distant, because they're his blood too. If you don't come clean with Josh – about *everything*, then we're denying our son a very basic right – to know the truth – and I won't deny him that.'

'So you want him to know his mother was a junkie, that she left him for hours on end, that if it wasn't for me, he may never have survived?'

'It doesn't have to be so brutal. He doesn't even have a photo of her because you lied to him, you said they were destroyed in a fire.'

'Stop it, Alice, stop it!'

'You offloaded on me, swore me to secrecy, said if I ever told you'd take Josh from me. I had no choice. But *you* did – you could have come clean, but instead you used me like your therapist, only I wasn't a very good one. I allowed you to blame Sarah, stress, fatherhood, and even me. You said it happened because you wanted to be with me. I let you get away with murder. *Literally.*'

He stands for a moment, allowing the truth to float like a big grey cloud over us, as it always has.

'You clearly have no idea just what and who you're putting at risk,' he says, his voice calm but unsettling. 'Be very careful, Alice.'

He walks down the hall and I hear the door close. It isn't a slam, just a click, but still it makes me jump.

I catch my breath, heart skipping. I've been controlled by Jason, I've sometimes been intimidated by him, but never scared for my life. I think about Sarah, who didn't do as she was told, and ended up dead. To Jason she was the inconvenient woman . . . and now that's me.

40

In the aftermath of Jason's departure, I feel sick just thinking about the situation I'm in. Should I go to the police and tell them I'm frightened that my husband might try to kill me? Am I being ridiculous, and if I say this out loud will Jason go all out to try and prove that I'm mad, and take the children from me? Josh isn't even my biological child, so where do I stand there? And what would happen to Josh with no female influence, left solely with a misogynistic womaniser like his father?

Sweat gathers at the back of my neck. I feel like I'm breathing through cloth, the hall feels like it's closing in. I'm scared – do I have to carry on like this, and stay locked in this house with all the fear and lies?

I walk into the front room and gaze out of the window to see Mum's car has gone! During that whole thing with Jason I'd completely forgotten about her, assumed she was still here. She obviously sneaked out while I was in the office with Jason. I didn't realise the time, and wasn't at the school for the kids. I've never done that – how could I? My heart speeds up just to think of Mum driving them and I rush into the hall, grab my car keys, and I'm about to tear down to the school when I hear voices outside. I'm half expecting it to be the police on the doorstep to tell me there's been an accident, but suddenly the door opens and Mum and the kids come crashing in from school. I breathe a huge sigh of relief to see they're all fine, and glancing out see that Mum's car looks okay too. Thank God they're all in one piece. But from now on I need to be on guard, and can't let her collect them again.

Despite my fears, there's laughter and noise and Mum being bonkers to take me away from the current nightmare I'm living in.

'Nan's made a chocolate cake!' I announce, taking the cake tin from the cupboard.

'I *need* it now!' Ruby pleads, and even Josh smiles when he's offered a slice. Perhaps things are looking up, and as we all sit round the table eating cake and chatting, I realise once more that this is what it's all about. And as long as these three people are okay today, then so am I.

Obviously the words 'dick' and 'dickhead' pepper the kids' speech, which Mum is used to, and I make no attempt to chastise. For me this is a sign that all's right in their world, and it gives me great comfort to know they're as abusive to each other and lively as ever. I'm particularly pleased to see that Mum and Josh are maintaining the relationship they've always had: he's as protective, jokey and affectionate with her as ever. We sit round the kitchen island on stools, while the kids trade insults and Mum entertains them unintentionally with her almost-grasp on youth culture.

'I quite like that rap music, I was listening to it on the YouTube,' she says.

The kids look at each other, horrified yet amused.

'They kept talking about "the booty", I wasn't sure what it meant. So I looked it up – wish I hadn't.'

They both laugh at this. 'You've been vibin' to some filthy beats, eh Nan?' Ruby laughs.

'She's got that fire on repeat,' Josh adds.

'Will you all stop talking?' I act confused for the comedy, and the kids laugh at the role reversal. 'Mum, what on earth are you doing listening to rap?' I ask.

'Just keeping it real, Alice,' she chuckles.

I'd forgotten days like these, with no angst, no threats, no tension – no Jason. God, how much better life would be if he didn't exist.

A little later, Mum goes home, the kids head off upstairs to do homework and I go into my office and write an email to Daniel. It's businesslike but warm and polite, just asking if he's had time to look at and sign the contract I sent. I have other projects to work on, so I throw myself into them and stop for dinner with the kids.

When I get back to the office, I check my emails and am delighted to see Daniel's emailed me back.

> Hey Alice, please accept my apologies, I haven't had the opportunity as yet to check through the contract and sign, but it's on my list of things to do. I know you said you had a few more ideas, and I was thinking perhaps you could come over with them tomorrow? Could you be here at 2pm as Maddie and I will both be at home and we'd love to look through together and discuss. I'll also sign and return a hard copy of the contract then. Hope that's ok? Love Daniel x

I am elated. In truth I was beginning to think Daniel might be stringing me along, but I should have known that's not like him.

So I email him back to say I'll be there and go back to working on the final bits for Silvercliff to present to Daniel and Maddie tomorrow.

I put my heart and soul into this work. I want Maddie to want this as much as he does, and try to consider her as a new mum in the design. I want to give her a feminine, contemporary look, with practical elements like safe areas for the baby and plenty of toy storage. Meanwhile I'm still offering Daniel a slightly more traditional, old-money feel, with that Amalfi vibe we joked about.

I make detailed floor plans, find material samples, finish the mood boards and lighting schemes, and every now and then I check the time, horrified at how fast it's going. I've never been so tired. It's been a busy and emotional day and I didn't sleep last night, so I'm relying on caffeine and chocolate.

I have to have it with Daniel and Maddie by tomorrow at 2 p.m., he was quite specific, which makes me think that despite his constant whooping over my designs and my home, this may still fall at the last hurdle.

By 3 a.m. it's done. I check everything over, and instead of staggering up to bed, I'm still buzzing. So I sit in the kitchen, exhausted but elated, surrounded by sketches and fabric and general designer chaos. As I pour myself a small, celebratory glass of wine and drink it slowly, savouring each mouthful, I hear one of the kids moving around upstairs. Josh is probably awake – he's heavier-footed than Ruby and I often hear him on his way to the bathroom at night.

I think about Jason's threat, his angry face and my own fear, but working has channelled that fear; creativity has lifted me. I wander out into the garden and walk barefoot on to the lawn. The grass is cool under my feet from the early morning dew, and I stand on the earth, feeling grounded, sure of myself. In the glimmer of a sunrise, I finally see a glimpse of change. I'm shaking off the past and heading into a better future. Only I can do this, and I won't be scared by Jason, or his stupid threats. I am in control, and as soon as I feel strong enough, I will go to the police and tell them everything.

But for now, for the sake of the kids and for me, I need to make our escape, sell the house, and break free from Jason.

I go to bed about 4 a.m. and barely sleep. And once the kids have gone to school, I'm straight on the phone to the estate agent, who is coming over tomorrow. 'I know the house you mean, it's beautiful,' he says. 'I don't like to say before I've seen, but I doubt we'll have any problems selling for a good price.'

I spend the morning working on a smaller project, a nursery for the Robinsons, a young couple moving into their new house with a baby on the way. My design is all birds and clouds and lovely beginnings, and though it lifts my heart to work on something like this, it also makes me sad. The Robinsons are both so excited and happy about the baby, and they love each other so much, which reminds me of my optimism at the beginning. I want to tell them to beware, to nurture what they have, take care of it, but believe nothing, and trust no one, even each other. In the meantime, I'll fill their nursery walls with the clouds on which to place their fragile dreams.

41

An hour before my meeting with Maddie and Daniel, I gather all my files, photos and fabrics and pack the car. As I drive out to the beautiful house, I wind down the window. The air feels fresher – it's still warm but more bearable today than it has been for several weeks. My little car climbs the rugged cliff terrain, and as the road unwinds towards the clifftops, something inside me loosens. I feel my shoulders dropping as my breath deepens, and a quiet fizz runs through me. It's a strange and wonderful feeling, and I drive faster, my whole body leaning towards wherever I'm going, open and unafraid.

I pull up outside, and climbing from the car, salt and sunshine fill my chest, and the sound of gulls welcomes me as I stand high on the cliffs. I walk to the edge, as I did on that first day with Daniel, and I feel like I've come so far, and nothing will stop me achieving what I want to. I'll do it for my kids, and for me. I want to make them proud, and nothing's going to stop me being myself ever again. My bracelets jangle as I lift my design folders from the back of the car and walk towards the house. The breeze ruffles my hair and my heart as excitement sparks through me at the prospect of this job, and being paid to spend time in this gorgeous house.

I ring the doorbell, and wait. They must be busy, so I ring again, but there's nothing. Perhaps the doorbell's broken? So I ring again. And again. And I can hear the bell clearly, so it must be ringing inside too. Then just as I'm taking out my phone to call Daniel and tell him I'm here, there's a sound on the inside. Someone's unlocking the door, and relief floods through me – perhaps the maid's off and they were in the garden? Their home is on six acres of land, and who can blame them for being outside on a day like this? And in all that outdoor space, it's understandable they wouldn't hear the doorbell.

Finally the huge door opens with a shudder, and I'm smiling, and there's Daniel, and I wait for the usual hugs and accolades and compliments. But I'm not being smothered in charm, and though he's smiling with his mouth, it isn't reflected in his eyes.

'Hey,' I say gently, but the air feels different.

He looks confused. 'Hello Alice, you look lovely.' He's on autopilot, he isn't seeing me, he's just saying this because he thinks I expect him to say it.

'Thank you.' I pause, waiting to be asked in, but he doesn't open the door wider, just stands there.

'I'm here for our two o'clock.' I'm tentative, like I don't want to step on anything.

'Oh . . . oh, I'm sorry.' He bangs the heel of his hand on his forehead. 'I can't do this today, Alice.'

I feel like Alice in Wonderland: I'm shrinking, and everything I want is now moving out of reach, the smaller I get.

'I . . . did I get the wrong day?' I ask, lamely.

'No . . . but, Alice I'm so, so sorry, I can't offer you the work, I'm going to have to cancel.'

I honestly think I might faint. I can feel joy leaving my body. 'I don't understand. Is it Maddie?'

He nods.

'She doesn't like the designs . . . or is it me, she doesn't like me?'

'No, no, it's not you, Alice. Maddie's left me . . .'

I don't know what to say. He looks dreadful, his voice is croaky and he's clearly not slept.

'I'm so sorry, Daniel.' I think about what Martha told me. I can't begin to imagine what's happened. I want to ask him why, but he looks so closed off. He just stares at me blankly, his eyes damp.

'Is there anything I can do?' I ask, trying to put aside my own devastation at the sudden loss of the project that's vital for my future. I feel a surge of anger towards Maddie, not just for breaking poor Daniel's heart but for her bad timing. I want to be kind, and not just think of myself and my situation, but I can't help it. If only she'd waited a couple of months before dumping him, I could have finished the project and the money would be in the bank. Damn her!

'No Alice, I'm afraid there's nothing you can do.'

I groan as I breathe out, selfishly still thinking of myself and all that work I did, all the hopes I had for this job.

'Do you want to talk about it?'

'I can't, I'll say too much,' he replies, and all I can think is *she's made him sign something to keep him quiet.*

'Okay.' I step back, he's obviously not going to invite me inside. In fact, the way he's holding the door and his body language would suggest he doesn't want me over the doorstep.

'So . . . I'm so sorry, I hope that perhaps you guys can . . .'

He shakes his head before I've even finished.

'Oh. Well . . . call me if you need . . .' I realise I'm holding the folder containing all my work for the house. 'You should have this,' I say, holding it out. 'It's no use to me now, this house is unique, and it was all designed with you guys in mind – so who knows, perhaps one day you'll have some use for it?'

'No Alice, this is your work. I can't possibly take it from you.'

'Really, it's fine. You have my number, and if you decide later on you'd like the work doing . . .' I say, aware that in the circumstances this is crass and vulgar, but I'm desperate.

'No. You must keep it. I won't be staying here now, so perhaps whoever buys the place from me will be interested? I'll give them your number?'

'Thanks, where will you go?'

'I plan to move to France. Staying here is far too painful – houses tend to hold all the memories, good and bad, don't they? And when a relationship's over there's no point clinging to a place. We have to leave or we'll never recover.'

'Indeed we do,' I say, unsmiling. What a luxury to be able to run away like that, not to consider the money or the mortgage, even the cost of the move. So many of us stay in sad marriages and unhappy relationships because we've spent our lives working for the homes we live in.

'Most of us can't afford to leave, but you have no financial ties, you can just move around the planet, living and loving and leaving. I wish you well.'

He says nothing. I'm not sure he even understands me – we're from two different worlds, and there never was a what-if? He starts to close the door, and before it shuts, all I see are his eyes, cold and dark, and terribly sad.

I stand on the gravel path for a while, watching his windows to see if he's looking. It feels like the end of an affair that never was.

42

I get into the car, and as I slowly drive away I call Martha and tell her what just happened.

'Bloody hell. I'm sorry you lost that job, mate.'

'Not as sorry as me.'

'You were going to get rid of Jason with that money.'

'Yeah, well, there must be other ways of getting rid of him.'

'The kitchen knife in the conservatory, or the metal pipe in the kitchen-diner?'

'Something like that. I'm so disappointed, Martha, but I feel guilty even saying that because Daniel's devastated.'

'You need to stop with the guilt – your feelings of disappointment are just as valid as his devastation. Has Maddie run off with someone else?'

'I don't know, and I didn't ask.'

'I bet she has. Yeah, it's sad but I'm sure he'll find another young, beautiful and willing trophy wife to adorn the mantelpiece of his next home.'

'I really think he loved her, Martha. You could see it in his eyes.'

'Perhaps? Or is he just a good actor?'

'I believed him.'

'You believed Jason every time he said he'd change. You aren't a great judge of men, are you, love? I told you when you first started seeing him in sixth form that he was a cheater, and it took you twenty years to realise I was right.'

'I think I knew sooner, just didn't want to admit it, even to myself.'

'I know, admitting it to yourself is the hardest bit,' she says sympathetically. 'Hey, I'm working from home today, shall I call in at yours for a coffee when you're back?'

'I'd love that,' I say, and when I finally pull up at the house, she's waiting in her car with a bag of freshly baked pastries. I've never been so pleased to see her, and as we drink coffee and eat sweet almond croissants, we debrief the Daniel and Maddie split.

'I called Mike, left him a message, he'll get back if he has any intelligence,' she says through a mouthful of croissant. 'Shame about the job at Daniel's . . .' she continues. 'But he should have seen the writing on the wall. She was such a whacko, and so rude yesterday at yours. I was excited to meet her, but she was horrible.'

'Yeah, she was obviously checking out, which explains her reluctance to engage with me or you.'

'Had you planned a design for the nursery too?'

'No . . . that was so weird. When I mentioned it, Daniel kind of shut it down. At the time I thought it was odd, but afterwards I thought perhaps the upper classes like Daniel think nurseries are bourgeois or twee. They probably just throw a Moses basket in a room until the kid's about ten.'

'Or it could have been her? You know, Miss Lovey Actress with some new-age ideas about the cot facing east for energetic renewal or something. It wouldn't be the first time you've had to design a nursery for the parents.'

'True, but thinking about it now, it was bloody weird that he never mentioned a partner or baby on the way in that first meeting,' I remark.

'It was really messed up. What was he trying to hide?'

I wonder that too, as we continue to do a deep dive into their rather odd dynamic. And as it's a lovely day, and we're both invested in this debrief, I suggest we sit outside and have a cool drink.

'I should go home and work, but I reckon I could get away with another half an hour,' Martha says, checking her watch.

She wanders into the garden, while I make some elderflower cordial with ice, and minutes later I join her at the garden table with a tray.

'I can't deny I'll miss this garden,' I murmur, gazing around, seeing the roses I planted ten years ago. They were little root balls when I buried them in the soil; Ruby was still in nappies toddling around, getting her hands filthy 'helping Mummy make flowers'.

'Yeah, your bones are in the house, and this garden too. It must hurt to think about leaving it.'

'Yeah, but I feel ready to go. It's time to leave the past behind. Along with my husband.'

'We could bury him over there,' she shrieks, pointing to a small patchy area of grass that's turned blonde in this constant heat.

I chuckle. 'He'd kill the roses,' I say, looking at where she's pointing. Something suddenly catches my eye. 'What's that?' I say, still smiling, as I think of Jason buried there while trying for a closer look at a thing on the frazzled grass. 'Is it some kind of clothing?' I'm thinking one of the kids has left it out here, and go over, and now I'm closer, I see it's a school jumper. Folded.

It's the neatness that stops me cold. Not just the weirdness of it being on the lawn, but the precision of it. Judging by the size, it's Josh's jumper, folded into a perfect square, dead centre on the grass as if placed there in some kind of ceremony. Like a shrine? I think of the pieces of broken mug left on the window in a circular shape. My mouth goes dry.

I pick it up; the label has been cut out. That tiny stitched rectangle with his name in my handwriting that I lovingly sewed in has been removed. I turn to Martha, who's sitting at the garden table looking bewildered.

'What is it?'

'Josh's jumper.' I hold it to my chest. It feels weird to me, like someone's touched him without actually touching him. Someone's hands took away his name, smoothed the sleeves flat, pressed the wool into lines, thinking of him while they did it.

I don't move. The air feels wrong, thick, as though I've stepped into the space someone just vacated. Is this a message? A warning?

My eyes instinctively sweep the hedges. I walk around to the front of the house, breathless with fear. As far as I know, Josh's sweater was in a drawer in his bedroom. Whoever it is wants me to know they are close. Close enough to take my son's sweater. Are they letting me know they can also take my son?

43

I'm a mess. I really don't know what to do, and as yet I can't share the significance of this with Martha. She was away travelling when Michael (now Josh) and Jason returned to the UK. She knows Josh's mum died from an overdose, and I later adopted him. Like Mum, she assumed the adoption process was straightforward – that his biological mum had no family and it was all above board. But it wasn't, and the fact that weird things have been happening – Mum having a visitor from Spain, and her key for my house going missing – is, to my mind, no coincidence. I fear the chickens have come home to roost.

I stand in the garden feeling like my whole world is crumbling. But if I'm to save anything, I have to know what's going on and who's behind all this.

The house is going up for sale, but I can't afford to just take the kids and leave, I'm not Daniel with a lush farmhouse in France to escape to. I have to stay and fight; I have no choice.

'We need more cameras,' I say. How insane I sound. I turn to Martha, who's standing with me now, looking in horror at the sweater I'm holding.

'Those secret cameras, the high-end undetectable ones – you said Ryan installs them?'

'He does, and I have Ryan on speed dial.' Martha calls him and I listen as she tells him, 'It's a matter of life and death.' Usually I'd roll my eyes at her drama, but not on this occasion, because this time, she could be right.

I go and collect the kids, leaving Martha at the house talking Ryan through what's needed; a camera on the back garden is now paramount. But she's also going to ask him to install 'secret' cameras inside the house, where only me, Martha and Ryan know where they're placed. I wanted to tell Josh and Ruby, but Martha said I should just keep it to us.

'The fewer people who know about the secret cameras, the better chance you have of catching who it is,' she said. 'And if it is Josh, then you can talk to him – but if it's Jason, you just get straight on to the police.'

She'd touched my arm, her voice full of concern, and said gently, 'Babes, be prepared for all that's been happening to be Jason or Josh. After all, who else could it be?'

Who else indeed? I can't tell her about the possible alternative – that it might be a woman coming back to wreak revenge for someone else.

As I wait for the kids to come out of school, I call the police and tell them what just happened.

'You're calling because you found your son's sweater in the garden?'

My heart sinks. 'Yes . . . but it's a message, a threat. Two of your officers came to see me yesterday, they're aware of the problem,' I say, knowing they also probably think I'm unhinged.

'But what are you reporting exactly?'

I don't know anymore.

'Hello, Mrs Taylor, can you tell me what you're calling about exactly?'

Where do I begin? I don't even have the energy.

'Look, I just want to report this.'

'You want to report your son's sweater in your garden, Mrs Taylor?'

'Yes, no . . . look, I think my children may be in danger, my son particularly . . .'

'The same son whose sweater is in the garden?'

He's so taking the piss. I can imagine him putting this on speaker and the rest of the team sniggering.

'*Please* just log this call, or whatever it is you do. If anything happens it will be the police's fault and whoever is left can sue.'

'All the calls are logged, Mrs Taylor.'

'Can someone drive past? Or call in?' I ask, desperately.

'Would this be to see the sweater, Mrs Taylor?'

I end the call; I have to stop calling them until I have something concrete. They think I'm a lunatic, and I'm worried if I call them with a late-night break-in they're not going to take me seriously; they'll put me on speaker and order a few beers.

'I thought we'd go for pizza?' I say when the kids arrive. Josh skulks in the back of the car, as horrified as ever at the prospect of being seen out with his mum and sister. But he needn't worry, I drive them to a pizza place that's miles away. I need to give Ryan enough time to fit the cameras, and be gone when we get back. I also have this primal need to escape from the area with my children.

As we eat pizza, I wonder at the madness of fitting secret cameras in my own home. Outside is one thing, but inside feels so invasive, especially if the kids don't know. Am I being swept up in Martha's drama? It's not a bloody spy movie. I reach for my phone more than once to text and ask her to cancel Ryan's installation for inside the house. But something stops me.

By the time we're home, Ryan and Martha have gone, and I do a few subtle checks and see the cameras are now active. Later, when the kids are in bed, I read the text she sent with details of how to work the app, which is the same one the door cam is on, but I need all the help I can get when it comes to technology. She also tells me that I mustn't worry about payment, joking that she's 'paying Ryan in kind'. But I know she isn't, I know she's simply paid him for me, and I feel quite tearful at this.

You are my bestest friend, and I love you, I send.

She texts back: Call it an early Christmas present.

My friend knows I can't afford the cameras, and can't even ask Jason for the money because I don't want him to know there are secret cameras inside the house. This is about our safety, and my best friend knows this and cares. And I now have a chance of catching whoever is making my life a misery.

44

The following morning I'm up early. Robert Parks, the estate agent, is due just before lunch. So I spend the morning cleaning and spritzing and doing damage limitation in Josh's room.

'Beautiful place,' Robert murmurs as he walks down the hallway. I'm glad his first impression is favourable. And in the kitchen his eyes light up. 'This is a wow factor if ever I saw one,' he exclaims.

As we wander the rooms, he can't take the smile off his face. 'You'll have no problem selling this, it's stunning,' he says.

'How much do you think we could ask for?'

I hold my breath.

'I'd be looking at putting this property on the market . . .' He makes some notes, and I wait in agony until he looks up. 'At £999,999.'

'Wow! A million pounds?'

'Yes, assuming there are no hidden issues with the land or the building itself.'

'Can we put it up for sale now?'

'Of course. I'll need to speak to your husband before we proceed as he's on the mortgage as joint owner. It's just a formality really, a double-check that he's happy to sell too.'

'I'll call him now,' I say, taking out my phone and dialling Jason's number. I beg for Jason to pick up. He knew the estate agent was booked in today and I might be calling about the house.

Robert Parks and I sit awkwardly waiting for Jason to answer the phone. I think Robert's almost as anxious as I am to get this house on the market.

'I'm sorry, he's not answering.' I leave a message and Robert Parks's number, before hanging up.

'He's at work.' I smile, trying not to sound like I want to kill him. I feel quite stressed. Every moment we delay putting this house up for sale is agony for me.

I don't hear from Jason at all, but less than an hour after he left, I get a call from Robert Parks. 'Hello Mrs Taylor, I imagine you're aware that your husband has called me?'

No, I'm not.

I'm annoyed he didn't get back to me, but managed to speak to the estate agent. Still, this hopefully means we can move on this.

'Oh, okay. So what happens now?'

'Well, I can put it on the market for you, but have to say . . . I don't hold out much hope at the price you and your husband are suggesting.'

'I don't understand?'

'Mr Taylor said you are agreed on the asking price of one and a half million pounds.'

'I think there's some confusion here, Robert. I . . . he hasn't spoken to me. I had no idea he was even thinking about such a high figure.'

'He was insistent. He says he won't sell for less, but it's an extra five hundred thousand on top of my suggested price. I doubt we'd be able to sell your home at all.'

And that's exactly why he suggested it. He doesn't want to sell, as I suspected. He wants to prolong this torture.

I tell Robert I'll speak to Jason and try to come to a sensible compromise, knowing this will be damned near impossible. He has no intention of handing me my freedom on a plate; he'll need to extract a price first. And it won't be cheap.

Over the next hour, I text and call Jason, leaving voicemails and messages. I feel like a crazed stalker, but I'm desperate to talk, to somehow convince him to drop this stupid price so I can be released from purgatory. But there's no response.

But today is proving to be even more crazy than usual, and Robert Parks calls to say that despite having doubts about such a high price, he's uploaded the listing on to the company's website.

'Mr Taylor insisted I list the price instructed by him and yourself,' he says, so he's gone ahead and put the house on the market, which grinds my gears. I made it clear I hadn't agreed to that price, but sometimes men only hear other men – even when those men say stupid things.

'And to my surprise,' he continues, 'we've received a call from an interested party.'

'They're interested at £1.5 million?' I ask doubtfully.

'Yes! They live nearby, know the house, have always admired it and would like to do a viewing as soon as possible.'

'Do you think they'd actually *buy* it at that price though?'

'Hard to say, but they sounded keen on the phone, and if you're happy for them to view, we can take it from there.'

'Yes, let's do the viewing as soon as possible.' I'm not convinced it will sell, but even if they put in a lower offer, we could accept it.

'I took the liberty of asking when they were available and they both work during the day, and they asked if they might view early evening, tonight if possible?'

Sometimes the universe is with me as opposed to against me. Jason's in New York with work, or says he is – and he won't be back until tomorrow. Whatever price they're prepared to pay I reckon he'd try to put them off if he was showing them around. And I don't even want to imagine how he'd do that.

We agree on 7 p.m., and I go and collect Josh from school. Meghan's mum Yvonne is picking up the girls and taking them home for tea again before gymnastics tonight. Relieved to see she's safely in Yvonne's car, I wave, and they all wave back.

Meanwhile, Josh is wandering out of school, his reluctance evident by the agonisingly slow walk towards the car, with a face like thunder.

'There are a few things I need to talk about with you – that I don't want Ruby to know, okay?' He's in the back of the car as I pull away, and doesn't reply. 'Josh did you hear me?'

He grunts. Apparently, I'm now so annoying he can't actually speak to me. I hate this, but whatever I do seems to make it worse.

'The other night something happened – it was the night the wine went missing when Martha was here, after you'd gone to bed.' I pause, and look in the rear-view mirror to see his reaction before adding, 'Someone was standing in the front garden.'

I wait for this to drop, but again he doesn't respond. So I go on to tell him about the phone calls, the broken mug, my diamond ring, and his sweater. But instead of being spooked at this, he laughs.

'My sweater?'

'Yeah, it freaked me out to be honest.'

Neither of us say anything, for a while, and as we are on a roll, I go back in.

'I just wanted to let you know so you can be on the lookout.' I glance again in the mirror. He's gazing out of the window, is he listening? 'What do *you* think?' I ask, keen for a reaction.

'I don't know about any of this shit,' he says. 'It sounds fucking insane.'

'Yeah, agreed. It's pretty insane.'

'Who do you think's doing it?' he asks. It's the most he's said to me in weeks.

'I honestly don't know, and you mustn't worry because—'

'Mustn't worry? There's some creep hanging out in our front garden at night, making calls, and stealing your jewellery . . . and . . .'

'Yes, I know. But we have to stay calm and try to work out what's going on. I've reported it all to the police,' I say, inwardly cringing at the humiliating call I made about his sweater.

'And what are the police doing? Nothing, I suppose?'

'I . . . well, we're on their radar,' I offer, feeling rubbish. 'I'm collecting you from school so I can tell you this now, while Ruby's not around.'

'It's not school though, is it? I go to sixth form, has anyone even noticed?'

I hide my irritation at his nit-picking; he really is too much at the moment. 'Sorry, I guess we've always used that term, but I do appreciate you're a grown-up, Josh, and despite what you seem to think, I respect your feelings.'

He doesn't respond.

'And . . . I'm sorry to tell you like this, but you should know – we're going to sell the house.'

'When?'

'It went on the estate agent's website today. It's the only solution – this nesting thing has become impossible.'

'Yeah, it's pretty shit. Anyway, I'm away at uni from September, so you can do what you like. But what about Ruby, where will she live?'

'Nothing's been decided yet. It's very early days, but it's probably going to be a more regular arrangement. Dad and I will both get our own places and . . .' I'm not sure what the fuck's happening either, so I don't know what else to say. 'Okay, Josh?'

'Yeah, yeah.' He seems pretty indifferent, but at least there's no nasty remark or resentment in his tone, and given how he's been recently, I'll take this as a win.

Once home, Josh goes upstairs to revise for tomorrow's exam, so I prepare the house for the viewing. I've almost finished wiping down the surfaces in the kitchen when I notice a mark on the floor coming from under the fridge. I need to move the fridge away from the wall to get to it, and it feels like a workout to heave it away from the wall, to get behind and make sure it isn't a leak. As I pull at the fridge, it moves, and I hear something drop. So I squeeze in behind, hoping to God it isn't a mouse – or worse.

Once behind, with the waft of stale dust filling my nostrils, I can see what's fallen. A whole stack of envelopes is wedged between the wall and the fridge. As I move the fridge further out and open up the space, they land – so many envelopes, pale and jaundiced, now lying on the floor in a heap. The space is still tight and I can only just bend down to reach them, grabbing handful after handful. I finally have them all, and clutching them to my chest I edge my way out from behind the fridge, letting them fall in a dusty heap on the kitchen island.

I'm puzzled; I have no idea what these envelopes are, but as we gutted the place when we moved in, they don't belong to the previous owners. They must be ours.

Some look fairly recent, and others look like they've been behind there a while and are sticking together. So I gently prise them apart, and look at the address on the envelopes. Most are addressed to Jason. But some have my name on the envelope too.

But what bothers me the most is that most of them are stamped in thick red ink and are all variations on the theme of:

> *FINAL DEMAND, NOTICE OF DEFAULT, IMMEDIATE PAYMENT REQUIRED.*

Some are unopened. Others appear to have been read. The dates go back more than a year. Mortgage, electricity, household insurance, every bill that keeps this house alive. My chest is tight as I carry one to the countertop where my laptop sits. I sign in and start checking the accounts. *What has he done?*

45

This makes no sense. Red letters blooming across white pages. Each envelope another horrible revelation. I'm not really here but my hands keep opening one envelope after another as if the next one might change the story and give me a happy ending. This has been happening here in our home and I knew nothing about it. How could I be so blind?

I sign into our electricity account, again hoping this will obliterate what I've been reading, but it's just another stinging slap in the face. The same words, over and over, pulsing at me in both ink and pixels. As the paper bills have already revealed, the electricity bill is overdue by three months – and the online bills are obviously identical. My mouth is dry as I click into the water bill, and gasp to see our water is scheduled for shut-off. Then I have a terrifying thought – what about the mortgage? Logging into the account, I can barely move my fingers over the keys. I need to know, but I don't want to.

When I sign in, it feels like I'm being stabbed in the stomach. My insides twist, my breath is shallow, I'm beyond tears. '*Fuck*,' I murmur under my breath as my worst fear is confirmed.

Jason hasn't paid the mortgage for almost a year, and the bank is threatening foreclosure.

He's been logging in. Deleting and moving emails into obscure folders so I'd never see them. But he couldn't stop the paper bills and final notices from coming in the post, so he hid those too, pushing them behind the fridge where he thought I'd never look. Throughout our marriage he's taken care of the bills. Occasionally I might check that things were going through online if he was working away, or if he couldn't log on wherever he was. And there's never been a problem – no calls, no red warnings, everything was paid, until now.

I don't move. I just keep staring at the screen, my finger resting on the trackpad, one click away from opening the most recent message in the list. When I do, I wish I hadn't. It's headed: *Notice of Intention to Repossess.*

It's ten minutes to seven, someone's on their way to view our house, and it's about to be repossessed. It's too late to call the estate agent to stop the viewing, so I'll have to go through the motions and get rid of the couple as soon as I can.

I gather up the as-yet-unopened envelopes, knowing there will be even more revelations. I can't imagine anything worse than defaulting on the mortgage, but I take a deep breath and – putting the ones I've seen aside – lay the rest of the envelopes on the kitchen counter like tarot cards. And as I open the first one, my skin fizzes. *Your new credit card is enclosed.* But there is no card. I open the next one, another credit card. *Thank you for choosing us.*

I go through each one. *Dear Mr Taylor. Please find your new credit card enclosed.* Eight letters. Eight different credit cards from different banks.

But they all start the same. *Your new credit card is enclosed.* All have that faint rectangular shadow on the paper where the plastic should be, a ghost outline with a gluey residue.

I go back to the bills I found earlier, and shuffle them together with these letters, mixing them into one long paper chain of debt and denial. Mortgage arrears on one side, fresh lines of credit on the other. Jason's salary is large; in recent years we've had no money problems and he's always been careful, never decadent. My earnings are small compared to his, mostly because I was bringing up the children and being at home while he worked away. And how complacent, how trusting, how fucking stupid have I been?

I pick up another envelope at random. A card issued just last month. Limit: £12,000. But this one is way, way worse – it's addressed to me!

No, no, no. With shaking hands I go through all the other envelopes, desperate to see, and at the same time terrified of what I might find. And after I've gone through them all, I lean on the kitchen countertop, my legs about to give way. I was right to be terrified. He's taken out *four* credit cards in my name.

I scramble my thoughts together. It's such a mess, and it's all been going on behind my back. I immediately google if it's possible to apply for a credit card for me without me knowing – 'Shit,' I murmur, as the answer appears on the screen.

Yes, if that person knows your date of birth, address history, National Insurance number and bank details from shared accounts.

He has everything, and the more I google the more I want to cry. For online applications, ID verification is done via credit checks or scanned documents. He could use my passport or driving licence, which we keep with all the family documents. I thought he kept them safe. If nothing else, I thought he kept *me* safe.

He must have arranged for the cards to be sent to a locker, or PO box, because if they'd been delivered here I'd have seen them when they dropped through the letterbox. He must have set the monthly statements to paperless and given his own email and phone number.

Has he been drowning and not told me, but tried to navigate his way through using my name to get more money, hoping he can pay it all off and I'll never know? Or is this something else entirely? Has he just been spending money we don't have?

And what happened just over a year ago that set all this in motion?

I know the answer to that. *Ellie!*

The fridge hum deepens. The letters are still in my hands when the floorboard creaks in the hall, and I turn to see Josh standing in the doorway.

'Oh . . . you made me jump, love,' I say, far too brightly.

'You okay?' he asks, moving into the kitchen slowly, concern on his face.

'Yes . . . I . . .' My son keeps telling me he's a grown-up, and I need to treat him like one. 'I found these . . .' I gesture to the pile of envelopes and letters, and he starts to read through them, his face falling at each one.

Suddenly the front door bell rings, making us both jump. 'It's the people viewing the house. I need to hide them.'

I'm looking around frantically to see where I can push them. 'Go and answer the door,' Josh says. 'I'll hide them in the utility room.'

I head down the hallway, and open the door with my brightest smile, aware my son is now hiding his father's secrets.

'Please come through,' I say to the woman standing on the steps. She's a little older than me, in her forties perhaps. Her hair's cut in a dark, shiny bob and she's very smiley. 'My husband's on call this evening, he's a doctor,' she explains. 'We were hoping we'd be able to do a quick viewing, but he was called away.'

'Oh.'

I smile blankly, too busy processing all the other shit that's currently running through the sewage of my life.

'Don't worry. If I like it, we'll buy it – my husband does whatever I tell him.'

I give a fake chuckle that squeezes out my final spark, leaving me fragile and hollow. She smiles back, and I have a fleeting hope that perhaps this woman and her doctor husband might just save us after all, and buy the house before it's repossessed? Does it even work like that? I take her through to the sitting room, where she enthuses over the soft furnishings. 'Robert said you're an interior designer, and I said to my husband, imagine living in the house of an interior designer – that's the dream.'

Just at this point, the front door is being unlocked. Is this Jason turning up to stop the viewing? I want to throw up, and I dash out into the hall to stop him before he ruins our possible last chance of anything. But as the door opens and I see Ruby, relief floods through me. This is immediately replaced by panic.

'You should be at gymnastics, is everything okay?'

'Yeah,' she smiles as she passes me in the hall. 'I forgot my bloody leotard,' she yells from halfway up the stairs.

'Ruby, no swearing,' I call, embarrassed that our prospective buyer is listening. 'Sorry,' I say, returning to the sitting room.

'Please don't apologise, I have two of my own, and their swearing is far more . . . descriptive?' We both smile at this, and I lead her into the hall where we almost bump into Ruby thundering down the stairs.

She stops halfway, clutching her leotard, looking a little confused. And I realise in that moment I haven't had a chance to tell her we're selling the house. What a horrible way for her to find out. I could kick myself.

'This is Mrs Weaver, she's come to see the house,' I say, hoping that will be enough.

'Hello.' She doesn't smile, just slips past us both.

I long to run after her and explain, but I can't abandon Mrs Weaver.

We continue on through the viewing, and a part of me wants to come clean. I don't want this poor woman to get her hopes up.

'My eldest would love this bedroom,' she's saying as we stand in Ruby's room. 'We have a boy too, so the fact this is four bedrooms is perfect. Both kids have a room, which leaves a spare.'

'Yes, the other room is my son's but he's revising for an exam tomorrow. I hope you don't mind if we don't look in there?'

'No problem.' She smiles. She seems nice, and I feel guilty I may be misleading her.

After the tour I walk her to the front door, and she says she'll be putting an offer in. I should be delighted, and it may work out, but of course it isn't going to be that simple now.

I call Jason again, but there's no answer, and having not eaten all day I make a sandwich and sit with my thoughts in the darkening kitchen. At 8.30 p.m. Ruby comes home. She seems happy, like she's forgotten all about me showing a prospective buyer around the house.

I smile, and try to let go, but my head's still in the utility room with the final demands and new credit card letters. *In my name.*

'Was gymnastics fun?' I ask, longing to immerse myself in my daughter's wonderful trivia.

'Yeah good.' She opens the fridge, grabs a yoghurt and joins me on a stool at the island.

'We stopped for bubble tea after,' she's saying. 'I got the strawberry one because Meghan's mum was shady, said the brown sugar one's "basically a dessert". But I'm *so* getting it next time . . . can you and me go, Mum?'

'Of course.'

She continues to discuss the merits of bubble tea and how 'super-fake' her classmate Olivia's social media is while checking her phone. My daughter's voice is comforting background music. Until she says, 'Is that woman going to buy our house then?'

'I don't know. I'm sorry, Ruby, I should have told you . . . would you hate it if we moved?'

She shrugs. 'Dunno. But that woman, looking at the house with you, she was the one' – she stops talking, licks yoghurt from the lid – 'who talked to me and Josh in the coffee shop.'

My heart quickens.

'Don't you remember, she was the one asking us where we lived and all that. She must have kids at our school, I've seen her waiting for them in her car. She drives this really cute little green Fiat.'

46

My world has just slipped off its axis. 'Ruby, are you absolutely sure the woman who I was showing around the house tonight is the same woman who talked to you in the coffee shop?' I ask.

'Yeah, definitely.' She's now muttering about some teenage outrage she's just witnessed on TikTok, and reporting it directly to Meghan.

I'm not going mad. The woman *has* been following me. I've seen her at school, sitting there in her car watching mine.

'Honestly, Olivia is such a pick-me girl, I can't believe she even posted that.' Ruby's still speaking in teenage tongues, still messaging Meghan. And still completely unaware of the bomb she just detonated.

'Has the woman tried to talk to you since?' I ask, dreading the answer.

She shakes her head, doesn't look up from her phone, then delivers the line that floors me. 'No, but I think she talks to Josh.'

'What do you mean. When does she talk to him?'

'Dunno.' She's realised she shouldn't have told me. I know her, she won't tell me any more if I continue to ask questions. I need to be more subtle.

I have to keep her away from my kids, and my kids away from her.

'Thing is, Ruby, Mrs Weaver isn't who she says she is. She's so fake . . .'

'Oh?'

'Super-fake . . . such a thirsty trap.'

'It's thirst trap, Mum. Please stop talking.' She doesn't look up, just continues to scroll. How many teenage words can I throw as bait to get her attention? *Think, think, think.*

'I mean it Ruby, she's shady.'

'I thought she was super-nice.'

'Nah, she's up in everyone's business, I think she only came to our house tonight to have a super old nosey. She won't buy the house.'

She finally looks up. 'Ugh, and you showed her around?'

'I didn't realise then, but if she's the same woman who talked to you and Josh, then that's her. If she tries to engage you in conversation, or asks you or Josh if you'd like a lift, say no and call me immediately.'

She looks at me, intrigued. 'OMG, I'm getting total creeper vibes.'

'Just steer clear of this Karen,' I add dismissively, so I don't freak her out. 'Anyway, it's late.' I check my phone. 'I think you should jump in the shower and get to bed, Ruby.'

Without looking up, she moves out of the kitchen and up the stairs, never once taking her eyes off her phone.

I immediately call Robert Parks the estate agent, and ask him not to arrange any more viewings until I can 'clarify things' with my husband. But despite working for a company whose USP is 'We're here for you 24/7', Robert's phone goes straight to voicemail, and it's too complicated to explain in a message. I try Jason again, who also doesn't answer – but to be fair, he's never been there for me 24/7.

Someone that has been there for me 24/7 is Martha. She texted earlier, but I haven't had a chance to read it, so I flop down on the kitchen stool and click on the message.

> Hey Alice, hope all went well with the estate agent today. I didn't want to worry you and don't want to call in case the kids are with you. But have to tell you something. After finding that jumper in the garden, Ryan and I decided to check your door cam over the last 24 hours. We can't work out how someone took that jumper and placed it in the back garden, because to do that, they'd need access via the front garden. We checked and double-checked, and it's so weird because the recordings show no one walked into the front garden and down the side of the house. Not even you.

She doesn't spell it out because she doesn't need to.

So, I call her. 'Whoever took the jumper and put it in the back garden must have come from inside the house,' I say.

'Try not to worry love.'

'It's probably the same person who broke my mug, took my diamond ring . . .'

'Perhaps worth asking the kids if they saw anything?'

I know what she's saying, I can't even trust my kids – who else could come and go without being seen? I think fleetingly about Jason. He has a key of course, but he's in New York – and he isn't even here when he's supposed to be, so I doubt it's him, but who knows?

'I'll talk to the kids,' I say, defeated.

Then I tell her all about the paperwork I found behind the fridge. Her fury is tangible, I can feel the flames licking the phone as she speaks, which she can't do without inserting the words 'bastard' and 'fucking'.

'I can't believe he'd do this to you. And also, duh, you're going to find out, aren't you?' she's spitting down the phone.

'It makes no sense. I'm annoyed at myself for not checking though, because I noticed the mortgage hadn't gone out of our current account last month. When I mentioned it, he said he'd taken it from our savings account. I didn't question it, why would I? Jason's always been good with the household finances.'

'Has he incurred some huge debt that he doesn't want you to know about? I mean I'm filled with hate, but trying to give him the benefit of the doubt here.'

'I don't know. I give myself a wage from the business, and his salary and bonuses automatically go in there each month with mine on the same date, which was just yesterday.'

'So presumably losing his job isn't the answer to this mystery?'

'No, but as I can't get hold of him, I don't know what the hell is going on. He's away with work, supposedly. It's my last night here until next week, but I'm wondering if he'll even turn up tomorrow.'

'Wow. If I ever see him I will push his head into a brick wall, and that's just my opening.'

'He has money direct-debited every month into our savings, but that hasn't happened for twelve months, around the time he started getting the credit cards, which of course I know nothing about. Jason only ever had one credit card for work expenses, and a shared one with me. He doesn't even like credit – he only uses his in an emergency.'

'But if he's being paid a huge salary but not paying the bills, or putting anything into your savings, and possibly getting credit too – where's all the money?'

'I went through everything last night, and I can't even see his salary, that stopped months ago. I reckon he's having that paid into another account.'

'One shared with someone else?' she suggests.

'I wouldn't be surprised – he obviously doesn't want to spend it on household bills for the family.'

'Bastard,' she spits. 'I'm sorry, Alice, but for his own safety, don't let me near him. Honestly, I would kill him.'

'Well, don't end him before I get there, I want a go at him too. Might not even bother killing him first, just throw him into a deep grave and let the earth take him slowly.'

We have recently started playing this game, we call it 'Murdering Jason', and compete to come up with the most gruesome, painful way of causing his demise. Just being able to conjure up these awful endings for him is hilarious and a harmless way for me to get it off my chest. But today we aren't laughing, our anger is real, and I seriously wonder what Martha would do if she were to bump into him.

We say goodbye, and as I put down the phone, I hear one of the kids padding downstairs.

'Do you want more light?' Josh asks considerately, emerging into the dark kitchen.

'Hey love. Thanks, but I don't. I just want calm and quiet and dusk.'

He sits on one of the stools opposite me. He's making eye contact, seems more relaxed, less awkward than he's been of late.

'Did you ever meet my real mum?' he asks.

My heart beats faster. Why is he asking this now?

'I never met her. I'm sorry I didn't, because I know she was a lovely person.'

'Why?'

I smile. 'Because she had you.'

'Fair enough.' I know he wants more. But I can't give him more. 'You should ask your dad about her,' I suggest. 'They lived together for several years in a beautiful part of Spain. You could go there sometime.'

'I'm half Spanish, aren't I?'

'No love, your mum was English.'

'Oh . . .'

He knows his mum's name was Sarah. Jason said she was from Yorkshire, but he didn't know exactly where. And all Josh has is the little cardigan and shorts he travelled to the UK in. Jason brought nothing else.

'Mum.' He hesitates for a moment, and asks the question that he's never asked before. 'Did Dad take me away from my mother?'

'No love, as we told you, she was very poorly, and after she died, your dad decided to come home to the UK with you.'

He gives a vague shrug, and I think I may be losing him again, but he changes the subject. 'I looked at all the bills and the stuff Dad's been doing.' His voice is softer, more articulate than the usual grunts and sighs.

'Yeah, I can't get hold of your dad, he must be busy at work. So until I can speak to him I'm not sure what's going on.' I'm trying to sound reasonable, but don't feel it.

'He's really done a number on you, hasn't he?'

'Like I say, until I speak to him—'

'MUM!' His voice is raised, a flicker of anger. 'Stop. Making. Excuses. For. Him.'

'I'm not . . . I just don't know—'

'He wouldn't give you the same respect,' he speaks over me. 'And not answering his phone? He does it deliberately. I've been with him when his phone rings and if it's you he says "oh shut up" and turns it to silent.'

This hurts. 'Really, in front of you?'

He looks awkward, guilty. 'Yeah, Dad says you're only calling because you want more money. He says you're trying to ruin him then keep the house for yourself . . .'

This feels like a punch in the gut. 'That just isn't true. When I met your dad he had nothing, he came to live with me here in the UK. He trained to be a lawyer while I worked full-time and . . .'

'And looked after me.'

'Yeah. And it was the best job I ever had, looking after you.' Tears well up in my eyes.

'Mum. I'm sorry. I thought you were the bad guy in all this, I . . . I thought the stuff he said about you was true.'

'Oh Josh, it isn't . . .'

'I know that now, but . . .' I hear the tears in his voice. 'Mum . . . he lied and I never defended you.'

'It's okay . . .' I start.

'No, no, it isn't. I wanted to hurt you – I was the one who broke your mug. I put the broken pieces in the circle, and I . . . my school sweater, it was me who folded it and put it in the garden. I was confused, I dunno . . . I was trying to scare you, wanted revenge for you splitting us all up.' He puts his head down. 'Sorry, Mum.'

'Josh. You were distressed, something was bothering you and . . . I guess I should have realised. I tried to talk to you but . . .'

'I know, I wouldn't. I just felt like you hated me, you didn't want me around. Dad just kept saying all you wanted was the house, and Ruby because she's your kid and I'm not.'

This hits like a physical blow. How can he say that?

I'm still on the kitchen stool and he's standing close, so I reach out and grab his hand. 'You and Ruby come first, you always have, always will. And be sure of this – I love you *both* equally. I'd live in a shed rather than keep the house if it meant losing either of you.'

He sighs. 'Dad's been such a dick . . . I never realised. And he hasn't just done it to you, he's done it to all of us.' He shakes his head, and my heart breaks a little more. 'He says you're the one breaking us up, that he's the only one who cares, but how could he do something like that if he really cared about me and Ruby? He hasn't paid our bills, he's applied for credit cards without telling you, he's wrecked everything. I see him now.' He sighs. 'I'm sorry this happened.' Then he looks at his watch, and stands up. 'I'd better go to bed.'

'Try and focus on your exams. I know it's incredibly hard, but everything else can be sorted, I'll fix it. But this is your future, it's so important – it's your law exam tomorrow. How are you feeling about it?'

He shrugs. 'Okay, I've revised. Dad said he'd go through some of the old exam papers with me.'

'Right, well he's the lawyer, so I'm sure that's helped.'

'No – he *said* he would, but he never did. I called him yesterday but he never bothered to answer. I left a message, and he still hasn't called me back. I guess he's doing the same to me now, seeing my name, and saying "shut up" and muting me. Just like he does with you.'

47

I'm sad for Josh, but I guess he had to see who his father really is in order to move on. And as hurt as we all are by what's happened, I hope that Josh and I can start to rebuild our relationship in the rubble that's left.

He goes to bed, and I'm just pottering before going to bed myself when I think I hear a quiet knock on the door. At first I think I must be mistaken – it's after 11 p.m. But then I hear it again. Soft, but determined. I feel suddenly uneasy. Who would call round at this time?

I immediately check the cameras, and make out a shadowy figure standing on my doorstep. Daniel Prescott. The hairs on the back of my neck prickle – what's he doing here? I like Daniel, but Martha and Jason have both warned me about him, and the fact he's turned up at this time of night, knowing I'm on my own, makes me uncomfortable.

I stare at the camera screen; he's just standing there, and I can't pretend I'm out because my bloody car's in the drive and all the lights are on. Still, I'm in my nightwear, it's late and I don't want to open the door to him. But now Willow has sashayed into view on-screen, her big fluffy tail up, as she wanders towards the nice man. I hold my breath as he slowly bends down and strokes her head. She's now flopped at his feet and being a total slut.

I keep really, really still, and watch, and wait, and wait. Now he's picked her up, and he's looking down at her as he steps forward and knocks on the door again. I'm frozen to the spot. He doesn't move. I don't move. Willow doesn't move.

I hear Martha's voice in my head: *Natalie's cat went missing soon after Daniel was caught sniffing her shirt . . .*

After what seems like an eternity, he turns to go. But my instant relief seeps away as I realise that he's walking around the side of the house to my back garden, *still* carrying Willow. I continue to watch for a few more seconds, then check the cameras at the back, where I see him wander into the garden. Then, still holding Willow, he peeps through the bifold glass doors, and he's staring into my kitchen. I'm only in the next room! He moves again, and I see from the screen that he's now staring into this room, where I am. I slowly look up from the screen, and our eyes meet through glass. My finger ends tingle. *He's got me.*

He's now smiling and holding Willow up at the window, making her paw wave.

I pretend to look surprised, but I'm sure my irritation at this intrusion must be apparent on my face. This feels like such an invasion of privacy.

What's wrong with the bloody upper classes – don't they ever call ahead? I have to deal with this and get rid of him. So I stand up from the sofa, wrap my nightgown around me, and go to the front door.

I stand there for a moment, working out what to say.

Eventually I pull the door open, almost falling over backwards. 'Hello? Daniel?' I call into the darkness. I hear footsteps on gravel around the side of the house again, then Daniel's voice.

'Hey Alice, I assumed you must have gone out,' he says, walking into the light of the door.

'No . . . I, where's Willow?' He isn't holding Willow.

'Your cat? She's in the garden, chasing midnight mice.' His eyes widen at this. He's now standing in the doorway towering over me, and I feel slightly uncomfortable as he bends down to hug me. I can't explain it, but his energy is different; there's no exuberance, and even his smile feels like a grimace on the darkened doorstep.

'Are you aware a downstairs window is open round the back, Alice?'

'The utility room? No, I . . . wasn't.' Did *he* open it, and if I hadn't been here, might he have let himself in?

'I closed it from the outside.' I feel like he's waiting for me to thank him. 'The lock seems to be broken. I thought you should know.'

'It's fine, I'll deal with it,' I reply dismissively. 'I didn't hear you ring the bell, I'm surprised to see you, it's very late.'

'Oh dear, I have the most appalling manners. Keep doing this, don't I? My apologies for the late hour, I knocked quietly, in case the children are asleep.'

He's standing on the doorstep, like he's waiting for me to ask him inside.

'Yes, the children are asleep, so if you don't mind, I won't invite you in. It's been a bit of a day,' I add – the biggest understatement I think I've ever made.

Even in the dim light I see his jaw tighten at this. 'I understand,' he says, but I'm not sure he does, because he makes no move to leave. His tall frame is still looming over me. I feel like he's crowding me.

'I knocked, but when you didn't answer, I decided to check on you. I know you're alone.'

'Thank you, I'm fine. I have lots of good neighbours who keep an eye on me.' This is a lie, everyone on this road has a big house behind tall trees, and we rarely even say hello. But this doorstep encounter is creeping me out and I'd like him to think someone will hear me if I scream.

'Sorry, I know it's late, but there's something I need to talk to you about.'

'Now? I'm so tired, Daniel, perhaps we could chat over the phone tomorrow?'

He doesn't move, he stands on one foot then the other, and I wonder why I ever thought Daniel Prescott was the one who got away.

'Alice, when you hear what I have to tell you, then you'll understand why I came here tonight.'

I doubt that very much.

I don't respond, leaving silence to fill the gaps.

'I'm here because,' he hesitates, 'I have something to show you. It's most unpleasant.'

'Oh . . .' I can't begin to imagine what unpleasantness he's about to show me on my own doorstep. 'I really don't think now is the time for this, Daniel . . .'

'It won't take long, and you *should* know.'

This is starting to feel really sinister; the man who's always seemed so kind, and sensitive, so *safe*, is trying to get inside my house. Against my will. I'm feeling extremely vulnerable. I won't let him into my home, where my children are sleeping. *And where's bloody Willow?*

'You were holding Willow at the window, is she still out there?' I say. 'She recently went missing, we were all so worried, especially my daughter. I'd hate to lose her again.'

'Oh, that's awful. I lost a dog once, I was only nine years old. I was devastated, her name was Poppy.'

'Oh.' *What the fuck is going on?*

'My mother gave her to me before she died, and my father broke it to me that she'd run away. I cried every night, for months.'

'That's so sad.' Now I'm softening slightly.

'Yes, it was, I was devastated, never got over her loss. That's why I find it hard when people leave me. My mother left, then Poppy, and—'

'Oh, there's Willow,' I say, pointing at the cat disappearing into the trees in the front garden. My feet are bare so I can't run out on to the gravel.

'I'll get her for you,' he says, like an eager child, and disappears into the trees for a few seconds, returning with the prize. I thank him and take Willow from his arms.

'I'd better go, I don't want her out all night.'

'You don't have to invite me in, I can show you what I need you to see here. I understand you'd rather not have a man in the house late at night.'

I sigh openly, and quickly go back down the hall, put Willow in the kitchen and close the door, but as I return to the hallway, he's moved inside. A man I now realise I really don't know is inside my home, blocking my exit. And all I can think is: *I could die tonight.*

'What I want you to see is on my phone,' he's saying.

Why don't I just tell him to leave, push him out of my house? I don't want to anger him, or upset him. I hope when he's shown me whatever the hell is on his phone he'll leave.

'This is the reason my marriage ended,' he's saying, clicking on the screen.

'I don't wish to be rude, Daniel, but your marriage is none of my business,' I say, as he turns to switch on the light in *my* hallway. My power is ebbing away; he's taking control slowly, gently. He opens up his phone and hands it to me.

I don't want to look. I can't imagine what it is. Maddie naked? Maddie *dead?*

'Look at the screen,' he says, a quiet command I can't refuse. I'm too scared.

I allow my eyes to alight on the screen. At first, I can't make out the image. But I look more closely, and realise it's grainy, taken at night. I think it's Maddie. I don't want to look; it feels so intrusive.

'Look, Daniel, I'm sorry this happened to you. But perhaps talk to someone who can help you. I'm not that person, it's nothing to do with me.' I try to hand back his phone.

'Please,' he urges, pushing it at me. 'Please look again, it's *everything* to do with you.'

I sigh. This is uncomfortable and exhausting. If I play his game, will he leave? I feel like I have no alternative, so I take the phone and look again at the screen. I'm horrified.

48

I continue to scroll through Daniel's phone. Each photo, every video, pushing me further and further to somewhere I don't want to go. Maddie laughing, Maddie naked, having sex in the sitting room at Silvercliff. I can't see his face, but it isn't Daniel. All apparently filmed through the window, the camera like a peeping Tom. Floor-to-ceiling glass leaves nothing to the imagination.

I look up. 'I don't want to see this. Why are you showing it to me?'

'Keep watching,' he says, the urgency in his voice painful.

She climbs on to her lover, pushing him inside her, riding him like the waves, her breasts kissing his face. Then they move, and he turns her around, lays her down, and all I can see is his naked, muscular back as he pins her to the sofa. Their bodies twist and jerk together, so absorbed, so dizzy with desire, both oblivious to the prying camera at the window. I can't bear to watch any more, but can't stop. I scroll through and now they're walking along the beach near Maddie's home. They stop, and kiss, and within seconds they're down in the sand, his head between her thighs. Her ecstatic cries mingle with the crying gulls above their heads, where the camera, as high as a drone, records from the cliffs. Numbly I keep scrolling through; other days, other nights, other places, but always the same two people.

Daniel's wife and my husband.

Shock sparks through me, my mind unable to fully process what I've just seen.

Taking the phone from me, he shrugs. 'Your husband, my wife – the actress and the lawyer, they lie every day in their professions, and consequently are accomplished liars.'

'As painful as that was, I'm over my husband, but for you it must be so hard, and there's the baby to think of too . . .'

He shakes his head slowly. 'I really believed the child was mine.'

What? 'The baby isn't yours?'

'No.'

'But . . . no? No, it isn't . . . ?'

He's nodding slowly. 'Your husband's, yes.'

I can't even bring myself to think about this. All the cheating, all the betrayal, but he's never before taken things so far . . . 'But I don't understand. If Maddie's eight months pregnant they've been together for at least that long, but he was seeing a woman he worked with called Ellie around that time and beyond. Surely even Jason wasn't seeing two women at the same time while married to me?'

'He was seeing someone called Ellie?' he asks.

'Yes, I ended our marriage when I heard his voice note saying her name. That's how I know her name is Ellie.'

'Maddie's real name is Madelyn Eleanor Rose Lavender, but people tend to call her by her stage name, Maddie. Her friends and family call her Ellie, she prefers it to Maddie – says Maddie sounds like she's mad.' He raises his eyebrows for a moment, presumably for me to digest this, then carries on. 'I refuse to call her Ellie, she'll always be Maddie to me. My mother's name was Maddie.'

'It's all starting to make sense. I knew Jason's other woman was called Ellie, but I had no idea *who* she was, and I'd never have believed it if someone told me it was Maddie Lavender. Jason lied about everything – he told me Ellie was a colleague he'd met at work.'

'Well, actually . . .' He pauses. 'He did meet her at work.'

'How?'

'Maddie's currently dealing with a few . . . legal issues.' I know what he's referring to: the scriptwriter who's about to go to the press with his stalking story.

'And Jason's her lawyer?'

'Yes, that's how they met.' Daniel nods sadly. 'I'm ashamed to say I leaked her legal issues to the producers, and that's when they wrote her out of the show.'

'Oh, so it wasn't her choice to leave, or because of the pregnancy?'

'I was of course upset that the baby wasn't mine, but as Maddie's agent made me sign an NDA on our first date, I couldn't go to the press with stories about her, and had to be creative. The producers thought my little leak was an anonymous tip-off from a disgruntled cast member, and when they learned that her ex the scriptwriter was about to tell all, they were scared to death.'

'I can imagine. Did you do it for revenge?' I've always considered Daniel to be kind, eccentric, misunderstood. But I realise I don't know him at all.

'Revenge? Not at first. I found out about the affair quite recently. I had no idea it had been going on for about a year and he could be the father. I foolishly thought if Maddie lost her income, she'd need me to support her and our baby, and she'd end it with Jason and stay with me. I had no pride back then. People like Maddie make you lose all self-worth. It's so destructive. Love can be dangerous for your health.'

'And the baby's definitely Jason's?' I ask, thinking of how the kids will take it that they'll have a half-sibling.

'Yes, that morning you came with the designs she'd just told me.'

'I'm sorry, bad timing.'

'That's an understatement.' He smiles, the humour coming back into his eyes.

'Did you really *have* to film them in flagrante?' I ask.

'That wasn't me. It was a private detective appointed by my father's legal team. As the only child, I inherited everything when he died a few years back. My father always said I was a fool for a pretty face, and was determined to protect me and the family money from a beautiful gold-digger.'

'Do you think Maddie was a gold-digger?'

He shakes his head. 'Maddie and I were in love, until she met your husband. We'd talked about marriage and children, and so when she told me she was pregnant, I was delirious. All my dreams were coming true, so I bought the diamond, dropped it in the glass of champagne and got down on one knee . . .' He falters.

'What happened?'

'She said no, she wanted to wait until after the baby was born. I was disappointed of course, I could see no reason for that – we could have arranged a beautiful wedding in a matter of weeks at Silvercliff.'

'But presumably she knew it wasn't your baby and was waiting for Jason to end his marriage?'

'Yes, exactly, she was keeping me waiting, just in case he didn't come through for her. But when she discovered that you were divorcing, that was the end for me.' He takes a long breath. 'I knew none of this of course, but my father's lawyers had their instructions in the will, and went ahead with an investigation. It didn't take them long to discover a few skeletons in her closet, and they employed the private detective. Oh Alice, it was horrible when the lawyers presented me with those videos. I felt like my life was over.'

'I'm so sorry you had to go through that.'

'I don't want you to think I just came here tonight for pity, or indeed to upset you with the "evidence". And when I was peering through your window earlier, I apologise, that must have seemed quite out of character, but in truth I was concerned for your safety.'

'In what way?'

'Maddie is an extremely jealous woman, and she can become quite violent. I've been on the receiving end. I wondered if she'd see you as a threat, the obstacle to her being with *him*.'

'I doubt she'd come for me. After all, she's got Jason now, I don't want him.'

'She doesn't have him, he ended the relationship. It drove her wild, and she became obsessed. She'd regularly drive here and watch the house, watch you. She knew Jason had to come back here . . . and she'd stand in those trees for hours. I was watching her, because as crazy as it sounds, I still loved her, and she had to be protected from herself. Who knows what she'd do if pushed . . .'

My blood turns to ice. Will me and my kids ever be safe?

'She called me yesterday,' he continues. 'I had no idea where she was but she asked if I'd seen you, and were you back together.'

'We aren't back together, that will never happen. I haven't seen Jason for a while – he said he was in New York this week but I'm not sure I believe him. I thought he was with Ellie . . . Maddie. But obviously not. Where else could he be though? It doesn't make sense.'

'I wouldn't believe anything he says, Alice. It wasn't enough for him to steal you from me all those years ago – he had to take Maddie too.'

No one 'stole' me from anyone – Daniel's rhetoric around women is bordering on misogyny, and his hatred of those who he believes have wronged him is pretty permanent. Perhaps Martha's right, his parents messed him up, and his mother's death was the final flourish?

We stand in silence. I'm processing everything he's told me – these last few weeks have felt like a brutal fairground ride. Every now and then something else comes along to throw me up in the air.

'All I want is peace and quiet and calm, but now there's so much to get through before life can get back on track. The things I once took for granted have gone,' I say into the silence.

'Yes, I feel the same. I've gone from being in a happy relationship expecting a child . . . But it was never happy, it can't have been, I just saw what I wanted to see and heard what I wanted to hear.'

'Me too.'

He turns to me. 'The other thing I wanted to say about all this sordid stuff, the videos and such – I have these in my possession, and should you need any help with your divorce, I'd be happy to send them to you.' He holds up his phone.

'Does Maddie know you have the videos . . . does Jason?'

'No, and neither of them can know, it could get me in hot water because of the NDA if the pictures were leaked. But someone else could leak them . . . ?'

Daniel's not here to tell me about my husband and Maddie out of concern. He's here tonight because he wants me to leak the videos for him.

'Did you ever want me to work on your home, Daniel?' I ask. 'Was I just the toy you wanted to dangle in front of Maddie to play games with her?'

He looks uncomfortable. 'Maddie was threatening to leave me, and I was so desperate I'd have done anything to make her stay. I wanted her to see what she was doing, breaking up another family by loving someone else's husband. I thought if she met Jason's wife then she might think twice about leaving me for him. And of course, I knew who Jason's wife was, so I searched Facebook and came across your ad. There was your phone number.

'I felt like the universe was giving me answers, and when I spoke with you, I thought I could get Maddie and Jason in one fell swoop. I even harboured a very scandalous idea of trying to have an affair with you . . .' He's chuckling. *Like a fucking psychopath.*

'That would have been a big mistake, for both of us.'

'Do you think? You're probably right – I was trying to save my relationship, for the baby, but to do that I toyed with you too. Not emotionally I hope – but I let you believe that I wanted a complete design renovation . . . I'm so sorry.'

'Collateral damage.' I shrug. 'But I'm past hurting, and I don't feel bitter. I just want to move on now. And those videos are my past, they aren't my future. I'm moving on, so don't send them to me. I don't need revenge, I just want him gone.'

He looks at me, and his hand reaches out and touches my face, but this time I recoil from it, and I see the pain in his eyes.

'I *live* for revenge, Alice,' he says, his voice cold and unfeeling. The only passion in there is hate. 'I want him to suffer physically for what he's done to me – oh and to you,' he adds as an afterthought. His eyes are lit, I've never seen him so invigorated, and I think about him torturing Maddie by putting me in her orbit, and the humiliation of being held in front of her like bait. And I wonder what other cruelty he might be capable of.

'I hope you manage to end your marriage without too much pain – for you anyway,' he smiles. 'I'm always on the end of the phone, Alice.'

I don't respond. I won't be calling Daniel Prescott for help – ever.

'I'll go now,' he says, and I walk him to outside the front door, where we embrace lightly, none of his usual exuberance or hint at something more. And as he walks across the gravel, I call him.

'Daniel?'

He turns around.

'Your puppy dog . . . Poppy, the one you lost – did you ever find her?'

He stops, and in the dark, for a few moments, he just stands there. I can't see his face, he's too far away, but eventually he turns to me. 'My father said I was getting too attached. He had her euthanised.' And with a vague shrug, he walks away.

49

After Daniel left last night, I called out for Willow, who turned up immediately, thank God, then I locked the doors and checked the utility room window. He was right, the lock was broken; I hadn't noticed that before, and worryingly it's in a blind spot for the cameras. I jammed the window shut from the inside with a ladder against it.

Did Daniel break the lock, was he planning to come back? I shudder at the thought.

I hate the idea that he knows where the weakness is in the house. Daniel obviously likes to play on weakness, and vulnerability. I called the locksmith first thing, and he's coming later, but Jason will presumably be back from New York and be here by then, which is a whole new drama for me. I need to kick him out and take back my house, my life and my kids – I need to save all these things after the damage he's done. We need him to be out of our lives, and if he refuses to go, then I'll tell him about Daniel's 'video collection' and threaten to put everything online. It would ruin his career and reputation, and Maddie's too.

I would never do that, as I said to Daniel. I don't want revenge, I just want him gone. But Jason doesn't know that.

The kids rush downstairs arguing, and I make toast and coffee and pour juice and amaze even myself at how I can hide everything that's going on in my head.

'Don't forget guys, Dad's picking you up. It's his turn to be at the house for the next couple of nights,' I say as they run around the kitchen gathering water bottles and bags and leaving toast crumbs everywhere.

Ruby pulls a face. 'Yeah – if he turns up, you know what Dad's like. He's always so busy with work he forgets everything. Even us, his kids.'

'Yeah, well, you have to understand, Dad has a demanding job,' I reply, while I want to say *you have to understand, Dad has a shit-load of debt and a* celebrity *stalker girlfriend with a baby on the way.* But I'm putting off that conversation for another day.

However, as Ruby wisely predicts, Jason may not turn up for them later, so I'll make sure I'm not too far away when school gets out. I'm all for giving children their freedom, but right now I can't trust anyone – and I'm on high alert.

I turn in to the school gate, and the kids get out. I'm saying goodbye and giving out instructions that neither of them are listening to, when I see it, the Fiat.

She's here. And she's watching my kids. I've had enough. I need to sort this, face her head on and confront the unknowns, the shadows that hang around the edges of every day. I can't take another moment of this, so abandoning my car on double yellow lines I march towards the Fiat. I've been through so much these past weeks that everyone is a potential burglar/child snatcher/stalker/killer – they walk among us, and it's time I stopped fretting and hiding and instead fought back.

As I get closer to the car I can see this is the woman who, calling herself Mrs Weaver, came to view the house. It's the woman who spoke to the kids at the coffee shop, the woman who's been haunting us for weeks now in her mint-green Fiat.

'Mrs Weaver?' I call. Her car window's rolled down so she must be able to hear me. But tellingly she doesn't respond, because I'm calling her fake-prospective-house-purchaser's name. 'Mrs Weaver?' I shout more loudly and more angrily as I approach the car. I'm going to confront her, ask why she's stalking my house and my kids and tell her I'm going to the police.

But before I reach the car, she sees me, winds up the window, and tears off down the road. I manage to take a photo of the registration number as the Fiat disappears into the distance. 'Gotcha,' I say to myself, feeling like Cagney or Lacey. The blonde one.

I stand there for a moment. Why am I letting her go? Why am I allowing someone else to have control over me, to shape the narrative of my life? She's been haunting me and the kids for weeks, sneaking around behind my back. It's time I did something, not just stand here passively thinking *damn, she's gone*. So I run back to my car, jump in, and chase after her.

At first she's going really fast, and as I'm near a school, I have to drive slowly, but once we're on the open road, I put my foot down, and soon I'm right behind her. A little further on she jumps the red lights, and as much as I'd love to do a full-on Cagney and Lacey and put my pedal to the metal and chase her, I'm not an American PI, I'm a law-abiding citizen and mother of two.

Damn it, I've lost her after all. But I console myself that I have her registration number, and if nothing else I've scared her off.

I need a moment of calm, so sit in my car for a few minutes and decide to check in on Mum before going back to the house.

As soon as I arrive, she puts the kettle on and I flop on to the sofa and breathe for the first time in a while. 'What is it, love – something's upset you, hasn't it?'

'Where do I start, Mum?'

And despite promising myself I wouldn't worry her, I find myself talking about Jason's hidden paper stash behind the fridge.

'He can't do that, can he? How much money has he taken out on the cards? Why . . .'

'I don't know, I can't get hold of him, but don't worry, it will all be fine,' I lie. 'He won't get away with it. I've booked to see a lawyer next week; she's a friend of Martha's.'

'Good old Martha, what would we do without her? You can't let him get away with this, love, he can't do that.'

'No, he can't,' I say, but the problem is, he *has.*

'Well, let's hope Martha's lawyer friend can get him locked up.' She smiles and pats my knee. God bless her, she doesn't really understand the dilemma. As Jason hasn't been paying the mortgage for a while, the unpaid money will have interest slapped on it, and then there may be court costs because he hasn't dealt with the mortgage company and they've started legal proceedings. And that could all land on me, as the joint mortgage holder, along with the unpaid household bills which add up to thousands. Presumably he's taken out money on the credit cards too, and that will put a huge hole in anything that might be left from the house. The way things stand, we'll lose everything, and Martha's lawyer friend is nothing compared to my husband the lawyer – known in legal circles as 'the shark'.

'I think he's finally defeated me, Mum,' I say sadly.

'You'll be fine, love, you always sort things out. And you have that big celebrity client, don't you?'

'I'm afraid that's fallen through too,' I say, and tell her about Maddie Lavender leaving Daniel. I also tell her the scandal about Maddie being a bit of a stalker a few years ago, which she loves.

'Ooh, that must be why she was killed off in *The Seaside.*'

'*The Shore*, Mum,' I remind her gently.

'Of course, silly me, that's what I meant.'

'I always thought Daniel was okay, but I think he's as bonkers as she is.'

'I'm seeing Julie Lansing for lunch today, she'll remember him.'

'Perhaps don't mention his current romantic problems.' I'd forgotten that Mum has a teacher friend who taught Daniel. 'He might not want anyone to know. As there's a baby involved, I wonder if they'll share custody?' I don't tell her the baby is Jason's, she doesn't need to know – yet.

'Well, let's hope they don't do that nesting thing you're doing, love . . .'

'Did. The nesting thing we *did*. I'm done with that and I'm done with him. It's his turn to stay tonight, but when he gets back from New York this afternoon I'm asking him to leave. I'll stay there for a while, until they repossess the house, if you like you can come and stay.'

'I would love to, but I can't leave your dad. Oh.' She looks stricken. 'He's not here anymore.' Her face crumples, and my chest fills with the weight of sadness. I'm definitely losing Mum and it's heartbreaking. I feel like she's with me one minute, and gone the next.

'He has to go, Alice,' she says.

'Yes, and he will if it's up to me. I just want him out of my life, Mum. I never want to see or speak to him again.'

'That's not going to be easy, love, you share children.'

'That's so true. It's like a horrible, ugly knot tying us together for life. I sometimes feel like it's strangling me,' I murmur, almost to myself. Then I see Mum's crumpled face, and realise I shouldn't be saying stuff like this to her, so I pat her on the knee. 'But my kids are beautiful, so I can't complain.'

'No love, you can't, those children are so precious. And he left poor Ruby in the dark.'

I don't respond to this. I'm hoping she'll forget, but she's pretty fixated on the time he forgot to collect her and Meghan.

'I'll go over there in a bit. He'll hopefully get back about two, pick Ruby up from school at three-thirty, not sure about Josh but tonight he's staying over at Leo's and Ruby has a school disco.'

'Don't let him leave her waiting outside in the dark, Alice,' she warns. Again.

'I won't Mum.'

'He makes my blood boil. Wait until I tell your father, he'll sort him out.'

'If he was still alive, he would,' I say, my skin tingling with fear as I look into her eyes. They're empty, like she isn't here. 'You okay, Mum?'

'I'm fine, love, you get off and collect the children from school.

It's 9.30 a.m. and she doesn't seem to realise that I wouldn't be picking the children up now.

'Don't want them left waiting in the dark . . . he left Ruby waiting in the dark, didn't he?'

She's repeating herself. I wish I hadn't told her about Jason forgetting to collect Ruby; it's obviously playing on her mind. 'That was ages ago, she was fine.' I play it down as I walk to the door to leave.

I sit in my car outside Mum's apartment. I hate leaving her alone now, I'm concerned she might come to harm, but Dr Manjit said she's in the early stages and capable of looking after herself. He also said there are medications that can help slow things down, but I can't help being worried.

I'm also worried about 'Mrs Weaver' being at large, and won't rest until I know the kids are safely home from school, and as I haven't heard from Jason and can't rely on him to collect them, I might just hang around in the background during pick-up time.

Then later, once the kids have gone off to their sleepover and school disco, I'll go and confront him and tell him to leave, that the nesting is over and now it's time to live apart. I'm hoping that as the house is for sale he'll agree to leave and let me stay at the house with the kids until it's sold. I think he'll accept that it's a matter of time before we both move out anyway. And if he has any decency left at all, he'll be so ashamed about the unpaid bills and credit cards, he'll go quietly.

I'm still sitting in the car outside Mum's when my phone rings, and seeing Jason's name I pick up.

'Hey Alice. It's me.'

'I've been calling and texting since yesterday, but you probably had me on mute,' I say, recalling what Josh told me about how Jason would have my number on mute on his phone and laugh about it to Josh. 'I needed to talk to you urgently, but anyone would think I was your bloody stalker, not the mother of your children.'

'I . . . yeah, we need to talk.' He sounds different, subdued, with no comebacks. 'Where are you?'

'I'm at Mum's, what time will you get home?'

'Just landed, just off the red-eye. I'm at Bristol Airport now, so will be back at the house in a few hours, by about two o'clock.'

'Good, because after all my messages, and no doubt emails from the companies, you'll know about the non-payment of vital bills, applying for credit cards in my name . . . and—'

'Look, I'm about to go through security . . . Sorry Alice, the signal's weak here, I can't hear you.'

50

Once home, I wander into the kitchen, look up and see Jason's already here. He's at the island, eating cereal, and by the look on his face he's as surprised to see me as I am him.

'Thought you were at your mother's,' he says, his brow furrowed, clearly embarrassed.

'I thought you were at Bristol Airport, straight off the red-eye,' I say sarcastically.

'I was, it's just that—'

'Save it, Jason.' I hold my palm up in a stop motion. 'Everything that comes out of your mouth is a lie, I don't want to hear it.'

He doesn't object, or talk over me, because he doesn't know what the hell to say. He thought I'd gone to Mum's and wouldn't be back for three days, and I couldn't talk to him because I thought he was at the airport, then he'd be with the kids. He was trying to avoid a conversation about the money.

I'm surprised at how territorial I feel, watching him sitting at the kitchen island I designed, eating from one of *my* beautiful handmade pottery bowls. He's keeping his head down, eating the cereal quickly, hungrily, like someone's going to take it from him. I watch him discreetly as I wipe down the milk and cereal he's obviously spilled and abandoned. He's slurping up the cereal like he's rushing for a train, milk round his mouth, spilled orange juice on his shirt. It isn't like him. Jason's used to eating in fine restaurants with colleagues and clients; he usually eats with grace. These past few months have changed him. I walk around the kitchen island to find he has no shoes or socks on, he's gained weight, and it looks like he hasn't shaved for days.

'Christ, that flight knocked you about a bit,' I say.

He just continues slurping, lost in himself.

'So, the unpaid mortgage, the credit cards, what the hell are you doing? And I know about you and Maddie Lavender – what a fucking mess you've made, it's just off the scale . . .'

'It's not what you think—'

'Oh, it's exactly what I think. Trust me, there are no grey areas. Jesus!'

He shrugs, and it's the shrug that does it. It's like something inside me snaps – not cleanly, but with a tearing sound I can *feel* in my chest. That small, careless roll of his shoulders burns hotter than all the lies, the cheating, the quiet erosion of my dignity, I am not some mild inconvenience to be brushed away.

I lean on the island countertop facing him, appearing very calm despite the urge to grab a kitchen knife or a heavy object and end him. 'I've seen the videos of you and Maddie Lavender,' I start. 'She must be very worried. Well, you both must be.'

'What?'

Finally I have his attention. He had no idea; the shock on his face makes me want to laugh, but I'm swishing around the kitchen like a courtroom lawyer in a TV drama.

'Oh sorry, I thought you knew.' I do a wide-eyed fake-innocent face. 'You and Maddie were recorded having sex at Silvercliff – I think that's the title of one of the videos.' I say this almost to myself. 'I reckon a crazed fan got close-up and personal with their phone without you realising. What are you going to do?'

He's clutching his chest, and for a moment I think he might be having a heart attack, but he seems unable to speak.

'Thing is,' I continue, 'her career's already in the gutter, what with the stalking, the restraining orders, injunctions, her crazy threats. Got yourself a proper little catch, didn't you, Jason? Mmm, she's a keeper . . .' I pause purely for effect. 'And now these videos. I mean you're past your best with no shirt on, but she's still hot, so when they terminate your position as partner at the law firm, you guys could always start a couples Only Fans page? You'll need to do something Jason, can't have you sitting around all day – you'll need money for our divorce, no one's going to give you mates' rates anymore, are they? So, our divorce, her legal fees, your debts, and you'll also have a new baby to feed.'

He takes a breath, and can barely get the words out. 'Where did you see them? Are there videos online?'

'Why? Fancy a night in with a film and a takeaway?'

He looks down. There's no fighting back, no threats. He seems broken. I wish I could say I feel sorry for him, but he's done too much harm to too many people.

'Shit. I know it was that pervert Daniel Prescott . . . he filmed us, didn't he?'

'I've no idea who filmed them or what platform they're currently streaming on,' I add sarcastically.

I put the kettle on to make myself an instant coffee, and as he sits at the kitchen island, staring ahead, his cereal now abandoned, I quietly observe him. He's put on weight, his hair's unwashed, he hasn't shaved, he looks like he hasn't been to bed, and he just seems really shifty.

'You have no idea what I've been through,' he says, suddenly.

'What *you've* been through? Bloody hell, Jason, what about me and the kids? Mum's losing her memory, I'm losing the house, my husband's having a baby with a soap star who may or may not be my stalker. And I've just had a car chase with a mint-green Fiat.'

He sighs loudly, and I just know by looking at him that there's something else he's not telling me.

'You know who she is, don't you? That woman in the Fiat, you know her. She's connected to Sarah . . . this is about *her*, isn't it?'

He shrugs. 'I . . . I've been meaning to talk to you about it.'

'Who is she?'

'I . . . I'm not sure, can't be a hundred per cent, but I did some digging . . .'

'And?'

'I think it might be Josh's mum.'

51

'But the woman in the Fiat can't be Josh's mum, she's dead.'

Jason just looks at me.

'Sarah died, didn't she?'

'Her name wasn't Sarah.'

I'm back on that fucking fairground ride again. I feel my stomach dip, waiting for the fall.

'Her name was Gabriella. I didn't want you to know anything about her. I wanted to keep you apart.'

Another lie.

'So, okay, you lie about everything else, why not change everyone's identities – what makes you think it's Sarah . . . I mean Gabriella that's driving the Fiat, following the kids – it could be any one of your *Fatal Attraction*-type lovers.'

He takes a deep breath. 'The other day, I was here and saw her car. I watched her park up down the road and creep into the garden. It was Josh's mum, Gabriella.'

'I don't understand, you told me she was dead.'

'I was never completely sure. I'm not a doctor.'

'So can we just, for once, have the real story? You didn't leave her dead in that bedroom and get on a plane with Josh?'

'I . . . I *thought* she was dead, but . . .'

'So you left her for dead?! That's why you had no death certificate. You told me we needed to stay under the radar, that the adoption lawyers fudged the fact there was no death certificate because it was best for Josh.'

'And they did, they worked it so *you* could adopt him, no questions asked,' he replies, pushing this on to me.

'But you said the adoption was just paperwork – "a formality", you said. You never told me that the child's mother was likely to be alive and looking for him.'

'I didn't know if she was alive or dead . . . her pulse was weak.'

'And you let her lie there and didn't call an ambulance or try to get help for her?' I'm horrified.

'She LOOKED DEAD!' he yells angrily.

'You took a sleeping child from his mother's arms . . . while she lay dying. But she was still alive? And, not caring whether she lived or died, you left the country and changed his name so she could never find him, and he could never find her. And I colluded with you, believed you when you said it was all red tape and in the baby's interests to get him back to the UK and adopted as soon as possible.' I take a breath, and hear my own voice, firm and loud. 'I know you aren't a good man, Jason, but this is next level – you tore a mother and child apart, they lost more than ten precious years of each other, so you got what you wanted.'

'It wasn't like that,' is all he can say. He knows he did a terrible thing, but it's too late.

'So that's why you wanted to change his name? That's why you lied and told me her name was Sarah? They could never find each other, and I couldn't find her even if I'd wanted to, because everything you told me was lies. And when I asked if you had any photographs for Josh, pictures of his mother to keep by his bed, you said there'd been a fire and all the photographs and mementoes had been destroyed.'

Together we'd told Josh his story – a story I thought was true, and all the time I was lying to the little boy: whenever he asked me about his 'real mummy', I told him she was in heaven looking down on him. Later I explained that his biological mother had died of a terminal illness, and I'd chosen to be his mum because I loved him so much. I lied to him since he was three years old. And all the time, Jason knew the truth, that there was a chance she was still alive and grieving for her child, not knowing where he was, if he was alive or dead.

He stands up, and throwing his cereal bowl into the dishwasher he walks from the kitchen.

'Believe what you like, but everything I've done and still do is for my kids. I didn't want Josh to be mothered by a woman like her, to have his life ruined before it even started. I don't regret what I did, and you know what? I'd do it all again.'

With that he stomps up the stairs and I'm flooded with relief that he's gone. How I look forward to the final ending, the curtain down on our marriage.

I finish my coffee in silence. I can hear him upstairs, and I don't care. I'll come back later when the kids are out with their friends and ask him to leave. But for now, I just need to go and check on Mum. I walk to the bottom of the stairs.

'Jason, are you going to be okay for the school run?'

No answer, he's obviously still sulking. Whatever. But he needs to know the arrangements, and despite making a note on the whiteboard, I know he won't read it.

'You only need to pick Josh up today,' I try again, 'but could you also take the carrier bag with Ruby's leotard in? She's forgotten it again.'

But I hear him snoring, and decide it's actually easier to do this myself. And as there's plenty of time, I take the carrier bag. I can hand it to her at school, gives me an excuse to be there to see if Jason turns up for Josh.

I'm driving away from the house just trying to process what Jason has told me about Spain and Sarah – well, Gabriella. I know now who the woman in the Fiat is, and as much as I want to protect my son, I also want him to have the opportunity to meet his biological mother before Jason scares her off. I think he'll try to make her go back to Spain. He'll no doubt frighten her with legal threats, because while she's here she's dangerous and could make trouble for him.

I arrive at the school early. There's no sign of the green Fiat, and as I have nothing else to do, I take out my phone and check the film footage from the house. I've been feeling a little weird since Daniel's nocturnal visit, and I really just want to double-check that he left and didn't hang around outside, or try to get in via the utility room. I did what I could to wedge the window shut, so I doubt anyone could get in, but I didn't sleep very well as a result.

I scroll through the footage, and there's no sign of Daniel anywhere, so I keep scrolling, and at 3 a.m. I see something happened. It was just a movement downstairs on the internal cameras. I watch as Willow wakes up, stretches and wanders over to an area with no cameras, her tail up. And then the familiar sashaying across the room in the direction of some fuss – my eyes follow her to the corner, where the cameras don't reach, but I can see by her movements and reaction that someone is in the kitchen.

My skin feels prickly. Someone was in our home last night, while we slept upstairs. That's terrifying. They are standing out of the camera range, so whoever it is knows I've installed them, and where they are. It can't be the kids, and the only people who know about the cameras are me, Martha, and of course Ryan, but he's the installer. But I think I know who it is, because Willow ran with her tail up to whoever was standing in the corner. I stop the film and zoom in. It's a man, and the way Willow's tail is up, it seems like she knew it was the nice man from earlier.

Daniel came back?

Last night may not have been the first time the night visitor broke in, and as uncomfortable as this is to watch, I have to know. So I take a breath, gather my courage and start going through the footage from the previous night. And sure enough, around 3 a.m., there's movement, the camera's picking something up, and Willow is doing her thing again. Woken by someone moving around, she wakes and climbs down from her cat tree to go and greet whoever it is. They are now standing by the fridge, opening it, taking out a bottle of milk and drinking it in huge gulps. And when they finally finish the bottle they leave it on the side, and wiping their mouth with their sleeve they turn and look straight into the camera.

I zoom straight in. I can't believe who I'm seeing.

52

It's early afternoon, I'm sitting in my car outside the kids' school staring at the film from the CCTV in my kitchen. It's showing me what happened in my home at 3 a.m. the day before yesterday, while I slept upstairs. My mouth is dry, my stomach tight. I've zoomed in, and I'm looking into eyes that once promised so much, that in the end gave me nothing but pain. And now, I'm scared of what the screen is showing me. My husband is standing by the light of the open fridge, having just drunk a whole bottle of milk in the middle of the night – when he was supposed to be in New York.

'What the hell, Jason?' I ask the close-up of the man staring up at the camera, at *me*.

I watch for the next ten minutes. He's wearing the same old tracksuit he was wearing earlier, eating his cereal hungrily, leaning over it like someone might steal it from him. It was the same with the milk, drinking like he was so thirsty he'd never stop. I continue to watch avidly as he sneaks around the kitchen, when he said he was in New York. So that's why he was home earlier eating cereal. *Just got off the red-eye.* He hadn't been in New York at all. No surprises there, but I know now that he wasn't with Maddie – so where was he, and why *did he lie about being in New York?*

I can't stop looking; it's like the climax of a film. My breath feels shallow, my heart's pumping, and I just keep watching. He's obviously aware of the cameras, because he stays in the dead areas the camera can't pick up, but still blunders into shot now and then. At one point he tries to cover one of the cameras with a tea towel, but he's so out of shape he can't throw the tea towel high enough and soon gives up. I guess if he's raiding the fridge, he has no choice but to risk being filmed, but I haven't checked the night footage until today, so he could have been doing this for weeks. He's now blundering around, and with a bottle of wine tucked firmly under his arm, he moves out of shot. I fast-forward, but he doesn't turn up again over the next few hours, until 9.30 this morning, when he's back in the kitchen, pouring the cereal and milk he was eating when I walked in.

This doesn't make sense. I'm confused. Where did he go for the six hours between 3.30 a.m. and 9.30? I assumed he'd been hiding out in some love nest with Maddie Lavender and lying to me and the kids about being in New York. I thought he was doing the classic Jason, avoiding responsibility and family, and sleeping with a woman other than his wife. But it doesn't look like that's what he's been doing.

And that's when I realise. We haven't been nesting at all. *My husband never moved out.*

53

Aware that the school bell's gone and kids are spilling out, I turn off my phone in a daze.

I'm still trying to process what Jason told me about Sarah/Gabriella, and now this. Sometimes I was awoken by noises – and the window to Ruby's bedroom and the utility room, both prised open. Was that Jason? If I'd bolted the doors from the inside, he wouldn't be able to get in with his keys, so did he try to break in? But how long has he been staying at the house overnight, and why? Where has he been sleeping? I have so many questions. I assumed on the nights he wasn't at the house that he was with Ellie – or Maddie as I know her. Come to think of it, where the hell is Maddie? I think of Daniel, who seems hell-bent on revenge, and what he said last night in my hallway: *I* live *for revenge, Alice.*

It makes me shudder. Should I be concerned about Maddie's safety?

Daniel is hurt and angry, and the more I think about it the more dark and twisted thoughts come to mind. But as always, the immediate trivialities of life drown out everything else, and Ruby's now running out of school oblivious to the fact that she doesn't have her leotard with her.

I quickly climb from the car and wave the carrier bag, just as she and Meghan approach the exit.

'Oh my God, Mum, my leotard,' she shouts, for theatre.

I smile and shake my head indulgently.

'What are you like?' I hand her the carrier bag.

'What's she like? She's delulu!' Meghan says, with an eye roll.

I chuckle at this, 'Have you seen your brother?' I ask.

'I saw him earlier, he went home.'

My stomach clenches. 'Why? What time?'

'Dunno, I saw him at lunchtime . . . so.' She considers this.

Ruby's vagueness only adds to my anxiety. Did Gabriella come to school early to avoid me racing after her? Has she convinced him to get in her car? Imagine thinking your mother died when you were three years old, and at seventeen being confronted by her at the school gate? The emotional impact would be huge. He might assume we both lied to him; he might never come back from that.

'Did Josh say why he was going home?' A low hum of panic is starting in the pit of my stomach.

'Dunno. Saw him at lunchtime, we were looking for Meghan's false nail and bumped into him.'

'And he was definitely going home?'

'Yeah . . . but I wasn't really interested, Meghan's nail was far more important than my ludicrous knob of a brother.' She looks at her friend. 'Your nails will *always* come before family.' They both crack up at this and skip off to Meghan's mum's car.

I watch her go, glad that at least one of my children is safe and happy. And climbing back into my car, I try to remember the last time I felt as free and joyful as my daughter does now. But after a few seconds, I give up.

I'm concerned about Josh, but I have to get this into perspective. He's seventeen and left school early, but he's in the middle of exams – no one at school would question this, and nor should I. He's fine, he's just gone home early to do some revision, and that's a good thing. I asked both the kids to keep me posted on their whereabouts, but Josh never has and never will, and I have to accept that. Besides, he'll be at uni in another city in a few months' time. I have to get used to it.

But as I pull away to head for home, dread sits in my stomach. Something isn't right. I've always been able to sense things – Mum calls me 'the prophet of doom' because I often know when something bad's about to happen. And that's what I'm getting right now.

I pull up outside the house, and that feeling is gathering momentum. Climbing from the car, all my senses are on full alert. I'm on edge, looking for something, someone. Irritation shimmers through me as I remember Jason snoring upstairs when I left. He didn't collect Josh, or take Ruby's leotard, he no doubt just stayed in bed. Like everything else, he assumed I would do it.

This makes me angry, and if Josh isn't here I'm going to finally pin Jason down on the money, hanging around the house in the middle of the night, and all the other shit he's put me through. I close the car door with a thud, and happen to glance at the road through the gap between the trees. I swear I glimpse a flash of pale green; what the hell is *she* doing here?

Suddenly I'm running down the drive and making my way to the road. The Fiat's going pretty fast. Too fast, but this is the woman who runs red lights, she must have seen me arriving home. I catch the registration number, and it's definitely her.

I don't want to scare her away now I know who she is. I want to talk to her, find out her story. I need to hear it from her, not from the liar I married. It's all so weird, but it doesn't occur to me until I walk back to the house that perhaps she's been here. Perhaps she knocked and tried to speak to Jason, or even Josh?

Opening the door, I walk inside and the heat and tension hits me like a body slam. 'Hello?' Is Jason finally up, or still having a siesta in my bed? 'Is anyone home?' I hear what sounds like whimpering. *What fresh hell is this?*

It's the smell that hits me first, a thick metallic stench of blood and urine.

I walk through the front door and down the hallway, my heart beating hard. At first I can't make sense of the tableau. Josh is on his knees at the bottom of the stairs with his back to me; the sound is coming from somewhere inside him. Is he laughing, is he crying?

'Darling, what is it? What . . . ?' I can barely get the words out; a lump of panic sits in my throat. Then I see the trickle of blood meandering along the black-and-white floor tiles. I bend down. 'Josh, are you hurt?' *Has he tried to take his own life?*

'There's no pulse Mum . . .' He moves away slightly, and that's when I see what he's been hiding. There's so much blood I don't recognise the body at first, but when I do I hear myself whimper in horror.

'It's . . . it's Dad . . .' He turns around, moves away slightly, so I can see what he's trying to show me. 'Dad's dead.'

54

For a few moments, the world stands still, wrapped in suffocating heat and silence. But it's the absolute stillness I'll never forget, like the house is holding its breath.

Eventually my brain allows me to drag my eyes from Josh to see Jason curled at the bottom of the stairs. He's lying on his side, eyes wide open, staring right at me. The shock on his face is like something from a horror movie, the blood on the floor the colour of Merlot. Josh is holding a blood-soaked kitchen towel to try to staunch the flow spilling from his father's head.

Josh is crying. Jason is staring. I get down on my knees and crawl through the blood to reach Jason. If I shake him, he'll wake up. His body is twisted, his leg is under his back in an unnatural way. It must hurt, I need to move it for him. I can fix him. 'Jason, wake up,' I say, lifting his head. Holding it in both hands. Horrified at the cold, dead weight. Like heavy pottery in my hands, I drop it, and his mouth falls open.

I turn to Josh. 'Has he fallen?'

My son is rocking backwards and forwards, his face contorted in a silent scream.

'DID HE FALL, JOSH?' I yell in his face.

He puts his head down, and nods.

'Was it an accident?' I hear myself, calmer now. I need to know what we're dealing with.

He shakes his head, and my world tilts. Still on my knees, I move away from Jason, move through the slippery blood, and try to reach my son.

Anyone except my son. His son. Please don't let it be Josh.

But he's already beyond my reach, shivering in the heat.

He doesn't need to tell me what happened, or how it happened. I *know*. I see it all. Josh home unexpectedly, angry with his father about the money. Jason caught off guard, as his son becomes the adult, behaving more like a man than his father, and the gladiatorial fight between father and son.

Like a pressure cooker, heat and tension and blame has been building all summer. Josh was hurt at the family break-up, and horrified about the way his dad had thrown everything away. He felt as betrayed by Jason as I did, and in a small way, I saw this coming. Something had to give, but I never imagined anything like this.

'Did you and Dad argue?' I ask.

He nods, but offers me nothing more. I stand up. I don't need to *know* any more.

'Do you want me to help you?' I ask quietly, as I look down on him, a crumpled heap in his father's blood.

He doesn't say a word, but his eyes slide up to mine, and I see his answer.

'I'm here, love,' I say.

How best to help him? I can call the police, who will see what's happened, take Josh away, interview him, possibly arrest him – and his life will effectively be over.

Or I can take control of the situation, and the story.

So I tell Josh to go and delete all the house camera footage from the last few hours. 'Just wipe it from this morning onwards,'

I whisper, knowing that if the police work this out, we might one day need to show Jason in a certain light. And the footage of him hanging out in the house after midnight, drinking from bottles of milk, behaving erratically, might be invaluable if we ever need a defence. He walks off in a daze, and does as I asked, while I attempt to make it look like I've tried to resuscitate Jason. I mess up the crime scene by wiping my hands in the blood, touching Jason's body, and spreading my DNA with Josh's. I don't know the first thing about forensics, but if things start to look bad for my son further down the line, my DNA will be here too. I'll say I did it.

It takes Josh a minute or two to delete the footage, and when he returns to the bottom of the stairs, I talk him through the story we tell the police.

'You came home at 2 p.m. to revise, which is true. You didn't see your dad, because he was sleeping on the bed. I can confirm that because he was snoring when I left, at 1.30-ish. You had your earphones on, you were engrossed in your revision – law, wasn't it . . . you have your second law exam next week, Josh, you were revising for it?'

He looks at me like I'm mad.

'You worked all afternoon, and then at 3.30-ish decided to come out of your room and go downstairs for something to eat. From the top of the stairs you saw someone lying in a heap. At first you didn't know what it was, and slowly as you walked down, the realisation hit. Dad has fallen! Okay?'

He's still staring at me, and suddenly his eyes change, like a robot that's just been switched on.

'That isn't what happened, Mum.'

'I know, love, but I don't want to know what really happened, because then I'd be obligated to tell the police. And I can't do that, because it would kill me. So, we need to stick with the story, and not waver.' He looks as terrified as I feel, and I just have to hope and pray we can get through this. 'What we do now will affect the rest of your life. Dad's gone, and he wouldn't want you to lose your life too. This was an accident, okay?'

I can only imagine how this looks, a mother and son at the bottom of a staircase. The body of her husband, his father, is next to them while they plan their story for the police. Both of them are covered in his still-warm blood.

I take out my phone, and call the police, then go in the bathroom and throw up.

55

Inside, I'm a mess, but I'm holding it together for Josh. I hope that between us we can convince the police that this was an accident, and that the faulty camera isn't seen as suspicious. I have no idea what the police will find out, but know how all-seeing they can be. We just have to stand by what we're saying, and get through this.

I'd take the whole rap myself if I could, but too many people will know he was home when it happened, and I wasn't. Today Josh left school early, there will be witnesses who saw him walking home; the school has cameras that will show him leaving, and his friends were probably aware he left. We can never hide the fact he was here, but by losing the footage, we *can* hide the fact that he was angry with his dad, and that they had a fight.

I sit by the body, waiting for the police. This is my first love, my husband, the father of my children, my forever person, and I think about our wedding, all the flowers, and sunshine and hope. Our horizons were wide, our path felt so long, but little did I know how rocky it would be. I cry silent tears for the past, and everything I'd hoped for but never achieved, and now I have to fight just to keep the light on. I've lost so much along the way, but this isn't about me, it's about my son, keeping him safe, keeping him sane – and keeping him out of prison.

The police arrive quickly, almost too quickly, their boots stomping through the house, radios crackling, voices loud. Then the paramedics turn up, a man and woman – sensitive, polite, efficient. There's no emotion here, just a job to do, but I see the look that passes between them as they check his body. Are they simply acknowledging to each other that their patient is dead, or is it something more? Do these professionals know, can they see something that I haven't thought of? Is murder or manslaughter obvious to medics and police?

My paranoia is at an all-time high as the living room is transformed into a mirage of notebooks and uniforms, the air thick with sympathy and suspicion.

Josh and I sit on the sofa like two children. It's our home, but someone died, and therefore we have no jurisdiction here now. The police are marching through like it's a thoroughfare. I glimpse through the window – someone's arriving in a white suit, with booties. There's crime scene tape everywhere, and Detective Harris, a gnarled older man with a scar across his cheek, invites Josh and me to talk at the station.

'It's easier, the lads are busy here and you don't want to get in the way,' he says, like he's doing us a favour. But I know, because I watch *CSI* and *Law and Order*, that they want us off the premises so we can't delete, destroy or hide evidence, while they go through the house with a fine-tooth comb.

'Just routine, Mrs Taylor,' Harris keeps reassuring me, but I know how this looks, and as we are escorted to a police car to go down to the station, I see the neighbours' curtains twitch. I know how they think this looks too.

The questions, when they come, are endless and obvious. The police playbook, probably born from statistics and past cases – all pointing to what the police think might be the issue, to help make their arrest and be home by teatime. *Has Jason ever been violent? Did he drink? Did he hurt you? Did you want him out?* I answer what I can, my throat dry, the truth and half-truths tangling the words as I try to say them.

'No, he's never been violent, and he didn't drink that much, but he spent a lot of time away working, so I'm not sure. And yes, I did want him out, but he wanted me out too.'

To steer them away, I mention others. 'My husband and I were about to start divorce proceedings,' I say, then try to explain the nesting arrangement, and Detective Harris looks at me like my mother did when I told her, in complete disbelief.

'So let me understand this thoroughly, Mrs Taylor, you both lived there, but not at the same time?'

'Yes, that's exactly it.'

I see the glance pass between him and DC Shah, his much younger sidekick, beautiful and scar-free, with more emphasis on academia than street smarts like her boss. If this was a police drama they'd be the clichéd odd-couple partners – chalk and cheese, but ride or die.

'Do you have any theories, Mrs Taylor,' he asks, with a smile. 'I mean, did your husband have any enemies . . . people who might' – he hesitates – 'forgive me, but want him dead?'

Yes! 'Well, there are other people who were angry with him.'

'And who might they be?'

'So, Maddie Lavender, his pregnant mistress, she's—'

'Lucy, from *The Shore*?' He's clearly impressed.

'She *was*, but after a rumoured stalking situation with her ex, she was killed off.'

'Stalking?' He raises his eyebrows and makes a note.

'Then there's her husband Daniel, obviously humiliated, furious. And there must be a lot of others, husbands of women he slept with, friends of women he slept with . . . oh, and women he slept with,' I add.

'Not bitter at all?' DC Shah remarks sarcastically.

'I was just . . . joking,' I reply, knowing how awful this sounds, but if I was the killer would I say stuff like that? No. However, in my attempt to seem completely innocent and detached, I think I may come over as cold and possibly psychotic?

I realise during the interview that I will throw anyone under the bus to distract from what really happened. Sometimes we surprise ourselves at who we really are. But this is for my son, and if I didn't know it before, now I know there's nothing I wouldn't do for him.

After the interview I wait for Josh, who emerges looking very pale. I drive us both to Mum's at Detective Harris's suggestion/directive. They clearly don't want us back there interfering with evidence and getting in their way, and it's actually a relief to be away from the scene.

'I'm not sure I could have slept there tonight,' I say, as Mum serves Josh and I her home-made shepherd's pie. It's welcome and comforting, especially now the weather's broken. We all eat together at the table, and discuss the situation.

'How was your chat?' I ask.

'Okay,' he shrugs. He's still slightly tearful, but that's understandable.

Mum keeps looking at me, acknowledging his state. She reaches out and touches his hand.

'Eat up, love,' she says, then suddenly seems to realise Ruby isn't with us. 'Where's Ruby? She's not waiting somewhere in the dark, is she?'

'No Mum, she was at gymnastics with Meghan. I spoke to Meghan's mum but I felt I should leave telling Ruby until tomorrow. I'd like to bring her home and break it to her gently. I didn't know how long we'd be at the station, or what might happen.'

My darkest fears were that the police may have had something on Josh, but I didn't get that vibe and neither has Josh by the sounds of it. Also, the truth is, I want Ruby to have one more night of being happy, laughing with Meghan about silly things before the daylight comes in. I couldn't bear to take her away from her happiness and bring her home to a flurry of crime tape and confusion.

For now, things feel as calm as they possibly can, given the circumstances. It's good to be at Mum's where we can look after her, and as she brings in her apple pie that she made with Ruby's help, the smile on Josh's face brings me some comfort.

But in the quiet places of my mind, I can't stop hearing his whimper, seeing his shivering, his blank eyes. I thought I'd saved Josh once, when he was a tiny baby with no mother, but turns out I was wrong. Unbeknown to me, I merely helped to take him from his mother's arms. And Josh did what he did *because* of me and Jason. I take full responsibility for that, and now is my chance to really show up for him.

56

I brought Ruby home to Mum's after picking her up from Meghan's the next morning, and we told her about Jason together. Josh was there, he didn't say much, but Mum held her hand, and between us we supported her. Ruby was obviously shocked, and very upset, so we didn't say too much, just that he'd fallen down the stairs and the police were called. 'A tragic accident,' Mum said in her best Bette Davis. I haven't told Mum what really happened; Josh and I agreed it will always remain strictly between the two of us.

It feels like we're in a kind of limbo at the moment, the horrible lull after death and before the funeral. There'll be delays too because the police are waiting for more forensic reports, which keeps my nerves on edge. But we're getting through each day. I'm ferrying the kids to and from school, and keeping an eye on Mum too. We're quite the team, and as sad as it is for my children to lose their father, there's no tension, no uncertainties about where he is or when he'll turn up.

I hadn't heard anything from the police for a few days, but this morning Detective Harris called me. I was hoping it was to tell me Jason's body had been released and we could go ahead with the funeral. My stomach flipped when he asked if I'd be willing to go to the station, 'for a chat'.

'We can send a car or you can drive yourself,' he offered, but I said I'd drive. Poor Mum's been through enough without a police car pulling up outside her apartment; she's gone from living alone to having three of us there. I remembered how, when they were little and I was working full-time, Mum was always there, taking care of all of us – and now it's my turn to take care of her. As I said to Martha earlier on the phone, 'Sometimes she's just like her old self, but the confusion comes and goes. And despite us all squeezing into her tiny apartment, she seems to enjoy the company. The kids have obviously been affected by the death of their father in their own ways, but I'm good, and as callous as it may sound, my life is so much better without Jason.'

I arrive at the police station feeling nervous, and I'm now in an interview room that smells of disinfectant, cold coffee and Polo mints. A tape recorder blinks red on the table. Detective Harris sits opposite me, next to DC Shah, the double act.

Apparently the forensic report's back now and they have some queries. God knows how I'll deal with this, but while I'm involved, I can continue to try to control the narrative of what happened on the day.

'Alice,' Harris starts, his voice low and measured. 'You understand this is a voluntary interview?'

'Yes.'

'So, we've had the chance to do a little digging and the forensic report has finally arrived. Today we thought it might be useful to tell you where we're at.'

'Thank you, yes.'

'Thing is, we're still searching for the murder weapon,' he says.

'Murder weapon?' I don't need to feign surprise. I am surprised.

'Yes. Forensics found traces of metal in your husband's skull.'

'It was an accident, he fell down the stairs!' I say, alarmed.

Harris shifts in his seat, shuffles a few papers then looks right at me. 'According to Forensics, your husband had severe head injuries not wholly conducive to a fall. Their investigation revealed the injuries to the skull may have been caused by a heavy blow.'

He's half reading from his notes, but looking up every now and then as if to check on me. Is he looking for a reaction? Am I giving anything away?

'I realise this is probably very distressing for you, Mrs Taylor, but if you can help us . . .'

'Of course,' I croak, swallowing hard.

'So, we're looking for an object that might cause the kind of injuries sustained by your husband . . . a golf club, metal curtain pole, a poker. Anything like that? At this stage we're just making educated guesses as to what might have killed him, aren't we?' He turns to Shah for confirmation. She nods, unsmiling, without taking her eyes from mine.

'Well, if someone *did* kill my husband, presumably the weapon would be in the house? And you did an extensive search, so did you find anything?' I ask, hoping to God there was nothing under Josh's bed.

'We haven't found anything concrete so far . . . but we did pick up a couple of objects from the house that *might* fit the description. They're currently with Forensics.'

Fuck!

'Well, I can't think of anything. The curtain poles are fixed, we don't have open fires, so don't have a poker . . . and none of us play golf.'

'Your husband and son aren't golfers then?'

'No and neither am I, or my daughter,' I say, wanting to add *you old-fashioned, sexist pig* – but perhaps now isn't the time? Then I have a flash of inspiration, and God forgive me, I throw it out there like confetti. 'Daniel Prescott plays golf, and he turned up really late at the house the night before Jason died.'

'We've already spoken to Mr Prescott. He has an alibi for the day your husband was killed . . .'

Damn.

'Look, Detective, I don't want to seem unhelpful, but I just think it was a terrible accident . . . or the banister, could he have hit his head on one of the spindles on the banister?' I'm desperate, and it's showing.

'No. Forensics found metal in his skull.' He leans forward. 'Thing is,' he pauses, 'the angle of the injury isn't conducive to the fall either, and suggests the blow landed *before* your husband fell down the stairs.'

I force myself to hold his stare.

'And you maintain you had no physical altercation with your husband that day, no arguments over anything?'

He's fishing.

'No. I *saw* him that day, he was at home earlier when I came back from the school drop-off. He was eating cereal, he wasn't himself – he'd gained weight, was listless, a bit out of sorts. That's why I wasn't surprised that he'd fallen down the stairs. He was blundering around all over the place.'

'See, thing is,' Harris continues, 'Forensics say it most likely wasn't an accident. The angle of the injuries and the blood spatter on the wall isn't consistent with a fall. They reckon he was struck. Hard.'

Shah slides a photo across the table. Blood on the tiles, Jason's body collapsed at that grotesque angle. I look away, gripping the table with my hands. 'I didn't do that.'

'So how do you explain your DNA on him?' Shah chips in.

'I . . . I touched him, I held his head to try and rouse him, I checked his pulse. I thought—' My voice cracks. 'I thought at first he was alive, and I could help him.'

Harris tilts his head. 'Or finish what you started?'

My throat burns. 'NO. Look, do I need a solicitor?'

Harris leans closer, lowering his voice so only I can hear. 'Do you think you need a solicitor, Alice?'

I don't know, so don't answer him. I'm terrified. Does he think I killed Jason?

'You were angry that day, weren't you? Only the day before you'd found out your husband hadn't paid the mortgage, he'd been applying for credit cards in your name to run away with his mistress. I wouldn't blame you for—'

Shit. He does think I killed Jason.

'We went through this in the last "chat" we had. And as I told you then, yes, I was angry, but not enough to hit him in the skull with a golf club we don't own at the top of the staircase.'

'Is that what it was . . . a golf club?' Harris and Shah are doing that double-act thing again, looking at each other in mock horror.

'NO. There was no golf club. I was being sarcastic when I said golf club. I still believe it was an accident.'

'Have you spoken to a lawyer, Alice? About the unpaid bills? The credit cards, the way he was ruining you and your children's lives.'

'You and your friend even talked about burying him in the back garden,' Shah adds. Wow, so my neighbours weren't around when people were breaking in, or stalking us, but they could hear me and Martha larking about.

'Oh, for God's sake, that was me and Martha, we always joke like that.'

Harris raises an eyebrow. 'You always joke like that about murder?'

I feel the blood drain from my face. 'Yes – but we didn't *mean* it.'

He tips his head, as though considering this.

They've obviously seen messages on my phone that I had to surrender. God knows what else me and Martha have said in texts. They're staring at me. I don't know what to say. In the silence, just the faint hum of the overhead lights. Then Harris changes tack and his eyes narrow. 'Josh knew about the money, didn't he? Your son was furious with his dad, he hated him for what he'd done, didn't he?'

The words slam into me. 'I wouldn't say that.'

'Oh . . . because he did, we have it in the notes.' He glances over at Shah and she nods in confirmation. He leans forward, lowering his voice. 'We've spoken to your neighbours. They heard shouting that afternoon, voices, male *and* female?'

'Perhaps I shouted?' I offer.

'No, this was earlier, about 2 p.m., before you returned.'

I shake my head, but my chest is tight. I feel like there's a vice around my ribs.

Shah speaks quietly, almost kindly. 'If you know something, Alice, if you're protecting someone, we need to hear it. This is your opportunity.'

My eyes sting. 'I've told you everything.'

Harris sits back, watching me as if he can see the war inside my head. The red light blinks on the recorder. Steady. Relentless. They're waiting for a sacrifice.

'What about Maddie Lavender, Ellie Rose, whatever her name is? She's a known stalker, she also has a temper, and I know for a fact she was hanging around outside our house, Daniel told me.' I'm now offering up human sacrifices randomly, desperately.

'She's with him in France.'

'What? So they're back together?'

'Apparently.'

'That was quick, she was still with my husband only last week,' I say, in a vain attempt to put her back in the frame.

'Look, I may be being a little indiscreet here,' Harris says. 'But I'm going to bring you up to date with what's been going on with your husband – you have a right to know.'

57

It seems that Harris has been to France and interviewed both Daniel and Maddie in his luxurious farmhouse somewhere near Cannes.

'Apparently Maddie Lavender's affair with your husband ended several months ago.'

'What? But she was pregnant with his child . . .'

'According to her, your husband ended the affair.'

'Did she say why?'

'We had some information about previous issues, and we put those to her,' he says, obviously being discreet about her bunny-boiler career. 'And your husband had discovered her in the house one evening when he was there alone with the children. Maddie insists she just wanted to meet them, but it seems your husband felt threatened by her breaking and entering to do this,' he adds with a hint of sarcasm.

'So, he wasn't using the money from credit cards on Maddie?'

'Not completely, but she did extract quite a lot of money from him. When you and Mr Taylor first split, Maddie assumed he'd just whisk her off to a love nest somewhere, but he didn't have the money for that.'

'Really?'

'No, because a year ago, his partners discovered that he was having an affair with their big new celebrity client – Maddie

Lavender. He was let go – and hasn't worked for twelve months. We spoke with his friend Oliver Burns, and according to him, Mr Taylor made several attempts to find work, but the one or two companies he started with received phone calls from Miss Lavender with accusations of sexual harassment. Obviously no law firm wants that potential problem, especially with a high-profile celebrity client – even if it may not be proven.'

'So that explains why he hasn't been paying the bills.'

'Yes, and he had no money to pay for lodgings. His friend Oliver Burns also told us he stayed there for a couple of weeks when he first left the marital home. During this time, he ended the relationship with Miss Lavender, but she couldn't accept this and the police were called out several times to Mr Burns's property to deal with various issues involving Miss Lavender. Mr Burns became concerned for his own young family at this point, so asked your husband if he could find somewhere else to stay on the nights he wasn't at your house.'

'I assumed he was staying with Maddie all this time.'

Again, they do the double act of looking at each other, and then Harris says, 'You mentioned things going missing at some point, Mrs Taylor – in fact you filed a police report because you thought someone was watching you, and may have broken in?'

'Yes, I did, it was really strange.'

'Well, when we did the search of your house, we discovered clothes, some food, crockery, even cat food and empty wine bottles in your attic. We also discovered a diamond ring, which we presume your husband was going to try and sell.'

'I realised he was somewhere in the house, I saw him on CCTV in the kitchen the night before he died. So *that's* where he was living, the attic?'

Harris continues. 'According to Oliver Burns, your husband was trying to escape from Miss Lavender, who made violent threats to burn the house down if he didn't resume the relationship. Mr Burns said your husband called or texted him, and had by then become agitated and a little paranoid, because she was always around, standing in your garden, or sitting in her car, watching your house at night. But Mr Taylor was hiding inside, and he started by using your daughter's bedroom window to get in and out at night . . .'

'That explains Ruby's nightmares. She probably did see a man climbing into her room in the dark, but didn't realise it was Jason, just closed her eyes and thought it wasn't real.'

'According to Oliver Burns, your husband then broke the lock on the utility room window downstairs and would enter and leave from there. By then Mr Taylor was in permanent hiding and he had no money. Mr Burns said his friend had nowhere else to go, and in a way it was the safest place for him to hide because Maddie Lavender had no idea where he was. And while the nesting arrangement was happening, it never occurred to her – or anyone else – that he was hiding inside the house.'

'In the days before his death, he told me he was in New York.'

Harrison looks at his notes. 'No, according to Mr Burns, in the weeks before his death he was permanently in the house. He'd take food from the kitchen at night, and just lived in the attic. When he called to tell you he was in New York, he was calling from the attic.'

'The calls were coming from inside the house,' Shah says. She's clearly been dying to say that.

Too soon.

'It's like something from a horror film,' I say, dully, my brain working in overdrive. It's horrifying, but so many questions are answered now. It explains the noises in the night, the food and wine missing from the fridge, the way things just seemed to go missing. And why Willow would scratch and miaow all night on the landing, under the attic door. She knew Jason was living up there.

'We wonder if either you or your son discovered his hideout, and found him there, on the day he died,' Harris says. 'Was it you, or was it your son who killed your husband, Mrs Taylor?'

I blink back at them, steady as the red light on the recorder. 'I told you it was an accident.'

58

Nine Months After Jason's Death

I met Daniel for lunch last week – he's back in Devon. Maddie met someone else while they were in France and she and the baby are living in a chateau with a French baron.

We ate mussels and made small talk in a beautiful harbourside restaurant, and as we drank coffee and admired the boats, he suddenly said out of the blue, 'I'm not convinced his death was an accident.' He picked up his cup, sipped at his coffee, then put the cup back in the saucer.

My blood went cold. 'What makes you think that?'

'I know someone who wanted to kill him.'

My heart was in my mouth. 'You?'

'No.' Then he stopped to consider it. 'Okay, yes, two people who wanted to kill him, if you include me.'

'Who else?'

'Maddie told me herself that she wanted to kill him for ruining her life.'

'Do you think it was her?' I asked, knowing he didn't suspect Josh, thinking she might be a useful distraction should Josh ever have to face Harris and the team again.

'Who knows? She was the one with the biggest motive.'

'I think to some degree we all had a motive, but I can see what you mean. Maddie was clearly a woman on a mission – she even called new companies he tried to get work with, and told them he'd sexually harassed her.'

Daniel smiled at this.

'It's not funny, it obviously wasn't true.'

'Of course not – but I had to do something, I told you I wanted revenge.'

'It was you?'

He nodded, proudly. 'Well, my housekeeper made the calls. She's quite amusing, very good at impersonating Maddie, especially when Maddie was in a strop.'

'Daniel, that's terrible.' I drank my coffee and looked at him. 'Did you get him sacked in the first place by telling his partners he was having an affair with their celebrity client?'

'I couldn't possibly comment,' he smirked, biting into a large, chocolate petit four.

Every time I see him he just seems madder than ever, but he's about to move into a mansion in Cornwall and has asked me to completely renovate it. I was there yesterday, and this time it's a genuine wreck – I was thrilled. Martha says I never learn, but he's amusing, and the fee will help take care of a few of Jason's debts I'm still paying off.

Meanwhile, life goes on, and Josh passed his driving test today. Ruby baked him a cake and we're drinking prosecco and have toasted him. And Gabriella, his mum, has joined in the celebrations. She is slowly becoming part of Josh's life, which hasn't been easy for me, or for her.

Learning that the mother of my son was still alive was a body blow, and it's taken time to come to terms with what that means.

When I heard the story from her, it was different to the story Jason told.

'I wasn't a bad mother. I'd had drug issues when I was younger, and managed to get clean before and during the pregnancy,' she explained. 'But I suffered after the birth, I had postpartum depression, I should have seen a doctor, but I didn't have the heart or the mind to seek help.'

Meanwhile, Jason was having a fling with a waitress who worked at the bar with him, and Gabriella was so distressed – along with the baby blues she was weepy and tired. He told her she was a mess, and that's why he was sleeping with the waitress. Apparently they fought all the time, until one night he came home with some pills. He said they'd 'calm' her down, and she felt so wretched she took them, and continued to take them for the next three years. And all that time, he provided her with the drugs that kept her so 'calm' she often slept all day. She didn't bond with her baby, she hated herself and her life and said she would have gladly died. 'I tried to get off them,' she said, 'but the reality of living with Jason was so painful, I would rather be asleep, or dead.'

What she needed was kindness and support, and love – and instead he gave her drugs to keep her down, so he could live his life.

And after he took her baby and left for another country, she was devastated, but had no way of finding him, and for several more years, she continued to self-medicate and give up. 'But I'd wake up every day with this emptiness, this yearning in the pit of my stomach. I was grieving for my child, and eventually I realised I would die and never see him if I didn't turn my life around. I had to help myself. It was a turning point,' she said. 'I got help, got clean, and got on a plane to find my boy. It's the best thing I ever did.'

When I came to tell Josh about his mother being alive, I was shocked again to discover that he'd known for a while. They'd already met in secret, having connected first on Facebook. Gabriella had done her research, finding Jason through his company. His profile boasted of 'a beautiful wife and two perfect children', and she hoped he'd changed and become a good husband and father – for their son Michael's sake.

'Why didn't you just knock on our door and tell us you were still alive?' I asked her.

'Because I couldn't do it to you,' she replied in her Spanish accent that sounds like summer. 'I watched the pretty wife and the two perfect children coming and going from the beautiful house – and I had to consider the consequences of the truth. I needed to know first what Michael . . . sorry, Josh wanted. And if he wanted to know me, and it didn't break up a family, then I would try and make that happen. If he didn't, then I would walk away.'

'Is that why you came to view the house as Mrs Weaver?'

She nods. 'I wanted to meet you, to see where my son lived. It was deceitful, I feel bad about that, but I was desperate.'

'I understand, I'm not sure I would have then, it might have tipped me over the edge. But you were convincing, and you do a good English accent.'

'I'm familiar with it, remember I lived with an Englishman once.'

'Yes, how could I forget.' I smile, glad she didn't walk away and something inside her made her stay and fight. And as we both sip prosecco and celebrate our son's driving test success, we smile and clink glasses. I'm so glad to have her in our lives.

'Congratulations, darling,' I say, grabbing Josh and holding him tight, glad he can at least have this now. But as always, I feel that shadow slipping over the sun, knowing that if Detective Harris finds one shred of evidence, how fragile and temporary his happiness and these watersheds could be.

I know in my heart that it wasn't the right thing to do morally, but the alternative is too horrific to bear. Josh is suffering enough, he misses his dad, he cries for him, he regrets what he did I'm sure, but would spending the next ten or twenty years in prison help him?

We both promised each other that day that we'd never speak about it, and we haven't; it's between the two of us, and as long as we stand by that, my son stays free. The police have looked high and low for the murder weapon – a golf club or curtain pole or whatever the forensic people thought it might be. I don't want to know what it was, or where he hid it, and I've never asked.

I spent my married life keeping Jason's secret so I didn't lose Josh, and I'll spend the rest of my life keeping this secret – so I don't lose Josh.

But I sometimes look at him and wonder – if it happened once, how can I be sure it won't happen again? If he lost his temper, or someone hurt him, if he was really tested emotionally, what would happen? I don't know. He was so angry with Jason for what he'd done to us, he couldn't help himself. And I'm ashamed to say, that since that day, I've never left him completely alone with Ruby.

His university offer was held over for a year as the police were still inviting him in for impromptu 'interviews', and after the chaos we all just hunkered down together. But it's now spring and there are new green shoots, a little hope in the air, and he's starting university in September.

I'm happy for him, but I also lie awake at night, worrying. If he's away from home, I'm not around to keep an eye on him. I can't protect him from the police – or himself.

59

One Year After Jason's Death

I knew today would be a difficult one, but I had no idea how hard it would be. Mum finally had to move from her apartment and go to a place where she can be cared for properly, and though we'd come to realise there was a problem, it was still a shock. We looked after her for as long as we could, but it's time now for her to have professional help and support. So, tonight, Josh, Ruby and I are staying with her in her apartment for the very last time.

Ruby is crocheting with her, but Mum isn't so great with the crochet hook anymore. I cook dinner, and afterwards Josh makes us all a cup of tea, and we sit around the fire talking. Mum's memory still goes back years, and she tells us about her childhood – stories we've heard many times, but that are always worth a retelling.

In the middle of her storytelling, she has one of her fleeting moments of clarity that are quite remarkable.

'It's lovely to have you all here,' she says. 'My Ruby and my Joshy, and you.' She's looking at me, not quite sure who I am. 'I hated him, your husband,' she suddenly says. 'He left Ruby to stand outside in the dark, he didn't look after the children. I told him, I said, "You don't deserve such a lovely family."'

Ruby's looking at me now with a half-smile, as if to say, *Nan's off again.*

Josh understandably looks guilty, and sad. 'Let's not talk about that now, Nan, tell us that story about when you met Grandad, eh?'

'NO!' Mum shouts. 'I want to talk about *him.*' Then she turns to me and says quietly, 'I knocked her husband's block off.' Then she giggles, and Ruby giggles, and I glance over at Josh, who's looking at me with a strange expression.

'Knocked his block off I did.' Mum's repeating herself; she does that all the time now. 'I hated him, he left Ruby in the dark, he spent all my daughter's money. Where's my daughter?'

'I'm here, Mum,' I say.

'I gave him such a whack on the head, he won't do that again.' She laughs at this, and I see Josh wince, his eyes sliding to the fireplace.

'No you didn't, Nan, you mustn't say that, you'll get into trouble.'

Mum seems to slip into more confusion, and hugging Alexis her Russian doll she says, 'You know, don't you, love? You're like a daughter to me.'

'Come on, Mum, time for bed,' I say.

'Joshy was there, he was there. I told him, "You left Ruby in the dark", he was a terrible father, didn't deserve a beautiful wife and family. He ruined my daughter, and her children . . . he spent all the money too!'

She turns to me. 'I had to do it, love, I was at the top of the stairs, he was being very disrespectful, told me to shut up, he was shouting at Joshy too. You can't leave children in the dark, Jason, and then I did it, and he fell and I was happy. He was a horrible husband . . . and he left Ruby and her friend waiting in the dark.'

I help Mum to bed, say goodnight to Ruby and return to the living room where Josh sits alone by the fire.

'What happened, Josh?' I ask.

'What do you mean?'

'You know exactly what I mean.'

'I couldn't tell you, Mum.'

Reality sets in slowly and then rushes in all at once. 'It wasn't you, was it?'

He shakes his head, and in a voice that feels heavy from its forced silence he tells me the truth. 'I came home early to revise, and I was in my room and heard Nan shouting. Nan was screaming at Dad. She just kept on about him leaving Ruby in the dark.'

'Oh God, it was something that happened ages ago. Dad was late picking Ruby and Meghan up and I made the mistake of telling Nan. It obviously played on her mind, she wouldn't let it go.'

'I think it was more than that, Mum, she was saying things like, "You've ruined my daughter's life and the only way she'll have a chance is if *you're* dead." That was when I came out of my room.' He stops for a moment, and I see the pain in his eyes as his memory rewinds to that horrible, horrible day. 'I saw everything . . . Nan was standing at the top of the stairs, and yelling, but Dad was walking down the stairs away from her.'

Like an echo from a faraway time, Dr Manjit's warning comes back to me. He said dementia is different for everyone, in some patients it can manifest in aggressive ways – like the way Mum reacted to me spilling the cup of tea. Her illness caused her to act on impulse, as Dr Manjit had predicted, her anger and aggression towards Jason must have built up until she couldn't control herself.

Josh fixes me with an intense gaze, steady, controlled. 'I think she went to the house that day, saw or heard Dad wandering around upstairs, and just saw red. She just wanted to hurt him, I guess, and . . .' His eyes fill with tears.

I'm in shock. 'Perhaps he just fell?' I'm willing him to lie, I want him to say yes, because I can't face the fact that my mum is a murderer any more than I could face my son being one.

He shakes his head slowly. 'No, Mum. I saw it all.'

'You never told me any of this, Josh.'

'You said you didn't want to know, and never to talk about it. And it made sense, I couldn't talk about it – imagine if I did and Nan had to go to prison, be with murderers and . . . I couldn't even think about it.'

'So . . . Nan did it?' I hear my voice, an almost-whisper, thick with unshed tears.

'Dad started to walk down the stairs. She was behind him, on the step above. I saw her lift the poker over his head and she brought it right down with such force I couldn't believe it. And I'll never forget what she said: "That's for Alice!"'

Epilogue

The mint-green Fiat pulls up outside our new cottage, and after checking the camera, I open the door. Gabriella opens the car door and climbs out.

'Alice, I love this cottage – it's so cute.' Her accent is light, just a hint of Spain in her voice; it sounds like sunshine, and she's always smiling.

Josh, Ruby and I have moved into the rented cottage recently. This place is tiny and nothing like our previous home, which we had to sell to pay off the debts incurred by my husband. But I'm still working, my business is small but doing okay, and I'm happier here than I ever was in that beautiful house with Jason. I think I believed if I could create beautiful surroundings for us to live in, then my marriage would be better, my husband would be kinder, more faithful. But the answer isn't in expensive paints and high-end furnishings, it's in this little cottage with its old sofas and cracked wooden beams.

We're still living in the same area, but it's more remote, surrounded by countryside, and not far from the sea. There are no neighbours for miles, just sheep and moorland and no unexpected visitors, or bumps in the night. We all need this time to heal and the peace and quiet out here is restorative, and we're melding into a family again, this time a happier one.

'Ahhh, my sister,' Gabriella sighs, putting her arm around my shoulder as we walk through to the garden.

Hard to imagine that 'the stalker' in the green Fiat turned out to be our saviour. She's pulled us all through this in so many ways, and she's now teaching me, Josh and Ruby Spanish. I always wanted Josh to know where he came from, and spending time with Gabriella when she's here is so good for him. Later in the year when she returns to Spain, he'll visit her and, as she says, 'He may not have a father now, but he has two mothers – and that's so much more.'

'Come through, let's sit outside,' I say, and we walk through the cottage to the tiny garden that overlooks the sea.

'This is beautiful,' she sighs again, putting her arm around my shoulders as we gaze out to sea.

It's the first time she's been to our new home, and we've been here a few months now.

'It's not as big as our old house, but I can afford the mortgage, and look at that view.'

'I admire you so much, Alice. You have your life sorted, you've picked yourself up from a very dark place, and made a new life out of nothing.'

'You've done the same. We didn't know it, but we both turned out to be warriors – especially when it comes to our children. There's nothing we won't do.'

I'm a different woman than the one Jason knew. I used to think I needed him, but the more I discover about him, I realise he needed me more. I feel truly free for the first time in my life, and I haven't lost a son, instead I've gained a friend in Gabriella.

'Did you hear the news?' I ask her now as we crunch across the gravel to the backyard. 'The police have finally closed the file on Jason's death.'

I glance at her for a reaction, and she just smiles, almost as if to herself.

'I've always wondered,' I start, 'about that day, what really happened?'

'I guess we'll never know,' she murmurs, putting her head down, and she keeps walking.

I slow down, and touch Gabriella's arm. 'Do you know?'

She stops and turns to look at me, alarm flickering in her eyes. 'Do you?'

'I know it was Mum.'

'Your mum had been poorly for a long time, she wasn't a killer. I used to go and see her, took lemon cake, she seemed to like that. Once I visited her and the door was open, so I walked in. I heard her shouting, she sounded distressed and I was concerned about her. But when I ran to help her, you were there in the shower with her, but she saw me and looked so terrified. In that moment, I almost stayed, I wanted to help – I also wanted to talk to you because I knew what you'd been through. We shared a son, and we'd both once loved the same man. I knew what you'd been through, and wanted to help. But your mum saw me standing in the doorway, she didn't recognise me and was terrified. I just ran away, probably made things worse – but I didn't want to cause any more distress.'

'So that was you? I knew someone was in her apartment that day, but then thought I was going mad. It was a time of complete emotional chaos and there was nothing you could have done. Mum's illness was horrific, but Jason's death – and Josh being a suspect – that was the hardest,' I say. Gabriella sighs, and pats my hand, she's been on this journey with me. Thanks to her I haven't been alone. 'But the case is closed now, so the police won't ask me any more questions. I always told them the truth, that I didn't know what the murder weapon was, or where it was hidden, but . . . you know too, don't you?'

She sighs. 'Alice, don't ask me.'

'I have to, don't you understand? I wasn't eavesdropping, I was in the kitchen the first day you came to visit, just weeks after his death. We were still at the old house, and I heard the two of you whispering in the hall – Josh asked you "where's the poker?"'

Gabriella shakes her head sadly. 'As you say, the case is closed . . . I guess you should know, but we swore to each other that we wouldn't tell anyone. Your mum was a lovely lady. I went to see her, not long after I first contacted Josh.'

'She told me, she said you'd had a really nice afternoon together.'

'He spoke about you and his nana a lot, and she really loved him.'

'She did,' I say gently. 'Tell me about the murder weapon, where is it – no one can ever find it, can they?'

She takes a breath, fixes her eyes on mine, and somehow she understands I have to know.

'On that day, Josh called me. He was in tears . . . I didn't know what had happened, we'd only met for the first time a few weeks before, but he was my son, and he needed me. So, I jumped in my car and went straight to your house. When I arrived, Josh was hysterical and your mother was in deep distress with blood spatter on her clothes. She was desperately trying to wipe it away, in a horrible sort of panic, she seemed more concerned about the bloodstains on her dress than the dead body at the bottom of the stairs. Josh wouldn't leave his father, but at the same time he understood the consequences if he didn't remove his nana from the scene. He wanted to save her, and his father. But when I checked, it was too late for Jason, but not for your mother, someone Josh loved very much. He just kept saying, "Nan can't go to prison, get her out of here!" I realised what had happened, I knew Jason, and

Josh had hinted to me about what he'd done, and how his nana was only trying to protect them.'

Gabriella took a deep breath, before continuing. 'So I took a leap of faith. I know it was wrong in many ways, but your mother wasn't a killer, she was a confused old lady taking revenge on someone I knew to be cruel, someone who'd taken my son from me and ruined my life. At this point I wanted to help my son, so I took your mother away from the scene. I helped her out of the house through the back gate, avoiding the cameras as much as possible. Then I made her lie on the back seat of my car, so no one would see her. She was exhausted, in shock, and still clutching the murder weapon all the way back to her apartment. Once there, I cleaned it thoroughly and put it back where it belongs, in the fireplace.'

'The poker . . .'

Gabriella nods.

It crossed my mind that Josh might have hidden it from the police, but I never asked any questions, because I didn't want to know.

'Soon after Jason's death the police visited Mum to question her, mainly to ask her about Josh,' I say, remembering how worried I was that Mum would say something to incriminate him. 'And all the time, the murder weapon was right in front of them, in Mum's fireplace – that was so clever of you, Gabriella.'

She shrugs. 'I saw it in a film once – the killer had to hide the murder weapon. It was an ornamental sword, with his fingerprints all over, so he hung it on the wall. It was so obvious that it wasn't obvious,' she says. 'And when the police came to investigate, they never realised the murder weapon was there. In plain sight.'

We share a smile, which feels inappropriate when discussing a murder weapon, but both Gabriella and I were Jason's victims, and we understand each other. Her quick and clever thinking on the day saved Mum, and though she barely knew us she kept a dangerous secret. She chose to care about my family more than telling the truth which would have destroyed us even further after everything.

'I can't thank you enough,' I say.

'What else could I do?'

'You could have told the police, you could have taken Josh away . . . but you let him stay with me. I'll never forgive myself for the fact that I had him for all those years. I just hope you forgive me.'

She touches my arm affectionately. 'Of course I do, and how could I take him from you? You are his mother too, and now he has the best of both of us. I wasn't good enough for him then, and you looked after him for me; you were a better mother than I could ever have been back then, Alice.'

We walk down the garden together to join the kids, who turn towards us, smiling. Gabriella goes to Josh and they hug, then Ruby, never one to be left out, joins the throng as Willow appears from behind a tree and curls around their legs, her tail high, her purr loud; she played her own part in the family drama, but no one paid attention to her scratching and miaowing under the attic door. Next time Willow tries to tell me something, I'm going to listen – because cats know things.

At times like this, when the family's together, I miss Mum. But she's happy at the care home, drinking tea and eating cake while telling everyone how she killed her son-in-law on the stairs. No one listens, and even if they did, they wouldn't believe her – it's just the ramblings of an old lady with an impaired mind. Sometimes I worry that one day someone might take her seriously, but the murder weapon is now in my cottage fireplace, and no one could connect it to Mum or the murder – I hope.

My phone suddenly pings; it's Martha texting to say she's on her way, with a bottle of pink. She loves Gabriella, the three of us sometimes go out for dinner, and there's always a lot of laughter. Martha and I were talking recently about what would have happened if Jason hadn't fallen down the stairs. 'Shall I tell you what would have happened if he hadn't had the accident?' she said. 'I would have helped him and pushed him down those stairs myself,' she joked, and I laughed, a little too loudly.

One day I may tell Martha the truth, but for now I'll let her think Jason fell down the stairs and incurred a fatal head injury. I think the fewer people that know, the better. Only me, Josh and Gabriella are aware of the truth, and as the police aren't pursuing the case anymore, I feel the pressure has lifted. And if for some reason the police ever stumbled across the truth, Mum's now far too poorly to be charged with anything.

So for all of us, it's about looking to the future now. Jason can't take Josh away from me as he'd always threatened, I'm not tied to a man I don't love because of his child. Gabriella hadn't been able to be a mother to her son, but when she got the chance, she came through, she was there when he needed her. She also saved my mother, and though she isn't my blood, she's closer than any sister, and the bond we have through Josh is unbreakable. So until the children go off on their own journeys, we'll start this new life and make memories together. Unlike our old house, this one hasn't known fear or death, but will become infused with the lives we will live here. It won't be perfect all the time – nothing is – but we won't live with the ghosts of the past, or be haunted by our secrets. And out here, no one is watching.

ACKNOWLEDGEMENTS

So many talented people contributed to this book, and I'm grateful to every one of them.

Thanks to my lovely editor Hannah Shaw for stepping magnificently into the role, making the process calm and seamless and giving me such great support. And to my editor Victoria Oundjian, thank you for your wonderful ideas, infectious enthusiasm and delicious humour. And thank you both for having faith in the original idea, and for the fun we had talking it up into a book.

My huge thanks and apologies to copyeditor Gemma Wain, who deserves a medal for untangling the chaos of my timelines and inconsistencies.

Thanks also to the cover designer, Lisa Brewster and proofreader, Sadie Mayne, who provided the polish and packaging!

Big thanks as always to my wonderful reader, friend and safety net Harolyn Grant, who never ceases to amaze me with her forensic eye and ability to see what I don't.

Thank you to my family and friends, who show me a world beyond writing, on those rare occasions when I'm not attached to my laptop.

Finally, if you take one thing away from this book, it's to always listen to your cat – because cats know things. So to Cosmo our clever cat, thanks for working out those plot twists in the small hours, while I write, and the world sleeps.

ABOUT THE AUTHOR

Photo © 2024 Nick Watson

Sue Watson was a TV producer at the BBC until she wrote her first book and was hooked.

Now a *USA Today* bestselling author, she has sold almost 2 million books exploring the darker side of life, writing psychological thrillers with big twists. Originally from Manchester, Sue now lives with her family and Cosmo the cat in leafy Worcestershire, where much of her day is spent writing – and procrastinating.

Follow the Author on Amazon

If you enjoyed this book, follow Sue Watson on Amazon to be notified when the author releases a new book!
To do this, please follow these instructions:

Desktop:

1) Search for the author's name on Amazon or in the Amazon App.
2) Click on the author's name to arrive on their Amazon page.
3) Click the 'Follow' button.

Mobile and Tablet:

1) Search for the author's name on Amazon or in the Amazon App.
2) Click on one of the author's books.
3) Click on the author's name to arrive on their Amazon page.
4) Click the 'Follow' button.

Kindle eReader and Kindle App:

If you enjoyed this book on a Kindle eReader or in the Kindle App, you will find the author 'Follow' button after the last page.